Abo

CW00420611

Joel Hames lives in r
two daughters, chopping wood, burning things and
fending off herds of rapacious country-beasts. Back in
the dim and distant past, however, he was a Master of
the Universe in the Big City, buying and selling and
securitising and generally raising hell. Joel writes what
he wants, when he wants to (which by coincidence is
when his wife and children choose to let him). *Bankers
Town* is his first novel.

BANKERS TOWN

Joel Hames

For Sarah, Eve and Rose, who keep me sane and keep me smiling.

Our revels now are ended. These our actors,
As I foretold you, were all spirits, and
Are melted into air, into thin air:
And, like the baseless fabric of this vision,
The cloud-capp'd towers, the gorgeous palaces,
The solemn temples, the great globe itself,
Yea, all which it inherit, shall dissolve,
And, like this insubstantial pageant faded,
Leave not a rack behind. We are such stuff
As dreams are made on; and our little life
Is rounded with a sleep.

The Tempest, Act IV, Scene i

It's all just a big fucking game, mate.
The thing is, you've got to know you're playing it.

Jason Kennedy, Milton Shearings, 2007

Contents

THE PLAYERS

The Bankers

Milton Shearings

Alex	Hero, villain, Essex Boy, lover, thief
Jason	Alex's closest friend
Liz	Banker, spy, unluckiest girl in the world
Marcus	Head of many things; "the Spider"
Rachel	Alex's colleague, legs up to here
Russell	Alex's friend, confidant and boss
Jane	Alex's razor-sharp and rather posh colleague
Stephen	Ex-head of securitisation and as close to a saint as a banker can be
Jessica	Cool-as-ice head of Jason's team
Anthony	"The Bloodsucker"; widely-loathed colleague of Alex
"The Beast"	Security. Don't ask.
Karl	Thoroughly unpleasant German with far too much power for anyone else's comfort

Lorraine	Jason's PA; purple nail varnish, Krispy Kremes and cats
"The Witch"	HR. Don't ask.

Greenings

Grace	Clever, evil securitisation banker
Graham	Clever, evil M&A star and husband to Grace

The Deal

Ahmed	Excitable CFO of Mintrex, the client
Harvey	Talented partner at Sommersons, Miltons' lawyers
Christine	One of Harvey's juniors

The Real World

Paul	Member of the Dagenham Mob
Sally, Emily, David	Jason's wife and children
Charmaine	Jason's mistress. Yes, I know.
Jasmine	Alex's ex-girlfriend; an artist of questionable talent
Starbucks girl	Girl who works at Starbucks. Come on. Do I have to spell everything out?

PROLOGUE

No One Was Supposed To Get Hurt

No one was supposed to get hurt.

It's best to start out honest. That's what I used to think, anyway, even if the things I've done might point the other way. What is it they say? *You can trust me, I'm a banker.* Except they don't, and you can't, and there's no reason on earth you should. But I might as well be honest now. I've done some bad things, and there's no point pretending otherwise. It'll all come out one way or another.

But the thing is, I didn't set out to do any damage. I might have taken more than I was due, sure, but no one was supposed to get hurt.

Or look at it this way. Who's lost the most? Well, yes, I suppose some have lost more than me, that's true. I'm still alive and in reasonable shape, and that's better than a couple of others I can think of. But take a look at what I've got coming, and compare it to what I had.

One minute I'm a successful investment banker, raking in the money, living the high life. The next, I've got no job and no chance of getting one, and I'm staring down the barrel of a good long stretch at Her Majesty's pleasure. In anyone's book that's got to be a pretty sour turn.

If I can be a little less self-absorbed for a moment (it is possible), I'm not the only one facing the lean years after a decade stuffing my pockets with fifties. We all had it good in my world. We'd had it so good for so long that we forgot what it was like to be normal. We used to talk about the world out there as the "real" economy, and that says everything. We *knew* we weren't real. We sat there, in our Edens of steel and glass, making money out of nothing. And now it's over. Half of us are out, and the rest are getting used to a salary that's more than enough to live on, but not exactly enough to make a Rothschild blush. The end of an era, and no one cares. No one pities the bankers.

So who fucked up?

As far as the global shitstorm's concerned, the list is too long. And here's the thing: the way I see it, there's nothing to gain by blaming anyone at all (unless you're a journalist or a politician, I guess, but if we're talking about bankers living in an unreal world then you can be sure they've got politicians for neighbours). So many people fucked up that if you stacked them head to foot they'd reach the moon, and if you decided to leave them up there no one would blame you. Everyone who loaned money, borrowed money (yes, you), talked about money, regulated money. It's not just the bankers who were in cloud cuckoo land. We were just living it up on the classiest, most expensive clouds. And then, of course, it started to rain. Toxic asset rain.

Here's what it was like. Think way back. You're a kid. You're in the back of the car on a long journey. It's dark outside. Lights flashing past. Gentle murmur of adult conversation from the front. You're safe and warm, and you don't have to do a thing. Don't even have to think.

Well, that's us. All of us. The bankers, the borrowers, the same old suspects. We got in the car and never thought to question the driver. We just assumed they knew what they were doing, where they were going. And now we're stood by the side of the road in that cold bitter rain wondering how the hell we ended up here. Should we be allowed to just shrug our shoulders and say "*not my fault, someone else was in charge, and look, everyone else did it too*"? Or those of us who *were* supposed to know what was going on, shouldn't we be thinking "*perhaps I shouldn't have shut my eyes in the first place*"?

So maybe we should just learn from our mistakes and start again, right? No use pointing the finger.

Think I should try that line before m'learned friends, when the time comes?

No. Thought not.

Let's ask again: who fucked up?

And this time, I'm talking about my own personal Paradise Lost. Here's the tally: one deal in freefall, one guy dead, another at death's door, a marriage on the rocks, and (apparently) an entire economic recovery stalled on the starting grid (*oh please*). The good times have rolled, the revels are ended, and I've got one hell of a hangover.

Now there's a school of thought out there, and I'm guessing it's a pretty popular school right now, that says the answer's very simple. Me. Alex Konninger, tool of the devil, scourge of the righteous and curse of the markets. It's easy, really, just like the myth of all those wicked, nasty bankers. People like their baddies bad. With an English accent, for preference (tick) and ideally horns and a pitchfork, but we've come on a bit since the middle ages and I haven't worn so much as a goatee for years (it went ginger after a couple of weeks and had to go).

So you could look at it this way. I got swept along, too. I didn't set out to do what I did. I was guided, by people I trusted, and everything that's happened is the inevitable result. There's others involved. I *wasn't responsible*.

But there – I would say that, wouldn't I?

So I guess I'm going to have to do better. I'm going to have to justify myself. Not my actions: mea culpa, they're beyond justification (some of them), laughable or sordid (most of the rest). But I'm going to have to prove I'm not the serpent of the piece – or at least, not the only serpent, or even the most poisonous. And that, unfortunately, means telling my story. *Apologia pro vita sua*, Konninger, published (no doubt) Wormwood Scrubs, 2010, on toilet paper. If I'm lucky.

If I'm going to offer up my own version, now's as good a time as any to do it.

Time to take the wheel, Alex.

MONDAY

1: Credit Committee and All That Bollocks

Monday 14th December, 2009

"Over the last three years, Mintrex has introduced international standards of transparency and corporate governance."

There are better ways to start the week than a 7:30am grilling from four bored execs. Not that I could blame them. Not that I could pity them, either: they only had to read the stuff. I was the one who had to write it, and now they'd got to the bit where I'd nearly lost my way at half two in the morning. Five hours ago. I'd barely been able to keep my eyes open then and I wasn't doing much better now.

"At the same time efforts have been made to streamline internal management and all that bollocks."

The voice trailed off.

And *what?*

An uncomfortable silence. I opened one eye, then another. Three other pairs of eyes (my colleagues) were gazing fixedly at me; another four pairs (the executives, here to decide the fate of our application) flicked from one of us to the other.

"All that bollocks," continued the voice, as if nothing unusual had happened. "An unusual turn of phrase for a credit application, although I appreciate your candour."

He allowed himself a chuckle. So did my colleagues,

nervously. I didn't. Couldn't believe I'd let this slip through. Sure, it was boring. Sure, it had been the middle of the night and there were better things I could have been doing. Sure, it was true: no one gave a damn about how much our client gave to charity or how nice they were to their accountants. The only thing that mattered was whether they were going to pay us back and how much we were going to make out of it. But still. It wasn't the kind of cock-up I made.

Maybe I needed a holiday. Only a few days to go and the deal would be closed. Then two weeks in the office, two nice, calm end-of-the-year weeks. And then America. A week in the Big Apple, where I was hoping to rekindle some happy times with Jasmine. Four days in Vegas, to lose some easy money with Paul and the Dagenham mob. I couldn't fucking wait.

"I know this application was somewhat last-minute, and perhaps it didn't get the attention it should have done, but we do have to get these things right."

Last-minute? Just a little bit. On Friday some bastard somewhere had decided to bring everything forward by half a week. There were a lot of balls in the air already, and suddenly there were another four or five, and I'd let one fall. And now I was going to get a rocket from the head of equity capital markets, about twenty rungs up the ladder from the likes of me, notoriously sarcastic, vicious and known for firing employees at the drop of a hat. Let alone a ball. I mumbled an apology, closed my eyes and braced myself for the onslaught.

There was no onslaught. I opened my eyes. The executives were talking amongst themselves, calmly and quietly, discussing the application like nothing had happened. I'd got away with it. If I'd not been so relieved, I might have been surprised at how quickly they came to a decision. One by one, they pointed out that this was a high profile deal with a lot of money in it; that the risks were long-term but manageable; and that therefore, in their considered view, we ought to proceed.

Now I know it's coming up for Christmas, season of peace and goodwill to all men, but this was 2009, folks. We were supposed to be diligent. We were supposed to be questioning things, refusing credit, all that stuff we'd been told to do in 2008 and been told off for doing earlier in 09. And this was the Credit Committee, too: the guys who are *supposed* to give us hell, whatever the deal, whoever the client. But not this time: application passed, four-to-zero, no conditions, no reservations. Should I have noticed this was unusual, realised we were in uncharted waters? Would it have made a difference if I had?

Who knows? All I saw was cock-up forgiven, application passed. Result.

After that and right up to around 10:13 this had been about as normal a day as you could expect to see at our shop, given where we'd got to on the Mintrex deal. Now we were through credit, all commercial terms had to be agreed by close of business so we could round up first thing Tuesday and price the deal. If this is starting to sound like jargon, well, it is, but you'll know it as well as I do by the time I've finished. Just in case you need it, I've even shoved a glossary in at the back, so you've got no excuses. (The "shop", by the way, is Milton Shearings. You know them well. These days, chances are you own a chunk of them, whether you want to or not).

When I'd shown up at 7:00 it was still dark outside and would be for another hour. The place was quiet as the grave, which gave me a chance to start ploughing through the 75 or so emails that had arrived overnight and I hadn't been able to deal with on my BlackBerry on the way in (*"checking your emails on a motorbike, sir?" "What do you think red lights are for?"*). Most of them could be ignored, which was a blessing, because by half past – when we stepped into Credit Committee – the floor was buzzing and my phone was ringing off the hook. I could tell this was going to be a long day.

I'm not trying to say I'm horribly overworked – I know a banker's not going to get much sympathy on that. And fair enough, it's not like we're chained to the desk making iPhones for a dollar a day. And it's not usually all systems go, red alert, no matter what some millionaire might tell you when he's trying to justify his (our) pay and bonus. But this deal, for a London-based global mining company called Mintrex, had been in the works for close to a year now, and had gone through so many changes that by this point its own mother wouldn't have known it. We had half a dozen law firms, five investment banks, four hedging counterparties, three rating agencies, two three-hundred-page offering circulars and a client who knew shit-all about how the deal worked but laboured under the delusion he was running it.

The reality was that if anyone was running the deal, it was me. I'd brought in the client, nursed them through the bumpy bits, been out there in the trenches with them the whole time. There was one person, in the cast of hundreds, that knew exactly which piece fitted where, when it should be slotted into place, and who had to sign it off. That guy was – is – me, and without wishing to blow my own trumpet, if I fell under a bus today, there was no way this deal was closing. Well, not on time, anyway.

Maybe not the most magnificent epitaph: *"here lies Alex Konninger, whose untimely death delayed a City deal by a couple of days."* But you've got to take your ego-trips where you can.

The first few calls I had to deal with were from our lawyers. They're not traditionally early starters but these guys were still on yesterday. They'd been up all night amending documents, reviewing documents, arguing with other lawyers, bitching about their clients, the other lawyers, the other lawyers' clients, and sending me increasingly frantic emails and voicemails asking for instructions on new problems that had only just come up despite the thousands of lawyer-hours that had already gone into this deal. The way it usually went, a problem that started out as a crisis at 1am generally got fixed by 4 or 5, so by the time I got round to actually speaking to the zombies we were down to half a dozen points plus whatever new shit came up during the day.

OK, so maybe I'm being a little unfair. Our lawyers on this deal were Sommerson & Co. Heavy hitters in the legal world, a Magic Circle firm, and even I could see they'd done a good job. The partner was a smug, floppy-haired son-of-a-bitch called Harvey Simmons-Smith, and the best thing about Harvey was that he was on my side. He'd managed to keep his cool when he needed to, kept his own team cool, for the most part, and kept the rest of the lawyers on the deal in their place, which was more of a challenge. No one else I knew could have done it. Smooth as martini most of the time, but when you've seen him taking some other lawyer apart you just want to hand the poor guy a cocktail stick to ram in his own eye and end it all there and then. Harvey had a whole army of keen young lawyers assisting him and, to my shame, after a year I still couldn't have named more than three, and two of them I wouldn't have recognised in the street.

I'd have spotted the other one a mile off, though. Christine. Scots lass. Mid-twenties. Long red hair, green eyes, and it looked to me like that suit was hiding something worth getting to. I'd spent more time discussing the deal with Christine than was strictly necessary, probably, but I enjoyed talking to Christine, particularly if I was looking at her at the same time, and even if we were talking about mining companies and contracts. When this whole Mintrex thing was over we'd all have some drinks to celebrate, and maybe a dinner, and I'd make sure Christine was close by the whole time. Sure, New York was coming soon, and Jasmine with it, but that was just an interlude. I needed something in London to come back to.

I made a few decisions (we'd kill this, concede that, and ignore the other because I just didn't give a fuck). The rest could wait. The rest had to wait, anyway, because that near-catastrophe of a Credit Committee was sitting there like a tumour in the middle of my morning. The lawyers, the other banks, even the client, I could deal with all that when it suited me. But the Credit Committee was a fixed object, and even though I'd thought it would be a breeze I was relieved enough to get through it. Especially after I'd come so close to screwing it all up.

By 8:15 the floor was beginning to fill up. I was a little surprised to see Jane slip into her chair opposite at what for her was a pretty ungodly hour. Jane was in the same team as me, the corporate team, but most of the time she did her own thing and she did it well. Utility companies. Gas, water, electricity. She'd bring in two or three deals a year, palm off all the slog on the juniors, get stuck in for the last couple of weeks, and win all the glory and a fuck-off bonus at the end of the year. If you didn't like her you'd wonder how the hell she got away with it, probably guess it was all down to accent, school, breeding, polo with half the clients and regattas with the rest. That's what I'd assumed when I'd first sat down opposite her and introduced myself, but it hadn't taken me more than a few weeks to see how wrong I was. Because for all it looked like she was bringing in the meat and leaving it to everyone else to cook it, if something did go wrong – and in our world, something *always* goes wrong – then it would be Jane the client would call to sort it out, Jane who would somehow understand all the complexities of the deal everyone thought she'd forgotten about, Jane who would cut through the crap and come out with a solution everyone was happy with.

I liked Jane. She could be a bitch if she needed to, but not to me, not so far, anyway.

But with none of her deals on the home straight it was difficult to see why she'd bother putting in an appearance before her customary 11am – until, during a brief but merciful lull in my telephone schedule, I overheard a snatch of her own conversation:

"Question is," she was saying, "who do you want filling his shoes?"

She was talking on her mobile, and quietly, but from where I was sitting the words were clear as day. I didn't catch any more, because a moment later I got another call from another exhausted lawyer, but it was enough.

Russell was on the move. I don't know how she'd figured it out, it was supposed to be some big secret, but you know bankers, we can't keep our mouths shut any more than anyone else can. Russell Calman was our boss, king of the corporates, not yet forty and already one of the bank's rising stars. And he was leaving. Jane wasn't supposed to know.

I wasn't supposed to know either, not really, but Russell could never keep much from me. We both knew I'd reached my level, or close to it, and I was happy to stay there, which meant Russell could tell me things safe in the knowledge I wasn't gunning for his job. And the thing was, once he moved up to the executive floor there'd be a gap at the top of corporate, and bankers abhor a vacuum – especially if it's one they'd like to fill. Jane had found out, somehow, and started her scheming early. She knew people everywhere, she had friends on the executive floor, and she wasn't unpopular in corporate. She had a chance.

Of course she wasn't the only one. There was a rival within the team, one I knew about, anyway. Anthony. Russell had brought Anthony with him from Paller Beaton, back when he'd been hired in 2003. Nobody could see why at the time and nobody could figure it out now, either. Sure, he worked hard. Sure, he had a decent analytical brain, nothing special. But the only things he was really good at were kissing arse, dodging bullets and stealing credit, and everyone except Russell could see it. I couldn't stand him, and nor could the rest of the team. Bloodsucker, they called him, but Russell liked him and I liked my job too much to make it any clearer than I already had that my boss's golden boy was a piece of shit.

Jane wouldn't take working for Anthony, and nor would half the rest of the team. Anthony wouldn't take working for anyone except Russell. So there was going to be blood, for sure, and Russell might be leaving us but he didn't want blood on his turf. He had a plan. At least, he claimed to have one, but he hadn't yet told me what it was and given he seemed to think Anthony could fit into it, I wasn't much looking forward to seeing what he'd come up with.

Meanwhile I'd been working through the emails that were starting to hit my inbox at the rate of four or five a minute (from past experience, I expected this to peak later this afternoon at around fifteen to twenty – and anyone who tells you they can stay in control of that much information at that kind of speed is either a freak or a liar, and probably both). Most could be ignored, but one caught my eye. One of the rating agencies had some concerns over what they referred to as "the impact of the highly-complex interest rate derivatives structure on the tax position of the deal as a whole."

Now that might sound as dry as a night out in Mecca, but to me it was important. You want to know how important? Twenty million pounds worth of important.

Let me explain.

The idea behind this "derivatives structure" was that Mintrex (a mining company with customers who paid in every currency you've heard of, and a few you haven't) wanted to be able to pay whatever they had to on the bond, and relax about interest or exchange rates going mental and screwing everything up. We'd take that worry away from them, with our clever swaps, and everyone would be happy. Most important, the rating agencies would be happy, which actually mattered because for some reason, even after all their fuckups, people still seemed to care what they said.

This could have been a nice straightforward single-line swap. They give us their rand and schillings and bolivares, we give them their pounds, end of story. And a nice straightforward single-line swap might have done the job, but it wouldn't have turned much of a profit for us, so this thing had wound up looking like a Jenga tower put together by a gang of particularly dextrous lunatics. A delicate edifice of carefully-placed parts, and if you so much as looked at one of them the wrong way the whole thing would be on the floor before you had time to blink. It had all been in place for three months now, so part of me was wondering what had suddenly changed and why the fuck the rating agencies hadn't spoken up a bit earlier. The rest of me knew it didn't matter. The agencies had probably only just got round to reading the stuff we'd been sending them since the end of summer, and that made them useless, idle tossers, but the problem was still my problem and I needed to figure out how to solve it before it put a multi-million pound hole in our bottom line.

Derivatives were important, you see. Oh, not all that stuff about hedging risk and getting the rating agencies happy. Forget about all that. What was important about derivatives was that we could make serious money out of them without breaking a sweat. Every bank on every deal wanted more than their share of the derivatives action, but we had something the others didn't. We had Sergei.

Back before people used to call bankers dumb, there was this myth that we were rocket scientists, and for the most part that's what it was, a myth, a fucking joke if you ask me, not that anyone did. The thing is, even though it was mostly crap, sometimes there's gold in crap, and Sergei was that gold. He *could* have been a rocket scientist, him and Anja and the rest of the analytics crew. They looked at a screen full of numbers and saw what made those numbers tick, they saw cars or pints or mortgages or record sales or whatever it was lay behind those numbers. And it worked the other way, too. Sitting there in a room with a client and a few bankers and lawyers and accountants talking over sales and bank accounts, you'd see their eyes start to glaze over as the words turned into numbers, rows and columns of them. Like those guys in *The Matrix*, but with spreadsheets for guns.

So Ian from our derivatives team had got hold of Sergei and told him to make them something that would blow the client's mind, something that looked better than anything the other banks could come up with. Something that looked cheap, so Mintrex would love it, but wouldn't end up that way, so we'd still get our millions. Sergei worked his magic and Mintrex liked what they saw. I'd helped along the way, translating Sergei for the guys at Mintrex – you had to know Sergei for a year or two before you understood more than one word in four. After that I'd just stuck around, keeping one eye on the derivatives side of the deal, sorting out all the little problems that popped up, quietly and behind the scenes, while the other banks were running around like headless chickens and freaking out the client. They didn't seem to understand that Mintrex were just like everyone else. They didn't want to have to deal with problems; they didn't even want to hear about them. Five banks on the deal, and every one of them had worked all out to win more than their twenty per cent. We looked like being the cheapest and the smoothest, the best team on the block. We got sixty; the others shared the rest, and none of them knew who it was that had bagged the golden goose.

Except now they did. Some time last week the other banks had learned the details of the derivatives carve-up and two of them had started screaming blue murder. Screaming blue murder wasn't a big deal: if you can't handle another banker screaming at you then you need to find yourself a new job. The other two banks knew when they were beaten and had the sense to keep calm, look reasonable, and take a better shot at it next time. And the client wouldn't have understood what the fuss was all about anyway, because as far as he knew, this derivatives stuff was just a side-line. It looked cheap, remember? Mintrex were paying out a couple of million in arranging and distribution fees between all five banks, plus another million or so for various other services we were providing. The swaps looked like two hundred thousand, maybe three. On the surface. But if you put on your mask and looked a little deeper, you'd see us booking a profit of somewhere between fifteen and twenty million, right from day one.

So you can see why the banks who'd been frozen out were angry as the devil, and you can see why we were smug as big fat cherubs. The more they whinged, the more the client complained about them to us, and the better we felt. Pretty much as perfect a situation as you can get, really, because if you're not getting abuse from the sidelines you haven't pissed anyone off, and if you haven't pissed anyone off you're doing something wrong. Only now, all of a sudden, the rating agencies had woken up and decided to fuck it all sideways. If the other banks got word, they'd go running straight to Mintrex, act all concerned that things were going wrong, and offer to step in and make all the problems go away. That's what I'd have done, and I was pretty sure they weren't dumb enough to miss a chance like this. There was £20 million at stake, and more than that, there was Claire, the nightmare on the ninth floor, the Queen of Rates, the toughest, least sentimental person I'd ever had the misfortune to meet. We'd got Claire from Greenings a couple of years back and she still scared the crap out of anyone below her and probably most of the ones above. Most of that £20 million was hers, or her team's, at least. I didn't like to think what she'd do to me if I lost it.

The problem needed solving before things went too far down that road, and it was my job to solve it, to get the rating agencies onside again without doing anything that would affect the structure too much. Remember, we'd built this thing with one aim in mind: look cheap enough to win the deal, but pay enough to be worth it. Whatever I did, I couldn't change that. I'd have to go right back to the beginning and unpick everything that had gone into it, all the conflicting demands of all those people droning on about cashflows, operations, tax, accounting, legal, credit, and see if I could pull out one little brick without the whole lot crashing down.

But first things first. Whilst commiserating with another one of Harvey's exhausted lawyers (lawyers talk about sleep like the rest of England talks about the weather, all the time and with obsessive interest in the forecast), I looked up and saw Rachel stroll in (bang on 9 as usual). Coffee time.

2: Coffee and King Lear

Monday 14th December, 2009
9am.

I don't drink much coffee. I don't really like the stuff that much, so my particular poison's a double espresso. Means I can get the whole thing over in a couple of seconds. But the taste isn't really the point, it's all about the hit, and the coffee break itself, five minutes, maybe ten, and maybe a cigarette if I'm in one of my smoking phases (right now, I wasn't). I'd a habit of taking the first coffee break of the morning with Rachel. The two of us would rip the rest of the office to shreds, and I'd sip my espresso and drink in those legs. Christ, those legs. Aussie legs, tanned-on-the-beach legs, surfer's legs, and the rest of her probably just as good, not that I'd ever know, because her husband was all she was interested in and twice the man I was.

(I'm not being modest, by the way. If you've seen Greg and his muscles and his long golden locks, you'll understand that being half a Greg is something to aspire to.)

Small wonder that first coffee break took closer to fifteen than five, often as not. I caught Rachel's eye; we were in the lift in two minutes and at the front of the queue in another three. I felt in my pocket. I'd left the BlackBerry on my desk, and even though I had better things to look at than another round of Mintrex emails I felt like a small part of me was missing. It was probably a good thing. We tried not to talk deals unless there was something really interesting, Rachel and I, so we didn't talk deals too often. She'd been to the ballet the night before and started off on that, but then she remembered she was talking to me and not her husband (Greg's a choreographer), and Russell and the succession plan took over before the first couple of sentences were out. Rachel was like me. Prettier, obviously, and probably cleverer, too. But she wasn't in the frame for the big job and she knew it. She knew *about* the big job because I'd told her. And she had no idea what Russell was planning, which wasn't any great surprise because I didn't either.

A twelve-minute oasis of calm, that break, and maybe I should be thankful, but twelve didn't feel like nearly enough, and by the time my feet were back under the desk it was 9:15, another twenty emails had come in, and not one of them solved my Mintrex problem.

One, however, was from Jason, asking if I fancied a coffee. Too late. Gave him a call. It rang three times and got answered with a couple of bangs and a deep breath. Lorraine. Lorraine was the main PA on Jason's team. She looked good, in a dumb sort of way, but the dumb outweighed the looking good by a mile. Once she'd figured out who I was she thought for a moment. There was something. Yes. Jason. He'd popped into a meeting with Marcus but he'd wanted to speak to me this morning, or was it yesterday, let's see, I wrote it down somewhere, I was wearing the purple nail gloss so that's right it must have been today.

A meeting with Marcus. The Spider. I tried to let it wash over me. It could mean anything. Lorraine might have got the whole thing completely wrong. It had happened before. I sighed and thanked her. No use speculating, especially when there was real work to be done. I'd find out eventually.

Toiled on with Mintrex. Anthony was on the floor, chorused by high-fives and back-slapping from a couple of colleagues who wouldn't have pissed on him if he was on fire. Not that he thought much more of them, I imagined:

useful drones at best; disposable losers more likely. I swivelled my chair and took a look behind: Russell was in his office, shielded from the rest of us by three partly-frosted glass walls and that "Head of" on the front of his business card. His door was ajar and I could see him looking out, watching Anthony. Did he realise how hated the guy was? I'd tried to tell him; I couldn't go any further. He closed the door and retreated from view.

The phone rang; I looked down; as if summoned by the power of my thoughts, there was Russell's number. He wanted a chat; I strolled in and took a seat.

Russell's office was nothing special – once you got past the fact that for a banker, having your own private office is pretty special in the first place. You might be a trader taking home ten million a year and pulling in fifty times that for the bank, but unless you're a manager with a good-sized flock and an upward trajectory, you're still sitting out there in the noise and the bad lighting, next to the fat guy who cycles to work in the height of summer and hasn't yet found the showers on the tenth floor. Of course you might be next to your boss's foxy PA instead, but your chances aren't good – there are a lot more fat guys than foxy PAs.

Russell's desk was a quarter-length version of the thing half a dozen of us were sitting at outside. Front covers from banking magazines evenly spaced along the wall, award after forgettable award. Perspex tombstones on the desk and on top of the filing cabinets, memories of deals long-dead. The oval conference table of polished oak I was sitting at looked like a nice touch from a distance, but you didn't have to lift it to tell it was just veneer. The wood wasn't wood, and the frosted glass wasn't glass, either, because plastic was cheaper and a hell of a lot easier to move. They got moved a lot, windows and walls, whole rooms suddenly appearing and disappearing whenever someone got fired or promoted. No space to spare for an empty office, no time for those who were left behind to look at a room and remember who'd sat in it. When you were gone you were gone and you might as well never have existed.

"So what do you reckon? Time to move on?"

Russell was sat at his desk, facing the screen. I don't know how he knew for sure it was me he was talking to, or whether he really cared that much any more. Some secrets seem more valuable than they really are. So what if Russell's move went public? It wouldn't stop it happening.

"What do you mean, mate?"

"Come on, Alex. You're the one guy who knows what's going on."

Yeah, sure, I thought. But I didn't say anything. Russell turned around and grinned at me.

"I mean, look, why not stick around here?"

I frowned at him. Last week he'd sketched out the job he'd been offered, or at least he thought he had, but all I'd got out of it was a bunch of words that could have meant anything. I didn't know how many people he'd be ruling over or precisely how much money would be added to a package someone like me could only dream of. But still. It was going to be bigger and better and more than he had now.

"You're joking, right?"

"Look around you." He stood, arms outstretched, more like a tourist guide at a beauty spot than a drone in his little plastic cell.

"I've got it good here, Alex. Why should I give this up?"

The question was so ridiculous it took me a few moments to come up with the right answer. But there was no point being gentle.

"Russell. Listen to me, mate. This place is a shit-hole"

He stared at me. We had nothing in common, really. He liked golf, and fine wines, and skiing in the kind of place where the guy in the next chalet has the word "Prince" in front of his name. I liked beer and fast cars and women. He was going to be a star, had "star" written on him from the day he walked in, hand-picked by the guy whose office he was now sitting in. I was going to be a solid dealmaker no one outside my own deals would ever hear of. But I didn't think there was anyone else he'd talk to like this, and there certainly wasn't anyone else who'd talk back to him the way I was doing. People like Russell need a bit of honesty in their lives. Lucky for him I was there.

"Really, Russ. Look at it. A few feet of plastic. Look, mate, you've got a great job, you've done a fantastic job with this team, but for Christ's sake don't get hung up on your office. You can't stay here forever."

I meant it, too. Just because I was never going to get the kind of offer he had didn't mean I wouldn't have taken it if I could. You get a lot of bankers talking about how they'd hate management, how they need to be at the coalface, doing deals, and sure, doing deals can be fun, but if you're a banker then at a certain point you've got to admit you're in it for the money and the power – and they tend to sit upstairs. And Russell hadn't actually run a deal for a long time.

Russell folded his arms, nodded at me.

"I guess you're right. I'm just, well." He paused. Unsure where he was heading. "I'm just nervous. I know it's crazy. But, well, it's a big change."

I shook my head. He grinned. Now was as good a time as any.

"So what's the big plan, then?"

The grin broadened. He sat down next to me at the table.

"It's just an idea, Alex. But, well, whoever I put in, there's going to be trouble, isn't there?"

More than you know if it's Anthony, I thought, but just nodded.

"So I thought why not do something different? I mean, look, we've got the structured deals, we've got the utility deals, we've got the transport stuff, we've got long-term asset-backed, right, we've got all kinds of things going on in the one team."

I frowned. We did a lot of different deals on the team. So what?

"So why not split things up?"

"Split the team up?"

"Yeah."

I thought for a moment. I hadn't been expecting this. I hadn't been expecting anything this stupid. I don't know what my face looked like but I think he could tell I wasn't impressed. He carried on.

"There's at least two people I can think of who could lead this team, Alex, and I don't really want to piss either of them off."

I couldn't let that one go.

"It's not your job to make sure you don't piss anyone off, Russ."

He started to speak but there was so much wrong with what he'd been saying I couldn't stop myself.

"Seriously, you think this is a good idea? Split up the empire, make sure there's no one powerful enough downstairs to come after you? You think you're King Lear or something?"

Russell had studied English lit at university. He might not have liked what I was saying but at least he got it. He frowned, then grinned, then frowned again. Not that Lear wouldn't be an improvement. With Stephen it had felt more like Macbeth. Most of the time it was like a revenge tragedy round here.

He hadn't given up on the hard sell, though.

"It's easy for you to shit on it, Alex, but if I don't do this I've got to pick someone and I'm buggered if I know who."

"Pick someone, Russ. But one. Not two. More than one and they'll tear each other apart. That list you just did, those categories, Mintrex fits at least two of them. And that's just one deal I happen to be working on right now. A big one. They'd eat each other alive for any deal, for the shittiest little tap right up to an elephant. I would. You would, too."

For a moment he looked like he was going to argue, but it was only a moment. He must have known it was stupid. Maybe he was just looking for someone to say it out loud. He nodded. He looked thoughtful, sad, like he'd finally realised this was real, and it suddenly hit me that maybe it was true, what he'd said when I came in, maybe none of it was what he really wanted at all.

And then the phone rang and the spell was broken. By the way Russell jumped to answer, it looked like senior management. Or anyone more important than me, really, which took the field a lot lower than senior management. But ten seconds of hand signals was time enough to arrange a drink for later in the week. We'd continue the discussion then.

Back to Mintrex, then. I'd dug up the history on the derivatives and now I had a good idea why it looked like it did. Unfortunately, I also knew that it had to look like it did or the whole thing would fall apart. Sergei had been very eloquent on the subject.

"Alex," he'd said, "you must never change these swaps. Never. I will have you fucking killed if you change these swaps."

I'd laughed at him, and he'd shaken his head and looked as serious as man with a potato for a head could look. "I am not joking, Alex. This is delicate, Alex. *Very* delicate. You do something to this swap, it's like disarming a nuke when you're full of fucking vodka and your hands are shaking because it's winter and you're in Siberia and you're in the middle of a fucking field."

"At three in the morning, right, Sergei?"

He'd shaken his head again, pityingly, and said "In Siberia in winter is *always* three in the morning, Alex."

Not that he'd spent any more time in the Gulag than I had; not that he could get me killed any more than he could get me elected Prime Minister. Sergei had gone from middle-class Moscow to studying maths and money in London, and followed that up with a very expensive MBA in the States. He might be smart, and he could talk the talk, but he was just another well-padded, well-heeled banker with a nice flat in Islington.

But he was right about the swaps. Like a line of over-sensitive dominoes. Make the change the agencies wanted, and the accounting treatment of the hedge would change with it. The lawyers who'd written the tax opinion for the deal would spot this and make their own little changes – a "will" would become a "should", a "satisfied" would get a "reasonably" shoved up its smug little arse. And when they saw these tiny little tweaks, our own tax team at Miltons would throw their toys out of the pram and veto the whole damned thing, because now, suddenly, there was a one in a million chance of something going ever-so-slightly wrong.

Back in the day (by which I mean the glory days, the before-2008-days, the halcyon days when everything we touched turned to gold) the answer would have been simple: call the rating agencies, shout at them, and threaten to throw them off the deal until they agreed to drop the point. There were other agencies out there, after all. We hired the fuckers, or our clients did; we could fire them just as easily. Maybe it wasn't the cleanest, most transparent system, now I think about it.

But it didn't work like that any more. The whole dynamic had changed. First off, the agencies would rather drop the deal themselves than take the chance they'd be caught with their trousers round their ankles and their faces in the trough (again). They might not be subject to banker levels of scorn and abuse, but they weren't far behind. And secondly, as they well knew, on a deal like Mintrex, which was "groundbreaking" (risky), "innovative" (flaky) and "exotic" (liable to fall apart at any moment), there weren't any other agencies out there. Mintrex was weird enough to need the blessing of all three of the big ones if we were going to convince investors the deal could wash its face. This time, I'd have to find someone else to bully – which is how it should have been in the first place, really. And, helpfully, I knew just the victim.

My phone was ringing, so the victim had a reprieve. Lorraine on the line. What the hell did she want?

"I think you should come down."

Jason's team worked down on the fourth floor, we were on twelve. Nothing to do with status; the execs were on the exec floor, and the rest of us weren't, that's all. And these days even we didn't know where we were half the time, because whoever happened to be empire-building up there liked to keep us all moving, once, maybe twice a year.

"What's up, Lorraine?"

"Please. Just come down."

It was on the tip of my tongue to tell her to piss off. My head was full of Mintrex, and I didn't have time for whatever non-crisis had got stuck inside the subatomic particle she called a brain. But there was something in her voice, something different, something almost mechanical like she was upset, really upset, and trying not to let it show. Now I might be a soulless banker but I'm not a complete bastard.

And anyway, first on the scene is first with the news.

3: The Spider, the Witch and the Beast

Monday 14*th* December
10:13am

Lorraine's desk faced the lift lobby, so you could see her through the glass doors the moment you stepped onto the floor. Even from here I could tell she'd been crying. There was no sign of Jason. No sign of the team head, Jessica, either; of course, she was on holiday. A few others sitting around, shrugging and shaking their heads. No one seemed to know what was going on.

As I got closer I spotted a couple of cardboard boxes by Lorraine's desk and everything fell into place. Someone had finally decided to get rid of her. They'd waited till Jess was away, too; Jess had a soft spot for Lorraine. Box your stuff and get the hell out – it was brutal, sure, but Lorraine wasn't going to be the greatest loss to banking. I glanced over my shoulder, like I always did these days when I happened to be on four. There was an unfamiliar face watching us, stood outside the corridor leading to Marcus's office. A kid, hardly twenty I guessed, but built like two twenty-year-olds stuck together. I'd not seen him before, and I couldn't imagine why they'd decided to stick this kind of security on Lorraine of all people. Worst case she'd walk out with a dozen pictures of kittens from her Facebook friends. I reckoned the bank would survive.

When I got to her she was slumped in her chair drying her eyes. She had a loose knitted top on and I could see that for once she'd chosen to wear a bra. I fought back the disappointment. This wasn't the time. The boxes were to the side, in front of Jason's desk (and where that bastard was I'd no idea, he couldn't still be in his meeting, and this was his problem, not mine). More stuff in there than I'd have guessed, document after document, even the odd book. I hadn't thought Lorraine could manage a whole book.

"I'm so sorry Lorraine. When did it happen?"

She was dabbing her eyes with a lipstick-stained tissue. The results weren't pretty, but I wasn't going to mention it.

"It's still happening. He's still in there, talking to Marcus. HR just called me and told me to start the packing."

SHIT

Suddenly everything fell into place. The papers, the books, Jason's call earlier, Marcus's unending pressure.

SHIT

Two questions flew across my mind in quick succession. *Is he just getting fired? What's he saying about me?*

"Just" getting fired.

SHIT!

That could be me in there.

I had to calm down. I'm not the kind of guy who usually thinks in caps, and last time I'd used an exclamation mark I'd still been at school. I took a step back from Lorraine. I'd been staring at her without saying a word for maybe ten seconds. She hadn't noticed. Maybe she was used to people just staring at her. I had to find out what was going on but I wouldn't know the details until Jason got out.

But there was something I could do. I could give Lorraine a hand. If there was anything there that shouldn't be, maybe I could get to it and get it out the building before the wrong people got hold of it. Lorraine wouldn't find anything, she wouldn't even know what she was looking for. As it happened, I had no idea whether Jason kept anything to do with our little sideline inside the office. I knew I didn't, and I hoped to hell he didn't either, but I didn't want to take any chances.

Turned out I didn't have much choice. I'd got as far as crouching down, one hand on Jason's desk drawer handle and the other in a near-empty box, when a much bigger hand fell gently on my shoulder.

"Excuse me sir."

The voice was surprisingly soft. I hadn't noticed him leaving his post. I'd have thought the floor would have shaken.

"Is there a problem?"

"Excuse me, sir." The touch was still gentle, but the pressure ever so slightly firmer.

I could feel myself getting warm. I didn't like this at all. I needed to stay calm.

"What's going on? I'm trying to help out a mate so please can you get on with letting me do what I'm doing here?"

I hadn't stayed calm at all. I couldn't even manage a coherent sentence, but the point was pretty clear. Unfortunately, so was the response.

"I'm sorry, sir."

I turned round to face the guy. I definitely hadn't seen him before. I'd have known him if I had. Not one of our usual security team. Gentle and terribly calm, and you could tell you wouldn't want to be around if the storm broke. He reminded me of one of those giants standing stone-faced guard outside the celebrity bars. Perfectly round face, short, thinning brown hair, boxer's nose, huge body crammed into the dark blue of Miltons security. A real Beast.

I wasn't going to be able to talk this guy round. I stood up and stepped back a couple of paces, arms out, palms facing. He nodded, slightly, and returned to his station by the corridor. I returned the nod, walked over to the empty desk the other side of Lorraine, and sat.

On further questioning, she didn't have a whole lot else to say. Jason had been called in to see Marcus just before I'd returned his call. Half an hour later, Lorraine had taken a call from HR asking her to go through Jason's desk, identify anything personal, and box it. She didn't know when the security guy had taken up his post. She'd made a start, going through drawers and staring blankly at random articles before applying some arbitrary brain-filter and consigning them to the box or back to the desk (where she'd probably come across them again a few minutes later and make the decision all over again). It took another ten minutes for her to realise this wasn't normal, and maybe something was up. No one she'd asked had known what was going on, and Lorraine had figured it out all by herself, so that was something worth celebrating, at least. She'd broken down and reached straight for the one person she knew Jason trusted. Me.

All of which meant it was now nearly three-quarters of an hour since Jason had gone to meet his doom, and he still wasn't out.

The range of possibilities was broad, and the worst case was pretty fucking terrible. Jason fired, police called in, Marcus's back well and truly covered, Alex exposed. Of course, there might be no police; I might have been kept out of it; maybe there had been no firing at all, and Jason was just being encouraged to leave, politely, with excellent references and some money in the bank.

I didn't think that was likely. Not with the Beast standing watch.

Ten minutes passed, the longest ten minutes I could remember. Lorraine had nothing left to say, I had nothing left to ask, and everyone else was pretending to get on with their work. And then movement, in the corridor, behind the Beast. Jason was on his way out. He was flanked by security guards, familiar ones this time, and behind I could see Marcus, the Spider, expressionless. Beside Marcus, talking quietly to him, her lips almost in his ear, the Witch from HR. No one knew her name, but she was only ever seen when someone was being fired. We'd seen a lot of her over the last couple of years. No one else, or no one I could see. So no police at the interview, thank Christ, unless Marcus had left them in his office. Marcus, the most careful, the most paranoid man I'd ever come across. No, there'd been no police.

Jason was ashen, lips pursed, giving nothing away. Fugue state or poker face, I couldn't tell which. The men either side of him were steering him towards his desk and the haphazard selection Lorraine had made on his behalf. As he reached the desk it was still impossible to read his expression – clearly nothing good had happened, but there was a world of difference between bad (for Jason) and very bad (for both of us). At least it looked like he was being allowed to correct Lorraine's mistakes.

I'd never heard it so quiet. The rustle of every bit of paper, even the creak of desk drawers opening, everything Jason did sounded like someone shouting in a metal room. Four wasn't a trading floor, so there was never much of that squawk-box chat and friendly abuse you'd have got on two or three, but usually there was something, doors closing, printers clattering, phones ringing, people talking. Silence. Looked like Lorraine hadn't done such a bad job after all – either that, or Jason didn't have the stomach to do the job properly, what with the security guards and the having been fired – because after a couple of minutes he stopped. A promising career, a man going places. Two small cardboard boxes.

Then he looked up, looked around, and saw me. And turned and gazed at the two security guards and Marcus. My mind was screaming *"Don't be so fucking obvious,"* but I couldn't say anything. Sure, I wanted to know what had happened in Marcus's office, but I didn't want to find out in front of the combined cast of Macbeth and The Sopranos. I raised a hand, palm out – with the Beast it had been *calm down*, but now it was *shut up*, and then closed the hand to a fist and raised it to my ear. We'd have to speak later. Nothing strange about that, was there? We were friends. Everyone knew that. Even Marcus would have known that. Nothing suspicious. I'd call Jason's mobile in five minutes and get the goods then.

Or not, as I realised watching Jason pull out his *office* mobile phone and hand it, together with BlackBerry, security pass and corporate Amex, to the Beast. I'd have to wait till he got home. No problem. I caught Jason's eye again and shrugged. He shrugged back. Fine.

All fine. No reason for me to stick around for the end of the show. Just walk out like nothing's happened. Past the security guards. Straight to the lift. No problem. Keep walking. Look ahead, not to the side. All fine.

Except one thing, one small thing: as I passed the end of the bank of desks, almost in the clear, Marcus strolled over to me. Expressionless as ever. Disproportionately small eyes, too: gives nothing away. Strolled over, patted me on the shoulder (as if in commiseration) and said, so quietly it was all but a whisper:

"I'm watching you, Konninger."

4: Following the Money, 1993-1999

I never wanted to be a banker.

Not at the start, anyway. First time I worked in a bank, I didn't know what a banker was. I'd just had a row with Dad. I don't even remember what this one was about, but I was fifteen and he was angry and for a while, we argued every day. We'd argued over breakfast and I'd stormed out the house before he left for the Plant, and as luck would have it, that morning at school we had to pick work experience assignments.

Everyone knew that was a joke, to be honest. This was Dagenham. There was cars, and there wasn't a whole lot of anything else. Dad was at the Plant, everyone I knew with a job was either at the Plant or doing something connected with it. And the truth is, I didn't much mind the Plant. It might not have meant the things to me that it meant to Dad, but I'd have worked there happily. I was fifteen years old, for fuck's sake. What did I know?

So if it hadn't been for that row I'd have signed up for the Plant that morning alongside everyone else. It was only a couple of August weeks, after all. It would have been a laugh, we'd have got up to all the old tricks, pissed around, played jokes on the old men, and as usual everyone would have turned to me when we got caught and I'd have come up with some line to sort it all out. I'd have signed up, I'd have steered clear of Dad and the rest of the union men, and I'd have enjoyed it. But that morning I was sick of Dad and the union and the whole lot of them, and I flicked down the list of options and saw a box that said Milton Shearings. I'd seen the name on the High Street. It was a bank. As far as I was concerned a bank was the place people put the money they didn't hide under the bed, and I didn't have a clue what went on in one, but it didn't matter. It wasn't the Plant. Ticked the box, and that was it, the rest of my life.

It's not like those two weeks blew me away. It was OK, I guess. But still. It wasn't awful, and it wasn't the Plant, and by now I'd convinced myself that I really didn't want to build cars. Dad had been furious when I told him about it but come the beginning of August, when I actually went there and came home each day looking a tiny bit interested, he'd bitten back all his lectures about capital and workers and oppression and nodded and smiled and tried to look like he was pleased.

A year later I was out of school and at the bank for good.

Most of the people at Miltons in Dagenham had worked there for years, and they still thought it was just the place people put the money they didn't hide under the bed, but I couldn't believe that was all there was to it. Cars I understood. Dad could price the parts for me, the supply, the materials, the energy costs and property costs and the rest, everything except labour, and then he'd show me how much a car sold for, and I'd whistle at the difference. He meant to show me how much money the workers were being cheated out of, and on a basic level I understood what he meant, that it was all a closed system, and if there was that big a gap between what was coming in and what was going out then that gap should go to the workers. But all I got, really, was money: how you could make it by building cars.

What I didn't understand was how you could make money by putting it in a box and sending it out at the end of the day in an armoured car to a place with a bigger box and thicker walls. I'd seen the numbers, even back then they'd announce the profits the banks were making each year and everyone would whistle and get back to their cornflakes. But if that money was sitting in boxes the whole time, where did the profits come from?

I wanted the answer, and the only way I could get it was by following the money once it left the bank. I'd ask people in Dagenham and they'd shrug. The men were too busy eyeing up Sam, the pretty blonde cashier. The women were too busy bitching about her roots and her fake tan. I guess the manager knew how it all worked, but he was too busy to talk to the likes of me, or at least he pretended to be. Peter McGinley, a pompous, old-fashioned fat man who liked to wear a bow-tie for work and seemed to inhabit a different world from the rest of us. What he really got up to for the four or five hours a day he spent sat by himself in his dark wood-panelled office was anyone's guess. The only people who might have been able to help were the people who came to pick up the money, not the ones with the blue uniforms and scowls and menacing bulges but the ones who came with them, to check everything was how it was supposed to be. And they *really* didn't have time for the likes of me, not when they were off almost as soon as they'd arrived, to the next branch or back to Head Office to do more important things I couldn't understand.

So I did something Dad would have been proud of, even though he never saw it, because six months after I started at the branch he was dead, a heart attack, early shift at the Plant, and nothing to do with his disappointment at the choices his son had made. I read. I'd go to the library at lunchtime and read books about economics and finance, half of them written half a century earlier and half of *them* still mourning the demise of the gold standard, but it was enough to get me started. I read newspapers, nothing like the papers Dad used to read, papers that still turned up at home sometimes, left behind by Dad's friends who dropped by from time to time to see how I was doing and maybe how Mum was getting on and if she was ready to start thinking about the future yet (she was, but not with any of them). I read and I read and finally I started to understand. I knew what happened to the money when it drove out of Dagenham. I knew how a bank made a profit. I knew what a banker was.

And I wanted to be one.

Back in those days a list would come round once every couple of weeks, a photocopied sheet of paper working its way around the branch for people to ignore or point at and snigger. They didn't even know what they were laughing at, a list of jobs they didn't understand in places that weren't Dagenham, it was the laughter of the ignorant and the envious. But *I* knew, now. I wanted something different and I thought it would never come but one day, finally, nearly two years after I'd started there, I got out.

I don't know what I'd expected. I was from Dagenham, not Dagestan. I'd been to London enough times to know my Whitechapel from my West End, but I'd not really spent any time in the City. And now I was off to work there. Head Office, it was called back then, before it got torn down and rebuilt and became a number in an office complex that looked like something designed by Darth Vader. I suppose I thought it would be just a bigger, grander version of McGinley's office, all wood and sombre elegance, maybe a little marble. Instead I got a tall, dirty, run-down tower block that wouldn't have been out of place on one of the East End housing estates the train took me past on the way in.

But the job was the thing, and it was exactly what I'd hoped it would be. Don't get me wrong. I wasn't a banker, not by a long shot. I was just a bloke running backwards and forwards between floors, between different buildings, delivering bits of paper between the teams and the people who worked on them.

Miltons had always been a high street operation, a retail business that had started out as a gang of regional banks and building societies and turned into one of the biggest mortgage providers in the country. When it came to investment banking, these guys were only just getting started, and even I could tell they were making it up as they went along. I was working with the government bonds team, gilts, they were called – working *for* the gilts team, really – and they were just starting to wake up to the fact that they needed to keep records of what they were doing, needed to let other people know what they were doing, needed someone to approve their trades – and this is mid-nineties, it's not like they can just pdf the stuff and shove it on an email. There were people like me all over the place. Monkeys, they called us. Each and every team – bond sales, traders, you name it, they all had their own monkeys, recording and settling and trying to keep tabs on chaos. Which meant dozens of monkeys like me, all reporting to a few traders or salesmen, all with their own unique system of getting the job done. It shouldn't have been a surprise that things were going wrong. Trade details getting lost, papers mislaid, mistakes all over the place, because the people who had to deal with all this stuff had no idea what it was they were dealing with.

Thing was, I'd done my reading. I *did* understand the importance of what I was doing – kind of. So instead of just running around with bits of paper and forgetting about them, I started copying those bits of paper and sorting them into files. And when someone needed to find one, instead of having to chase it halfway across London, they could just come to me, and chances were I'd be able to lay my hands on it by the end of the day. They liked that. They gave me a desk. They gave me a ledger and I started putting numbers into it, adding them up, taking them away. They took away my ledger and gave me a computer. I still wasn't a banker, but I wasn't a monkey, either. And then Kemp arrived, and everything changed.

In 1997 Henry Kemp, the socialite head of a small British merchant bank with blue blood flowing through its veins (alongside vintage claret and some lucratively-financed nineteenth-century opium, but they didn't talk about that any more), was handed the top job at Milton Shearings. To the surprise of employees, the financial press, and the informed public, all of whom assumed him to be a toffee-nosed twat who'd got where he had on the strength of his contacts rather than his brain, Kemp proved a ruthless and efficient leader. He wanted the investment banking side of the business run properly, professionally; he wanted the retail bank to grow its market share and take more deposits. The more money the retail bank churned, the more useful it could be to the investment bankers, who could attract clients to their high-margin products with the promise of enormous loans funded by deposits from the man in the street. But only if the investment bankers could be trusted not to lose the client, the trade, the deposit.

The story went that shortly after his appointment, Kemp hosted a dinner with the various heads of the investment bank in the Miltons boardroom. I saw that room, once, before Head Office got pulled down; the one place in the building that *did* have the wood and the marble and the rest. It was meant to be a getting-to-know-you thing, the bankers all happy and relaxed and looking forward to some decent food and a lot of wine. They must have been surprised when Kemp started questioning them over the rumours he'd heard. Lost trades, missing data, embarrassing fuckups which had left Miltons red-faced and out of pocket. Maybe he thought they'd deny it; maybe he thought they'd have a decent excuse. But when he realised there was no centralised back office, when he learned about all the monkeys running around doing their own thing, he hit the roof – literally, flinging his plate across the room in fury, leaving gravy dripping from the ceiling and some very expensive suits needing a good dry-clean. He told the assembled heads they had three days to get together and come up with a detailed plan for a unified back office. If it wasn't there, or he wasn't happy with it, they'd all be fired. If it met with his approval, they might live to fight another day.

The plan was duly presented, and Kemp did approve – so much so that only half the poor fuckers who'd witnessed the "night of the steak knives" (as it was dubbed by one wag in the business pages of a Sunday broadsheet) lost their jobs that year (the rest were gone by the following Christmas, but that's banking). And so the back office was created.

Kemp being Kemp, it wasn't all about unification and efficiency. There was money to be saved and jobs to be cut, which meant I ended up applying for one of forty jobs alongside a hundred and fifty fellow-monkeys. But like I said, I'd done my reading. I understood what I was doing. And of the hundred and fifty, seventy plus really *were* monkeys – just about capable of doing the running and copying, but nothing more – and a few more had serious black marks against them for the sins of the past. One fifty to forty might not sound like great odds, but I knew I'd breeze it, and I did.

The back office was a revelation. No more blown lighting circuits, no more blocked and overflowing toilets, no more Head Office. A new building, just across Bishopsgate. Head Office was being torn down and rebuilt, in a spot no banker would have set foot in a couple of years back when it was called Shoreditch or Hackney. The City had moved north, though, and Shoreditch and Hackney had retreated a half mile further up the road. And while the new place was rising from what rumour had it was a seventeenth century plague pit, we were in a new building. A whole floor, just for us. Back office. No more ancient filing systems; no more shared phone lines; no more traders shouting "FUCKING CUNT" at no one in particular while you were trying to have a civilised conversation with an agent or a clearing house. It was heaven.

A year went by. I was still working with gilts but now I was sitting alongside people doing the same thing for all the other bits of the investment bank. The bank was growing, the profits were growing, the deals were growing. We weren't screwing up so much now we had our own base, but when we did screw up, it was costing us the kind of money that would have made Kemp turn over an entire dessert trolley. Kemp was gone, Lord Kemp, as he was now, striding into Westminster full of youth and sound and fury, and suddenly a hundred years old, dozing quietly through speeches and voting the way he was told to. But the people who came after Kemp didn't like losing money any more than he had, and when the new bureaucracy in the back office told them they knew how to fix the few problems that remained, they believed them. Hire, more and more, grow, bigger and bigger, until the back office that had just been forty ex-monkeys keeping records turned into a monstrosity that dwarfed the traders and dealmakers it was supposed to serve. I don't know if it worked or not but with the time I'd already put in I suddenly had something like seniority, and I wasn't just doing my job any more, I was looking out for the new guys and making sure they didn't screw up.

By the time the new building was up, the back office was so big there was no room for us there. We stayed where we were, just across the road, getting on with business while new faces flooded in and the people in charge changed our titles and the names of our teams like they changed their suits and hairstyles. I did a stint in corporate bond settlement. I did a stint with one of the cash teams, the guys whose touch of a button sends a billion dollars fizzing round the world. And then came securitisation.

Back then, you said the word "securitisation" and outside a few bankers, accountants and lawyers, no one would know what the hell you were talking about. Now, at least, they know it costs a lot and they don't like it. It's a start.

No one at Miltons really knew what securitisation was, either, but they'd heard about it and how it could make them a lot of money. So they did what bankers always do when they want to learn something and they don't have time to do it themselves. They threw money at it.

Just four people, that's how it started. Four hires, in the front office, bankers who called themselves "structurers", which made them sound like they were putting up scaffolding and made the rest of us laugh because if they weren't lending or trading or selling then what the hell were they doing in a bank? Two Americans, two Brits, stolen from four different banks, with one thing in common: they were costing us a shitload, so if they wanted to last more than a few months they'd have to hit the ground running. Which is where I came in, because while these new guys were structuring their deals, whatever that meant, they needed a team in the back office to cover their backs and make sure everything else was running the way it was supposed to. Someone had the idea that I should be that team. I didn't know why at the time and I still don't, but it changed everything for me.

I went to meet them. I don't know what I was expecting, aliens more than people, but they looked just like the rest of the bankers over there in the new building. Spoke a different language, though. I recognised the words, or most of them, but to me it sounded like these guys were just throwing everything together in a great big fucking finance soup. They must have seen me looking blank and they might have told me to piss off and found someone cleverer who knew what they were talking about, but they didn't – they'd have struggled at our shop, anyway, back then. Instead they sat me down, patiently, for an hour one morning, two hours the next day, another couple at the end of the week, and again the week after, and they told me what it was they did, and why they did it, and how they got paid for it. They took their deals, the ones they'd already done, back at their old shops, and they dissected them for me, the thousands of pages of documents, the billions of pounds, the payment waterfalls, credit default swaps, liquidity facilities, interest rate hedges. A few weeks earlier I'd never heard of securitisation. Now, I was hooked.

After everything the media has screamed at you over the last few years, you probably think you know what securitisation is. You might even be right, although the chances aren't good. Let me give you the bare bones. I'll keep it nice and short.

First thing you need to know is that securitisation is a complicated way of arranging a loan for a company, your client. It's complicated because the company wants to pay fuck-all interest or as close to fuck-all as they can, which is fine if they're Apple or Microsoft or BP, but they're not. Most of them aren't even Easyjet. So the only way your clients can get a low rate of interest – "cheap money", we'd call it – is by having something the lender can take off them if things go wrong – like mortgaging your house when you borrow the money to buy it. And just like a mortgage, the more the house is worth, the happier the lender and the cheaper the loan.

Instead of a house, your big corporate borrowers have cashflows – sums of money someone else will be paying them in the months or years to come – and it's these cashflows that they promise to use to pay off the loan they'd taken out. The cashflows could come from almost anything. Most commonly, your client's a bank or a building society, and the cashflows are payments from a whole host of mortgages – yours and mine – that they've loaned out in the first place. Your client parks all these mortgages and cashflows in a brand new company, called an "SPV", and it's the SPV that does the actual borrowing, by issuing bonds – usually hundreds of millions of pounds worth – to pension funds, insurance companies, hedge funds and other faceless pits full of cash. So on the fifteenth of the month, when you and me and everyone else make our regular monthly payment, that money goes from us to the bank, and from the bank to the SPV, and the SPV uses it to pay a bit of interest and a bit of principal back on the bonds. Anything left over at the end gets funnelled back to your client. Everyone's happy.

Now, what I've done here is give the classic example of a securitisation. There are a thousand variants, and a hell of a lot of jargon to go with them. You don't have to use mortgage loans in the first place – you don't even have to be a bank. You can use anything that'll pay out some money over the next – well, the next whatever, because some deals can run for a few weeks, and some can run for 30 years. Pubs and hotels securitise their takings. Property companies securitise lease payments from office buildings and shopping malls. Mining companies, like Mintrex, might securitise the expected income stream from whatever it is they're digging out of the ground. Music companies – and David Bowie – securitise royalties, and football clubs, and Bernie Ecclestone's Formula One, securitise ticket and TV revenue (hence Bowie Bonds and Bernie Bonds – bankers have a great sense of humour).

Of course, bankers are bankers, so that's just the starting

point. It's got to be a whole lot more complicated than that to justify the fees we all squeeze out of it. You've got your senior bonds and your junior bonds, your fixed rate and your floating rate, and your thousand optional extras that bolt on to the basic structure until you end up with something utterly monstrous – so monstrous that now they're telling us we've brought the world to its knees. As if.

What it all boils down to is more and more complicated ways of doing the one thing anyone cares about: raise as much money as possible for your client, as cheaply as you can, and squeeze yourself a decent fee for doing it. Once I understood what it all meant, they didn't have to work very hard to sell it to me. I was their man.

I'd stopped going back to Dagenham after work, now. It started with a girlfriend in West Ham, far easier to stop at her place than go all the way back home each day. And then we'd split up, it was never really that serious, and I'd found my own place in Holloway, which was almost as grim as Dagenham, to be honest, but there was no one left in Dagenham any more. Even Mum was talking about leaving. They were still making cars there, but not so many, and the decision I'd made back in school everyone else had made in the years that followed. They'd got out, and now my childhood friends were scattered to the winds. The Dagenham mob, we called ourselves, when we met for a weekly drink or a monthly curry in Brick Lane. They grumbled about that, the rest of them, because most of them worked in the West End now and Brick Lane was no good for them. Good for me, though, right on the doorstep of Bankers Town (that's what they called the City, back then), and cheap, and far better than anything we'd grown up thinking of as a curry. There were eight of us, and I won't bore you with their names or their lives. Except for one, Paul, my best mate, who'd got out before the rest and not long after I had. Paul had joined a call centre to make more money than he could pull in making cars, and found he had a talent for it. Now he managed a floor of that call centre and was pulling in more money than Dad had managed after nearly forty years at the Plant.

And that was still less than me.

5: Choices

Monday 14th December, 2009
10:40am

"I'm watching you, Konninger."

Seriously, all the way back up in the lift, back across the floor to my desk, even after I'd sat down and taken a couple of deep breaths and tried to read some emails, I could feel him there, breathing over my shoulder, watching me. And (in case this hasn't been made sufficiently clear), this was not a good thing.

There was no one I could talk to. Jason and Marcus were the only people who knew what was going on. Jason wasn't going to be in touch for a while yet, I had no idea where he was heading, and Marcus was the enemy. Might be the enemy. I still didn't know, not for sure, although that parting comment hardly seemed friendly.

I sat there and tried to think about something else. Christine. Jasmine. Even Mintrex. Nothing worked. I couldn't wait for Jason to call me. He didn't have a mobile any more so I tried to work out where he'd go. I could call. Leave messages. Track him. Where would I go? The Nightingale wouldn't be open for half an hour. So there was home, or the flat. Sally and the kids, or Charmaine.

I chose the flat. It wasn't the more likely option, really, even though it was just twenty minutes away against forty-five for the house. But I didn't really want to speak to Sally if I didn't have to. If he wasn't there, if it hadn't all come out already, she'd want to know why I was calling, and I didn't trust myself to say the right amount of nothing. With Charmaine, there wouldn't have to be any explanation. If he wasn't there, he wasn't there.

It was a good little flat. Docklands, two bedrooms, expensive furniture, nice river view. Buy-to-let, that was the idea, boom times, everyone wants their own place and most of them can afford it. Jason hadn't got a day's rent out of the place because Charmaine had been in there the whole time, the only tenant, and she wasn't paying. Charmaine had arrived on the scene just before Jason completed on the flat – he had bought it as an investment, that much was true – and it wasn't difficult to see why he'd fallen for her. I'd have fallen for her, too. Of course I didn't have a wife and two kids to worry about so it was easy enough for me, but I'd never had the choice because it was Jason she'd set her eye on, from that first moment when we all barged into the marquee, a dozen of us, excited and full of bravado and maybe a little nervous too. Except for Jason, because nerves weren't his style, at least, not back then.

I thought I'd been bold getting out of Dagenham, but it turned out I was just another Essex boy on the make. The City was full of people like me. Jason was different.

It could all have been so simple for Jason. So straightforward. Bright lad, middle-class family, a bit of money and a lot of brain. He got himself into Cambridge, that kind of brain. But he didn't last there. Jason was a man in a hurry, even then, too much of a hurry to sit and read books for three years while everyone else was out there doing things. One of his old school friends – one without so many brains but more money and a bit of luck – one of them had decided to set up a business, digital photography, it was the future back then and even if none of them knew a thing about it, it still sounded exciting. Jason couldn't resist. He'd always been a chancer, that's what he said, and two terms at Cambridge were enough when he could see big money and more fun working with his friends in the big city. It hadn't worked out like that in the end of course, because it turned out you did need to know something about digital photography if you wanted to make much out of it, and the little they had made hadn't been shared out like Jason thought it should be. But it didn't matter. Jason was a chancer because he saw chances, and he'd spotted one of them while he was trying to stave off the banks that were about to gobble up what was left. You didn't need a degree to be a banker. He'd negotiated the loans in the first place, complicated things, they were, because who was going to lend to a company like this without the founder's family backing things up? By the end it wasn't like it had all collapsed into nothing, they hadn't needed to go after houses or cars or anything like that, but they'd thought, the banks, that they could just walk in and take whatever they wanted, and Jason had shown them that wasn't the case after all. He'd made life so damned difficult for them that they'd hated him and then been worn out by him and eventually admired him so much that one of them, the tech and telecoms unit at Milton Shearings, had made him an offer. Chance made, opportunity taken.

Jason's route from there to securitisation was no more interesting than mine had been, just faster. He saw something he liked, and he went out and got it. Another opportunity. But he'd settled down. He'd got married, to a beautiful girl he'd known most of his life, and they'd moved to the suburbs, and had a couple of kids. He had a platform now, a family, something he could put his weight on and it would still be there in the morning. No wonder he'd put all that behind him, all the risk-taking, all the danger, life in the fast lane. Until Charmaine showed up. Maybe he was just addicted to taking chances, maybe he'd just managed to bury it for a few years and she brought it back to the surface. More likely she was just in the right place at the right time, fluttering those baby blues right in his face at the very moment he'd looked down, seen a gaping hole in the platform, and realised there was nothing he could trust to take his weight forever.

I dialled and let it ring. Nothing. She'd probably be at the gym, or swimming, or jogging. No chance of finding Charmaine stuffing her face with cake or a Big Mac. Whatever you might say about her, she knew how to look after herself, but it didn't look a whole lot of fun to me.

It didn't matter where she was, really. She wasn't at home. Jason had realised Charmaine and the apartment were a mistake years ago, but still too late, and he'd spent so long convincing himself there was nothing he could do about it that it turned into the truth. Now he might have to do something after all. I put the phone down and looked around, hoping for an idea, hoping I'd see Jason walking towards me with his sideways grin, hoping I'd imagined the last hour and none of it had happened.

But I hadn't, and there was only one thing I could do if I wanted to speak to Jason now. I picked the phone back up and dialled the house.

I'd known Sally five years, nearly as long as I'd known Jason. I was one of the few people who could show up at the house without Emily having a screaming fit the moment she saw me, the only one at the bank who even knew about Emily. And I was David's godfather. So this wasn't going to be an easy call to make. If she knew everything, what would she think of my role? If she didn't, what should I say? Was it up to me tell her her husband had been fired? Did I have the balls?

As it turned out, she didn't know, and I didn't have the balls. Bankers aren't known for moral courage. Jason wasn't at home. We exchanged pleasantries, I laughed at something amusing David had done and forgot what it was straight away, and I found myself having to think up some bullshit excuse for why I'd be trying to get hold of Jason at home on a weekday. But Sally wasn't the suspicious type.

Why would she be? What was there for her to suspect – well, apart from Charmaine, and the fraud, and the firing? Christ, I could have told her anything and she'd have swallowed it, and thinking on my feet – or lying, you might call it – is one of the few things I'm good at. In the end I came up with some story about a call from Jason which seemed to have come from home rather than the office, a confused tale redeemed by the reasonably credible premise that Lorraine had screwed up in passing on a message.

So now there really was nothing to do except wait. Or, in fact, work. If I wasn't about to get fired (and possibly arrested) for fraud, then I might as try to do my job and avoid getting fired for incompetence. So it was back to Mintrex with as much of my brain as wasn't busy fighting off visions of P45s and prison cells. Didn't leave a whole lot of my brain for the job, but there's enough to go round.

First thing was to find myself a victim. Someone I could take all that fear, and rage, and frustration out on. If I couldn't take down Marcus, and I couldn't scream blue murder at some box-ticker from a rating agency, then the least I could do was put the fear of god into a lowly minion in our own tax department.

The great thing was that for once, the facts were on my side. The added spice the boys in tax had thrown into the mix a few months back was something brand new, something they'd never needed before, and this was the ingredient that had the rating agencies all hot under the collar.

But facts are never enough. Being right doesn't win the argument, not in banking. What wins the argument is money, and risk, and I had both of them on my side too. The money we stood to make was enormous. And the risk was tiny. Even tax should understand that. The hedge would make us nearly twenty million up front, booked against a high investment grade counterparty who had agreed to post top-quality collateral (translation: lots of money, a client who won't go bust, and who'll hand over valuable low-risk assets as security for the money they owe us). The down-side scenario? If, by some twist of logic too bizarre for me even to fucking imagine at this point, we chose to move our own investment banking business offshore (thus losing billions in tax-revenue for the Treasury, who pretty much owned us at the moment), *and* the courts interpreted a little-known regulation in a way that even our notoriously conservative tax lawyers were prepared to state was "not, in the view of this firm, a reasonable interpretation of the Act as modified by the amending legislation and as further clarified by the Guidance Notes issued from time to time by Her Majesty's Customs and Revenue" – *if*, as I say, these never-gonna-happen events *did* go and happen, then what would be the result?

I'll tell you the result – it would cost us up to four million pounds.

I'll put that down again, in case you think you read it wrong. That's *up to four million pounds*. Probably much less. In a one-in-a-million scenario. Against twenty million, in the hand, by the end of the week.

This was such a no-brainer it was a decision I'd have been happy to take for myself, but things don't work that way in a bank, much less a big bank, much less a big bureaucratic government-owned monstrosity like Miltons. Probably a good thing, really. I've got some sense in me. I can tell the decisions I should be able to make from those I shouldn't. But I can't speak for anyone else, and the rules have to take into account the stupid as well as me. The rules said it was someone else's call, which meant I had to bully that someone else into seeing my kind of sense.

The Tax department, alongside Legal, Finance and others too numerous to bore you with, had to bestow its blessing upon each and every deal before we could close it. One of the most painful tasks, as the finishing-line approached and you started to see the dollar signs and the champagne flowing and a few days' R&R, was to gather in all these blessings (which was a bit like herding cats) and then make sure the bastards didn't change their minds at the last minute (which was a bit like persuading cats to sit still, outside, on a cold, wet day).

The element of surprise is crucial in war. You need your enemy on the back foot. This was war and I'd chosen my enemy, even if they didn't know it yet. They would soon enough. I picked up the phone and put the call straight in to tax.

Mel, she was called. Seemed nice enough on the phone, pleasant, but wary, which was what I'd have been in her place. I'd never met her, I'd spoken to her half a dozen times on half a dozen deals, but I might be living next door to her and I wouldn't have known it. All that mattered was that she'd put herself between me and twenty million pounds.

Poor woman never had a chance.

I started low-key enough, murmuring gently about significant problems, last minute hitches, lots at stake, and then, as if off the top of my head, I reeled off all those other deals I'd dug up where she and her colleagues had let the exact same point slide. And then I sat back and suggested she have a chat with her team and get back to me when she could.

Now, I knew this wasn't enough to win the battle, I even knew what the response was going to be (that the Government wanted everything whiter than white, because some day they'd want to sell this bastard of a bank and they didn't want any problems when they found a sucker willing to buy it). But I also knew that Mel wouldn't manage that response herself and would have to drag in her boss. And it was her boss I needed to speak to, since it was only her boss who'd be able to make the call on whether it was worth jeopardising twenty millions pounds for the slim chance of a four million hit.

The phone rang the moment I hung up. Unknown number. Back before things went tits-up in 2007 "unknown number" meant recruitment consultant; guys who would ring up promising the earth without the faintest idea what you did or what they were offering. Then, for a brief time, "unknown number" meant press. All of a sudden, just as the rest of the bankers were pointing their fingers at us and shaking their heads, the news media were all over us. Inevitably, certain ill-judged comments made their way directly to TV and radio – including the now-infamous: "I get paid a fortune because I'm fucking good at what I do and if I want to spend it on a Maserati then I'll fucking well spend it on a Maserati. Communist twats," from a trader on the second floor who enjoyed a short spell as the biggest hit on YouTube as consolation for his summary dismissal. After that, the word came down from on high that anyone talking to the press without clearance from the smiley faces in the PR team would be out the door by the end of the first sentence. So all we got to say was "I'm sorry, I'm afraid I can't comment on that." Needless to say, after a while the press calls went quiet, too.

This time "unknown number" was just what I'd been waiting for. Jason. A lot of noise and interference in the background, not clear enough to hear what was causing it, but I'd have known that voice in a hurricane.

"Alex? Is that you?"

"Jason! Thank Christ. Where the hell are you mate? I called the flat and the house."

Sharp intake of breath.

"What did you say to Sally?"

"Come on man, don't worry. I spun it. Played the

fuckwit. She's seen that often enough. Where are you?"

"Out and about. Can't talk for long. Just wanted to give you the main headlines."

"I'm waiting."

Deep breath.

"They fired me."

What I was thinking was *come on, Jason, for fuck's sake. Hardly news. Tell me what I need to hear.* But that wasn't what he needed to hear from me.

"I guessed that. I saw the Witch. I'm sorry, mate."

"All he said was they'd found some irregularities in my deals. Said it was enough to get rid of me on the spot. Had some papers, some invoices, cashflows, proof enough I guess."

"Hardly a fucking surprise, is it? We probably gave them to him."

"Right. And he didn't say anything about the Big One."

The Big One. The mother of all frauds, and the truth behind the firing. Not that we'd actually done it, yet. But none of this was news; from the moment I'd realised Jason was being canned, it was obvious this was Marcus's gameplan: revenge on Jason for not playing ball, and the chance to bury him before he got the whistle to his lips. If he came back bleating about Marcus's involvement, who'd believe a word of it? No one. Not even Lorraine, probably.

And it wasn't as if Marcus had been forced to look hard for the evidence. We'd put it in his hands, all those scams, the little hops before the great big leap we'd never even taken.

But this wasn't telling me what I needed to know.

"Anything else?"

I hadn't meant to be obvious but Jason knew me well enough.

"What, about you? Don't think so. Still don't think he knows. At least, he didn't say so in front of the Witch. He did say they'd be looking into all this in more detail, you know, but that's the kind of crap they have to say. If he's got any sense he'll chuck it all in some archive and forget about it."

Maybe. But there was another way of looking at all this. If Marcus thought there might be a third man, he'd dig until he found him. And when he did, he'd keep on digging until that man was buried so deep no one would ever hear a word he'd say.

The third man was me.

"Alex? You there mate?"

"Yeah Jason. Sorry. Just thinking. No more clues?"

Jason laughed. "Nothing really. Listen mate, I've got to go."

"Where are you going? What are you going to tell Sally?"

Long pause.

"Jason?"

"Not a fucking clue. Gotta come up with something. To be honest I think I'll just tell her the truth. Don't call me for a bit. Don't speak to Marcus. I've got to clear my head."

The truth? Bold move. I didn't mention Charmaine. There weren't a lot of options for him there.

"Good luck. Call me when you can."

"Will do mate. Good luck yourself."

And that was it.

I put the phone down and closed my eyes. I hadn't learned much, really. Jason might not have landed me in it, but I still didn't know where I stood with Marcus. "I'm watching you," he'd said, and my first thought had been that was it, he knew everything, I was dead. But maybe not. Because if Marcus had anything on me, anything serious, I'd have been out the door about twenty seconds after Jason was. Maybe he just suspected me. Which might not be ideal but was a hell of an improvement.

What could I do?

Just three choices, really.

Go to Marcus. Confess everything. Swear my eternal silence. Offer to go for the Big One.

I didn't like that option at all. The Big One was enough to send me to jail.

Go to Marcus. Confess everything. Swear my eternal silence. Throw myself on his mercy. Don't offer the Big One.

I wasn't too keen on that one, either. If I didn't give Marcus the Big One, I wasn't giving him anything he didn't already have. Eternal silence? Why would he believe that? He wasn't the kind of man that put much stock in heartfelt protestations of loyalty. As for mercy, he hadn't got where he had by being Mr Nice Guy.

And there was the nagging hope that maybe, just maybe, he didn't suspect me at all. His little comment down on the fourth floor might not mean a thing. A word of warning to the best mate of the guy you've just caught defrauding the company: I'd keep an eye on me, even if there wasn't anything else to go on. If that was all the suspicion Marcus had (and that was probably a fifty-fifty shot), then I'd be crazy to give him any more.

Which left option three: do nothing, keep working, keep my head down, and hope that it'll all blow over. If Marcus had nothing on me, then Jason was probably right: he'd bury the whole thing and make damn sure the police weren't called in.

And in the spirit of option three I turned back to my monitors only to find that now, of all times and on all days, there was nothing there. Three plain, blank, blue squares staring back at me. The blue screen of death.

6: Back to Front, 1999-2004

In 1999 securitisation at Miltons was nothing. It was me, and four guys in the front, and they were scrambling around trying to grab any deal they could get their hands on. Fact was, they might have been stars back in their old shops, but Miltons was just starting out, and no one wanted to risk the learners losing all their money. You couldn't blame them, either. I wouldn't have trusted us with my two hundred million pound deal.

But someone did, finally. We started winning deals the only way you can, when you're a nobody and you need to become a somebody fast before the rest of the bank realises you're costing them money you're never going to earn back. We bought the deals, offered to do them for free, or close enough, and threw in access to Miltons' giant balance sheet, whopping great corporate loans paid for out of all that cash from Dagenham and branches like it all over the country. Somebody very important must have said this was OK because bankers don't like giving stuff away for nothing, but we did it, anyway, did one deal, and another, residential mortgages and car loans and credit cards, thousands of pages worth of stuff that had me sitting in a cold bath with a wet towel over my head and groaning, but by the end of that first year, by the millennium, we'd done a dozen deals and we were being invited to every pitch going.

I still couldn't see where we were going to make any real money out of all this, but in March two thousand we sold our first swaps line and suddenly everything became clear. This was before Claire, this was back when Rates was a big shambling bull of a guy called Frank with a look on his face like someone had let the air out of his tyres, again. Frank spoke his own language and operated in his own world, with a desk on the sixth floor and another on the third, but every now and then I'd see him talking to the boys in the front office. *Why aren't you selling my product?* he'd ask, and the answer was always the same, *we're trying, but they don't know you, Frank, they hardly know us, once we've done a few more deals it'll be easier.* Frank would shrug – he was Italian, and he shrugged a lot – and he'd say *OK, but you know there's more money with me in one of your deals than half a dozen deals without me, and what I make, I share,* and the guys would smile and nod, and when Frank had gone they'd shake their heads and tell each other Frank was crazy, no one would trust their swaps line to Frank, why would they?

But that March someone did. It was a building society, and we'd got sole lead on the deal, for the first time, which meant there were no other banks in the mix trying to stir things up and get all the juicy bits for themselves. We were making a few basis points – that's a few hundredths of a per cent – on the actual deal, and it was only a hundred mill, so that was forty grand or so, which isn't going to pay a whole lot of bankers' salaries (much less a bonus). And Frank was down every morning, every lunchtime, every evening on his way home, taking Stephen to one side – Stephen was leading the deal, the most senior of the four, an Englishman we'd poached from an American bank – whispering in his ear, telling him this was the chance, this was the best opportunity we'd had, and if we couldn't make this one stick we'd never manage it at all. Finally one afternoon, while I was talking to Stephen about the deal and trying to understand how it all hung together, Frank wandered over, and Stephen smiled and said "It's your lucky day, Frank."

"Whaddya mean?" said Frank, who wasn't used to good news, at least not from this floor.

"They'll meet you," Stephen told him. "Southern & County."

I wasn't there when Frank met the client but Stephen

made sure he was. Turned out he needn't have worried. Frank might have looked like the kind of guy who couldn't sell drugs at Glastonbury, but that was just the face he showed us. When there was business to be won, he was a different man, and the client, who'd only really agreed to meet Frank because Stephen had begged him to, was nodding along and shaking hands and smiling and sold to before he realised what he was buying.

Forty grand, we made from that deal, on the bonds. Four hundred grand on the swaps, and half of that went to Frank, and the other half to us, and suddenly three months into the year things weren't looking so bad after all. By the end of that year four people in the front office had become eight, and my back office team wasn't just me any more; I was a boss, a manager, with a couple of monkeys of my own.

Two years went by fast. The Dagenham mob still met up, less often than we had, now there were a couple of wives and a sprinkling of kids. The rest of us shook our heads and knew that would probably be us, one day, but not for a decade at least. There was too much fun to be had for now. And meanwhile, the nights didn't go on as long as they used to, and on the rare occasions they did, we'd find ourselves three or four men down by the time we left the curry house and moved to the bar. I wondered what Dad would have made of it. No one seemed to miss the old world, Dagenham, the Plant, the cars. Closing the factories was supposed to have killed the place, but I doubted it, and even if it had, it was only a place. Just another grimy bit of a grimy city. You could get out if you wanted, even Mum had got out, gone East to the coast and away from the attentions of Dad's old friends. I hadn't been back for ages, I didn't even know what it was like there any more. I didn't have any reason to.

Meanwhile, in the front office, eight people turned into thirty. Stephen was still there, running the show, but the other three had left, lured by the hedge funds and the private equity boys, with the kind of money that would make even a banker blink. Stephen had turned that front office team into four teams, now, each with their own leader, each with their own field of operations and their own way of working. There were the conduit boys, Fat Paddy and his team, putting together smaller deals and financing them short-term by CP, commercial paper, which was as cheap as money could get and rolled every month or so. All the other teams financed their deals through longer-term bonds. There were the FI guys, Financial Institutions, doing the same credit card and mortgage deals that we'd started with, deals that didn't pay a whole lot of money but had propelled us from being nobodies to figuring on the league tables, which got us noticed by other clients who might one day give us something better. There were the real estate guys, who hadn't done a deal yet but were promising big money when they did. And there was the corporate team, Darren's gang, who had done a deal, just one, but that one deal brought in more money than half a year's worth of mortgage securitisations so Darren could do pretty much what he wanted.

Which was a good thing, really, because Darren liked to do what he wanted. He got on well with Stephen, the guy had recruited him, after all, but I'd never met someone so determined to go his own way. They had these weekly meetings, the team leaders, Stephen and Paddy and Darren, Andrea from FI and Barry from real estate, and they held them in the only room on the floor with walls and a door you could shut, because even Stephen sat out in the open with the rest of them, but if you happened to be on the floor walking past that room at eight on a Monday morning chances were you'd still hear what was going on behind that door. What you'd hear would be Darren, swearing, usually at Andrea or Baz (no one else called him Baz, no one would dare, if you'd seen his face when someone did you'd know never to do it yourself, but that just encouraged Darren to do it even more). If you opened the door a crack and took a look in, you'd see Darren sitting back in his chair and ranting, loud enough for a room ten times the size, but his face calm as you like, his eyes steady and cold, like it was someone else doing the ranting and he was just listening in. You'd see Andrea looking like she was about to cry, Barry looking like he was about to hit someone, Stephen with his hands out trying to calm everyone down, and Paddy sitting to one side, blonde hair all over his face, silently wobbling, anything not to laugh out loud.

It was all just jealousy, really. Andrea didn't like seeing Darren's team getting paid the same money as hers for a tenth the work. Barry didn't like the fact that he couldn't get a single deal, and he didn't like Darren, so Darren tore him to pieces every chance he got. Paddy didn't care and found the whole thing hilarious. And Stephen just wanted to keep the peace. I could have told him how to keep the peace, but he didn't ask, and he didn't need to anyway, because Baz wasn't there more than a year before even his own team were so sick of him they were running to Stephen and begging him to get rid of the guy and put someone, anyone, in his place. Baz jumped before he got pushed, and no, I don't know where he went and I don't know where he is now and I couldn't give a damn, either. Emma took over and I don't know if it was her brilliance or blind luck or just good timing, but suddenly the real estate team had so many deals there weren't enough hours in the day to do them.

The real estate boom in Milton Shearings' securitisation department had several unexpected results. People who hadn't done a stroke of work in months suddenly found themselves calling home and telling their partners they wouldn't be seeing them for the rest of the day, maybe the rest of the week. New recruits arrived to take up the slack, including a certain Liz, who'd just quit hunting down terrorists at MI5 when she walked onto the twelfth floor one wet morning in March. Remember Liz. She's important. Darren wouldn't take crap from anyone, that hadn't changed, but he liked Emma, and he'd warmed to Andrea, so it looked like it was Baz that had been the problem after all. But he saw Emma's team winning deals and making money and he didn't want his to be left behind – it was rivalry, but not the kind that ends with a knife in the back (that all came later). There were other teams out there in the City doing what Darren's team did, and doing it well, and he could have walked into the number one spot in any of them, but with just a handful of deals under their belt it was already starting to become clear to the few people that paid attention to that kind of thing that Milton Shearings had the best corporate securitisation team in the market. The only thing he could hope to do was to make it even better. He knew the brightest people already, the ones who might make a difference to the team. He'd worked with them, against them, stolen deals from under their noses. Most of them would have left their jobs and come to work for him in an instant. In the end, he picked just one, an unheralded new hire in mid 2003, and that one insisted on bringing a junior with him. If Russell could have left the Bloodsucker back at Paller Beaton it would have saved a lot of pain for a lot of people, but he wouldn't be parted.

The big surprise, though, came six months later. I had a team of seven behind me now, decent guys (and one girl), smart but not brilliant, more than capable of doing the job. I'd trained them myself, after all. There were desks and computers for everyone, piles of paper everywhere, filing cabinets blocking the windows. I made sure I knew what was going on in the front office, who was pitching where, how many deals each team might have on the go in a week's time, a month's time, at the end of the year. And I could see, everyone could see, that even with Liz and the three others who'd joined around the same time, Emma's team had bitten off more than they could chew. There just weren't enough teeth. So I wasn't surprised when Stephen and Emma turned up unannounced in our dark little den across the road one afternoon to talk over how the hell they were going to manage. I knew precisely why they were here and what they were going to say. I'd seen this coming. I had seven capable people in my team, and some of the work Emma's gang were doing, it was, well, it was process, wasn't it? It was mechanical and time-consuming and it would make sense, wouldn't it, if some of the form-filling and signature-seeking and box-ticking, if the unglamorous stuff was passed onto people who could handle it and weren't already spending twenty-five hours a day fighting fires and trying to stop their new clients from running straight out the door to another bank with more people in it? A slight redrawing of the line between front office and back office, that's what they were going to ask for, that was all, and while it wasn't entirely fair, because my own team were only just keeping on top of the workload as it was, I could see their reasoning. As long as they paid us for it, because all this new work was making lots of new money, and if we were going to share in the pain it was right that we'd share in the gain, too. I had my answers ready the moment I saw them walking towards me, I knew exactly what I'd say, how much I'd ask for, and I thought I'd judged it well enough to give them just a moment's pause before they said OK.

I had it wrong, of course. I misread the situation, not for the first time, and (more unfortunately) not for the last. I didn't know how their minds worked after all, not these two, even when I had all the same facts and forecasts they did, and that was probably why they were making names for themselves as hotshot bankers and pulling in seven-figure bonuses whilst I was trotting along in the backwater across the road pressing buttons. There was a problem, that much was right, and they did need more teeth, and they were hoping I could help. But the way I was going to help wasn't the way I was expecting to. They didn't want my team to do their work. They didn't want to redraw any lines.

What they wanted was me.

Stephen thought I was wasted in the back office. Emma hardly knew me, but she agreed. Because I'd had a hand in pretty much every deal the team had done since it started, I knew the business better than anyone except Stephen himself, and as for the commercial stuff, negotiating, doing deals, they'd seen how I could fight my own corner with the agent banks and the other back offices and the lawyers and accountants and, more often than not, with their own front office teams, and they had no doubt I could do just as much or more with clients and rivals and investors.

Six months, they said. Come and work with us for six months, and if you don't like it you can come straight back here. They'd pay for some new blood in the back office, we needed it anyway if the deals were going to keep coming in the way they were; but whoever sat in my chair would just be keeping it warm for me, *if* I decided to come back. They didn't think I would. I should think about it. Take my time, take a day or two to mull it over, and then let them know. And incidentally, smiled Stephen, if I did choose to join the front office, then I'd be paid like the rest of the front office for as long as I was there. He was six foot four, Stephen, slightly grey but completely unlined, and although I'd never said so to him or to anybody else for that matter, I pretty much worshipped the guy. If he'd asked me to go and work for another bank, or take a demotion, or sit in a box for six months, I'd probably have done it. And now he was asking me to come and work with Emma, with him, to get right into the heart of the action. And he was going to give me more money to do it.

I like to think I gave the offer the consideration it deserved. I didn't actually get back to them until the following day, and I did spend the odd moment during the intervening twenty-something hours trying to think of a reason, any reason, to say no, something to pitch against the excitement bubbling away inside. Anything I came up with got batted straight back down again. How would my team cope without me? They were smart enough, they'd manage fine, and anyway Stephen had just said he'd bring in new blood. Just say I hated it? I wouldn't, but it didn't matter anyway, I could give it up and come back if I wanted. Would I be able to manage, was I cut out for being a front office banker, did I have what it took? I'd seen what it took, I'd seen the front office team, and sure, there were the Stephens and the Emmas and the Darrens, but there was just as much dead wood sitting there nodding and getting through the day, and they seemed to cope just fine. Yeah, I'd manage.

The funny thing was, when I went round to see them the next day, the deal had changed. Not a lot, but just enough to make me think for a moment. They still wanted me, and they wanted me because they needed a hand on Emma's deals, but they didn't know how long the real estate boom was going to last and they didn't want to give me a job only to chuck me out of it a year later as the last man in. Instead, they were going to put me in Darren's team. It was a strange combination, but that's how things worked back then, now that Baz had gone and everyone was getting along nicely. You did your deals and then if things were slow and someone else needed your help, you gave it. It turned out half Paddy's team (including another new guy, name of Jason) were shoring up real estate; some of Andrea's, too, although most often they were the busiest of the lot. I'd be on Darren's team but I'd be helping out Emma until she didn't need me and Darren did.

It was Stephen telling me this, and Emma sitting next to him nodding, but no sign of Darren.

"What does Darren think of this?" I asked. I'd seen enough of Darren not to want to piss the guy off by turning up on his team uninvited.

"Darren's fine," said Stephen, and then Emma spoke up, finally.

"It was his idea. Said he'd had his eye on you for a while."

I didn't think he even knew who I was. I could smell the bullshit but I didn't care. If they want you enough to lie about how much they want you, then that's got to be good enough for me. The deal was done.

7: The Unluckiest Girl in the World

Monday 14th December, 2009
11:30am

Normally the blue screen of death would have me swearing and kicking whatever was unfortunate enough to be under my desk at the time. On a day like today, at such a crucial point in a deal, it would have me threatening the IT team with biblical punishments until my computer was back up and running.

And yet now, for some reason, I kept my cool. More important things on my mind, I guess. Didn't want to draw attention to myself, either. So I dialled the helpdesk, and quietly, calmly, I explained what had happened and asked them if they could get it fixed as quickly as possible. They promised they'd be on the case as soon as they could. They always promised that.

What could I do in the meantime? Sure, my BlackBerry was working, but with big fat fingers and the amount of stuff queuing up to be dealt with, BlackBerry wasn't the answer. I could find a free terminal and set myself up there, but that would take up too many precious minutes before I could even get started. The sensible choice was to step away from it all for a moment, to step outside, grab some lunch, and hope everything was better by the time I was back.

I called Liz. Liz had got sick of real estate securitisations quick enough and got out as soon as she could, but she'd stuck with Miltons. She had the beginnings of a career with the leveraged financed team, lending big bucks to private equity funds looking to snap up companies using a little bit of their money and a lot of ours. It was a role that promised great things for bankers as clever as she was, but she'd got out of there, too, and into a credit trading team tucked away somewhere on the ninth floor. I didn't know what she actually did for a living; I didn't really know what credit trading was, and I still don't, and whenever she tried to explain, I'd nod and sit back and let the words wash over me. All I knew was, she dealt with numbers, mostly; I preferred words. But whatever it was, it was a better place to be these days than leveraged finance – her old team was all but gone.

We were only talking for two minutes, but by the time I'd got off the phone the IT guy had arrived and started working. Maybe staying calm and not swearing was the way to get results from the Helpdesk. Looked like I'd stumbled across one of the great business secrets of the twenty-first century.

Although you'd never have guessed from the way she looked, dressed, walked or spoke, Liz was as Essex as I was. Posh Essex, village Essex, but still, East is East. She'd stormed Oxford with a first in PPE, which I thought was something to do with pay TV until she put me right. After university she'd worked for the civil service for a couple of years, which, as she confided in me one drunken night, meant the Security Service – MI5 to you and me. It was all bureaucracy and dead man's shoes, she said, and it hadn't taken her long to get bored, jump into banking and find she had a knack for it.

Liz was a looker, or at least I thought she was, but when she walked in the room, you wouldn't even notice it. I might, but that's me. For you, for everyone else, it was simple enough: she had better brains and bigger balls than the best of the men I'd come across at Miltons (a list I wouldn't feature in myself). She didn't need to trade on her looks, so she didn't bother. We'd had a brief fling way back in 2004, just a month, and no hard feelings on either side when it was over. She thought an office relationship was a bad idea, she said, and she'd have done well to take her own advice, but that's a story for later. As for me, well sure, I liked her, I thought she was attractive, but I couldn't help finding her a little intimidating, and that's not a great start.

We met outside the building, opposite the Evening Standard board that announced in stark black and white that our "Day of Reckoning" was due. Well, not ours, not this time: our international cousins, the American banks spattered like ink-stains all over Docklands and the City. Bonus time for the big boys (ours was still a few weeks away), and time for the public and the politicians to seethe with righteous indignation. We'd heard it all before, but somehow things were different now. Even we could see change was coming.

Gossip travels through a bank like any other workplace, like lightning, always looking for the path of least resistance, always getting where it needs to be. Liz knew something was up, something had happened on the 4th, Jason walking out with his stuff in a box. *Two boxes*, I nearly corrected, but didn't. She asked if I was OK, she knew we were friends. I shrugged, turned on a grin, realised that was the wrong thing and turned it off the instant it hit my face. She had no idea why Jason had been canned and wasn't tactless enough to ask. I managed to change the subject.

I don't remember what we talked about, really. There have been so many conversations with Liz, over a beer, over a curry, over a half dozen tiny plates of gambas and patatas and tortilla and ham, like today, that sometimes they run together. That's OK. They're always fun. They always take me away from what's bothering me, and today that was Jason and Marcus, and Mintrex and rating agencies and tax departments, and the paper-thin layer of ice my size elevens were stamping across. The food helped, the wine would have done too. There was a table-full of drunk and flirtatious secretaries next to us, and that wouldn't have done any harm, either. But most of all, it was Liz.

There's something about a nice meal with a pretty woman that pushes my buttons, but there was one other thing, too: she was married now. Just a few months ago, and in some style – bespoke vows, boutique hotel, vintage champagne, a famous DJ, string quartets and a chill-out room. As someone else's wife, Liz was suddenly even more attractive than she had been.

And look, before you start up and tell me I'm an idiot, my brain's in my dick, and neither of them are much to boast about, I'll hold up my hands and say *guilty, your honour*, but really, where's the harm? A bit of flirting, some light innuendo, nothing to offend anyone (assuming they couldn't read my mind). And nothing would come of it. An hour after we'd left the building I was back at my desk.

The good news: my computer was working. I had three monitors – I didn't need more than one, to be honest, but they sprouted out of the desks up here like flies on cowshit, and anything less would have looked like I couldn't even multitask. The bad news: the bad news was shouting out from all three of them, and it was shouting one word, very loudly. "MINTREX". I'd left my desk, but I'd done worse than that: I'd (deliberately) chosen a restaurant below ground level, where no emails or phone calls or texts could reach me. I could have checked my messages on the walk back to the office, saved a couple of minutes, but I hadn't. I'd been enjoying talking to Liz instead.

There were a lot of messages, as it turned out. It started with the tax people, and it started calm, with Mel, the woman I'd been talking to that morning. But I wasn't there, I hadn't called back, and pretty soon her boss was calling asking where the hell I was if this was so damned urgent. Then there was the usual last-minute deal stuff, requests, pleas, demands and threats from the other banks, the lawyers, the rating agencies and Uncle Tom Cobley. Usually I can keep on top of all this but today I was struggling to hold my focus. The smell didn't help much, either, cheap chicken tikka masala oozing in styrofoam boxes on half the desks and most of the bins on the floor. Even Jane's. I don't think I've ever seen Jane eat, but I'd not have had her down for that. Water, oysters and champagne, diamonds and pearls. Not chicken tikka masala. Not *this* chicken tikka masala. The canteen must have got a good deal on yellow food dye.

I carried on through the in-box. Joe was panicking. He'd just joined, straight out of university with a CV that said he only had to look at something to get a first in it, but if he couldn't handle me being out for an hour he wouldn't last long in our team. I'd hold his hand for Mintrex, for the deal, but after that he was on his own. I hammered out a couple of short replies and then, suddenly, the shadow fell. I could feel it behind me, malignant, far worse than the curry. Anthony wasn't welcome at the best of times but there was a fair chance he'd be my boss before long, so I had to play nice. I swung round and arranged my face, aiming for keen but harassed. He was looking over my shoulder and smiling. I didn't like that at all.

"Alex, glad I caught you. How are things?"

"Bit frantic on Mintrex to be honest, Anthony – we're pricing tomorrow."

"So I hear. I was wondering if I could pick your brains on something this afternoon."

Pick your brains. Sounded about right. Eviscerate, take what he wanted, and leave the rest. Well, boss-to-be or not, he wasn't having mine, not today. I offered him the midnight slot, as in *I'll be free, but not till midnight,* and suddenly whatever it was he wanted wasn't quite so important. I'd seen him holding the suit carrier when he swanned in earlier. At midnight he'd be halfway through *Secured Finance Magazine*'s annual awards ceremony – a first-rate hotel with a second-rate meal and a third-rate comedian. I'd turned down the invitation before I even knew Mintrex would be in the way. I liked myself too much to sit through that shit.

News about our problems with the rating agencies must have filtered through to Sergei, because he'd left me a voicemail. "Do not fuck with these swaps, Alex. If you do, I bury you. I bury you."

The agency that had stirred the whole thing up in the first place was back in touch, pushing again for the change to be made.

Claire and Ian were walking towards my desk. I liked Ian. He kept himself a step or two behind Claire, like he didn't really want to be there. I knew how he felt. Claire reached my desk and leaned forward, utterly expressionless. She spoke quietly enough, but the volume didn't matter.

"I can see you've got a lot on your plate, so I won't keep you. If we lose the Mintrex swaps because of your incompetence, you'll be out of here faster than you can blink, and I'll personally ensure that you never work in the City again."

You can take the girl out of Greenings, but you can't take Greenings out of the girl. I swallowed.

"OK. I'll sort it. I will."

"Good."

And she was gone.

Claire had only been there twenty seconds and my phone was blinking. Another voicemail. Grace, from Greenings. Greenings were everywhere, they'd even got themselves a spot on Mintrex, not that they'd lifted a fucking finger, and no one was happy about it, but it was impossible to keep Greenings off a deal these days. Still, Greenings was one of the banks that were pissed off over

73

what we'd pulled with the swaps, so that was some consolation. "Hi Alex." (Pause, dripping with venom). "I hear you guys are having some issues on the hedging." (*Where? How? Can no one in this business keep their fucking mouth shut?*) "We're here if you want us to help out." (*I bet you are*). "Call me" (*Not in a million years*). Bitch.

And yet another voicemail, this time from Ahmed, the Mintrex CFO, asking me to give him a call as soon as possible. There were a bunch of other things to go through but it was pretty unlikely they'd trump the client. Clients are everything to a banker; that's what sets the banker apart from the trader, who's his own client, best friend, probably lover. Reluctantly, I dialled his number. We'd met when I'd been sent in to pitch for the deal, and that was strange enough, thrown into it with a day's notice and a blazing hangover, but it turned out the easiest pitch I'd ever done, this smooth, Indian guy in a nice suit just smiling at me and shaking hands and acting like I'd won him over before I'd told him my name. Everything about Ahmed was smooth, everything was easy, and that was how he liked it. He had no idea how painful this deal had been, all the frantic paddling under the surface. I'd done a decent job keeping everything calm as far as he was concerned. When it looked like there was trouble coming, I'd dealt with his lawyers, his accountants, his underlings, people who knew him better than I did and understood what it took to justify bothering him. We sorted the problems between us and Ahmed coasted along in blissful ignorance. I wanted to keep him that way.

"Ahmed speaking."

"Hi Ahmed, Alex here, just returning your call."

He exploded. I'm not sure what I was expecting but it wasn't this.

"What the fuck is going on over there Konninger?" He stopped, for a moment, but ploughed on before I could think of anything to come back with. "I've had it up to here with your problems." He'd not seen one tenth of them. "I want this swaps point sorted and I want it sorted now." I could practically feel the spit.

I switched into soothing mode.

"It's OK, Ahmed. This isn't going to be a problem."

Soothing didn't work.

"DON'T JUST TELL ME IT'S NOT GOING TO BE A FUCKING PROBLEM! MAKE IT GO THE FUCK AWAY!"

Some amused looks from the desks either side of me, and the desks the other side of them. And I wasn't on speakerphone.

"I'm working on it Ahmed. I just need to make a few calls, that's all."

"You'd better. There's other banks want to do this deal, and they've told me they can get in and agree everything by the end of the day. I'll give you till five to sort this completely, yaar? If you don't, I'm going with the others."

Jesus. This is worse than I thought. Just gone two. Twenty million quid on the line and less than three hours to save it.

8: Noodles, Beer, and Revenge

It's possible I've given the impression I'm unflappable. Stiff upper lip, nerves of steel, sang-as-froid-as-ice. Well, everyone's got their limit. I'd sailed past mine under Ahmed's onslaught, and right now I was waving in panic as it receded into the distance.

Banking's a bit like politics, really. Something's always going wrong, or about to go wrong. And it doesn't matter whose fault it is; the idea's to pin the tail on the donkey before the donkey can pin it on you. I've always been pretty good at this – I can spot an incoming iceberg before anyone else realises we're in the North Atlantic, and I can steer my way round it with one hand and suggest it was someone else's problem with the other, just in case. Covering all the bases. It had worked well enough for me in the past.

Out of control was fine. Things were supposed to be out of control, at this stage of a deal, everyone running around shouting about their own little problems and how there wasn't enough time to fix them. I was used to that, I could handle it. But this time things were more out of control than they were supposed to be, and my one hour out seemed to have landed me right in the middle of the shit. This time everyone else had their ducks lined up and every last duck had "Alex Konninger" written in bold marker-pen on its forehead. If I didn't crack this, it wouldn't matter that our tax guys should have caved in, or the agencies should have spotted it all earlier. Those ducks would be shot, shredded and rolled into pancakes before you could say "hoi sin sauce".

But (I had to remind myself) I'm still good at this. I'm the best. No need to panic, because if anyone can deal with this, it's Alex Konninger, however close he might be to the oven. I needed time to think and the ping each time a new email came in wasn't helping. I turned off the ping, but I could still see that little envelope out the corner of my eye. I turned off the monitors, all three of them, and it was like I was in a different place, suddenly. A cool, dark cave. In the background there were fifty different conversations from fifty different phone lines, but that wasn't so bad. I stared at the blank screens and willed myself back to my immediate problem. Getting tax to fall into line. Getting them to understand that sometimes risks were worth taking. No one short of the man at the top was going to make a call like that, not now I'd pissed off the rest of them.

And that, of course, was the answer. I turned the monitors back on. A few clicks of the mouse, and there it was, six digits, the direct line (internal) for Mr. Edward Griffin. The head of tax, for the whole of the bank. The guy's one step away from the board, and not, in normal circumstances, to be bothered by scum like me. But these weren't normal circumstances.

It started well enough. He was there, he answered his own phone, he had a few minutes to discuss the problem. He was calm, by his standards, he spoke slowly and he chose his words carefully. He'd probably have real gravitas if it weren't for the high-pitched Belfast whine and the fact that he's five foot two and built like a fucking ball. And the words he chose didn't help, either. If this had been a video call, I don't think I'd have been able to keep a straight face.

The way he saw it – "*The way I see it, sonny,*" was that his team had a job to do and they weren't just there to roll over whenever we asked them to. What he actually said was "*to lie down and let youse all fuck us up the arse,*" but it meant pretty much the same thing. Followed by *"And look, we're not fuckin morons, whatever you lot in the front office might think."*

He paused, and for a moment I wondered why, and then I realised he was waiting for me to agree.

"Oh no, no, that's not it at all"

He understood what was at stake, he said. It was a commercial call. *"It's one for the fuckin money men."*

I knew where this was headed. He'd let me make the call as long as his misgivings were down on paper. He might talk like a gangster but he was as scared as the rest of them of getting something wrong and being on record doing it. On he droned. I was starting to relax, I'd almost switched off, and then, suddenly, this:

"And I think in this case, the man to make the call is Billy D."

I was speaking through a headset but if it had been one of those old-fashioned things you hold in your hands I'd have dropped it like it was on fire.

Billy D?

The name might not be familiar to you, but outside the business he was plain old Sir William Ogilvy Donahue, and that should ring a bell or two. Or some more, if you've got the time and the patience to sit through Treasury Select Committee hearings. Billy – his own choice, the name, and if it sounds ridiculous it still suits him better than Sir William – Billy runs Miltons' investment bank these days, which puts him in charge of a lot of money and a lot of people and in the sights of the press every time they're short of a banker to hammer. Impressive enough to get there, even more impressive that he'd been there in 2008 and still hadn't been axed, unlike pretty much every senior banker in every major bank in the western world. Billy's big time. Billy is not the kind of guy you want to bother with the tax implications of a paltry billion pound structured debt trade. Twenty million in swaps income was piss-all to him.

I started to say something, and then stopped. Billy D was out of my league. I'd never even met the guy. A conversation with Billy D was like an audience with the Pope, and I might be good at what I did but I was no cardinal. But Edward Griffin probably spoke to him every day, and if he thought it was OK, who was I to argue?

It was too late, anyway. Griffin had patched him in.

"Gentlemen."

I pictured him, sitting back. Leather chair. Cigar and a brandy. I don't know why I saw his office as the Athenaeum or Whites. It seemed to fit.

Edward took the lead, explained the background, and by the time he'd handed over to me I'd got my breathing back under control and decided to go with it and not worry about how we'd got where we were. I set out what was at stake, and it was all pretty clear as far as I could see: £20 million to be made, with a low-risk £4 million hit if things went wrong. To my immense relief, Edward agreed with my view of the risk.

"Fine."

"Is that all OK, then?" (this was Edward. I wouldn't have dared).

"You heard what I said. Fine. Do it."

And that was that. Four o'clock. There was still an hour till Ahmed's deadline. All I had to do was let everyone know. I threw out a quick email to various lawyers, rating agencies and other teams involved. Joe and Sergei got a personalised one-liner: "Nuke deactivated. World saved. Prepare vodka and potatoes."

Then the ones to savour. I strolled down to the ninth floor and over to Claire's desk, where I waited patiently while she quietly applied the death sentence to some unfortunate trader on the other end of her line. She shrugged when I announced the good news; all I'd done was my job, really. I thought about mentioning Billy, but if anyone was going to be impressed by a name, it wasn't Claire.

Next up was Ahmed.

"Ahmed speaking."

"Ahmed, it's Alex. Everything's sorted."

Followed by a burst of over-exuberant jubilation: "Fantastic! Man, I gotta say I was getting worried there. I didn't want to deal with these other guys and I really didn't want to stiff you, but I gotta tell you I thought you were fucked. This is great, man. I'm happy for you, I'm happy for me. This is gonna be one hell of a deal."

As usual when he was excited, Ahmed spoke in a range of accents. Indian, Eton English and New York all in one thirty-second burst. Bi-polar? The guy was all over the place.

"Thanks, Ahmed. I thought you'd want to be the first to know."

"OK Alex. Thanks for the great news. Speak to you tomorrow. Let's get this fucker priced, yaar?"

It was no wonder he wanted the deal done fast. No wonder he was over-excited. Between you, me and the next couple of hundred pages, we'd got more out of the rating agencies than we had any right to hope for. Let's put it this way: if I was an investor, I wouldn't have looked twice at this deal. Don't worry. I'll explain later.

An email came in from one of the lawyers. For Christ's sake. A request for a conference call (*don't bother telling us what for; more fun to guess*). Nine tonight. Everyone invited, too, which meant it was set in stone before I had a chance to shoot it down. I should have expected something like this the night before pricing. Never mind. I'd take the call at home, with a takeaway and a cold beer and the 60 inch Panasonic in the background.

The last, most satisfying call was to Grace. It went through to her voicemail. Maybe if she'd answered I'd have played it straight, told her the truth, enjoyed it, left it there. And I was about to, I was starting to explain how everything was fine, actually, and she didn't have to worry about us, when a little idea popped into my head and before I could stop myself, it was out.

"Grace, thanks for the offer to help out. Looks like we've hit a few problems. Could use your help, I think. I have to head into a meeting now," (she'd assume this was me getting my arse beaten for screwing up the swaps) "but if you're around after eight it would be great if we could chat." Eight was safe enough. I knew Grace. She'd stick around till doomsday if she could get our share of the swaps, and later if she knew she was getting it off me.

She'd spend the rest of the afternoon on heat, prepping her swaps guys to take over the trade. By the time I broke the sad news to her I'd be relaxing at home, beer in hand, while she'd be sat in the office with a bunch of structurers, swaps salesmen and lawyers. The only thing I regretted was that I hadn't said midnight.

Does this make me a bastard? Maybe. But this was Greenings, and Grace was typical Greenings. Vicious, rich, arrogant and rude. Maybe you think that sounds like the rest of us, but Greenings were different. Half the City would have been queuing up to shake my hand.

I should probably come clean. Grace and I had history of a more personal nature. If there was bad blood between Greenings and the rest of the world, the stuff between us was more like plague-ridden pus. It wasn't an unusual story: drunken night out with lawyers, bankers, assorted hangers-on; boy meets girl; boy gets drunker than he should and takes girl home; boy regrets it in the morning and is perhaps a little colder than he needs to be when he shows her the door. Girl leaves, in a hurry. Some less-than-friendly emails ensue. At home the next night boy stumbles across her underwear and other personal items that she's left in her hurry to get out. Boy puts them in three separate packages and posts them to her office with his compliments.

Grace was away, as it turned out, and when packages arrive for a banker who's on holiday, well, who knows whether there are important documents inside? The packages were opened by her secretary, in full view of most of her team, and no one had let her forget it. Humiliated, angry, and very, very bitter, that was Grace, for months after the event. I really hadn't known she was away. I hadn't expected everyone would see what they saw. But she blamed me. This was years ago, but since then we seemed to come across each other on practically every deal we did. She kept it cold but professional, but I knew she made a habit of bad-mouthing me to clients, other bankers, anyone she could, really. I rarely missed a chance to do likewise.

Why, given all that, would she fall for my voicemail? Because she was ambitious and greedy and had the morals of a robot. And I'd sounded desperate enough, I thought, to lure her in. She'd love that, the desperation, she'd be drunk on it by now, rounding up her team and her rates people and thinking of all the money she'd be making and I wouldn't. Would I have fallen for it? Maybe – I'd certainly snatch at the chance. Would she? Hell yeah.

Not yet five and there wasn't much left to do. A quick call with Ahmed's underlings and my old colleagues in the back office (or "ops", as they were now known). Dull enough, but important work, closing cashflows, spreadsheets and flowcharts and making sure the right money went to the right place. And (as people like Anthony never really understood), it paid to play nice with the back office boys, because however high you rise, there's always someone in the back who can do you a favour or make your life difficult.

A few more issues to run through with Joe and the lawyers. Pretty much everything was in the lawyers' hands now, and unless it got nasty it would be up to Joe to make sure they kept at it. The other banks got patched in, including our friends at Greenings (but not Grace, who, apparently was "in a meeting" – and I knew what that meeting was). I was a little surprised they'd bothered putting anyone on the call, even a junior. Probably wanted to make sure there wasn't any money floating around without someone else's name on it. I gave Joe the "*I'm not here*" signal, and I kept my mouth shut even when people started saying stupid things. I was supposed to be "in a meeting" too, at least as far as Grace was concerned, and I didn't want news getting through to her that I was back in the game.

A couple of mind-freezing calls with accountants, trustees and the like. You don't need to know. I'm not even sure I do.

Final emails to our own Legal, Credit and Finance teams to update them. This was their last chance to prise open any new cans of worms, and I let them know it: "If you have anything to say, speak now or forever hold your peace."

Time to get home and prepare for the evening's entertainment.

Home, for me, is West London. Not ideal for the office, it's true, but who wants to work on their own doorstep? It's young, it's rich, and it's smug, so I feel pretty much at home there. A good-sized – oh, who am I kidding? – a *massive* three bed apartment on the first floor of a portered mansion block with a pool, a gym and parking in the basement. There's a nice pub on the corner, some of the best restaurants in London within a five minute walk, wall-to-wall Bose, a grand piano in the living room, a model of expensive German engineering in the basement – alongside a two-wheeled Japanese monster with a growl like an earthquake – and right now, sitting on my dining room table, a banquet for one from a famous Chinese restaurant that only does take-out for its favourite customers.

I started on the food and kept an eye on the clock. *Surely Grace would have figured it out by now*, I thought. *Surely she'd realised.* But she hadn't. I'd diverted the office line to my mobile, and she called bang on 8, keen as mustard. She was in a meeting room, on a conference line, and I couldn't help smiling to myself as she introduced all the others in the room with her. A couple of juniors, some guy from legal, and the big boys, too, the MDs of her own department and the London rates team. She was talkative, excitable, I hadn't heard her like this before. I let her talk. As far as she was concerned, it was a done deal. She hadn't spoken to Ahmed (why would she?), and she didn't know how we'd priced our swaps, but as long as the numbers weren't crazy her people would take them off our hands and it wouldn't cost us a thing (which was generous, considering the money it would make her). She was enjoying herself. She was probably picturing me in a meeting room too, grim-faced colleagues all round me, staring at me with hate in their eyes as I gave away their twenty million. She was on a high, and it took a few minutes before I had a chance to say anything past "hello".

"Grace, thanks for calling. As you can imagine we've been scrambling all afternoon to fix this problem."

"Yeah, we really feel for you guys on this."

I could actually hear them sniggering in the background. Which made my next line all the sweeter.

"And I appreciate your stepping up, but I'm pleased to say we'll be able to handle it from here after all."

Stunned silence. After a few seconds, the rates guy burst

in, a nasal New Jersey whine:

"Are you saying that you guys are still taking all the swaps?"

"Is that Alan? Hi Alan. Yeah, we're still doing what we were doing. Nothing more, nothing less."

"Then what the fuck am I doing here?"

Was he *trying* to make me laugh?

"I don't know. I was just hoping to catch up with Grace. But it sure is nice to speak to you."

That was probably going too far.

"Fuck off, arsehole."

So Alan was *really* unhappy. Good. He'd take it out on Grace. So would her own boss. And the juniors and the lawyer? They'd just seen her look a fool.

"Come on Alan, no need for that. Let's all try to pull together and get this deal closed, shall we?"

Click. They'd hung up. I kicked myself – I'd forgotten to record it. Never mind. It had been short and sweet, and I wouldn't forget a word of it. Whatever his problems, Jason would laugh his head off when I told him.

A few bowls of duck, crab and noodles down the line, and I was waiting beer in hand for the conference call to begin. The Panasonic was on in the background, sound turned right down, Sky News with yet another demonstration against this year's villains (you guessed it): angry faces, illiterate placards, text alongside telling us, in case we'd been on Mars for the last week, that it was bonus time for (speak of the devil) Greenings. An otherwise pretty young girl (assuming removal of facial piercings, washing of hair, maybe a little make-up) screamed soundlessly towards the cameras. "YOUR DAY OF RECKONING IS COMING" – clearly the phrase of the moment – was scrawled on her scrap of cardboard.

I didn't think the call would take more than a few

minutes, and assuming it didn't, I'd head down to the Freemasons on the corner. If anything came up while I was there, well, it wouldn't be the first time I'd handled BlackBerry, beer and quiz machine together.

The agencies were on first, then Joe and Ian – both still in the office – then Ahmed. A few juniors from the other banks. Doug, from our own syndicate desk, who judging from the hastily-muted background noise clearly *wasn't* in the office (unless Milton Shearings' trading floor had set up a champagne bar and was hosting a spot from London's premier R&B diva). A couple of accountants. Sergei and his trademark heavy breathing. As usual, we had to wait a while for the lawyers who'd asked for the call in the first place and who seemed baffled by their own conference call system. They beeped themselves in, and out again, and back in, until finally everyone who was supposed to be on the line was, plus who knew how many who hadn't bothered announcing themselves, and it turned out no one knew what we were doing there anyway. We took five minutes on mechanics for pricing the next day. A few lawyers took the opportunity to raise their pet concerns – opinions, letters and documents that hadn't yet been finalised and were causing the usual last-minute palpitations. One of Ahmed's guys tried to bring up the closing cashflows and settlement process, but we'd been through this half a dozen times already by now, so I broke in and told him we could talk about all that after pricing (and felt the relief flowing from everyone else). No one mentioned the swaps. As we were winding up I asked Joe, Sergei and Ian if they could stay on the line; when everyone else was gone I told them about the call I'd had with Greenings an hour earlier. They loved it. Everyone likes being on the winning side.

Time to wind it up. Time for a beer. "OK guys," I said. "Let's price this fucker, yaar!" (in my best Ahmed-Indian).

"Yaar!" came the enthusiastic response.

"And let's thank fuck the agencies never did check the tail, yaar!"

"Yaar!"

Beep. Beep. Beep. Beep. Alone at last. I hung up, job done.

And so to the pub. I'll explain the tail later. If I'm sober and can be bothered, anyway.

9: Alchemy, 2004-5

Turned out Stephen was right. So was Emma. Darren, too, if he'd really had any interest in the matter, which I doubted.

I *was* good at this front office stuff. I *could* handle the deals, the negotiation, all that commercial stuff that was supposed to be beyond the back office boys. Darren might not have known who I was when I sat down for the first time at his bank of desks, and he might have wondered what the hell was going on when I got straight back up and walked over to Emma's team and sat down there, but it didn't take long for him to give me the nod.

That was Darren. He didn't say much, unless he had something to say, and then he said a lot and he said it loud enough that anyone on the floor could hear it. But if he liked what he saw, he nodded at you. That was all, to start with, but it was enough, and even though I was spending most of my time helping out Emma, I got my nod in the first few weeks. I didn't even see it, myself, but Russell did; we were already friends, Russell and me, he hadn't been with the team for long before I rolled up, and we complemented each other perfectly. He knew banking and the wider business; I knew Milton Shearings. He was on a roll, was going to be a star; I was quite happy just being a banker, finally, because up to joining Darren's team I still had a faint suspicion that I was never going to be anything more than a monkey. Russell sat opposite me at the time (the Bloodsucker was a couple of desks down and what with settling in and working with another team most of the time, I didn't even figure out who the guy was for a couple of months), and one morning I looked up to see him grinning at me like he knew something I didn't want him to know. For a moment I searched back, what had I been doing last night, how much had I been drinking, who had I been with, and then I remembered that I'd just gone home by myself after a quiet evening at the pub. He leaned forward and told me what I'd missed, that Darren had just walked past, quiet as the grave, and paused behind me for as long as it took him to nod, pointedly, in my direction. If you didn't know Darren it sounded like instructions for a hit man. I'd been in a meeting with Darren that morning, Jane had dragged me along to help her sell him on some electricity deal she was trying to push, something new and complicated, and I'd not understood more than one word in every four, but to my surprise when she turned to me and told me to explain how neatly it would all hang together and how the whole idea was beautiful because it killed half a dozen birds with a single stone, I'd found the words coming as smoothly as if they were a speech I'd been perfecting for a month. Bullshit, I suddenly realised, worked just as well on the twelfth floor of a City bank as it did in the front room of a council house in Dagenham. And bullshit was something I'd always been good at. Darren had stared at me and said "OK", and that had been it, really, back to my desk, over to Emma's, and some work with Liz on trying to lend a hundred million pounds to a couple of retired Irishmen to buy an office and retail park in Milton Keynes.

(I'm not joking, by the way. An ex-dentist, an ex-accountant, Milton Keynes. A hundred million pounds. And we were fighting to get the business. That's how things were).

I'd forgotten all about the meeting, until the nod, and then I was in a good mood for the rest of the day. So much so that when Jason wandered over mid-afternoon he got on his hands and knees and peered under the desk.

"What the fuck are you doing, Jason?" I asked.

"I could see the smile on your face from the other side

of the building, mate," he said, straightening back up. "I just wanted to see who she was."

Russell smiled. Jane shook her head, but I could see she was laughing, too.

Jason was my closest friend at the bank, already, even though I'd only known him a few weeks. Spend an hour with the guy and you could see he was a genius; spend another hour and you'd realise he was a lazy bastard, too, which was why he was on the slow track with the guys like me rather than the express line with the likes of Liz and Russell. He worked for Paddy, and he'd not been around for long, either, but Paddy was already farming him out to Emma because she needed everything she could get. I'd met Sally already, the dark-haired exotic beauty from – well, from Slough, but no one held it against her. They'd known each other most of their lives, on and off for a decade, and finally got hitched a few years back. Jason claimed he'd been a bit wild when he was younger, and Sally agreed, but she'd tamed him, she said, moved him out to Clapham and got him a kid to play with on the Common. Emily was just three, and I'd never really seen the point of kids, but either I was wrong or this one was special, because whenever I went south of the river I found myself looking forward to Emily almost as much as Jason and Sally. And spending time with Sally was always surprising, the way she'd sit there quietly, watching me and Jason talk endless shit, with her big dark eyes like some mystic oriental doll, and then come up with a line that floored us, that either had us rolling on the floor or realising everything we thought about whatever we were talking about was just bullshit. The way Jason smiled, every time, you could see how proud the guy was.

What with Russell, Jason, and Sally, the front office, and some genuinely interesting work, those first six months flew by. But by late 2004, life was starting to get complicated.

You could blame the Irishmen with their little bit of money and their dreams of so much more. You could blame Doug, the syndicate guy, with his never-ending requests for a little something here and something else there. You could point your finger at Liz, although it was hardly her fault I found her so compelling. Or maybe Jason, for putting the idea into my head in the first place.

And then, you could blame me.

I fell into bed with Liz after a drunken dinner to celebrate the deal we'd been killing ourselves over for half a year. We'd finally done it and we'd done it together, against all the odds, and we'd fought everyone else and each other, half the time, just to get within sight of the finishing post. It wasn't just the drink that made both of us drop our guard so much that we did something neither of us had really thought about doing at all (not that I hadn't imagined it, but there's a difference between dreaming and planning, isn't there?)

The deal we'd finally completed was a landmark. There was a boom going on, and we wanted to be part of it, to keep on lending, but at a certain point we were going to run out of money. And long before then, we were going to look at our own books and realise that the amount of real estate risk we had on there was a recipe for the kind of disaster we could only imagine.

(Don't need to imagine it any more, of course, but who knew, back then, how bad things were going to get?)

There was an answer, though. Securitise them. Bundle all these loans together and sell them, which was a piece of piss, because it turned out everyone else wanted in on the action, too. We'd make a profit every time and get fistful of dollars back in the door to start the ball rolling again. And since we knew that selling the bonds was going to be the easiest thing in the world, we loaned money to pretty much anyone that wanted it, even where the real estate collateral wasn't as solid as it should have been – a shopping centre in an area hit by mass unemployment, say, or a business park with an anchor tenant whose lease was up in six months and hadn't yet committed to stay on. Or a couple of Irishmen with an eye on Milton Keynes. But these were the kinds of terms everyone else was offering, and we needed to be competitive. Once we'd sold the risk on to investors, it wouldn't be our problem.

Alchemy, we called it, which must have meant that even back then someone in the bank knew we were turning shit into gold. And if you turn shit into gold, you must know that the day might come when it'll all turn back again.

But that's hindsight. At the time, everything seemed just fine. We didn't realise that our big, cheap, easy loans were fuelling a property bubble; it never occurred to us that if the investors ever stopped buying our bonds, we could be left holding a book of loans that would make War and Peace look like Topsy and Tim. Everyone was doing it – this was 2004, we'd come to the party late, and everyone else in the City had already pulled. They were ahead of us and we were racing to catch up, pedal to the metal, which meant roaring around like idiots making as many loans as we could to whoever happened to want them. The idea of the loans actually going wrong didn't really occur to anyone as more than as a theoretical possibility. Not to anyone other than Stephen, perhaps, who set up a dedicated unit of two analysts to monitor what we had on the books. That way, he reasoned, we'd get an early heads-up if things started to turn bad.

So Alchemy was a big deal for us. It was also a freak, because instead of doing things the easy way and *selling* the loans to our SPV (Alchemy 2004, we called it), we bought a bunch of insurance contracts off it – credit default swaps, they were called – against the loans going bad. The bean-counters didn't like it. "Finance", they were called, which sounds harmless enough, but they could crush us with one stroke of their little red pencils because they were the ones who decided whether we needed to set aside any regulatory capital, and if we did, how much. "So what the hell's regulatory capital?" I hear you ask – either that, or someone's snoring. Well look, it's important. Every bet, every loan, swap, investment we make, we have to set aside a bit of cash. The riskier the bet, the more the cash. Risky bets are the ones we like to make, because they pay the most. But that means more regulatory capital, cash sitting there just out of reach, making nothing, doing nothing. So forget raising cheap money for your clients, forget selling bonds and topping the league tables. Most of the brain-power that went into these deals went on twisting the rules, finding the loopholes, doing whatever we could to cut the regulatory capital and make the risks look smaller than they really were.

And yes, you're right. When you've got that many clever people (because we were clever, even if we were as misguided as a guy in a wetsuit in the Sahara), and the thing they're most focussed on is trying to work their way round the rules, then one thing should be clear: everyone involved is heading for a crash.

So on the one side we had Finance, who (helpful as ever) had written us a checklist. Forty-seven pages, about a thousand boxes to tick, and every box a bastard.

On the other side we had Doug. Twenty-three years old and already cocky enough to wear a brilliant all-white suit to work, Doug's view was that he alone knew what we had to build if we wanted to sell it, and he didn't miss an opportunity to tell us. Every day, some new feature, some minor tweak, sometimes several, and normally we'd have told him to get lost and just sell what we'd built because we couldn't change it now. This time, thanks to the credit default swaps, we could, and he knew it. One occasion I remember looking up and seeing that white suit heading my way for the fifth time that morning, and Jane and Russell whispering across the desk at me "here comes your wife," and I finally lost it and told him to fuck off before he'd even reached me. He looked hurt, clearly didn't get why I was pissed off, and I felt guilty watching him turn and trudge away, and by that afternoon he had everything he'd asked for and more. As usual. We ended up with a bunch of loans, and a bunch of credit default swaps, and they looked similar enough, but thanks to Doug and his never-ending tweaks, they weren't. There was a mismatch. And the biggest bastard box on Finance's checklist was the one that asked us to confirm that there wasn't.

Liz was seriously pissed off. She'd been involved in Alchemy from the start, had hit the ground running with her Irish dentist (Primora, they'd called the company, which for some reason made me think of cheese). It was Liz that had come up with this freak of a deal when the traditional approach turned out to be unworkable and it looked like the whole thing was going to bite the dust. Me, I'd drifted in and out, helped on Primora, wandered back to Darren's team and done some work with Jane and Russell, wandered back again when Emma came calling and found myself thrown together with Liz to drag Alchemy across the line. So I was a bit low, sure, but hardly suicidal. There'd probably be a way round it, and if there wasn't, it wouldn't be the end of the world. I guess it was easy for me, with my real home halfway across the floor, to look at it all a bit more casually. Take an all-round view. Not so for Liz.

While she flapped, I paid some visits. First port of call was Anja, who'd been responsible for the analytics on the deal and could tell me if anything could be shifted around without fucking it all up. Like Sergei, Anja was another rocket-scientist, creating financial models for everything from rainfall in the Serengeti to the price of wallpaper in Walsall and its impact on your client's car-lease business. Again like Sergei, Anja was had been born the wrong side of the Iron Curtain, but there the resemblance ended: twenty-five years old, six feet tall, Anja was an East German maths prodigy who looked like a supermodel, dressed like a prostitute and talked like a premium-rate phone number. And however drunk she got, she'd still managed to turn down every advance from everyone who'd tried anything on – which included not only yours truly, but also a number of significantly richer and better-looking men.

Skirt riding three-quarters of the way up her thigh, pen poised provocatively between her lips, Anja thought for a moment and gave the response she'd given dozens of men at Miltons, and no doubt elsewhere:

"No."

"No as in you can't think of a way round it?"

"No as in there eez no way round it. Normally I find thees kind of thing exciting but this time, my juices do not flow. I am sorry."

Which was a shame, but hardly a shock.

Next stop was Finance. "Any get-out here?" I asked Walter.

Every bank has a Walter. Most banks have hundreds. Mid-forties and pleasant enough, he got by on tales of his antics at Eton, stories of the latest weekend's fishing and shooting, and the odd snippet of racy gossip about someone we might stumble across in the Sunday papers but who to Walter was simply "George". A perennial survivor, too: he'd been shifted from role to role each time his deficiencies were spotted, but never fired, and always, somehow, on a faint but unmistakeable upward trajectory. What he was doing in Finance, for which he was eminently unqualified and which required technical skills that he couldn't even have named let alone mastered, was a mystery. But whatever the reason, there he was, in charge of half a dozen people who actually knew what they were doing, and directly involved in Alchemy because of its high internal profile.

There was never much chance with Walter. Someone really, really smart might just have thought of something, but not Walter. Still, we had a pleasant enough chat, he said something about the deal using a rugby analogy that was probably very witty but made no sense to me, and I left him bellowing good-natured idiotisms across the desk to his underlings.

And on to the next: I strolled over to the syndicate desk and asked if we could change the CDS terms without losing investors. Doug actually laughed at me, but at least he had the brains to look worried when I snapped back at him that he'd better call them all up and tell them the deal was dead. But looking worried wasn't enough if he wasn't going to back down.

I called Jason, and he said we should have a coffee. Sat in the nearest Starbucks, he frowned and shot looks round the room like a bad actor in a bad spy movie. Once he was sure the coast was clear he didn't waste any time.

"How much does this mean to you?"

"Well, it's a big deal. There's a lot of money to be made. There's important people watching."

"No, not to the bank. To you."

Not a lot, really, not to me. But to Liz, it was everything. If it fell through, it wouldn't kill her, but she wouldn't stay, either. She'd been at the bank less than a year but she had offers coming at her from other departments and other banks every week. Alchemy was her baby, and if her baby didn't come through she'd take one of those offers and go make some money for someone else. To my surprise, I found that I *really* didn't want that to happen.

"So?"

"So, yes, I guess if it's that important to Liz then it does mean something to me."

Jason shook his head and smiled. We both knew nice guys didn't get very far in banking.

"Alex, you really are a moron."

"What?"

"It's so fucking easy I can't believe you haven't thought of it already."

"Eh?"

"Who fills in the form?"

"I do."

"Who sees it?"

"Finance."

"And they assume it's all right, don't they? Whatever you put down, they take it as god's honest truth?"

"Yup." I had an idea where he might be going with this now.

"And after that, the form gets filed and forgotten about unless anything goes badly wrong."

"Right."

"What's the rating on the bonds?"

"Mostly AAA."

"So between us, nothing's really going to go wrong, is it?"

"No."

"So, do what you gotta do."

He was right, of course. It was so fucking simple I couldn't believe it hadn't occurred to me, but it hadn't. I could write whatever I wanted on the form, and the chances were a thousand to one against it would ever come back to bite me. I wasn't happy, but Jason kept on talking. Everyone was doing it, he said. This was the game; these were the rules. How the hell else did I think everyone else was moving so fast? If I didn't play it this way, I'd always end up coming in last. At the time I wasn't sure; I only half-believed him, and most of that half was because it suited me. But after everything that's come out over the last few years, I guess he must have been right after all. You can't bring down an entire global financial system through incompetence alone. They must have been at it all over the place.

I'd like to say it troubled me. I'd like to point to sleepless nights, wrestling demons in my dreams and waking to a chorus of conscience and care. And I suppose I did struggle with it, for about an hour. I thought about Dad, and what he'd said about bankers ("They're crooks, Alex. You're walking into a world of crooks. Don't turn into one.") I thought about Liz and whether she'd thank me for it, not that she'd ever know. I thought about whether it really made any difference, what I was considering, whether it was really crooked at all, because I was sure as I could be that nothing would go wrong and no one would find out and if no one finds out, where's the harm? I thought about what would happen if I got caught, and for a few minutes I was about to back out of it, and then I remembered that I wasn't going to get caught because nothing would go wrong, and I was back where I'd started. Liz was looking for me, close to tearing her hair out trying for a straight answer. I found myself an empty desk on the third floor, in amongst the sales teams, and I logged on and answered a few emails and ignored her calls and messages, increasingly frantic, increasingly black. And for an hour, down there on the third floor, in amongst those emails and a call or two, I did wrestle with demons.

Everyone was doing it, Jason had said. How do you think banks make the big money in the first place? You take some risks, you make them look smaller. That's the game. If it all goes to shit, chances are you'll be long gone. That's how it's done. And there's no other way.

Well, if there was no other way…..

One hour, it took, to make the decision. If I'd not made that decision, would everything else have followed anyway? Was that the moment I climbed in and shut my eyes, or had it already happened and all that one hour did was take me a little bit further away from where I thought I was? But one thing I hadn't figured out in that hour was how I'd sell it to Liz. Because I might not have known her long, but I knew she wouldn't like what I was doing. I couldn't think of a line, which was unusual, for me. I'd have to wing it.

I ticked the boxes that needed ticking, I signed my name, and I walked that fucker of a checklist right up to Finance on the ninth floor. I even took a couple of minutes to go through it with Walter in person – and breathed a silent sigh of relief as he nodded and told me that everything looked right. All that remained was to break the good news.

Liz was on the phone as I approached, but she glanced up and saw me when I was still half a dozen desks away. She looked almost tearful as she said a quiet goodbye and hung up. She turned to face me, shaking her head – it looked like she'd just about given up.

So she must have been astonished to see the smile on my face and the extravagant thumbs up.

"It's sorted."

"What's sorted?"

"Our little problem with Finance. It's gone away. No capital. Full relief."

Dumbstruck silence. After a few moments:

"How?"

Ah. The moment of truth. Time to wing it.

"I spoke to a few people. Don't worry about it. It's OK."

Obviously, she pressed – wouldn't you?

"But who did you speak to? We've been through

everyone. Finance were no fucking use at all."

I love a girl who swears. She was right, too. Finance were supposed to help us, but most of the time they were as much use as a pig farm in Iran.

I tried again. I thought maybe a shrug would help. They say body language is just as important as what comes out of your mouth, don't they?

"Don't worry. It's sorted. Between Finance and the people I've spoken to, everything's agreed. Full relief. Zero capital."

Even as I said it I could tell it sounded weak. Just repeating the words wasn't good enough. It wouldn't have been good enough for me, and it's not like I even cared.

"Who was it you spoke to? Come on, Alex, what's going on."

Now she was sounding suspicious. I'd played it like an amateur. I suppose I was an amateur, in this game. But then – a moment of inspiration.

"Sup Comms. I went through it with them. They're OK with it. I filled in our bit of the form and explained the background. It's not a problem. They're reasonable people."

She stood back and looked at me.

"Sup Comms? Really?"

I could see why she was surprised. Supervisory Communications had been called many things, but "reasonable" wasn't one of them. I nodded, she shrugged, and I breathed a silent sigh of relief.

"Well good for them. They've finally got something right. Won't miss the bastards, though."

Supervisory Communications were the new boys in Finance. Finance usually knew the rules and how to deal with them, but sometimes those rules were so badly written or our deals so complicated that they needed some guidance from the people who'd written them in the first place. So a new team had been created, Sup Comms, and their job was to get answers from the regulators when we needed them. They'd been around just three months and already everyone hated them. We hated them because they were a bunch of interlopers who'd just shown up and started fucking up our deals. The rest of Finance hated them because they acted like they were the guardians of some religious fucking mystery, and set themselves at the top of the Finance tree. Being hated by Finance was like being considered unclean by a leper, but it didn't matter. Everyone hated them, no one knew them, and they'd caused so much grief to so many people that in three weeks' time the whole unit was going to be shut down, split up and spread round the bank. That was the beauty of the lie: if Liz ever decided to follow up on it, there wouldn't be anyone left to follow up with.

"Yeah, maybe I just got them on a good day. But it doesn't matter. We've done it."

And she bought it. Or maybe she just thought it wasn't worth pushing any further. Maybe she knew the truth: that was the game, those were the rules. But either way, it was done. The deal closed. I'd committed my first fraud. And my reward was Liz, for a few fun weeks.

Now, I'm a banker, so no one's going to think I'm some kind of saint. Especially when I've just put my hand up to lying to a regulator and misleading a colleague, all for a month of surprisingly good sex. But you can see it wasn't really like that, right? I didn't know what would happen. I wasn't planning the steps – break the rules, close the deal, pour the wine, bed the girl. I saw my friend was upset, that was all, and I wanted to do her a favour. There really wasn't much in it for me. And another thing. It wasn't like I invented the game. I was only doing what everyone else had been doing all along. I was just along for the ride.

A few weeks later, Liz and I were history. Still close friends, of course, but nothing more. And a couple of months after that she'd embarked on an ill-fated relationship with another colleague (we'll call him Graham, because that's his name) which eventually led to their engagement, her discovery (in the space of three consecutive evenings) of his cocaine, porn, and prostitute habits, their breakup, his breakdown, sacking, and eventual reappearance at, of all places, Greenings. I've told her before, and now she's married I probably won't be able to again, but Liz's taste in men really is shit. Graham was an arsehole (I'd told Liz that just after she hooked up with him, which hadn't done me any favours), and being an arsehole made him a prime candidate for Greenings, but I didn't think they'd have all that much room for an ex-junkie with a documented history of mental problems. What did I know? Graham turned himself into a big swinging dick in Greenings M&A, got rich and well-respected, and didn't even bother making a secret of the past. He was proud of it, the sinner reformed. He'd become patron of a well-known mental disability charity, and he hosted an auction every year where hundreds of drunk City types threw their money at a couple of rehab clinics he'd helped set up.

Can people change? Maybe. But my guess was that he was still an arsehole. And neither I nor any of my colleagues could touch the bastard.

But he was married now, to another bastard straight out of the Greenings bastard-factory. Worked in securitisation. Name of Grace. And she, well, as you've seen, she was a much easier target.

TUESDAY

10: The Sting in the Tail

Tuesday 15ᵗʰ December, 2009

I woke to the taste of metal and mild stomach cramps. I had no idea what time it was so I lay there, grimacing and swallowing and hoping the discomfort would ease, until the alarm clock went off. Nothing unusual, really; an everyday kind of hangover.

I'd stayed in the pub till closing, chatting with a few of the regulars and Mandy behind the bar (young, blonde, inevitably Australian). Back in the City every bar and pub would be full of drunken bankers, brokers and lawyers on the Christmas drinks trail, out since lunchtime and still there until they threw up or got thrown out. Much more civilised here – no drunks, no office parties. No calls came through but I had to deal with a few emails, which earned me the expected abuse from the others – a bunch of "serious" drinkers that included two accountants, a lawyer, a doctor and the marketing director of the country's best-known pharmaceutical firm. Serious drinkers my arse. By the time I got home I was sober enough to register that I still hadn't heard from Jason, and to be a little concerned. I called the apartment, but no one answered. I thought about calling the house, waking the children, after midnight, and decided no. I poured myself a large whisky instead. I may have followed it up with another. I'm guessing it was the whisky that did the damage.

Ah, the tail. I promised an explanation. This won't hurt a bit.

The Mintrex deal was what we called a monetisation of natural resources. Mintrex were raising cash based on the minerals they had in the ground. To work out how much money they can get (and how the agencies will rate it), you need to know how much there is in the ground, and how much they can expect to get for it over the next 25 years – that was the life of the deal. You take these numbers and you fuck around with them, running "stress tests" like what happens if Mintrex goes bust and you've got to pay someone else to get the stuff out, what happens if some dick with a metal detector finds a billion tons of the stuff in a field off the M4 and suddenly it's worthless, what happens if the Government goes green and gets regulation-happy. You do all this work and then the rating agencies pluck a number out of the air and tell you that's how many bonds you can sell if you want them rated.

The thing is, all our predictions showed that after about fifteen years, everything Mintrex could lay their hands on right now would have run out. Those last ten years – that's the "tail" of the deal – Mintrex would have to find some other way to pay their debt. That was OK, though, because while they were running through this stuff, they'd be getting planning permission on other sites, looking for new sites, finding more minerals in the old ones.

Planning permission wasn't a gimme, but you could factor that in, too. If you've got a ninety-five per cent success rate, you call it a five per cent failure rate, stress that (say) three times for a fifteen per cent failure rate, and assume eighty-five out of every hundred sites would eventually get their permissions.

That's the way it looked, on the surface, and that's the way the agencies took it.

Which seems fair – except for one thing. We'd skipped a stage. Mintrex aren't idiots, you see, so when they don't think they'll get planning consent for a site, they don't apply for it; they sit on it and wait. One thing they've got plenty of is time. Over five, ten, fifteen years, the picture could change; regulations, governments, markets, local authorities, resource requirements, these could all move in their favour. But they're not going to apply when they know the odds are against them.

So, in reality, ninety-five successful applications out of a hundred was ninety-five successful applications out of every *two hundred and fifty* that had been through Mintrex's internal planning committee. The other hundred and fifty never even got to the local council, because any fool could see there wasn't a chance in hell they'd be allowed to put an access road through the primary school, bulldoze the care-home or vent toxic waste into the babbling brook. The five per cent failure rate the agencies were working with, it should have been sixty-two per cent, and the agencies should have laughed us all the way back to the quarry.

It wasn't like we hid any of this. The pack we sent them included planning committee minutes going back ten years. We even put together a summary table to save them reading the thousand pages of minutes. Fairer than fair, right? They'd spot the problem and tell us to cut the deal in half, we thought. We'd negotiate, settle somewhere in the middle, and everyone would be happy.

But they didn't spot it. OK, it was hidden away at the bottom of half a ton of dull-as-fuck legal documentation. But still – it was there. We spent weeks waiting for them to spot it, and as the weeks turned into months we started to realise that they weren't going to unless we actually sat down and told them and waved the bits of paper in their faces. And if you think there was a chance in hell we were going to do that then you, my friend, have a lot to learn about bankers.

Meanwhile today was pricing day, which meant I'd have to drink, lots, on top of whatever beer and whisky was still sloshing round my system. The radio warned of ice on the roads and snow to come. I wouldn't risk the bike.

It was a horrible journey, even by Central Line standards. There was ice everywhere, the delays worse than usual, the platform and trains so busy I couldn't get on the first three that stopped. After a lot of ungentlemanly pushing I finally got myself onto a carriage that still stank of last night's beer and kebabs. My feet sank an inch into a cold, gluey mixture of slush and tattered newspapers ("Arsenal Rampant", "Millie Splits from Paul", "Day of Reckoning" – again). Even more trouble when we got to Bank, part of the station shut, so the platform was packed and I only just made it off the train. The crush continued all the way up the escalators, past the ticket barriers, to the stairway and into the blessed light and air. I was going to miss the pricing call, and I might not be indispensable, but I wanted to be there. As I elbowed my way through the mob I looked up and saw the security guard from yesterday, the Beast, doing the same thing. He turned and looked back down and something he saw there must have scared the crap out of him, because I've never seen someone so big looking so helpless, little eyes wide, face the same colour as the soggy mush on the floor of the train. He didn't seem to spot me, so I couldn't take the credit, much as I'd have loved to. He was staring down for a couple of seconds, no more, and then he turned and shoved and was gone.

By the time I made it to my desk and dialled in, everyone was at the "congratulations" stage. They sounded genuine enough; the deal must have priced well. The email confirmation came through as the call wound down: all the tranches, from AA down to BBB, fixed and floating, had priced "inside price talk", which meant that Mintrex had sold everything they wanted to and would be paying less interest than we'd been expecting.

Moments after the call was over, the sales and syndicate

teams were among us, all gleaming teeth and high-fives. A six-strong sales team had pushed hard for three weeks, a lifetime in bond sales, to build up demand. Doug stood out, though, in the white suit and the perfect hair. He was still only twenty-eight, and brilliant, and he knew it. He'd have stood out at a David Bowie concert.

If you want to know what a syndicate banker actually does, the best thing to put it is to compare him to the sales team. Those guys know the investors. The syndicate banker, on the other hand, "understands" the investors, what they're thinking, what they want. If the sales team are the waiters, taking orders, pushing the specials, then the syndicate bankers are the executive chefs. Of course there's also my team, you know, the ones who actually get the client and put the deal together, and if you asked any of us we'd say we were the ones at the top of the tree, but tell that to Doug and he'd just laugh. As far as he's concerned we're the guys he sends out to market at five every morning to grab the best cuts we can. And then, you know, we cook the stuff. And every now and then Doug and his friends wander past, have a sniff, a little taste, suggest a pinch of controlling creditor rights on the class Bs, or tell us the early redemption provisions are overdone. Yeah, they fancy themselves.

And in Doug's world, in the world of the sales team, the deal was as good as over. Everything had been agreed, as far as they were concerned. Just a matter of getting everything tied up before closing on Friday. "Just".

For instance: other than the offering circular, all of the documents still had to be finalised (there were about a hundred of them). Which meant that whilst we thought we'd agreed everything there was to be agreed, we'd inevitably come across a few big commercial points (and a few hundred fiddly legal ones) that needed to be settled at the last minute.

For instance: settlement instructions had to be finalised and confirmed with banks, agents and clearing houses, bonds had to be listed on a stock exchange, legal opinions had to be finalised, financial statements had to be drawn up, due diligence reports from insurers, valuers, geologists and environmental consultants had to be agreed and confirmed, swaps and liquidity lines had to be "booked", and a three-hundred item list of "conditions precedent" to closing had to be ticked off.

For instance: the rating agencies had to confirm they were happy with the deal, and to issue their final ratings. They'd already issued their presale reports, which meant they liked the way things were heading, but they could change their minds if we didn't play ball on anything else they spotted. Like the tax mess I'd spent the previous day sorting out.

For instance: I'd have to head out for some celebratory drinks later today with all the guys whose work really was over. Sure, I'd have some fun, especially if a certain attractive Scottish lawyer was there, but she probably wouldn't be. Harvey knew how to keep his galley slaves pulling away until they'd got where they needed to be, and that wouldn't happen till Friday. But whatever happened, I needed to show my face later and that meant a little less time for all the things that still needed to be done. It's a dog's life in banking.

All of which meant the next three days weren't going to be a walk in the park. And my phone would be ringing and my BlackBerry would be buzzing every minute of every hour till we hit Friday afternoon.

So I took the opportunity to try to get hold of Jason the first moment I got to myself. Again, nothing at the apartment – I left another message, but more in hope than expectation. Of all the things Jason was going to have to sacrifice now he was unemployed and hardly likely to get a cracking reference, Charmaine was probably top of the list. It wasn't like he hadn't been looking for the chance. At the house I got nothing at all, not even the answerphone. I held for twenty rings, to be sure, and gave up.

I got little peace the rest of Tuesday morning, but for every bit of crap that landed on my desk I handed out half a dozen bits of my own. Boring, maybe, but this is when I come into my own: when everyone else thinks they can slack off, when you need a mean bastard to whip them into shape, out of the pub and back to the office, what you need is me, because let me tell you, I crack a mean whip. I had a list of people to deal with, to threaten and guilt-trip and frighten and coax into doing the jobs they should have been doing anyway. It wasn't like I expected anything to fall into my lap. No one I spoke to was happy to hear from me. They might grunt and give a grudging "yeah, OK," but it wasn't raining down the bits of paper I needed. Yet.

After a dozen calls I paused to catch my breath but the moment the line was down it was ringing again. I looked down to see who it was. Doug. He'd run the pricing call, he should have been halfway drunk by now, so whatever he was calling me for was probably important. I tried to sound cheerful.

"I've been trying to reach you for an hour, Alex."

That explained why he wasn't drunk, at least.

"Sorry, Doug. Still plenty to do at my end."

"Yeah, sure. Listen, Elaine's on with me."

Elaine. I struggled for a moment and then remembered. Sales. Perfectly pleasant, reasonably smart. She had a big account, a pension fund named Westhaven that had put two hundred million into Mintrex. I felt suddenly cold.

"Hi Alex," she said.

"Hello Elaine. What can I do for you?"

There was a moment's silence, like each of them was

hoping the other one would start. Doug was the first to cave.

"Erm, Alex" (he said), "it looks like we need to make a change."

"Eh?"

"We need to change the deal."

"Doug, you know we can't change the deal now. We've just priced."

A funny thing, pricing. The main legal documents hadn't yet been signed, but the call that had taken place that morning, and the orders that had fed into it, all that added up to an agreement between the investors and Mintrex. Mintrex would issue the bonds, and the investors would buy them, and the deal would look the way it was painted in the Offering Circulars. Hundreds of pages of the kind of detail that only a lawyer could care about, but any change would screw the deal. Might even kill it. Would probably cost some people their jobs – and if it did, those people would include Elaine, Doug, and poor innocent Alex. No wonder Doug wasn't drunk.

Time for Elaine to take over.

"I'm sorry guys," she giggled nervously. "I guess I just wasn't thinking. The people over at Westhaven asked me if we had full fixed security on everything. I just kind of assumed we did. They just called back to check that was definitely right. Apparently they've read the Offering Circular now and it looks like it isn't."

"Shit." That was me. "Shit, shit, shit."

Full fixed security is what you give the bank when you get a mortgage. If you're running a massive operating business like Mintrex and someone asks you for full fixed security over all your assets, you laugh and tell them to fuck off. You can't run a business like that, with someone looking over your shoulder telling you what you can buy, what you can sell, how you can trade. And even if you could, it takes so much time and money to grant it in the first place it probably wouldn't be worth doing the deal. So you end up with a negotiated position, a halfway house: a bit of fixed security, over things you don't expect to sell that often, like your offices or your warehouses or your factories or mines; and for pretty much everything else, something called "floating" security, which can turn into fixed security if things start to turn sour. That's easy enough to agree. What isn't easy to agree are the triggers, the numbers that tell you that it's happening, the end is coming, and it's time to bite the bullet and hand out the fixed security. This is when the rain starts to fall, and there's nowhere to run, and the crocodiles are circling, and you're throwing out bits of meat, throwing out anything you can to keep them away. No one wants to be there, not if they're the guy throwing out the meat, but the crocodiles don't want to be hungry, either, so negotiating the triggers for the Mintrex deal was probably the most painful thing I'd done since I started at Miltons. In that time I've come off the motorbike, fallen through a glass door, and had my balls almost crushed by a madwoman – so yes, I know a thing or two about pain. Nearly a year, it had taken, slowly edging our way towards agreement. In one corner we had the crocodiles: rating agencies, other lenders, trustees, swaps teams, all snapping their jaws and wanting their meat the moment a wisp of cloud appeared. And in the other corner the company, Mintrex, Ahmed and his friends, shaking their heads and offering up bugger all until they got a hurricane and a lunar eclipse in the same week. I'd lived that fucking negotiation like it was the only thing I cared about, I'd played referee, mediator, confidante, late-night drinking companion and I'd heard more secrets, whinges, complaints and moans than I cared to remember, and finally I'd dragged them all to a place they could just about live with. And now Westhaven wanted to blow it apart.

Where we'd got to, the triggers, the assets, the whole lot was set out in the Offering Circulars in more detail than anyone could ever have needed, and Westhaven had seen those Offering Circulars in draft after draft, they'd had them for weeks now, so they had no excuse other than laziness to have got it so spectacularly wrong. But now, on a recorded line (all sales lines were recorded), Elaine had fucked it all up.

Doug spelled it out, not that he really needed to. "It's two hundred mill, Alex. If these guys pull out, we're screwed. I'm serious. We need to sort something out. Think you can work something out with Mintrex?"

No. No, I couldn't. Even if there was time to reopen the year-long negotiations and start all over again, the actual security process would take months, not the hours we had. The only option was to try and smooth things over with Westhaven.

Doug couldn't have expected anything else, but he needed to hear me say it. And since I knew how this whole thing hung together better than anyone else on the planet, he needed me involved. I told him I'd keep myself available for a call with Westhaven for the rest of the morning, and he and Elaine hung up, full of worthless apologies, to try to set one up.

I had a few minutes before anything could happen, so I tried Jason again, a couple more times. The house line was engaged. Rachel was at her desk, and there was time for a quick coffee, but she was too busy, she said – which wasn't like her. She kept glancing over towards Anthony, Jane, Russell's office: no prizes for guessing what was on her mind. She was right to be worried, too – Jane knew she was good value for her job but she'd never played up to Anthony. She had a problem with Anthony, she said, which was that she couldn't stand being in the same room as a prick who thought he was cleverer than he really was, and when she'd first told me that I'd shrugged and told her we all felt like that about the guy. What I didn't realise at the time was that she hadn't bothered to hide her feelings. She wore them front and centre, which meant at least Russell knew someone hated his golden boy. But it also meant Anthony knew, too, and if he got the job it would be a tight call whether she'd get to walk before he fired her.

After a third try at Jason I got a call from Rob. Rob was an internal credit analyst who'd joined the bank shortly before I'd switched to front office. I'd worked with him on my early deals in Russell's team, and he'd helped push through a few of the Alchemy loans, too. I didn't come across him so much these days, but we still managed the odd drink together from time to time.

"Have you heard?"

No "How are you?" Not even a "Hi". Straight to the point. He sounded breathless, too.

"Yeah. Sad state of affairs. I've been trying to get hold of him actually."

I couldn't really say anything more, given the circumstances of Jason's dismissal.

"What are you talking about?"

"Jason. Got canned yesterday. What are you talking about?"

I heard Rob sigh. I'd missed the point, obviously; Jason was yesterday's news, and in a bank things move too fast to dwell on the past.

"Yeah. I heard about Jason," he said. "A real shame."

He didn't sound exactly distraught. Not that he didn't mean it, but something else was on his mind. I let him continue.

"No. It's Alchemy. The default."

Now, there are a few things everyone hopes they never have to hear. *'You're fired'*, say. *'I'm seeing someone else'*. *'There's been an accident'*. Hearing "*Alchemy*" and "*default*" that close together was right up that list as far as I was concerned. For an instant I could see everything falling apart and blind terror seized me. But only an instant. I didn't think Rob had noticed anything.

"What's happened?"

"Remember Primora?"

Of course I remembered Primora. Still sitting there, the single biggest loan in Alchemy, with a mismatched credit default swap no one knew about. I paused, briefly, and pretended to search my mind.

"Yup. Hundred mil, office and retail, right?"

"That's the one. Interest and a chunk of principal due yesterday."

"And?"

"And it didn't come in. Not a penny, and seven million was due. They're scrambling to get the cash together in the next few days before it's a formal default, but between you and me they haven't got a prayer. Word is they're a couple of hundred grand short."

"Shit"

"So it looks like we're gonna have to use the CDS."

There wasn't a lot I could say to that, so I didn't. Rob laughed.

"At least we don't have to take the hit, eh? Good job we put that one through Alchemy."

I was trying to think. Was there a way out? Any way out at all? He was waiting for a reply. I forced out the words.

"Yeah. Good job. Thanks for letting me know."

The credit default swap in question had expired three months ago. That was the "mismatch" I'd conveniently forgotten about when it came to the form. Three more months to go until the loan was done and dusted. Primora would pay us back our money, and no one would ever know the truth. And now this happens. Looked like Mintrex wasn't the only tail with a sting in it. I let my head fall to the desk and hit the wood, hard enough to hurt. I looked up. No one had noticed, so I did it again. It didn't help. If good comedy's all about timing then the dentist and his pal were fucking laugh masters.

And I was the punchline.

11: The Ferrari Games, 2005-6

Miltons was not, traditionally, a venue you'd associate with fun. A bank, full of bankers, banking. Need I say more?

But in early 2006, one afternoon shone through a grey, wet February. Eight gleaming red monsters, racing round the office. Ferraris – remote-controlled models, not real ones, because we were bankers not movie stars, but still, they moved like bullets and we all felt a little like Steve McQueen. For that one afternoon, dozens of people who usually got through the day with little more than a polite nod between them, these men and women were friends, laughing together, abusing management together (and management were right there with them), racing, winning, losing, fighting, swearing and making it up again. And it was all down to Jason, and me, and a touch of fraud.

Just a touch.

Not long after we got together, Liz and me were history. I had other fish to fry, though. Till now, I'd been helping Jane and Russell with their deals, but Darren had suddenly decided I was ready to fly solo. My own deal. Sure, it was an easy one; a client we'd known for years, a tap – which meant we were just issuing new bonds off a deal we'd already closed a couple of years back, a market (electricity) we knew back to front, the kind of deal we'd done so many times the whole thing was second nature. But it was a big thing for me, a rite of passage, and even if it looked easy from the outside, there were still a hundred-and-one things that might have gone wrong if I hadn't been on every single one of them from the moment I opened my eyes in the morning to the moment I went to sleep nineteen hours later. I did it in four weeks, which got me a good word from our client and another nod from Darren.

Over on conduit Paddy had welcomed Jason back with a deal of his own. Maybe I should remember what it was about, car leases or frozen goods or music royalties, it could have been anything, but I was so wrapped up in my own deal I didn't have time for anyone else's. He did it, too, took him a little longer, but that's probably because he still rocked up an hour after everyone else and sloped off to the pub most lunchtimes.

We owed ourselves a celebration, we thought. We'd done the celebrating with our clients, and I know what you're thinking, twenty-thousand pound bills in Michelin-starred restaurants, but it wasn't like that, not for us, even at the best of times. We'd had a nice time, but it was a nice, normal time, nothing to get irate about. And we'd had to behave ourselves, because our clients were there and heaven help the banker who lets his client see what he's *really* like.

I don't know how Jason did it. *Kurami*, the place was called, no idea why or what it meant, and it only lasted a couple of years, so you might not remember the name, but while it was there it was the hottest club in the West End. We'd fixed on a Thursday, decided to make it a big one, but neither of us had any idea where to go, or at least that's what I thought. Straight to the pub after work, with a few extras; then off for a bite to eat, and I'm throwing ideas out, this bar, that club, all places I'd been before, often enough with the Dagenham mob, I still didn't have the imagination to think big.

And then Jason chucks down a credit card and I do the same, and he picks up mine, hands it back to me and says "Come on then, let's go."

I'd had a few drinks already by this point, so we were in the taxi by the time I asked him where. And when he told me, I couldn't do anything more than gape.

It was eleven when we got there, and the queue looked like it was going on forever, but somehow we were inside before I had a chance to laugh at him and tell him we'd never make it. Two guys, no girls, neither of us particularly good-looking or well-dressed, and certainly not famous. I'll never know how he did it, but there we were, with our own table, looking around and spotting the occasional person who *was* famous, and plenty who weren't but were hoping this was the night.

We got a lot of attention, and even if Jason was still the responsible married man, I sure as hell wasn't. They must have thought we were celebrities, and we weren't telling them otherwise. Except – there was a lot of champagne. Really. And I knew I should keep my mouth shut, I knew it, but there was one girl I was chatting to, stroking her leg and kissing from time to time, and I couldn't help myself. "I work in a bank," I told her, when she asked what I did, and the moment the words were out of my mouth I realised I'd screwed up, but all she did was nod and shrug and move in to kiss me again.

I made sure I got her number.

Most of the rest of the evening was a blur, and every time I looked round for Jason there he was in the middle of a crowd, laughing, shouting, an A-lister on a high. The focus got a little bit sharper when the bill arrived. I don't know why I was shocked, I shouldn't have been, but even at a place like this, even with everything we'd drunk ourselves and bought for the girls who all seemed to have disappeared by now, the numbers hit me like a fist. I looked at Jason and was surprised to see him still smiling. He had his card out, and I reluctantly put my hand in my pocket but he shook his head and said "I've got this," and I was so relieved I didn't even argue.

Next morning, fairly late, in the shady haven of

Starbucks, I could remember just enough about the night before to apologise.

"Not a problem."

"You can't pay all that, mate."

"No, you're right. I can't. But they can."

Who were *they?* I wondered. And then I saw he'd taken out his credit card and laid it on the table, the same card he'd paid with at the restaurant and the club. I had one that looked identical, same logo, same colour. The corporate Amex. Miltons had paid for the whole night's entertainment, a little for dinner and not far short of a grand for our night at Kurami. I looked at him.

"Sure this'll go through, Jason?"

"As long as I client it up a bit, yeah."

I'd never heard the expression but it was obvious enough what he meant. As long as there's a client involved, you can get away with almost anything.

And something else began to make a little sense, too. Jason had been up and down like a high-tempo porn star for the last couple of hours last night, chatting to the man behind the bar, asking questions, getting answers. And then finally he'd grabbed me and told me it was time to go. I hadn't thought to ask what was going on, I'd spent most of the evening with Jasmine – Jasmine was the girl who hadn't minded me being a banker, and she hadn't minded what my hands were up to, either, so I reckoned on staying in touch with her if I could. Turned out Jason had been checking the tab. As long as that bill stayed below a grand and we could point to a client, no one would bat an eyelid. It would get paid and forgotten about, I knew that, I'd hired half the people in the back office who sent out the forms and made the payments. And Jason knew it too, apparently. Not that he made a habit of it, he said. He wasn't setting out to rip off the bank. But if he was going to spend that kind of money celebrating a deal, it wasn't going to be at his family's expense. He said it like it was just a normal thing, and maybe he was right, and if a little part of me wasn't so sure, there was a much bigger part telling me it wasn't like I'd actually done anything. I was just along for the ride.

As 2006 swung round, I'd just finished my first full year in the front office, and that meant I could look forward to a real banker's bonus. At least, I hoped so. I'd closed my deals for Darren, and everyone on Emma's team had seen what I'd done to get Alchemy finished off. Except the checklist. No one knew about that, except Jason and me, and I was planning on keeping it that way.

It's a strange time, bonus day. Everything seems to shimmer, and I don't mean with gold. There's so much nervous tension in the office you think you're going to fry when you put a hand on the photocopier, and when you step outside and everyone's just going about their daily business like nothing's happening, you don't understand how they can do it, how they can't be infected by what's happening a dozen floors above their heads. And when your phone rings and you look down and see your manager's name there, when you stand up and walk towards the closed door, you feel like you're floating, and every eye is on you, and just getting there and turning the handle and walking in is almost too much.

I've been told a hundred times that when you get the numbers, you've got to look pissed off. Whatever those numbers are. If they give you a million, you expected two. If they give it in shares, you wanted cash. And you know, I'm not a bad liar, not when it comes to making things up, getting myself out of the shit. But this was poker, and my poker face has never been my strongest suit, so when Darren called me in and slid that low-key manila envelope across the table, every nerve in my body was focussed on one thing: give nothing away.

Here's what I read:

"Dear Mr Konninger,
In view of your contribution to the business and to the bank as a whole this year, we are pleased to inform you that as of February 1st, 2006, you will receive a one-grade promotion to Associate Director"

This was a pleasant surprise. I knew I was good enough, but I didn't realise Darren knew it. The letter continued:

"Your bonus for the calendar year 2005 will comprise the following:
Cash: £150,000, to be awarded on February 28th alongside regular salary payment.
Stock: Milton Shearings Ordinary 'A' shares to the value of £75,000 (by reference to the closing price quoted on the London Stock Exchange on January 31st, 2006)."

I'd been expecting something decent, but nothing like this. Two hundred and twenty-five grand. I read it and read it again, and added the numbers up three times in my head to make sure I hadn't got it wrong. And all that time I completely forget the one thing I was supposed to be concentrating on: give nothing away. I glanced up and Darren was grinning at me, at the expression on my big dumb face. I closed my mouth and put on a frown, but it was way too late for all that.

There was some nonsense about tax and national insurance, and hanging onto the shares for ninety days. I could live with that. The world wasn't going to end in ninety days.

The final item was almost an aside:

"Alongside your promotion, your annual salary will be increased from £50,000 to £62,500, effective from the date of promotion.

This has been an excellent year for Milton Shearings and we hope, with your help, to go on to even greater things next year.

Wishing you a happy festive season.

Yours sincerely,

Erik Mortensen."

You know things are going well when you can look at a twenty-five per cent payrise and shrug, and mean it. I'd managed to keep my mouth shut for the last bit, and was concentrating on looking blank again, but in my head I was running through all the apartments I'd seen just out of reach. They weren't out of reach any more. I was still in Holloway (not that I was spending many nights there these days), and Holloway was no place for a man on that kind of money.

Incidentally, and you probably won't believe this: I don't like talking about money; never have, never will. It's crass, it's embarrassing, and no good ever comes of it. The amounts either seem pitifully small (to your more successful colleagues, hedgies, private equity players), or enormous, unjustified, and disgustingly overblown (to everyone else in the country). I don't talk numbers unless I have to. On Bonus Day, you have to.

Mortensen, by the way, was a hard-arsed Scandi who'd been brought in by Kemp's successor as his Business Manager. No one knew what that meant at the time, but it turned out to mean he sacked everyone who crossed him and a fair few that didn't, and replaced them all with more hard-arsed bastards just like him. Kemp's successor had moved on by now, and so had the guy who came after him, but Mortensen was still there, Chief of Staff, Chief Whip, Chief Axe-Wielder, and he was still chopping up whole departments and scattering their remains to the wind whenever he felt like a change.

The first rule of banking is *don't talk about your bonus.* I took this about as seriously as everyone else at Miltons, so half an hour later I was huddled over a coffee with a less-than-happy Jason. Unlike me, he'd been expecting a big pay-out. Unlike me, he hadn't got one. Paddy had sat him down and told him he'd done a good job, but the cupboard was bare, the conduit hadn't had a great year, the bonus pool was down. Everyone, apparently, had suffered, most of them more than Jason.

But you know how it is with bonuses, salaries, anything about money: if you're happy, you're happy, and if you're not, you're not, and it doesn't make a blind bit of difference if they tell you you're Osama Bin Laden or Jesus Christ almighty while they're dishing out the dough. I was happy. Jason wasn't.

The bonus wasn't the only thing I was happy about, to be honest. I'd waited a couple of days after the Kurami night and called Jasmine. Now I'm not the best-looking man on the planet. I'm not even second. But I've always had a gift for easy talking, so I was surprised how nervous I was as I dialled her number. There was something different about Jasmine, I thought. I didn't want to screw this one up.

I didn't screw it up, either, or at least, not at first. We met up that weekend and within another month I'd moved half my stuff into her flat in Holland Park. Even an Essex boy like me knew that Holland Park was about as far from Holloway as Dagenham was from Dallas. Jasmine, I soon discovered, was an artist, or at least that was what she called herself. Where an artist got the money for Holland Park and all those nights out, I couldn't figure out, at least not at the beginning. I thought maybe she was really good, maybe she was actually a successful artist, maybe she was making a proper living out of it, but then I saw the stuff she painted and made and even I could tell it wouldn't pay.

She owned up to her real name pretty early on. Rebecca, she'd been born, and never got round to actually changing it, and when I asked her what was wrong with Rebecca she looked at me with pity and shook her head. Du Maurier, and Hitchcock, she said. They'd screwed it up. Might have been a perfectly nice name but now it was gothic and doom-laden and she'd been over all that shit by the time she was a teenager.

She looked like she had, too. Whatever you could say about her, she knew how to have fun. I spent half an hour, after she told me about the name thing, thinking *what an oversensitive, self-indulgent idiot*, but later that same afternoon in bed, it was back to *what a girl*. She had everything, or at least everything a shallow banker like me was interested in. Great looks, a fantastic body, and an insatiable sexual appetite. She didn't seem to care where we were or who might be looking, and more than once I found myself thinking she might be too much for me. It wasn't just the sex, either. Her approach to alcohol and drugs, to driving, to everything, was reckless, like she thought she had nine lives and didn't mind wasting a couple. It turned out the money came from her family, car import millionaires who passed themselves off as landed gentry and didn't want anything much to do with the wild daughter any more, which suited her just fine as long as the cheques kept coming. It had been just a few months for me and I was having fun, but already I kind of saw their point, her family. I didn't think Jasmine and I would be together for the long run. But I'd enjoy it while it lasted.

A few days later over a couple of beers I managed to get a smile back on Jason's face. We were in the Nightingale, the nearest pub to the office, and the place was packed because it was freezing outside and everyone seemed to want a cold beer in a warm pub. We were talking tombstones.

You know the things, even if you think you don't. You'll have seen one in the financial pages of your daily newspaper: looks like an advert, gives the size and name of the deal, maybe a logo, and lists all the banks involved. Everyone fights to get their bank's name as high up and as far to the left as they can – careers have been made or broken on a centimetre's difference. And at the end of a deal, you get a real version, a physical 3D memento of the trade you've just given months of your life to. They're usually made of Perspex, and they look just like the ones you see in the newspaper, and they sit there gathering dust on shelves and desks throughout the City.

Over the years, the tombstones had got bigger, flashier, weirder, and more ridiculous. It wasn't enough to get yourself a slab of Perspex. Do a pub deal, make a tombstone in the shape of a pint-glass. Finance some aircraft or ships – well, you can guess. Tombstones had turned into executive toys – the chance to get creative with something other than money.

Jason had just closed another deal, a securitisation of loans for a bunch of car showrooms. That was where we were looking for some fairly obvious inspiration.

He was still pissed off and inclined to be reckless; I felt untouchable after my bonus and promotion. So when I started thinking out loud, and found myself talking about remote control Ferraris with names and logos painted on the side, he didn't dismiss it out of hand. There were half a dozen of us there, and the others probably thought I was joking (although Anja might have had them thinking again when she ambled into the middle of the conversation, purred "Now that would get me *very* hot," and strolled back to the bar to a brief stunned silence). We carried on drinking and one by one people drifted away, and soon it was just me and Jason and there were other things on our mind besides tombstones. I was talking about Jasmine – I say talking, it was boasting, really, but we were both on our fourth pint by now so I figured that was probably OK. Jason was quieter than usual, and at first I thought he was just bored with what I was talking about, so I changed the subject to who might be screwing who in the office. After thirty seconds I could see that wasn't doing it, either.

"You OK?" I asked, and it was two words but I guess it was the right two, because he shook his head and opened his mouth, and when the words started coming they didn't stop for another ten minutes.

It was Emily. The bright, happy three-year-old of eighteen months back wasn't so bright or happy any more. I'd seen it myself, noticed the blank moods, the tantrums sparked by literally nothing at all, but I knew fuck all about kids, and anyway, she soon flipped back to herself, most of the time.

Turned out she was autistic. *Like half of fucking Clapham*, said Jason. Everyone knew someone with a kid somewhere on the spectrum, but it didn't help, just knowing other people were going through it too. Nothing seemed to help, not money or drink or medicine, and I could see how that would eat him. Jason's way of dealing with a problem was to crush it, without mercy, without warning. He had brains, money, charm, a decent job and a lovely wife, and there wasn't much life had thrown at him he hadn't been able to deal with. But this was a problem that wouldn't be crushed. I could see it, now he'd opened up, how tense he got when Emily's face went blank, not knowing which way she'd go when the blank ran out, how calm and patient he forced himself into being, the most impatient guy I knew, when the face crumpled and the tears started raining down, how his head dropped when she pushed his arms away and ran from the room screaming. It had all been happening right in front of me and I hadn't even realised there was anything wrong. I couldn't believe what an idiot I'd been.

Don't tell anyone, he said, and I said I wouldn't. We sat and talked and after an hour I thought I'd lifted him, a little, so we carried on drinking and by the following morning it was hardly surprising I'd forgotten all about tombstones and Ferraris.

Jason hadn't, though. At 11 next day he called to tell me he'd spent the morning chasing down quotes and he'd finally tracked down a guy who could get him twenty-five cars for two hundred quid a pop.

So there we were, a few weeks later, racing around the office trying to keep track of these monsters, blazing red, seriously fast and *seriously* loud. After the necessary tribute to the client and the lawyers, eight remained. Me and Jason, obviously. Sure, I'd had nothing to do with the deal, but least said, soonest mended. A couple for the guys in rates, one for the fat, red-faced relationship manager (for services rendered to the restaurant trade); one for the credit team who'd helped push through a couple of tricky lines. Two left, and these went to Paddy and Stephen.

Sucking up to the bosses, right? I've got nothing against sucking up to the bosses, in the right way and at the right time; if you don't do it every now and then your mistakes start to count against you. But this wasn't one of those times. Because unthinkable as it might have seemed just a few months before, both Paddy and Stephen were leaving.

It was the end of an era. Paddy had built the conduit team, turned it from a money-pit into a profitable business, and finally had enough. The derisory bonus pool was part of it, sure, because despite the sugar Paddy had coated Jason's pill with, everyone on the floor knew that the conduit guys had been shafted, and Stephen hadn't been able to do anything about it. But the bonus was just part of it, and not the main part. That role fell to Mortensen, who was still there making life hell for anyone senior enough to swing into his orbit. And even when Mortensen wasn't there, there were his minions, an army of mini-Mortensens who knew his play-book back to front. The call of the hedge funds was just too strong to resist.

But if Paddy's departure had come as a shock, Stephen leaving us seemed unbelievable. True, he wasn't what he had been. It wasn't like he'd slipped up, he still seemed to get every call right, but his word, which used to sway the likes of Kemp, didn't open the doors it had done; his glare, which back in the day could freeze a credit committee at ten paces, left you feeling a little chilly, maybe, but nothing more. And this, too, was down to the Mortensen army: or, more precisely, Marcus and Karl.

Marcus and Karl were Mortensen appointees. On his "business advisory committee", whatever the fuck that was, because no one really understood how Mortensen and his men fitted in anywhere. Billy D was already running the investment bank, but Mortensen seemed to have his own parallel lines of authority, a shadow bank within the bank that meant he could issue his own orders and shoehorn people like Marcus and Karl in where they weren't wanted. Both were external appointments, both had worked for Mortensen before, and both had what appeared to be good CVs until you looked more closely and saw that neither of them had stayed in the same place more than eighteen months. Marcus had skipped around the international banking world with stints in London, New York, Hong Kong and Paris. Karl had stayed for the most part within Germany riding wave after wave of deregulation and consolidation, and appeared to have done little more than survive successive coups, culls and purges. Word was they'd been recruited on some hefty guaranteed bonuses to shake up any business that needed shaking up, and maybe a few that didn't, *pour encourager les autres*, as Karl would have put it (his claim to high culture being based solely on a sprinkling of inappropriate French idiom). Karl was responsible for business planning for corporate clients; Marcus had the same role for FI: the banks, insurance and pension funds. Neither had any real direct authority over Stephen, but they did have the ear of the people who did. Their very presence was enough to diminish his. Suddenly, the eminence grise seemed a little less eminent. And now our guru, our Yoda, was leaving us.

He wouldn't say where he was going, either. At first we all assumed he'd be heading up a team at one of our rivals, but it's impossible to keep that kind of thing under wraps for long, and nothing had leaked out. Personally, I thought maybe he'd had enough of it all and wanted out. I had no idea what kind of money someone like Stephen earned, but my guess was he had enough to live on in style for the rest of his life. So why bother any more? I'd see him, from time to time, in his little office, sat there facing away from his desk with Marcus standing above him talking and talking, and Stephen shaking his head and looking tired and worried and never having a chance to say anything himself. At some point Stephen must have given up listening and turned back to his desk, because even though I never saw the knife it was obvious enough that Marcus had shoved it in his back.

That afternoon, none of it mattered. What Jason had done looked like magic: he snapped his fingers, got his Ferraris, and got the paper-trail to disappear. We were all there on the twelfth floor, eight two-foot long monsters unpacked, fully charged and ready to show what they could do. The sales and syndicate teams had heard what was up. Even Legal and Finance put in an appearance. And it was worth it.

We had an inkling those things would move, and we

thought they might cause some damage. We needed space. I don't know how he did it, but Jason wandered over to the commodity finance guys, about twenty of them who sat just across from Darren's corporate team, and had a quiet chat to them, and next thing they were clearing their desks of anything they cared about and walking over to join us, smiles on their faces.

Turned out we were right. Those things shifted. And they took chunks out of bits of wall, desk, whatever got in their way. There were a few damaged shins, too, but no one could say they hadn't been warned: apparently you could hear them in the lift as soon as you got within two floors. The RCs were handed out to anyone who wanted them, and everyone got their turn. Race after race, chase after chase. Russell hammered Paddy in my car; Jane took over and managed to crash it into Stephen's, being driven by Doug. No one cared.

On it went. If Paddy and Stephen hadn't been on their way out anyway, no doubt Mortensen would have had their hides. But they were beyond retribution now, and (Christ knows why) the rest of us felt somehow sheltered. I remember seeing Marcus walk by, looking thoughtfully at us, like he was taking note of names and faces. Today, of all days, I couldn't give a fuck, and nor could anyone else. Even when it looked like things had gone far enough, there was further to go – someone had decided to see if the cars could fly. The desks were already cleared, and a couple of staplers and some lever-arch files made a decent ramp. And they *could* fly – but could they get higher? Paddy thought they could, and so did Jessica, his second-in-command and heir apparent. Russell thought otherwise. The cry went up: "put your money where your mouth is," but Jessica had a better idea, and five minutes later she and Paddy were sat on two of the office swivel-chairs, back-to-back, *tied* to the chairs, and blindfolded for good measure, so they just had the noise to tell them the car was getting close, and since it sounded close when it was the other end of the floor Christ alone knows what it sounded like in the dark, inches from your head. Inches was right – it turned out the car could get higher after all, but not further, so it ended up missing the landing ramp by a hair and smashing straight into a metal filing cabinet. One down, and I don't know whose it was, because I went home with mine.

The Ferrari Games, we called it afterwards, a legend that's grown with the telling like all legends do. But the truth is, we had a great time, and we drew everyone in, the whole department, the whole floor. I'm not even sure it was really a fraud, but I can't pretend I didn't know what was going on. I walked into this one with my eyes wide open, and I walked, I wasn't pushed. But it was hardly the crime of the century. Christ, by the standards of some of the celebrations I'd heard about, our Ferraris were restraint itself.

12: Beetle-Browed Nemesis

For a minute after I put the phone down, I just sat there, elbows on the desk, head in my hands. If Primora was fucked, then so was I, and I couldn't see the point in trying to cover it up. I knew precisely what would happen, every little step, and precisely how those steps would dance themselves into a nice little ring with me trapped neatly in the middle.

Someone in Miltons would contact the trustee for Alchemy to explain that there had been a default and we'd like our money, please. In the background, there would be a gang of little fellows drafting up all the little documents, notices and requests, that needed to be sent and signed and copied and received, they were what really mattered, these documents, but this fellow from Miltons would make the call anyway, just as a courtesy, and the trustee would act all confused and say "Oh, I thought that CDS had expired, and I rather hope it has, because we've just repaid the investors, you see, and there's nothing left in the bank." My Miltons chap would bluster and say that couldn't possibly be true, and while he was blustering away one of the little document johnnies would come and stand behind him, quietly clearing his throat, until the Miltons chap noticed him and, turning his great beetling brows on him, placed a hand over the telephone mike and demanded to know why he was being disturbed. (I wasn't even sure what *beetling* actually meant, and how a brow could do it, but it still felt like the kind of attribute this guy would have.) And the document fellow, who now looked something like one of the munchkins from *The Wizard of Oz*, would stammer and point to the bits of paper in his hand, including the all-important credit default swap with the all-important expiration date, some time in the past. And my beetle-browed nemesis would dig his bloody claws into the mass of paper and come out holding the form, the infamous Alchemy form I'd never thought to see again, and he'd see the boxes I'd ticked that shouldn't have been ticked, and he'd turn to the end of the form, paper shredding in his razor-sharp talons as the pages went by, until he came to my name, and that would be it, I'd be dead, and there wasn't a thing I could do about it.

In that minute all I could see was that they'd find me and in no time at all my neck would be on the block waiting for the executioner's swing. But it didn't take long for me to change my mind: maybe I'm just an optimist, maybe I place more value on the health of my neck than I should; take your pick. Either way, the only option was to try to head this off (no pun intended) before it got much further.

The first job was to check the documents and work out what the next steps would be. Within seconds I had the loan agreement open on screen to see how long I had before things *really* hit the fan.

Five business days. If the money wasn't paid in five business days – effectively, next Monday – Miltons would be entitled to call a default. From recollection, we could then claim straight away under the CDS (if it existed, which it no longer did).

Which gave me till the end of the week to somehow turn this around and make sure we got paid. To find whatever they needed to make up the missing seven million.

And before that, I had to head off both the munchkins and my clawed nemesis, because the moment anyone started doing any calling or digging I'd be out in the open with as much cover as a nudist in the middle of Wembley Stadium. If you want something done, they say, do it yourself. The same thing applies in reverse: if you want something not done, make sure you're the one that's not doing it.

Step 1: an email to Rob.

"Rob, thanks for letting me know about the Primora default. I'll get cracking on the notices right away – please can you tell the other teams involved they can leave it with me for the moment. Could you also send me all the info you've got on this and any background on where Primora are business-wise. I'll give the trustee a call and let him know what's coming."

Any number of things might go wrong here. The call might already have been made, the documents might all be out on some munchkin's desk right now, but if it hadn't and they weren't, I might have just bought myself a couple of days. Maybe I could find out how close Primora were to getting the seven million together. Though where the hell I'd scrape together the cash to get them over the line was beyond me.

The last thing I wanted now was a load of Mintrex shit to deal with but the wheels I'd set in motion earlier had started turning other, smaller wheels which had started turning even tinier ones and now I had emails about the minutest of details crawling all over my inbox. I dealt with the urgent stuff, but there wasn't much of it. Now I'd got the wheels turning, they could probably keep going a little longer by themselves.

In amongst the less weighty matters, Doug called back. He had Elaine on the line, and a fellow called Charlie Henderson-Scott, a chinless wonder from Westhaven's investment arm.

Henderson-Scott had clearly decided on the aggressive approach.

"Hello? Are you this lawyer chap?"

I wasn't, not in any way, but he didn't give me the chance to deny it.

"What's this I hear about security? We were clearly offered full fixed security. Now I hear it isn't in the deal. Are you playing with us?"

If he could be aggressive, I could too. I knew I'd have to end up bending over backwards for this guy if we were going to get anywhere, but at least if I started off bullish it might end up being slightly less painful for me.

"Mr Henderson-Scott? Alex Konninger here. I understand your concerns, but as you're aware we've already priced – on the basis of the Offering Circulars, which you've had for a few weeks now, and which fully disclose the actual security position."

"Are you calling me a liar?"

"I beg your pardon?"

"I said, are you calling me a liar? You want to check your recordings, chum. Elaine offered me full fixed security. I don't give a fuck what it says on page six-hundred and wanky-toss of some legal document. You offered us something and our commitment was based on that offer."

"I'm not calling you a liar. I understand your concerns. However given the stage we're at it's completely impossible to give you what you want now."

"WHAT?"

"There's no need to shout, Mr Henderson-Scott. I can tell you're not happy with the situation. Why don't we try to work out what we can do to get you more comfortable?"

"I want to know what you propose to do about this cock-up."

Isn't that basically what I'd just been saying? Meanwhile, no surprise, Elaine and Doug were conspicuous by their silence.

"Tell me, did the request for full security originate from your legal department?"

"Yes, yes it did."

As expected. A silly technical point from a lawyer without the faintest understanding of the mess he'd caused. A lawyer who was withholding his own signoff from the investment, leaving Mr H-S red-faced and itching to take it all out on someone else. I'd do. The vicious, ever-decreasing circle of banking abuse. Somewhere at the top there would be a private equity fund knocking seven shades of shit out of a leveraged finance banker; further down the line, I'd be cracking the whip down onto Harvey's bare metaphorical buttocks if he couldn't sort this out, even though it was no more his fault than mine. It's not right, and it's not fair, but that doesn't stop it happening.

"Could I speak to the lawyer in question? And maybe get our own counsel on the line too so they can perhaps hammer something out lawyer-to-lawyer?"

"I'll see if I can set something up." Abrupt, but slightly warmer than he had been. Mr H-S wanted this resolved as much as we did, and if it could be done between geeks so much the better.

I handed over my contact details, said goodbye, whacked out a short email to Harvey and Christine, and went back to all the other Mintrex crap that was piling up around me.

I was just getting started when Anthony strolled in. People walked in and out of our area every two minutes and unless you were looking right at them you wouldn't notice, but Anthony always liked to make an entrance. Usually he'd preen, or boast, or make loud reference to someone else's fuckup. Today he was complaining.

"Fucking chaos out there."

He wasn't talking to anyone in particular, he just assumed we'd all be listening.

"Station's shut. Some idiot under a train." He looked around, didn't seem to notice that no one was joining in, and laughed. "Bad bonus, I expect."

I caught Jane's eye and she raised an eyebrow. I shrugged and shook my head. How Russell couldn't see what was wrong with this guy was beyond me.

I'd managed another half hour on the little Mintrex wheels when the email I've been waiting for came through. As that half hour drew on I'd been worrying it wasn't going to happen, but here it was, Rob's reply, short and to the point.

"Thanks Alex, your help is appreciated. I've attached everything we've got. Lease income down on where it should be, but we could let that slide while they were still paying us. Now it looks like the anchor tenant's about to go bust, and that's left them 185k short for this quarter. There's a couple of other tenants close to the end of their leases and they haven't renewed. If these guys can't manage an interest payment and they've got tenants going down this fast I don't know how the hell they're going to manage the bullet next quarter, but they claim they've got refinancing on the table. They would say that, I guess. Christ knows where from. Looks to me like they're in trouble."

Christ knows where from indeed. Not us, that was sure enough. This was looking so ugly now that we wouldn't have liked it back in 2006, when we liked almost everything. The "bullet" was the great big dollop of principal due next quarter when the loan was finally repaid, but they weren't going to get a new loan to cover it, and they sure as hell weren't going to sell the thing, not for what they needed, so "in trouble" was putting it mildly. Not that they were the only ones there.

There was a second paragraph.

"Thanks for your help, anyway. I've copied in George from Distressed Assets who wants to keep on top of this, so please can you

keep him in the loop and send him your documents when they're ready.
Kind regards
Rob"

George from Distressed Assets. I didn't know him and I'd never heard of the team but it was obvious enough from the name what they did. Screw as much as they could out of deals that had gone bad. This one had started to turn, wasn't yet rotting, sure, but there was a smell wafting out of it that wouldn't have left you in much doubt what was coming. It was George's job to cut it down and get something out before the rest of the flies turned up wanting their share. George, if he spoke to the wrong people or saw the wrong things, would end up as my beetle-browed nemesis. I had to make sure George was too comfortable to do anything at all. I bashed out a quick reply about getting on with things and being sure they'd hear from me in due course and some more pleasant, meaningless tripe, and started turning over the meat of the problem.

One hundred and eighty-five thousand pounds. That was the shortfall, and it wasn't the kind of money I had in my wallet. There was twenty grand sitting in the current account, and everything else tied up in the apartment, the car, the bike, and shares in the kind of company you can't get yourself out of in a hurry. Give me a month and I could probably sell, borrow and mortgage enough to get there. Give me six and I could probably steal it, cover my tracks, and never have to think about it again. But five business days was pushing it. Covering my tracks would have to wait.

I could think of one place I could get that kind of money and I didn't like it at all. I needed another idea, a better idea, but for once the noise on the floor, the chat, the phones, all that background that I never really noticed, for once it shoved itself front and centre into every thought I had and turned my brain into soup. I had to clear my head.

I walked to the lift, hit the ground floor, wandered around for five minutes looking at my feet and came back again. It was noisy outside as well, of course it was, people and cars and drills, but it didn't matter, because there wasn't a place in the world quiet enough for me to find another answer there. There was no other answer, there was just the one, and if I'd known I was going to end up doing something like this I might as well have caved in to Jason and Marcus months ago and just done the Big One. Jason would still have his job and I wouldn't have Marcus breathing all over me. I sat back down.

This was huge. Aircraft-carrier huge, supertanker huge. It made every other scam we'd pulled look like a pedalo. And I was going to have to do it by myself, in a few days instead of the few months I'd always said we needed. I tried to think about it the way Jason had: it was a risk, true, a much bigger risk than any we'd run before, but the chances were still on my side. I knew how to do this, I knew the processes back to front and the deal better than anyone else alive. I'd probably be OK. Probably. And in a way, it didn't matter, because if I didn't get the money I'd be screwed anyway. Primora and Alchemy would come out and everything else would be sure to follow. I had no choice.

I took a couple of deep breaths and called up the Mintrex cashflows on my screen. It was a big deal, close to a billion, so there might be scope for nearly two hundred grand to go missing if there were enough places to spread it around. And if there was anyone who could find those places, it was me.

Let's see.

I started with the guys on the investor end of things. Paying Agents, Agent Bank, Common Depositary, settlement stuff. No one really understands how all that it works, which was just what I was looking for, but not here. You need meat if you want to find some fat, and these guys weren't charging enough to start with.

Bollocks, I thought, and moved on.

I looked down to our own fees. We were getting enough, but no more, and Ahmed was all over us with a pencil and a fucking calculator.

I was starting to panic now. Shitloads of lawyers, whole tower-blocks of the fuckers, fresh juicy meat by the ton, but Ahmed had been on at me day after day already, moaning about the lawyers and their fees. I couldn't do anything there. I shook my head again and started to move on, and then I stopped.

They'd busted their estimates months ago, the lawyers, every one of them, like we'd always known they would (not that we'd said as much to Ahmed). And yeah, the guy wasn't happy, but he had no more idea what the lawyers did for their money than I had about mining. My brain was suddenly racing ahead, seeing holes and opportunities that might be there or might not, so I forced myself to stop, took another couple of breaths, and looked at it again. Slowly.

When it came to the money, the lawyers went through me. All of them and every time. Ahmed might get pissed off but all he ever did was throw some more abuse my way. Ahmed was getting a billion quid. I could squeeze another eighty grand out of him on the lawyers without too much stink. And for eighty grand I could take some more abuse.

The lawyers were a start, but there was more.

Valuers, geologists, all those guys: I could probably add thirty or forty thousand there.

Accountants: another thirty thousand.

Rating agencies: they had pretty hard quotes, close as it gets to set in stone, but would anyone really notice if another few thousand was added to each of them?

I wasn't there yet, but I was getting close. It looked like there might be enough fat to chew on after all.

13: A Scam is Born, December 2006-June 2007

By the tail-end of 2006 Marcus and Karl were in charge, and they said we were all one big happy family still, but anyone with eyes could see which way the wind was blowing. The split was coming, and Marcus would be taking FI and conduit, and Karl would be taking corporate, and they'd already embarked on a slow, silent war over what was left. The battleground was real estate, and in Liz's considered opinion the whole situation was "a bit like when you spot a bit of mud on your shoe, and wipe it off, and it turns out to be shit, and it's all over your hands and your jeans, and the carpet." She was sick of it by now, she said, and the moment the right opportunity turned up she'd be on it so fast you'd think she'd never been there in the first place. It could have been worse, though. The best that could be said of Marcus was that he was never around when you needed him, but that was a lot better than Karl, who was always there when you didn't.

Karl had his nose stuck so far up every detail of every deal it was a wonder he could breathe at all. No one I spoke to (and I spoke to the lot of them, or rather, they spoke to me, and to anyone else that would listen, because annoying as Karl was there were only a certain number of times even the most patient person would sit through another series of the same complaints) – not one of them could figure out why Karl was so keen on micro-managing a business he didn't even run. They needed his approval to do everything short of taking a piss. Not that his approval was difficult to get: Karl's idea of prudent banking was staking only 99 per cent of your worldly possessions on black, so if it all went tits-up you'd have enough left for the taxi home. No, his problem was that Emma's team, and Darren's, weren't aggressive enough, and now he was pushing for bigger and riskier deals. He'd started off as a trader, and you could tell: he just didn't get the idea of an agency business that lived on fees and didn't bet its own balance sheet.

Marcus came from a sales background, so he was on board with the way our businesses made their money. Slowly, and reliably. Unlike Karl, he sat back in the middle of his web and let his teams get on with things. He knew everything that was going on. There was a short-lived rumour that he wasn't going to let Jessica take over conduit, that he'd kick her out and find another prick like him to run it, but that never happened, and she and Andrea seemed at least to be able to do their deals without someone looking over their shoulders every three minutes. But he was the guy who'd pushed out Stephen, and Paddy; that made him the enemy; and none of us planned on forgetting it.

As 2006 drew to a close, I found myself helping out Jane on a deal for a water company. It wasn't a massive deal and it wasn't particularly complicated or glamorous, and in normal circumstances Jane would have palmed the lot onto a keen young associate and just made sure nothing went too badly wrong. But there were timing issues, they wanted the deal done faster than we were comfortable with, and I was at a loose end, so I said I'd step up and I think Jane was grateful, although you never could tell. We had the swaps to ourselves, twelve years' worth of income and outgoings, with the one slightly higher than the other, we hoped. Sometimes, if you're lucky, you can put these things together so that the bank takes all that juicy profit from all those years in one go, up front, the moment the deal closes; when that happens the champagne's real and the glasses are made of glass, but it doesn't happen too often and it wasn't happening this time, either.

The thing is, I'd been hanging around in Darren's office more than I really needed to, and I'd seen and heard some things that I shouldn't have. Year end was so close you could almost smell it, and it didn't look like corporate was going to hit its income target. Normally this was the kind of politics and detail that wouldn't trouble the mind of a lowly Associate Director like me, but miss the income target and the bonus pool would take one big fucking hit, and the bonus pool was something I cared deeply about. I was spending so many nights at Jasmine's I hadn't bothered to find myself a new apartment yet, but I still wanted one, and I wanted a decent car to complement the two-wheeled brute of a Honda I'd just bought. I'd been through the deal pipeline, dragged every bit of information I could out of anyone who might have a finger in a pie I didn't know about, and I still couldn't see where the extra money might come from. Unless we pulled something remarkable out of the bag, there just weren't enough deals around to get us where we needed to be.

So there I was, with a form to fill in, consigning close to £5 million in swaps income (which looked, coincidentally, like being almost exactly how far we'd be from target) to future generations of Miltons bankers who'd done fuck-all to earn it. And then I saw how close we were, how very close, to being able to take the lot up front. It wasn't like we'd need to change the whole structure of the deal. We'd just need either a more credit-worthy client (which they weren't) or better quality collateral from them (which they weren't going to give us – believe me, I'd asked). It wasn't complicated, but it just wasn't going to happen, not in the real world. Anyone with an ounce of commercial sense would see that.

And then it hit me. Anyone with an ounce of commercial sense wouldn't be working in Finance. They'd spot a complex, technical anomaly a mile off, but tell them

Apple's flogging iPads for twenty quid a pop and they wouldn't bat an eyelid.

Do you really need me to tell you what happened next? Hell, I don't even remember the details myself. Just the broad brush – both the client and the collateral suddenly looked a little more solid than they had been.

A couple of nights later I was out with Jason, at a whisky club he'd just joined. I didn't really like whisky, but he was convinced he could change my mind (and he was happy for Miltons to pay for the experiment). I hadn't planned on telling anyone what I'd done but you've seen what I'm like with a poker face. After half an hour he put down his drink and asked me what the hell was going on, because I clearly had something to say and he was fucked if he was going to sit there all evening watching me work out whether or not to say it.

So I did. And he was impressed. He should have been, too. Unless the client stopped paying us, and all the collateral they'd given us went to shit, this was never going to be an issue. So simple, and so close to foolproof.

But this time, I couldn't hide behind any selfless motives or claim that it was all someone else's idea. It was my baby. It was fraud, plain and simple, I'd done it all by myself, and I'd done it so I could get myself a bigger pad and a faster car. Yeah, everyone else was doing it, or they probably were, and it wasn't exactly going to break the bank even if it did go wrong, but it was a big step.

I was a player now.

At least, I thought I was a player. But way over my head there was a bigger game being played, and Karl was winning. By the turn of 2007 his real estate fetish suddenly made sense. He'd made it his business to know everything that was happening, before it happened, and the result was that he could pass off all the good news as his, and distance himself from the disasters. "He spins the wins," that was how Liz put it, in disgust, still trying to work her way out but not sure where she should go. Karl must have been up there in Mortensen's ear every other day, and the way it looked, he was running real estate by himself already, so when the email came round to tell everyone Karl had officially taken over it didn't come as much of a surprise. But still, Marcus shut himself in his office, Jason told me (Marcus had moved his people down to the fourth floor by now), and didn't see anyone for the rest of the day. You didn't want to fight someone like Karl, we could all see that now, and we could see, too, how he'd survived as long as he had.

Sometimes you'd get a mauling before you even knew you were in a fight. I'd seen Karl baring his teeth, a couple of times, savaging people who had no idea what was coming, but it wasn't until he'd taken over real estate that he finally got round to taking a bite, and the man he bit was Darren. It was brutal, too. Full department meeting, everyone standing around thinking this is just one of those hour-long wastes of time you have to put up with every now and then, and Karl suddenly announced what he called a "change of strategy" for the corporate team.

"I want this team to make some proper money. Not the pennies you are bringing in."

I looked around the room. Everyone had fallen silent. *Pennies?* We'd brought in nearly forty million in the last twelve months. What the hell was he thinking?

"*Les jeux sont faits*, as we say on the mainland – but for some reason they never have been here."

He paused, again. He smiled. No one else was smiling, but that didn't seem to bother him.

"For too long we have just been servicing clients when we could have been selling to them, taking some risks, turning this team into the money-machine it should be. To that end, I have decided there will be some minor management changes."

Minor management changes. You didn't need to know Karl well to realise there was only one way this was headed. Darren stood up. Karl tilted his head and frowned, as if surprised, but he shouldn't have been. Eyes front, Darren walked straight out of the room. Karl waited until he had left and then continued as though nothing had happened.

"Darren will take on responsibility for managing the existing portfolio," (which meant doing nothing). "Russell will be given the role of managing overall origination strategy," (which meant doing everything – or, at least, everything Karl told him to).

By the time the meeting finished half an hour later, Darren had already packed up his things and left the building.

Marcus's methods were different but not much gentler. He wasn't chasing money, he was trying to save it, which meant taking an uncomfortably close look at what was going on in his teams and rolling some of the less profitable heads right out of the building. Having hung on to the cliff-face for so long, Andrea had finally crashed, moved sideways along with a couple of her right-hand men and then quietly dispatched when everyone had forgotten about them. Jessica had kept her team intact, so far, but now he'd started talking about closing the whole conduit down if it didn't make more money. "Trimming the fat," he called it, and it was hardly a radical thing in banking, but right now no one else was doing it. He might not have been slamming on the handbrake, but at least he was pulling over to the slow lane and letting the rest of the world race on by. Jason couldn't stand him.

I didn't have so much to bitch about, myself. Russell was a good manager, which came as a surprise to all of us, and he kept Karl away from the rest of the team, which was an added bonus. As for the actual bonus, the one I'd tried to bump up by lying on the swaps form, that hadn't worked out quite so well. Those commodities guys who'd been so accommodating when we were racing the Ferraris, they'd made some stupid bets that cost the bank a billion, give or take, and when something like that happens, everyone shares the pain. Piss-all for me at the end of the year and by now I was tired of waiting for the perfect pad: I'd found an apartment, the apartment, and if it wasn't quite what I'd had in mind it was good enough. Still is. The Porsche would have to wait; I was having enough fun with the Honda. I'd learned the importance of wearing the right gear, too. I'd thought I was unbreakable until I came off at not much more than a crawl and ended up looking like my left hand side had spent half an hour on a barbecue.

I was in and out of hospital in a couple of hours that time. It took an actual barbecue to get me seriously injured. Early summer 2007, and Russell got the whole team round his place. First question pretty much everyone asked as soon as they arrived was if Karl would be there, and you could see them all relax as Russell shook his head and the beers got broken open. I relaxed a bit too much; I'd been to Russell's place before, a massive pile in Hertfordshire among the brokers and the lawyers, so I should have known where the doors were, and the windows, and the walls. I should have known what was safe and what wasn't. I should have known not to climb along a high garden wall with iron spikes on one side and a plate glass window the other, and I should have known that no one there would be sober or sensible enough to figure out what to do with me while I lay there bleeding from what felt like a million massive holes waiting for the ambulance to arrive. Two painful weeks in hospital, that cost me, and I spent most of the time wondering what the hell Jasmine was up to because she'd spent pretty much every night the last six months with me, and I didn't know if she'd be able to spend more than one or two alone. It got me thinking, that fortnight, or maybe it did the opposite, because I'd decided before my unfortunate fall that me and Jasmine had run our course; now I found myself changing my mind. She seemed to have missed me, too, or at least she acted like she had and did it convincingly enough to sucker a dumb mug still loaded on morphine. She was gentle with me the first few days I was out, which I appreciated: one thing I knew about Jasmine was that being gentle didn't come naturally to her. On the second day she dragged a friend over to the apartment, another artist, dragged her halfway across London in a taxi loaded with bits and pieces from the girl's portfolio, and I thought I was going to have to be nice and pretend I liked the stuff, but another pleasant surprise: I did like it, I thought it was great, and even if I know as much about art as I do about astrophysics I could tell there was something special here. She was a nobody, the girl, if I told you the name you'd wouldn't have heard it, but I couldn't see that lasting, so I picked the biggest, boldest thing she had with her, a pop-art nude with a Rubens body, patches of red, yellow and blue on a dazzling white background four feet high and six feet wide. I glanced to the side of the room and saw Jasmine smile. The girl might have been a nobody, but I guess she saw the future as clearly as I did, because the money she asked was more Damien Hirst than struggling garret-dweller. I was about to shake my head and start beating her down when I remembered where I was, in my enormous new apartment, expensively-furnished, with my girlfriend – the artist's friend – looking on, so I stood up and shook her hand instead. The painting got hung in the bedroom, behind the bed, and it lasted longer there than Jasmine did.

Russell forgave me for ruining his barbecue. And a week

after I was out I was back at the whisky club listening to Jason, and thinking even with not getting the bonus I expected, and falling off a bike, and smashing through a plate glass window, I was glad I was me instead of him.

Because Jason hadn't got a bonus, either, and it was all a bit more serious for him. He'd put down a non-refundable deposit on a new-build apartment in Docklands, looked like easy money at the time. Sally was pregnant again; they'd been looking to move, been looking nearly as long as I had, but changed their minds and started work on a new extension, something that would work better for Emily and the new baby. Jason had his eye on a new BMW, too, but what with everything else, that toy got set aside for the future. The toy costing the money was a blue-eyed, blonde-haired beauty by the name of Charmaine, who'd wandered into Jason's life at a once-a-year Miltons client event on a race-track somewhere out in Bedfordshire. It cost nearly a grand a head, the track day, and when you're spending that kind of money you want to make sure most of the heads have clients attached to them, but a few employees have to show up, act friendly and lose gracefully, and both Jason and I got lucky that year. Him more than me, because the day hadn't even got started, we were just walking into to the welcome tent, pointing at each other's motors out in the carpark and laughing or nodding seriously, everyone a little nervous, a little excited, when the girl pouring the coffee caught Jason's eye and he smiled back at her and, well, that was that.

It wasn't like Jason. That night at the club, back when I'd first met Jasmine, he'd had women crawling all over him, or at least trying to, glamorous women (by my standards, anyway). And he'd bought drink after drink, and he'd danced and had a good night, but the whole time his wedding ring was shining out like the Olympic flame, and dancing and drinking was as far as it went. That night, Jason was on top of the world. But lately, he was as low as I'd seen him. Emily was getting worse, and Sally could hardly cope. He didn't have to tell me that. I'd seen the state Emily got in if the doorbell went or the phone rang and she wasn't expecting it. The blank was over fast, it only ever tipped one way, and the screaming fits went on so long that sometimes it seemed the happy child had disappeared for good. And there was so much to sort out. The forms, the assessments, the people wanting to get involved and seeming like the answer to all their prayers, and then steering them down another blind alley and leaving them there in the dark without a map. Jason didn't know what he could do to help. He threw in suggestions that Sally had already tried or knew wouldn't work, and eventually he decided that it was just another problem, and like every problem it could be solved by throwing enough money at it. There were places, he said. "Units". Places where children who didn't fit into everyone else's everyday life could learn how to lead a life of their own. Some of them seemed good, some didn't, but the one thing all the good ones had in common was that they were asking a lot of money. What with the lack of bonus and the extension there was less of that than he was used to and, he told me, he looked at himself from time to time and thought *if I can't even bring in the cash I'm no fucking use to them at all*. Everything that had seemed so solid felt like just another layer of ice.

And suddenly this bombshell's looking at him like he's fucking Apollo or something. I'm not trying to give any excuses and he wasn't either. It's just that the idea of Jason with a mistress wasn't something that came naturally. He threw himself into it with his usual enthusiasm, told her she could move into the apartment, and as soon as it was ready, she did. So his nice little investment was draining even more cash away. *No problem*, he thought, he could make up the difference with a little spread-betting on the side, financial indices, interest rates, commodity prices, that kind of thing, and he didn't do badly, but not well enough to make him the pile of money he thought he needed.

The way I remember it, it started out as a joke. Not that I remember it too well, to be honest, because we'd been drinking cask strength scotch for a couple of hours, without water or food, and we were both in the kind of state you'd expect at that point. My recollection of the conversation is a little hazy, but what I do remember went something like this:

J: "What the fuck am I gonna do Alex?"

A: Hiccup. "Eh?"

J: Belch.

J: "I need some serious – oops" (glass slips between fingers; neat whisky spilled onto crotch) "shit."

A: "You what?"

Pause.

J: "What was that?"

A: "You mean the whisky?"

J: "Yeah. I think it might've been a nice one but I don't remember drinking it."

A: "I think it's on your trousers."

J: Giggle. "Oh yeah."

Another pause, with (probably) a little hiccupping and some confused staring at the whisky list.

J: "So, yeah, I need some."

A: "Well go and get some then. And get me one too while you're there."

J: "No not that."

A: "Eh?"

Pause.

A: "What do you need?"

J: "Do you think you can help, then?"

A: "Help with what?"

J: "Oh yeah, I didn't say, did I? What are we drinking?"

A: "Spey I think. Nice."

J: "Very nice. Might take a bottle of that home."

Satisfied pause.

J: "Oh I remember what I meant to say."

A: "What?"

J: "I remember what I meant to say."

A: "I mean what was it?"

J: "I need some serious money."

A: "Better not take a bottle home then. Unless you're gonna smash it over someone's head and take their wallet."

Both: Giggle.

Pause.

J: "No really. I gotta give the builders something and there's another instalment on the flat coming up."

I looked at him. Even in this state, he knew what I was thinking. There was money in the flat if he had the balls to take it, but that meant a difficult conversation with Charmaine.

J: "I've fucked up, Alex. She had a set-up with her mates, she's handed her notice in now and they've got someone else already. I owe it to her."

I thought she was playing him, but what I thought didn't matter. Without either of us really noticing, the conversation had turned serious.

A: "How short are you?"

J: "I need thirty grand in the next couple of months. After that I dunno, I'm still gonna be short but that gives me a bit of time to see what else I can sort out."

A: "Look, I can probably lend you something. Not sure. Probably ten or fifteen grand. No interest but pay me back in six months, right?"

(I was drunk, true, but Jason was a mate – I like to think I'd have made the same offer sober).

J: "Much appreciated, mate."

Pause. Clink. Drink.

A: "What about the rest? Wish we'd kept all those Ferraris. Could have sold a few."

J: "Must be something else. If we can get cars and whisky out of the bank we can get cash."

A: (long drink): "Yeah, nice idea."

Pause.

J: "The ops guys pay whoever we fucking tell 'em too."

A: "Within limits though." Laugh. "Not twenty thousand quid."

J (long drink): "Too true. Shame though."

Long pause. *Thoughtful pause*, even, though I can't say much for the quality of the thought.

A: "Even for the big money, the hardest thing's just getting some company through KYC, right?"

KYC stands for "know your customer", a whole fucking forest of regulations and processes all designed to make sure your client isn't using you to launder money. Corporate documents, passports, utility bills, it's a bit like opening a bank account, only more so. It's probably the worst part of the whole job.

J: "Yeah but KYC's a pain in the arse when it's for real. Imagine how bad it can get when it isn't. And you've still gotta get someone to sign off the actual paper."

Which means someone looking at the invoice and nodding and saying *yes, OK, we'll pay it.*

A: "No you don't."

J: "What?"

A: Slurp. Belch. "Another?"

J: "Yeah but what are you talking about?"

A: "Another whisky. Some of that Spey."

Pause, return to bar to "try" some of the same whisky we'd just had.

J: "No, right, what we were saying?"

A: "Yup. You need money."

J: "No, I mean the thing about getting someone to sign it all off."

A: "Oh that, yeah, right. If it's Miltons money they're all over it. But client money's different. You want to pay something from a client or an SPV, the ops guys'll take your word for it as long as you've gone over the cashflows with them."

J (sitting up, frowning in concentration): "That's all you need?"

A: "Well, yeah, but you've got to have an invoice from the people getting paid."

J (sitting back again): "Fuck. An invoice."

Long pause.

A: "Yeah. Forget it. Mind you, any fucker can make an invoice. As long as it looks real. But you're right. Forget it."

J: "OK. But I need to come up with something."

The whole thing was in and out my head the same evening, and I didn't think about it again until a few days later when Jason called and suggested we grab a coffee down the road – not our usual Starbucks right by the office.

"I've been thinking about what we were talking about the other day."

Could have been anything. Jason had a whole heap of problems going on right now. I looked blank.

"The money, Alex. The SPVs."

"That was just whisky talk, mate."

"But we can do it. I'm sure of it. I've thought round all the angles. There's just two problems."

"There's shitloads of problems. Another two don't make much difference."

"I reckon we can get round the rest."

I shook my head and closed my eyes but he wasn't giving up that easily. He carried on talking, and I pretended not to listen, but I couldn't help hearing every word.

The idea went like this:

The boys in the back office have their fingers on a lot of buttons, and some of those buttons control the bank accounts of SPVs and clients, and from time to time, for a few hours, say, or even overnight, those accounts have hundreds of millions of pounds sitting in them. But if you want to get serious money out of those accounts, you need to be a company. Human beings aren't good enough, the checks would expose them in seconds, it would be like trying to break into MI6 with a penknife.

So if you want to get your hands on any of that money, the first thing you need to do is get yourself a company.

You need to get your company a bank account.

Then you need to get your company through all those KYC checks.

And you need to come up with a line of work your company actually does, so it's got something to charge for, and you need to draw up a plausible looking invoice.

On top of all that you need to be able to keep the bullshit going when you're on calls and talking cashflows with the ops teams, with the client's treasury team, with any other nosy bastard who might want to know what the hell you think you're doing with someone else's money.

Jason's first idea was to take a real company. One of the accountants, maybe, someone big, someone who'd already been through all the KYC. Copy one of their invoices, just change the bank account details. For about a day, he said, he thought that was the answer. But next morning he found himself on a call with Jessica and a real accountant, and he sat back quietly while the two of them started talking about all the deals the guy was doing with Miltons. If one of those deals had been a fake, if Jessica had started talking about the Sauerkraut financing and the guy had said woah, hold up, never heard of that one, and Jessica had said but look, you're supposed to be working on it, we've just paid you ten grand for a report, if all that had happened then whoever really had the ten grand would be fired by lunch and in a cell by suppertime. It was too risky, too uncomfortable. So he realised he'd need a new company. Jason would be one director and shareholder. I'd be the other one – suddenly I was in this with him, although as far as I could see, all I'd done was talk drunken shit with him and then forget all about it. We'd be in control, but when it came to getting the company through KYC we had to put someone else in there, because our names on the SPVs would show up like Sid Vicious in the House of Lords.

Easy, said Jason, and though my eyes were still closed and I was quietly humming, I had to agree. We'd just fake up some forms, Companies House filings, that sort of thing, that showed the company was controlled by a safe pair of hands Miltons already knew. There were professional directors out there, we came across the same names deal after deal, people who did this stuff for two, five, ten thousand companies at a time, and – more importantly – people who'd already run the gauntlet of Miltons KYC.

This was hardly major-league forgery. Jesus, you can download most of this stuff for free two clicks off your homepage. Write someone else's name on the forms. For the finishing touch we'd just scrawl some illegible lawyer's signature over the top and call it a certification. There's your company, and, with luck, your KYC. We'd set up a bank account somewhere, anywhere but Miltons, and we wouldn't even have to pretend to be someone else to do it.

Once we'd got all that done, we'd have to work out what the payment was going to be for. And this, Jason said, was the first problem.

I stopped humming. I opened my eyes and stared at him, trying to work out if he was serious. He looked serious.

"That's your problem?" I asked.

He nodded.

"It's not a problem."

Stuck under Marcus's watchful eye, Jason had been doing pretty much the same deal month after month for what seemed like forever. All he could see were the same old accountants and lawyers in every deal. You might be able to squeeze an extra one in, he thought, but he couldn't think where.

He'd forgotten that the bankers and the lawyers and the accountants aren't the only parasites in the securitisation business. He'd forgotten how infested it is with professionals and experts on everything you can imagine, all eager for the scrapings off the top of every deal.

There are the consultants who write market reports, guessing what's going to happen in a particular market over the next few years. They have no more chance of being right than anyone else, but for some reason we believe them. Then there are the real estate valuers, who are usually fairly accurate if you're talking about the state of the property market six months ago. If you want to know what something's worth now, ask them in six months. If you want an idea of what it'll be worth in six months, you might as well get your crystal ball out, because you're asking the wrong people.

Funding a giant, complicated takeover? You need "tax consultants". Financing a toll road? Don't forget to commission an "environmental impact report". There are experts in valuing everything from insurance contracts, to wine and whisky, to minerals, music royalties and football brands.

The accountants are everywhere, of course. They audit the data that's been sent to the rating agencies and used to create the financial models; they check the financial statements and other numbers that appear in the Offering

Circular; and on top of all that they might charge you a few thousand for a piece of paper which confirms you've correctly photocopied a four-line balance sheet, which even by our standards was the hands-down gold-medal winner for biggest waste of money in the business. They can also write you complicated accounting opinions and fiddly bits of analysis that I wouldn't pretend to understand if I were an honest man, which I'm not, but no one else understands them either, which makes them the perfect cover when you're trying to think of fictional services to add to a deal.

And – oh – the lawyers! The City lawyers, drafting, redrafting, amending, reviewing, arguing. Coming up with ideas, arguing over those ideas. Proof-reading. Chasing, hassling and panicking. Drafting some more. Saving the day (as, I hoped, with Westhaven), and charging the earth (you could count on that). And the other lawyers: Luxembourg lawyers, Caymans lawyers, Jersey lawyers, Bermuda lawyers, lawyers from everywhere from Teheran to Timbuktu, all squeezing a little bit more through the local tax laws or quirky stock exchange rules or whatever it was that made them absolutely indispensable. Even more than accountants, lawyers were a whole world of opportunity.

And this was supposed to be a problem?

Once you'd come up with your service provider and your service, drawing up an invoice would be a breeze.

There's one more stage. And one more problem. Whenever a payment like this is going out, the bank wants to make sure it's going to the right person. Instead of someone like Jason. So someone in ops will call up someone at the company receiving the cash, and confirm the details of the bank account. Sounds simple, but it isn't. We'd need to give ops the number to call. We'd need a new line for each deal, they wouldn't take a mobile number, and (since the call could come in at any time), Jason and I couldn't just sit at home waiting for it. We still had jobs, after all. What we needed was an accomplice.

Jason grinned at me. He knew who the accomplice was. So did I. And now I could see why Jason needed me, because he'd met the guy a couple of times, true, but that was all.

Paul was perfect for this. Most people might not want to be involved, but Paul would love it, anything a little bit dodgy, as long as no one got hurt, it'd be right up his street. He had hundreds of people and thousands of phone lines now. He could set up a new number at the drop of a hat, have one of his staff manning it, and deal with the call himself when it did come in. We'd have to slip him a share, but I didn't see any difficulties with Paul.

Now, I don't want to give the impression that we sorted everything out in twenty minutes over a macchiato one sunny afternoon. Once we'd figured out the basics we hit some more problems, and we'd go away and think about them, fix them, get a little further, hit some more and scratch our heads a bit. It took a couple of weeks and a thousand tiny potholes to fill in before we got it all worked out, but even then I was thinking most of this was detail, back-covering so solid we'd have been rated AAA if we were a bond. There was a lot of caffeine and a few too many beers, and one memorable lunch in Clapham, at the house, because Emily was so unpredictable these days Sally didn't dare take her to any of the cafés round the Common any more. As it turned out, that afternoon was one of the good ones. Emily smiled when she saw me, and asked me questions, and giggled at the answers, and squealed when Jason threw her in the air and tried to clap three times before he caught her. If I hadn't had my own memories of the bad afternoons to go on I might have thought Jason was worrying about nothing. But he wasn't. This was a one-off, it was obvious enough from the way Jason's jaw didn't move and Sally' smile stuck to her face for the first half hour, and from their relief as they started to realise this really was going to be a good day after all. After lunch, Sally played with Emily for an hour or so while Jason and I talked "business". We were upstairs in a box room Jason called his office, but we could hear Emily still laughing in the kitchen, and Sally's attempts at a witch or a talking horse, and after a while we looked at one another and realised we couldn't think of anything else to say. There were no more potholes to fill in.

There was one other problem, though, and it was me.

Sure, I could see why Jason was so keen. He needed the money. He could just about cover the extension and the flat and the day-to-day, but he needed more money for Emily, even though he couldn't yet figure out how much and precisely what he'd be spending it on. He was getting desperate, and he couldn't see anywhere else to get it, and the way we'd thought the thing out there was hardly a crack for us to fall through.

I just didn't like it. We'd pissed around with our expenses and I'd spun stories to the boys in Finance, sure, but this was crossing a whole new line, and I didn't know if it was a line I wanted to cross. And then one evening, in the last of the old red phone boxes in Chelsea, I was making love to Jasmine and felt her whole body go completely rigid. *Christ I'm good*, I thought, and a moment later, *sure, but not that good*, because it wasn't me that had done it for her. She was pointing through the smudged glass at a 911 Turbo growling its way slowly down the Kings Road like a thousand waking lions, and you could see from the way people were standing there, pointing or smiling or just open-mouthed, that she wasn't the only one affected by the car. Maybe the only one affected in *quite* that way, sure, but still. I wanted a 911 Turbo, and if I waited for my bonus to improve, Porsche would probably be Chinese before I got it. Up to that point, this whole thing with Jason was just an idea, maybe a possibility, but not something I could really see myself doing. Now, suddenly, I could.

Paul didn't know what to make of the whisky club. He'd made some decent money, sure, and he'd got out of Dagenham, but the idea of spending fifteen quid on a small glass of scotch, sipping it gently, talking about it – it really wasn't him. I suppose it wasn't me, either, but I'd learned to go with it.

The important thing, though, was that Paul liked the idea. He liked the whisky too, as it happened, so I made sure we explained everything to him before he was too far gone to understand. He had to know exactly what it was we were asking him to do, why it had to be a secret, why we needed to be one hundred per cent sure he could do it. I'd known Paul all my life and I knew he wasn't stupid.

"How often you gonna be doing this?" he asked, between slugs of a thirty-four-year-old Islay that came in steep even for this place. Jason and I looked at each other. We hadn't really thought that far, hadn't worked out how much we could take, from which deals, how many times a year. I plucked a number out of the air.

"One every couple of months, maybe. No more. Probably less."

Jason frowned at me. Looked like he had something a bit more regular in mind. Didn't matter. If it worked out and we all liked the way it was going, we could always step things up.

"And it's just the phones, right? You don't need me to do nothing with computers or signing shit?"

I grinned. I could see where he was coming from. He had his comfort zone and he didn't fancy stepping outside it. Asking some bozo to answer a phone with a fake company name, that was one thing. The bozo would probably be back at the job centre a few weeks later, wouldn't remember a thing. Putting something on paper, online, that was different.

"Just the phones, Paul."

He grinned back.

"You got it, Aliboy."

Jason looked at us both.

"Aliboy?"

I shrugged. "Haven't heard that in a while."

I hadn't. Aliboy. That was Dagenham, school, skipping lessons, getting in trouble, needing a line, an excuse, an alibi. Only one place to get an alibi. The aliboy. I'd come up with lines so fast and look so innocent while I did it, I'd see the faces of my friends' parents turn in a fraction of a second from suspicion to trust.

It was one of the littl'uns, Mrs D. Got mugged on the way into school. Paul was just making sure he was OK.

I don't think that's Simon's, Mrs Carmichael, some of the older boys have been messing around with our bags lately.

Alex the aliboy. Good old Alex, so polite and hard-working, they thought, all of them except my own parents, who knew the truth of it. It hit me that I'd been pulling scams like this my whole life. It was just the stakes that had changed.

Paul got it. Even with half a bottle in his gut, he didn't need us to spell it all out. He could see his bit was important, too, but not as important as ours. Or as risky. We'd changed the subject, we were talking about school, Jason was trying to drag some dirt out of Paul, when Paul suddenly stopped and held up a hand like he was about to burp. Instead, he said "Ten per cent, right?" and looked at us both, suddenly serious.

We'll think about it. That's what I was about to say, even though ten per cent seemed like the right number. But I didn't get a chance because Jason smiled and said "Yes, deal," reached across the table and shook Paul by the hand. I closed my mouth and nodded and joined in the handshake. Jason didn't want to do any more thinking about it. He wanted to get started. All we needed was a deal.

Just a week later the first opportunity came up, a conduit deal that Jason was set to run on his own. The client was the UK arm of a small Japanese bank, and the cashflows came from car loans, it was all technical, all about the maths, all very boring. Boring to work on, even duller to talk about, so I won't say any more than I have to.

We bought an off-the-shelf company and got ourselves set up as directors. Opened a corporate bank account at Sherman Trewitt, one of Milton's rival high street outfits. And then we started forging.

In the era of scanners and Photoshop, I did the old school thing. I went to a legal stationers, bought some supplies and locked myself up in an empty office with a pen, a pair of scissors and a Pritt Stick. Two hours and a trip to the most inconveniently-located photocopier on the floor later, I had some authentic looking forms – a "288a" (appointing the directors) and a Register of Shareholders, both complete with certification as "a true copy of the original" stamped across the bottom of each page. The final touch was the fake lawyer's signature; I settled on a scrawl that looked remarkably like the name of a dwarfish-looking bastard who happened to be a partner at Morder & Chay. Morders did most of Greenings' work in London, so I'd found myself crossing swords with them more often than I cared to remember. Nice for them to come in on my side, for once, even if they didn't know it.

As for our "safe pair of hands", the directors I named on the form worked for Structured Corporate Services Limited. We dealt with these guys on every other deal we did, so many and so often that no one could be expected to keep track of it all. They'd breeze through KYC without a second glance. Our shareholder would be another company within the same group.

Jason was all over the deal, could see his way round it with his eyes closed, but he still couldn't see where to come up with a service for our company to provide. It was an odd little blind spot, this. He had an eye for fraud, no doubt about it, he could see opportunities wherever he looked. But this one ingredient, finding something that wasn't there and making it look like it should be, that was somehow beyond him. Lucky he had me.

The accountants were already stuck right in there, providing financial statements to slot into the documents, vetting all the other numbers, auditing the raw data, and all this was being carried out by the same firm, one of the big boys, which was charging a whopping hundred grand for the privilege. There were two city law firms on the deal, they'd both agreed to cap their fees, and even I could see they were both going to bust those caps long before the deal closed. They'd look for an excuse to charge more than they'd promised – *it took longer than we thought, it was more complicated, there were more parties* – and they'd find one, and Jason would have to break it to his client that what was supposed to be a two hundred and fifty thousand pound legal bill was going to end up closer to half a mill. We were used to this. Every time, without fail. You know what they say about lawyers, you can't trust a word they say? I'm not so sure. Most of the lawyers I've known, they're straight as a die ninety-nine per cent of the time. The other time is when they're trying to win business and they're telling you what it'll cost you. Do me a favour. Double it.

The way the numbers were adding up, Jason was going to have some explaining to do. He'd bash the lawyers down as far as he could, the accountants, too, if they stepped out of line; he'd tell them the client wasn't paying a penny more than he'd said he was going to. Then he'd tell the client the lawyers were past half a million and the accountants were screaming for more sugar. He'd get everyone so angry and self-righteous that when he called them all up a couple of hours later and told them he'd managed to squeeze a bit more out of the client or beat the professionals down a hundred thou, they'd think he was Jesus Christ Almighty. Clever that, he'd shown me how it worked not long after we both started. It's easy to shaft someone as long as they think they're not the ones getting shafted.

With a glorious mess like that, hiding another ten thousand somewhere would be child's play. And the back office boys wouldn't be surprised to see another firm providing one of the accounting services (the data audit, say) alongside the firm who'd really done the work.

Creating the invoices wasn't much more than a fifteen minute job once we'd worked out everything else. There was a neat little bonus twist, too: we could charge VAT – hell, it would look weird if we didn't. And we wouldn't be handing it over to the taxman.

The company, by the way, was called AJP Consultancy Services – Alex, Jason and Paul. And consultancy, which in my experience means anything you want it to, and more often than not, nothing at all.

We'd printed our bank account details on the invoices; just a couple of hours after Jason had submitted them to the back office they called him to ask for a phone number. An hour later, Paul called and let us know he'd done his bit. I'd kept my old log-in details for the back office systems, which hadn't been upgraded in years, so even if I couldn't move the money myself, I could open up a screen and watch it fly.

I listened in on Jason's cashflows call, two days before closing. He was worried, beforehand, but he needn't have been; with all the zeroes being thrashed around, no one was going to notice ten grand (plus VAT) here or there.

That was it. Nothing left to do. The deal closed; we sat back; Jason checked the bank account and we were close to twelve grand to the good. Twelve hundred for Paul, more than five thousand each for me and Jason. Never before had I done so little for so much money – and coming from a banker that's saying something.

But that was just the beginning, because before the first deal had even closed we'd earmarked another three, including one beauty for close to a billion pounds that could stand to lose a hell of a lot more than ten thousand before anyone sat up and took any notice. We set up three new companies – we could start to reuse them in time, but for now we didn't want anyone spotting the same name twice and wondering who was behind it. I reached out to some of my old friends in the back office, tried not to be obvious, hoped I'd get a heads up if anyone thought about asking any questions. But there was no need to worry. Twelve weeks and three deals later, things were going quite nicely, and no one had raised an eyebrow at the fictional accounting, valuation, market consultancy and legal services we provided. I'd get on those cashflow calls and someone would ask a question, a question I hadn't thought of, a base I hadn't covered, and it didn't matter. Because the moment those calls started, Alex Konninger disappeared and the aliboy was there, the words falling from my lips without a second's thought. And it worked. Every time. Every lie I came up with on the spur of the moment, every bumped-up fee or new consultant or unaccountable change of banking details, every single one of them worked, even when I sat down and thought it through afterwards. It got so that Jason couldn't do a call without me, if it was one of his deals we were milking; he'd have me there, next to him, silent, ready to prompt him if a nasty question did get asked. I told him it wasn't necessary, I told him it didn't matter what we said, as long as you knew who was on the call and what they knew (and, more importantly, what they didn't). Nine times out of ten you could spin some line about tax and accounting services and everyone would stop listening before you'd finished the first sentence. Jason didn't care or didn't believe me, so I sat there and listened as nothing happened. No one was going to catch us. No one was even close. You'd think with the way the teams had got split up there would be more people watching, more people checking, more people making sure everything was done by the book. All that really happened was there were more holes to crawl through, more places to hide, because everyone who might have been watching us thought someone else was doing it. On a good day, I thought we could carry on doing this for another hundred years before anyone woke up to it.

But still, even though everything was fine, even though when it came to the calls, I was actually getting a kick out of it, even though I couldn't see any chance of getting caught, in spite of all that, I was starting to get nervous. And at the same time I was thinking *OK, we've had our fun, I've got a bit more in the bank, Emily's fund's kicking off, Jason's builders are happy, Charmaine's in the apartment, let's call it quits.*

But there was always another deal in the pipeline, another chance that was too good to miss. Over a coffee one morning I told Jason it was time to get out, but he wasn't having any of it.

"For Christ's sake Alex, this is the easiest money you'll ever make."

I shook my head, slowly.

"It is now, yeah, but if we do get caught –"

I didn't get to finish the sentence. Jason was leaning forward with his arms out and his palms up and an expression on his face like I'd told him I wanted out because there was a meteor on its way.

"How? Tell me how we're going to get caught. Tell me

who's gonna catch us. Do you really think someone's going to sit down and go through every deal and work out who's been spending and what they've been spending it on? Do you really think some ops guy on a closing call gives a toss what the client's spending his money on?"

Well, when he put it that way.

14: Favours

I could get there, I thought. There was enough fat in Mintrex to get what I needed, and hopefully there was still enough meat and blood and gristle to go round that no one else would notice. I was fucked if things went wrong, and I had to go on and try to make it work anyway, so by rights I should have been sweating like a Stilton in summer but I couldn't help it: I was enjoying myself.

And now, just as I was starting to get into my stride, the call comes in from Westhaven. No warning – that would have been polite. Just an assumption that I'd be at their service, and so would my lawyers. Thankfully, Harvey was available; I patched him straight in. Christine was in the room with him. The plan was to intimidate the box-ticker at the pension fund with a heavyweight name from a magic circle firm. The plan was a good one. But before the hellos were out I could tell it wasn't going to work out that way.

"Hello? This is Harvey Simmons-Smith."

"Harvey. John Cavendish here."

"Ah."

Significant pause.

"And, er, how are you, John?"

"Fine, Harvey. How are things with you?"

"Oh, good, good."

Something wasn't quite right here.

"Now, what's this security point that's come up at the last minute?"

"Hardly the last minute, John. It's all been fully disclosed in the Offering Circulars from the word go."

"I gather we had a verbal promise of full fixed security."

"You know that's not feasible."

A ping from my mobile: I looked down. A text had come in from Christine. I picked up the phone and read what she had to say.

"*remember that story I was telling you about, the dickhead at our place?*"

I couldn't see the significance, but Christine was on the same call I was and she wasn't going to be wasting my time on something irrelevant. Unless she was just flirting. Which was also fine. I replied.

"*there's plenty. Which 1?*"

"*the 1 who screwed up a whole bunch of deals and then went off on 1 when he didn't get partnership?*"

This was starting to ring a bell. Christine had told me a lot of stories, mind, and I hadn't necessarily been concentrating on what she was saying.

"*Is this the guy who flipped out in the meeting?*"

"*Yeah, he threw a carton of orange juice at 1 of the partners*"

Of course. It was a good one. I doubted it was true, mind. It had probably changed with the telling, like all stories do.

"*Yeah I remember*"

"*guess who went to work for westhaven after he was canned?*"

Oh.

"*oh shit*"

"*and guess who the partner was?*"

"*Harve?*"

"*got it in 1.*"

I put the mobile down and returned to the call. The sparring was still going on. However great it might have seemed in theory, my plan to dazzle Westhaven with our brilliant counsel wasn't working out so well in practice. Time to get involved.

"John, this is Alex again. Listen, you're aware of the

constraints we're under here. What can we do to get you more comfortable? Perhaps we can talk you through the timeline to get the full security package when the triggers are breached?"

"By all means."

The lawyers talked. Harvey explained, and John Cavendish said "hmmm" a lot in a way that you could interpret however you wanted. After what Christine had just told me, I was interpreting it as *"I don't believe you and I'm not really listening anyway."*

Harvey wound up the explanation. There was a short silence which I felt the need to fill.

"How does that sound to you, John?"

"This is all very well, and sounds fairly reasonable, but are Sommersons prepared to put their names to it?"

Harvey jumped in. "Meaning?"

"We want an opinion."

"You're not going to get one" – Harvey's instant, belligerent response. I had to step in before things broke down even further than they already had. And as I spoke, my hands were on the phone, sending another text out to Christine.

"Hold it, gentlemen. Let's work out what we can do here."

"That's all very well, Alex, but I don't see what we can work out. Westhaven want an opinion and if that's the only way they're going to get comfortable there's not a cat ..."

He paused, mid-rant. Silence descended. I could almost see him stopping, looking at the phone Christine was waving in his face, reading the message I'd sent.

The message said, simply: *"Don't you want Millcom?"*

Harvey was in an awkward position, I could see that. Cavendish had asked for a legal opinion, a signed statement that would put Sommerson's reputation and money on the line, for a subject that wasn't fit for a legal opinion, and an investor who wasn't even Harvey's client. To make matters worse, if Harvey did it, it would be an opinion offered in a secret back-room deal to a single investor, something so clearly against the rules I'd never even heard anyone try to justify it. It was a stupid thing to ask for and it would be a stupid thing to do, but the way I saw it Cavendish wanted something to show he'd screwed his old firm, and this was the something he'd decided on.

It wasn't really that awkward after all, I decided. Harvey could tell the guy to go fuck himself, which was what he'd been about to do when I sent the text, and no one would really blame him. It would damage the deal, might even screw it completely, and it was an elephant of a deal, but what Harvey was being asked to do – even an elephant was only so big.

Thing was, Mintrex wasn't the only elephant. And some elephants were bigger than others.

We'd just won the biggest of them all. Millcom, an ambitious telecoms outfit. Jane had run the pitch, and she'd come out on top as usual, sole arranger role for Miltons, and half a dozen other banks licking their wounds and trying to work out where they'd screwed up. A billion or so sterling, like Mintrex, but even more complicated and unusual and that meant more money for everyone who managed to get a piece of it. Every bank, every accountant, every advisor out there wanted a piece of it. And every law firm, too. I didn't know a whole lot about the deal, just the bare bones Jane had let slip. Chances were I wouldn't even be working on it. The fact we'd won it at all was supposed to be a secret, but towards the end of last week I'd noticed Jane getting call after call from lawyers anxious to get their names in the hat. Nothing that big could stay secret for long.

"Don't you want Millcom?" I wasn't promising I could deliver it, but I could put in a word, let Jane know we owed

Sommersons a favour, a big favour, an elephant of a favour. Harvey knew how these things worked. There were half a dozen law firms that might get our side of the deal, and it would come down to price, but also competence and trust and personal relationships. If Harvey could get his numbers in the right area, I might be able to do the rest.

"An opinion, then, John?"

Harvey said it like there hadn't even been a pause, like we were in the middle of a perfectly amicable discussion and this was where it had always been leading. Cavendish seemed taken aback.

"Erm – yes, yes, if you could manage it."

"I'm sure we can do something."

Ping. I looked down. *"Harvey says you owe him one." "As ever,"* I replied. Neither of us were going to mention the fact that Westhaven were getting something the other investors weren't, and I doubted Cavendish would, either.

"Gentlemen, I've got a deal to wrap up. Can I leave it to the two of you to agree wording?"

"Sure."

"No problem."

And all of a sudden it's happy fucking families.

I put the phone down and shook my head. We weren't quite out of the woods on this one, but there was some sunlight filtering through the trees. I dropped Elaine and Doug an email telling them we were on our way to getting somewhere with their investor, and let the pair of them know they owed me big-time if it all came through.

Back to work on my personal Primora problem. I ignored the phone, ignored the emails flooding in. There was a Mintrex ops call scheduled for later this afternoon, and if I was to have any chance of digging myself out of the shit I'd need my new cashflows ready by then. *And* I'd have to mock up a bunch of fake invoices to support them.

Within twenty minutes the numbers were starting to take shape; another fifteen and I could see what the cashflows would look like. I drew up a diagram – arrows everywhere, boxes that didn't really need to be there, all designed to get the people who might ask questions asking them in the wrong place. The art of misdirection.

The next job was the invoices. One invoice for a hundred and eighty-five thousand would raise eyebrows. Two for half the sum might, just as easily, but two was all I could work with. There were a couple of companies Jason and I had used before, and because we'd used them before they'd been through all the money-laundering checks already and would hopefully slip through the system a little more smoothly. If I was going to be caught, this was where it would probably happen. With a bit more time I'd have set up half a dozen new vehicles, nice clean companies, guided them slowly and carefully through all the checks they needed, and I'd have been able to breathe a whole lot easier with a bunch of invoices round the twenty-five grand mark. But time was the one thing I didn't have.

My phone rang. I glanced over and saw Liz's number on the screen. I picked up. Liz understood the way things worked. I could get rid of her easily enough if I needed to.

"Hi Liz."

"How's Jason?"

"I wish I could tell you. Haven't been able to get hold of him since yesterday."

"Halfway down a bottle of whisky?"

"Me or him?"

"You don't have the time," she laughed. "And I doubt Sally would let him."

Liz didn't know Sally well, but they'd met a couple of times and seemed to hit it off.

"Right on both counts."

There was a brief silence, broken by the sound of a siren passing by. I could hear it outside and coming at me from Liz's end of the line, too, a ghostly echo. I shivered. I felt rough, suddenly, like I hadn't slept in days and there was something nasty on the horizon. And I really didn't have the time. She was right about that.

"I'll let you get back to your spellings, then. Give him my best when you speak to him."

"Will do. Enjoy your sums."

Back to the task of drilling a little gold out of Mintrex. We hadn't commissioned any market analysis for the deal, because there was so much data out there we didn't need to pay yet another advisor a fortune for something we could do just as well ourselves. But who knew that? Eight, ten people, maybe, and none of them would dirty their hands with things like cashflows and invoices. A hundred thousand wasn't unreasonable for that kind of service. Let me rephrase that: a hundred thousand was fucking criminally unreasonable considering the heap of crap we usually got for the money, but it wouldn't surprise anyone in the business for a second. Which left eighty-five thousand, a plausible enough number for the structural engineering review which hadn't been commissioned for the Mintrex deal because there wasn't an engineered structure to review. Not yet one o'clock and I had the cashflows done, with a couple of genuine-looking invoices saved down and waiting to be printed and sent over to my friends in the back office.

If this is all looking a bit confused, you've got to remember a couple of things. I'd been doing this for a while now. I could run a scam like this with my eyes closed. Not this big, and not this quick, but the same general idea. The other thing is that it's *supposed* to look a bit confused. Not so much that it doesn't make sense at all, but just enough to convince anyone looking that it's probably OK and not worth looking into. Misdirection's part of it, sure, but no one likes to admit they don't understand what's going on, so there's another part which is just to make it look like a mess, but the kind of mess the people dealing with it shrug and pretend it's all fine. What it basically boils down to is three different stories.

Story one: Anyone familiar with the deal would see the usual cashflows, going out to the usual suspects, names they knew, people who'd been involved in the deal from the beginning. Lawyers, valuers, accountants, that kind of thing. Maybe a bit more money than you might expect getting paid to some of those usual suspects, true, but that was the kind of detail I could smooth over if anyone actually noticed anything.

Story two: The back office guys, who didn't know the deal so well but would be making the actual payments, they'd see the real numbers, the bona fide fees going out to the right companies. And they'd also see a couple of others, fees getting paid to two consultancies they didn't know from Adam but had apparently done some important, life-saving work on the transaction.

Story three was the simple, unvarnished truth. The lawyers, the accountants, they'd get everything they asked for. But those two payments were going straight to a pair of companies I'd set up with Jason. I hadn't thought to use them again, they were retired as far as I was concerned, but they were all I had to work with.

Clearer now?

Good.

Lunchtime and I was getting hungry. I glanced over at Rachel's desk. She was sat there in front of her screens, but it didn't look like she was doing much, just staring aimlessly into the distance. Or was it aimless? I followed her gaze just in time to see Jane step out of Russell's office, face set in a concentrated frown. No point in speculating. It could mean anything.

I'd just sent the invoices to print when the phone went again. Lorraine. I had work to do and food to get. I didn't have time for Lorraine.

Thirty seconds later, Lorraine again. And again. And again. This was getting harder to ignore. After five she'd ground me down; the sixth one I picked up.

"Yup."

Odd noises from the other end. Snoring or sneezing or snivelling, I couldn't figure out which.

"Alex?"

"Yup."

"Alex it's Jason."

Definitely snivelling. And the bad feeling was back, too.

"What do you mean?"

"There was an accident. At the station. He... he."

She didn't sound like she could talk. The snivelling had turned into full-blown weeping.

"Are you sure?"

She said something, it sounded like "yump," it could have been anything. I forced myself to think.

"Hang on, Lorraine. Why would he even have been there?"

This time she didn't answer, just carried on weeping.

"I think I'd better come down."

Deleted the invoices and locked the computer for good measure before I ran for the lift. Some things were even more important than fraud.

15: Never Had It So Good, June–November 2007

Six months passed. Six pretty lucrative months. We had a sensible system going: we kept it low-key, never more than twenty thousand on an invoice. We only chose deals one of us knew well enough to come up with the right story at the right time; we only chose deals where one us would be on the closing cashflows call. We didn't overuse our companies and didn't overuse the directors of those companies. There was the odd question, what did this company do, who are these people anyway, but nothing that caused more than a moment's panic.

You can look back now, maybe, and nod, and think you understand what happened in 2007, 2008, 2009, think suddenly it all makes sense. You can look at what we were doing, me and Jason, and you know it's small beer, it's not going to bring down a bank, but you can link it in to everything else. We were just the amateurs, after all. What about the lies they told at Greenings, the deals they built up just so they could knock them down again, what about the onshore-offshore-onshore-again tricks they played at Turney & Co, what about the half-truths Naylors span to the accountants and the rating agencies, to the Federal Reserve, to their own employees? What about LIBOR?

And sure, the stuff we did, the stuff they did, it hurt. A bit. A few billion, maybe, here and there. The stuff we did on purpose, the stuff we knew about, the lies we knew were lies.

But you'd be wrong, still. Because a few billion's nothing, in the big picture. There was no grand conspiracy. There weren't even enough little conspiracies to make more than a dime's worth of difference. What there was were tens of thousands of people all over the world who were just too stupid and too short-sighted and too unaware of what was going on right next door let alone in the other banks and funds and insurers and treasuries, too obsessed with their own little patch of ground to notice anything else.

When you've got that much incompetence, you don't need a conspiracy.

Izabella joined the team. Izabella was something different and I liked her from the moment I saw her. Early-forties and married with three kids, she was fed up with being a lawyer and knew banking well enough to give it a try. If she'd been a bloke, she'd just have been another bullish, aggressive middle-aged man in a bank, but she was a woman, so she was "feisty". She dyed her hair a different colour every week, favouring peroxide blonde and blood red over anything you might mistake for natural. She liked to party, she could drink as hard as any of the rest of us, and as it turned out she wasn't bad at the job, either.

Liz was single again, and moaning about it whenever we met up for lunch or a drink, but had finally got her wish and into leveraged finance. She didn't think much of it there, either, but hell would have been an improvement as long as Karl wasn't there, she said. Emma was still hanging onto her job, just about keeping Karl at bay by coming up with half-decent returns without stupid risks. Russell continued to surprise us all by actually managing the team, and by disagreeing with Karl from time to time. But something seemed to have shifted, subtly, for Karl himself. I'd have put good money on Marcus getting the next knife in the back, but instead he seemed to be edging ahead. You could tell, from the way people talked about him, still suspicious, but with a nod and a grudging respect; you could tell by the way executives were in and out of his office like there was a three star restaurant in there; you could tell from the way Karl himself kept a wary distance: Marcus had overtaken him and was stretching the lead. Marcus was still driving Jessica crazy, but no one could deny the results: more profit, less fat, and a little less risk on the balance sheet. He'd repaired a crumbling relationship with the swaps team, who'd been demanding a bigger share of the money they brought in through our deals; I don't know how he did it, but suddenly a couple of the older faces disappeared and there were smiles on the ones that remained. More important, he'd been the guy who brought in Claire, a star derivatives trader snatched from Greenings to their open-mouthed astonishment. Ours too, if we were honest, it felt a bit like Ronaldo turning up to play for your pub team. Our swaps people were clever, no doubt about it, but there was still a little bit of Frank about them, even though the guy had been gone for years. Claire put paid to all that, reshaped the Miltons team in the Greenings image, with the talent and the earnings, but without the attitude (well, with some of the attitude, I suppose, but she was fighting for the good guys now). Everyone was a winner; and now Marcus had a very powerful ally.

For Jason, life was just a little less stressful. Charmaine was in the apartment. Jason wanted her out, but he was still figuring out how to tell her. Now the money wasn't so tight, he seemed to think this could just run and run without anyone getting hurt, which sounded crazy to me, but I didn't reckon it was my place to tell him that, so apart from shrugs and frowns I kept my ideas to myself. There was a fund building up slowly but steadily for Emily, and Sally was too dewy-eyed over the apple of her eye, baby David, to care who was paying the rent (or notice who wasn't). Things were still tough in the conduit team, they'd had to lose a couple of juniors, and Jason wasn't expecting much joy come bonus time, but thanks to our little operation at least the crisis was over.

As the days got a little cooler and the trees started to turn, Jasmine just got wilder and wilder and I finally decided I'd had enough. It was Kew that did it for me, one warm, breezy Sunday afternoon, her idea, and I should have realised there would be more to it than a stroll among the buddleias. She found a spot, I'd like to say a secluded spot but you could see that tower clear enough from where we were. She lay the picnic blanket down on the grass, and I knew what was coming because I hadn't brought any food and I was pretty sure she hadn't either. I looked up at the tower. My mind had gone blank, I'd forgotten what it was called. If you were near the top you'd have as clear a view of Jasmine as you could have hoped for, but I didn't remember if you could even get up to the top or if it was all just a façade. Not this time, I thought, there are families around, kids, but she had other ideas, and her way of ramming the point home was to strip off and lie there, waiting and wearing nothing but a smile. "Get up," I said, but she just shook her head, and in the end there was only one way to get through to her when she was in that mood. I spent half the time looking around worrying about who could see us, worrying about that tower, and I won't pretend it was no fun at all, but the whole time I was thinking *never again*. When we'd finished, and I got up and started gathering our clothes together as quick as I could, she stood, still naked, grabbed me by the balls, and still smiling into my eyes, squeezed until it was all I could do not to scream. She didn't say anything, just let go, ambled over to her clothes and slowly got dressed while I collapsed into a quivering heap. If she wanted to let me know who was in charge, she couldn't have made it any clearer, but that *never again* just echoed stronger. Dressed a few minutes later and wandering through one of the glasshouses, she was acting like nothing had happened, but I was still limping alongside, not likely to forget in a hurry. *Pagoda*. That was it. A pagoda, and it was closed, there wouldn't have been anyone up there to see us. But anybody could have walked by.

We broke up that evening. I made sure I was dressed and there were no sharp implements nearby, but she took it well, so well that at first I thought she hadn't understood. I suppose a man who balked at screwing in the middle of Kew Gardens on a late summer weekend wasn't man enough for her after all. Jasmine was the longest relationship I'd had, and we'd packed a year's worth of excitement into each of the twenty months it had lasted, so as well as feeling a little sad and lonely I felt old and tired, but most of all I felt relieved. I decided not to buy the 911 Turbo. We said we'd stay in touch, stay friends, but I didn't believe it, so I was surprised to find we did, we even met up occasionally before she moved out to Manhattan. I made sure I kept my trousers on every time, but the trip I had coming up to her warehouse studio or whatever it was she called the place, well, I thought, I was single now, and as far as I knew, she was too, so maybe we could have some of the old kind of fun a few thousand miles from home.

Professionally, the last few months had brought me more than I could have imagined.

It all started with a call from Sam, an old intern I'd stayed in touch with. Sam had finished his training and been offered a job, but not in his favoured team, so he'd walked off and joined the London office of Sterling Walton. You'll remember Sterlings. US investment bank, what they used to call "bulge bracket" – or just plain "big". Sam worked on flow FI deals – credit cards and mortgages mostly – and we met up from time to time for a coffee, lunch or a beer. This time, we're chatting on the phone for a few minutes when he asks if I fancy joining him for a coffee later. And, he says, he'll be bringing Morris Schwartzman along.

I'd been about to say no, because Sam was a nice guy

and it wouldn't be a complete waste of time catching up with him, but I was pretty busy on a pitch to finance a new stadium for a football club. But when he said that name, Morris Schwartzman, my brain shut down and my mouth took over and said *yeah, sure, just tell me where and what time.*

Moe Schwartzman was a legend in our business. A big hitter. He ran fixed income for the whole of Sterlings' European operation, which put him way up over the likes of Karl and Marcus. What he wanted to see me for, I couldn't imagine.

We met in a quiet back-room of a smart Italian restaurant so discreet I'd never noticed it even though it was right across the road from the office. There was just one small, round table, there was Sam, little fat Sam with his big round glasses and his cheery smile and his golfing jumper, and next to him there was Schwartzman, a man I'd never seen in the flesh but knew from photos in the banking magazines. Sharp blue eyes and not a single hair on his head. You wouldn't mistake him for anyone else.

Schwartzman didn't waste any time. There was hello and a quick introduction, and then he hit me with it.

Sterlings had been in the City for years. They had flow, they had real estate. The one thing they didn't have was corporate. They'd drop into the odd deal, just before it closed, get their name on the documents and a few thousand pounds if they could, but they didn't have a team and they couldn't get in where they needed to, at the start, where the money was. They could see big money there and they wanted in. They wanted a team.

Oh, I thought, *how nice. They want me in it.*

That wasn't it. They didn't want me *in* it. They wanted me to run it.

Now, remember, I'm no good at this kind of thing. Give me trouble and I can lie my way out of it like nothing you've ever seen. But give me something *good*, something

I'm not expecting, and instead of saying *yeah, OK,* and shrugging like I'm hoping for more, I'll sit there with my mouth open like an idiot. This time I went even further, I sat there and asked Moe if he was sure, if I was really the right person, if he realised I had no management experience at all. It was like I was trying to talk myself out of the job.

Apparently this wasn't a problem. People – and he didn't say who, and I didn't ask – people at Sterlings had come across me, and no one had a bad word to say about me. What that really meant was that I hadn't screwed my competitors over as hard as I should have done, but it didn't look like they were holding that against me.

What did matter was that when I emerged blinking into the sunshine an hour later, I had an invitation to meet Moe's management team some time later that week, and a comment from him that I treasured, turned over and over in my mind for the next couple of days, and let it take me to places unimagined:

"And Alex," (he'd said, as we stood up to leave), "don't worry about pay. If we want you, we'll get you; and if we have to blow you away to do it, we will."

Things were looking decidedly interesting.

I don't need to say much about that meeting. A bunch of people in suits, sitting round a table, weighing each other up. I played it straight, because I figured these guys could find out what I could do and the money I was on if they needed to. We got on well enough, as far as I could tell. I met half a dozen of them there, including Marguerite Hanson, the woman I'd be reporting into if I got the job. They called her the ice-woman, outside Sterlings, and you could see why, tall and thin, pale, blonde and serious-looking, but once we'd all sat down and started talking it was clear she could laugh as much as anyone else. There were two others I'd come across before, on calls or in meetings, and I sat there sweating for a moment before deciding that I hadn't done anything back then to make them hate me. Ninety minutes, it went on for, and at the end Moe came in to say "Hi" and "Goodbye" and told me I'd be hearing from them soon.

Two days later, my mobile rang while I was sitting at my desk looking at shit on the web. It was Marguerite, and she wondered if I could come in for a few minutes that afternoon. Well, as it happened I had some important client meetings scheduled, but fuck 'em; they could be rearranged if they had to be.

This time it was just her and me. After exchanging hellos and handshakes we sat down at the glass table in her office and she pushed an envelope over to me.

"Look, it may not be what you were hoping for, I know Moe said we could blow you away but there are limits, even for American banks. But I hope it's enough for you to realise how much we want you."

Trying to sugar a sour pill, Marguerite?

No. She wasn't. She really wasn't. And, as I realised when I read the offer before me, Americans really did do things differently.

The salary would be pretty much the same as I was already on: a few thousand more, nothing to get too excited about. But after that, it all got very different. And look, I said earlier I wasn't going to throw numbers around and I meant it. So all you need to know is this: I'd be a managing director, reporting directly to Marguerite; I'd have a handsome bonus, which blew anything I could reasonably hope for at Milton Shearings out of the water and would be paid mostly in cash; and the total package was guaranteed not just for the first year, but for the first three years of my employment at Sterlings.

This was *not* the kind of offer people in my line of business could usually command, unless they were right at the top of the tree. This was, as Sergei would have said, "some serious fucking nuclear shit".

I managed not to whoop. I just smiled, said thanks, it had certainly given me something to think about, we shook hands, and I managed to get out of the building before I collapsed into a fit of giggles that wasn't helped by the two double espressos I downed as I sat at the nearest Starbucks rereading the offer letter over and over again. Moe Schwartzman had lived up to his word and then some. Sterlings had well and truly blown me away.

"You've got to get this in front of Russell. Do it, man."

To me, the offer was an offer. It was a job I liked the look of at a company that had impressed me, for a hell of a lot of money. I was pretty much set on taking it.

Which is why I wasn't a natural banker. To Jason, who was, the offer was leverage. It was something I could use to improve my position where I was. And, maybe, to get an even better offer somewhere else. He was convinced Miltons would match it, or come close. And that Miltons, an established British outfit, was ultimately a better home for Alex Konninger than the fly-by-night London operation of a US investment bank that didn't make the top four in its own country. Which is kind of a harsh set of standards to judge by, but did get me thinking.

I went to see Russell and told him everything. I also told him I'd rather stay at Miltons, but that there was such a gulf between what I was likely to get at the two institutions, I didn't see how I could. Russell looked at me and shook his head. He wasn't saying *no*, he was saying *not now, not me*. If he gave me this kind of money he'd have to fire someone else. He had a budget, after all. But if I went to see Karl myself.....

If I'd thought it would come to this I'd never have started the whole thing. I didn't want to be asking Karl for anything, I didn't even want to be in a room with the guy, but before I could think of an objection Russell had called Karl, whatever I had started was moving all by itself, and I couldn't see how to get out. I wasn't even sure Karl knew who I was.

Turned out that didn't matter, because one thing I'd forgotten about Karl: he hated to lose. And as far as Karl was concerned, the market set the true price for everything (to be fair to Karl, most bankers would have agreed, right up to 2008 or so, when they all simultaneously decided that the markets through which they were forced to revalue their assets were, suddenly and mysteriously, "inefficient", "inaccurate", "not reflective of true value" and so on).

Which meant that whatever Sterlings were prepared to pay me, I was worth it.

He may have been a waning power, but Karl could still make things move when he wanted to. His response came in less than two hours.

The trouble was, I was out. I was at the Nightingale having a drink with Jason, Liz, Izabella and Russell; I thought I'd be saying goodbye fairly soon, and I wanted to start the celebrating early. Rachel was stuck on a client call, said she'd try to make it along later, never did. The rest of us got so drunk I'm not sure we'd have noticed if she'd walked in and sat on us. It was packed there, and loud, and I didn't bother checking my phone or my BlackBerry, which meant I missed half a dozen calls from Karl, plus a couple of emails. It didn't occur to me to have a look until I was stretched out in the back of a taxi on the way home, stroking Izabella's leg (yes, we were that drunk, but nothing too bad had happened yet), and suddenly aware that I might have missed something.

The messages started off calm: Karl was still negotiating. He'd match the salary, make a little headway with the bonus. It was an improvement but didn't come close to what Sterlings had put on the table. Karl was counting on loyalty – all things being equal, I'd rather stay put. And maybe, perhaps, even if they weren't quite equal.

Then slightly less calm, asking me to call him back as soon as possible.

Then: "Alex, I've spoken to Erik" (Mortensen, that is), "and I can get you a bit more." He outlined what he meant by "a bit". It was more than enough to have me thinking, even if it didn't reach Sterlings' dizzy heights. Because, ultimately, Karl was right about one thing: I'd rather stay where I was.

A touch more desperate, now: "Alex, still trying to get hold of you. If you're with Sterlings, get out of there and give me a call please. If you're not with Sterlings, give me a call wherever you are. Karl."

And finally: "Alex, come on. We're doing what we can but you've got to meet us somewhere. This is the last offer."

And he set it out. Sure, it didn't match Sterlings. But it was as near as made no difference. There was no promotion, but that suited me fine. I didn't want management, not really. I didn't want Russell thinking I might be after his job.

"Pls call. Karl."

Now, I might have been drunk, and I might have had one hand occupied doing something it really shouldn't have, but I knew a good offer when I saw one. Jason was right – Sterlings looked good, but better the devil you know, particularly when they're nearly as attractive as the pretty little devil pouting at you, running her tongue across her lips, and slowly unbuttoning her purse.

Reluctantly I removed my hand from Izabella's behind (at which she gave a disappointed grunt and fell asleep). Both hands free, I managed to type and send the best response I could given the time, the place and the state of mind.

"Dear kal@." began my email, promisingly enough. "Thnks for ofer, does lk intresting to me, I need to slep on it tho so will call you tmorrow."

I like to imagine how Karl felt when he got that email. He'd been playing poker all evening, he thought. He'd been raising the stakes, little by little, till he reached my breaking point. And now he'd seen the truth: he'd been betting against himself the whole time, whilst I'd been off celebrating my winnings from the last hand.

And the beauty of it all was that having talked me up so high to Mortensen, he couldn't very well go back on it now, not without looking a fool. The 911 Turbo was back on, even if the woman who'd put me onto it was long gone.

Which is why November saw me arriving at David's christening in a car that cost more than Dad would have made in a decade. Did I feel bad about that? I might have done, if I'd have thought about it at all. There was a pretty young intern back in the apartment, a fling that had been going on a couple of weeks. I'd thought about bringing her along. Jason would understand, it wasn't like I was married, it wasn't like him rocking up with Charmaine on one arm, but still, there were going to be half a dozen colleagues there, and it was in a church, and it just didn't feel right. To my relief, she agreed. All she wanted to do was lie in bed, mess around in the kitchen, if I was lucky I'd be in for a great evening when I got back. Things were going well.

Having sworn to steer young David away from the devil's influence (fancy expecting an investment banker to do *that*), we all headed back to Jason and Sally's for a bit of food and drink. There was a good crowd there, Sally was a popular girl and Jason had made friends wherever he'd been. I was pleased to spot Paddy, who'd shed a little weight and was looking healthier than I'd ever seen him, and I stood there grinning at him while he chatted awkwardly to a pair of Jason's well-meaning aunts. He tried to catch my eye a couple of times and I pretended I hadn't noticed. Eventually I strayed too close and he managed to grab my arm and tell me loudly that we had to discuss the CP market. This is a long-standing SOS code: even people who work in the CP market wouldn't want to discuss it if they didn't have to. I took pity and pulled him away, leaving the aunts still smiling politely and nodding like little birds.

It was good to catch up with Paddy but the man I really wanted to talk with was Jason, and of course he was the one person it was impossible to get hold of. Until I grabbed his arm, pointed out of the window at the gleaming pile of metal I'd parked directly outside, and suggested we go for a spin. Unlike me, Jason was a few drinks to the good, and didn't need to be asked twice; Sally's frantic gestures at him to return as he staggered out of the room were dismissed with a wink and a blown kiss, and thirty seconds later we were cruising down the high street on our way to some wide open A-roads. Now was the chance.

"Jason, mate, we need to talk."

He hadn't even heard. Just carried on smiling, humming, and tapping his feet. *Dark Side of the Moon* was blasting out, and there were, apparently, eight speakers hidden round the car, but I couldn't find them all and wouldn't have known if they'd lied about a couple. I turned the music down and tried a more direct tack.

"Jason. I don't want to carry on doing this."

"Then let's head back. Not a prob, mate."

Christ. Not one of these conversations again. And not when one of us is sober.

"Jason. No more. I've had enough of scamming the SPVs."

Now that *did* get his attention.

"What? Are you fucking joking? This is so sweet we could keep it running forever."

"No, Jason, it isn't. Look, I'm doing pretty fucking well without the extras. And yeah, you might have needed it last year when things were looking bad but you're not exactly below the poverty line yourself. I know there's not much chance of getting caught, but there's not enough upside in it any more either."

Speechless, Jason took a moment to catch up. And then came up with the killer argument:

"No, no, no, no, no."

I had to laugh. "Don't sit on the fence, mate, tell me what you really think."

"We can't stop now. We need to do a few more."

It was always a few more, I told him. And then it would be a few more after that. Unless we made an effort we'd never pull ourselves out of it. And one day, we'd get unlucky, and we'd get caught.

"OK, Alex, I know about the law of averages, I know we'll get caught if we keep on and do thousands of these things. I get that. It's like the monkeys and the typewriters. But you don't get Hamlet out of two monkeys and a few dozen typewriters."

"Three monkeys. You're forgetting Paul."

Now he laughed. We both relaxed.

"OK, three monkeys, three opportunities to fuck up. But still, come on, the chance of failure is so low. Why don't we set ourselves a target? Five, six more deals maybe, but only go for bigger ones, and take more out so the upside is worth it."

Not a bad result, I suppose. I wanted out, but I could stay in if I knew the end was in sight.

"I don't see why you're so keen to carry on anyway, Jason."

"OK, you're right, it's not desperate like it was. But still.

There's Charmaine."

We were at a red light. I turned to look at him and he wasn't smiling. The shrugs and the frowns weren't enough. It was time somebody said something.

"Look, mate, she's living in the apartment, you take her out, you buy her clothes, what else can she want?"

"It's not her that wants it. It's me."

We were driving now so I couldn't see his face, but he sounded serious enough. He was tapping his hand on the door to the rhythm of *Money,* appropriately enough, but there was nothing easy-going about what he was saying. I'd done my bit. I let him talk on.

"It's gone on too long."

Thank fuck, I thought.

"I've got to get her out."

I could tell he'd turned, was talking to the side of my face. I concentrated on the road; suddenly it was pouring outside, we'd driven into the middle of an autumn storm. Jason had lapsed back into silence.

"What's stopping you?"

"Where's she gonna go?"

"What do you care?" I shot back. For a moment he was quiet again, just the rain smashing down and the legendary bass guitar.

"Look, Alex, I got her into this."

Like she had nothing to do with it, I thought.

"She had a place, now she's got nothing."

She still had her job at the track. She had a whole new wardrobe, she hadn't paid any rent for a while, or gym fees, I reckoned she'd done pretty well out of it all.

"I can't just dump her and kick her out."

"So, what, you're gonna give her a fucking severance package?"

He didn't laugh. I glanced to my left. He was looking straight ahead, into the rain and the wind.

"Look, mate, I know I fucked up, right? She might have done OK but fact is, she depends on me now, and I can't have that, I can't have someone else depending on me. But I'm not hanging her out to dry. It's not her fault."

So it was a severance package. It was on the tip of my tongue to tell him Charmaine wasn't just something he could buy his way out of, and then I thought about her and realised she probably was.

"I need a hundred thousand," he said, and I could tell he was looking at me again. If I hadn't been driving through the middle of Armageddon I'd have slapped him. I guessed by the way he hurried on he could see something in my face.

"Not all for her. It's not just Charmaine. Come on. There's still Emily. And David. It's not like Marcus is throwing money at us."

I didn't say anything, I just sighed, and Jason knew me well enough by now to figure out I was losing the will to fight.

"Come on, mate. We can do a few more, yeah? Give Paul a nice surprise, you'll get richer, I'll get less stressed. I need the money, Alex. What can I do?"

"You can make a choice, Jason. It's what people do."

That's what I should have said. I should have made my own choice, there and then. Stopped the car, closed out the game, and fuck the rules. But all I saw was a friend who wanted to make sure everyone he cared about was looked after, and if I didn't like the way he was doing it, I couldn't fault the motive. And it's not like I was Mr Clean, either. So what I actually said was:

"OK, fair enough. But let's stick to sensible amounts. OK?"

"OK."

As we pulled up outside the house, with the storm easing into a cold grey drizzle, it occurred to me that I'd started out determined to put a stop to the whole thing and somehow wound up talking Jason into "just" a few more deals. And I'd come out thinking I'd done well. Even drunk, he was a hell of a negotiator.

What the hell, though. A few more deals. It'd be fine.

I caught Sally's eye as Jason staggered back in, grinning as she slapped him hard on the arse. She looked good, still, a lot better than she should have done after two kids and thirty-five years. Laughing, I raised an invisible glass to my lips. Still stood in the hallway, she did the same with her champagne, and then raised it a little higher, and poured the lot over Jason's head.

Jason yelled out, astonished. Conversation ground to a halt, and then, as Sally doubled over in a full-throated roar, the laughter rippled out over the guests until those in the kitchen, the living room and on the stairs, they all drifted closer to see what they'd missed.

Sally finally managed to straighten up and licked a few drops from his ear; standing just behind I could hear her whisper:

"That's what happens when you step out of the christening party, lover. You get christened. Now if you're a good boy I'll lick the rest of it off you later."

He turned beetroot red and an idiot grin spread right across his face. He really had it all, did Jason.

16: Dead

Tuesday 15th December, 2009
1:15pm

Lorraine was sat at her desk. Slumped, more like. Three others there, guys from the conduit team I didn't know so well, standing around shaking their heads and looking confused like they'd just staggered drunk out of a noisy bar into the dawn. No sign of Jessica.

"Lorraine, it's Alex."

She lifted her head, slowly, and saw me. Nothing. Not a word. Her face was blank. She dropped her head again and I walked over and knelt beside her.

"What's going on?"

She opened her mouth.

"It's... it's...."

The words wouldn't come but it didn't matter, because the wailing wouldn't have let them. It started loud and sounded like something that had been going on since time began and would never end. I'd never really heard this kind of noise in real life; there was crying, sure, but this was something different. I didn't know what to do. The others were still standing there like bomb survivors, like they couldn't even hear her, but there were fifty more on the floor who could, putting their phones down, dropping their pens and going silent, standing up, wandering quietly closer. I put my arms around her and held her. She was shaking. There was a lot of Lorraine to get your arms around and normally I'd have relished the chance but somehow she just seemed tiny, like a kitten shivering in the cold. The volume started to ease. I stroked her arm and told her everything was going to be OK. It wasn't, that was obvious, OK was about as far as you could get from how things were going to be, but what else could I say?

After a while, the sobbing died down, leaving just the odd snivel and shake. She looked at me and smiled weakly, and leaned forward to stand up, but it didn't work, and she started to fall, right on top of me. That wouldn't do. Not now. Not appropriate. I pushed against the floor, hard as I could, and levered us both up, and she smiled again and pushed the hair out of her eyes.

"Jason. It was Jason, this morning at the station."

"What?"

She paused.

"The police called a couple of hours ago and asked if anyone called Jason Kennedy worked here. I asked them why and they wouldn't say, so I just said yes he does, and then I remembered and said no, he didn't work here any more but he used to and then just yesterday he…"

She tailed off, started to sob again, and then got a grip and continued.

"So they asked if his old boss was around and as it happened Jess was in."

"So Jess is back? Where is she?"

Lorraine ignored me.

"And I put them through to Jess and then I could see she started choking coz she was eating a doughnut, coz Keith brought in a load of Krispy Kremes and she got the chocolate one."

That was more like Lorraine.

"But she was speaking to them for just a couple of minutes and then she hung up and she just burst into tears and the first thing she did was charge into Marcus's office but he wasn't there and then she came back and we all said what's going on Jess and she was still crying and she wouldn't say and then she went to the ladies and we had to wait ages like at least five minutes and then she came back and she told us."

"What? Lorraine, what's going on? What did she tell you?"

And then I heard Jessica's own voice, the voice of sanity, behind me.

"Alex. You'd better hear it from me."

Jessica looked shaken. Jessica *never* looked shaken. She could have walked out of a fucking plane crash and not missed a beat. There was a story that she *had* climbed out of a smashed up taxi with her mobile still on and carried on negotiating like nothing had happened, and if you knew Jessica you'd believe it.

But now – mascara all over the place, face otherwise pale as the moon. She walked over to her own chair at the end of the row; I followed her and perched on the desk waiting for her to begin.

"What's Lorraine told you?"

"Nothing much. No, that's not fair. She's told me Jason was in an accident. But I don't understand. Why was he even here?"

"I don't know. But it's true. It happened on one of the platforms. The police said he must have slipped in all the slush. There was a train coming. I don't know. I don't know why he was here. He had his wallet with him, they said. That's how they knew who he was. And then they said, they asked me for Sally's number so she could go and identify him."

"Shit. Is she here?"

"No. I said I could do that. I gave them her number though, I had to."

Hang on.

"Hang on, you're going to identify him?"

"That's where I've just been."

"And?"

"It's Jason. He's pretty smashed up. But yeah, it's Jason. He's dead."

More crying. To my surprise, it was coming from both of us. I had my head in my hands and my eyes screwed up but there were tears falling down my cheeks. I looked up, looked around, there were people watching, dozens of them, just standing there silently, but I couldn't stop myself. At least I was quiet.

The whole story emerged over the next few minutes, but there wasn't much of it. Morning rush hour – that's why the station had been so crowded. He'd slipped just as a train was coming in, the witnesses said he hadn't even had time to call for help, and the driver had no chance of slowing down.

The police said they'd spoken to Sally. Jessica had tried to call her but hadn't been able to get through.

No one could think why he'd been at the station this morning. If anyone had known, it would have been me. But I had nothing.

I sat at the desk opposite Jessica and tried to get my head in order. Nothing made sense. And Jason was dead. The world had been trying to tell me all day and I'd been so wrapped up in Mintrex, and then Primora, that I'd not paid them any attention.

After a few minutes Lorraine disengaged from the small group standing around her and, taking something from her desk drawer, walked over to where I was sitting. In her hand was a USB flash drive, one of those little sticks people use to store photos or commit acts of industrial espionage.

"Here, Alex."

And she handed it to me.

"What's this?"

"Jason..."

The sobbing began. She couldn't say his name without

kicking off again.

"OK Lorraine. OK. Take it easy."

I started stroking her arm again. It seemed to do the trick.

"Jason…" (barely a sniff) "he gave me this. For you. When Marcus called him in the other day."

"You mean yesterday?"

"No, it was…. Yes. It was. Just yesterday. I can't believe it was just yesterday."

"And?" In spite of everything, I was starting to get a little impatient now.

"Yes. Marcus called and asked him to come in. I think he knew something was up. He asked me to give you this and then he went in and then they fired him and now he's dead. I'm sorry. I forgot."

"Thanks. It doesn't matter now, anyway. But thanks."

I stared at the drive. Whatever was on it I doubted it was something I should be looking at in the office. It would have to wait. I slipped it into my pocket and tried to work out what to do next.

The first thing was to try to speak to Sally. It wouldn't be pleasant, but I knew her better than anyone else at the bank, I was David's godfather. I had to try to help.

The first time I tried the line was engaged. The next time it just rang and rang.

Trouble was, I didn't want to do anything else. I didn't even want to think about doing anything else, didn't want to think about anything else at all, not until I'd got this done. So I kept on trying.

Finally, on what must have been the seventh or eighth try, the ringing stopped and I heard Sally's voice, strained.

"Hello?"

"Hello Sally. It's Alex."

Silence for a moment, or close as it could be. I could hear her breathing, shallow gasps. She'd been crying when I called.

"Sally, it's Alex. Do you want me to come over? What can I do?"

Then the sobbing stopped.

And the shouting started.

"JUST STAY AWAY."

"Sally?"

"STAY THE FUCK AWAY FROM US."

Click.

I didn't get it. Maybe she just wanted to be alone. That must have been it, surely. Didn't want to think about it, about Jason's friends, about the bank. You couldn't blame her. Still. *Stay the fuck away from us*. It sounded kind of personal.

A drink. I needed a drink. And the Nightingale was open. I waited until Lorraine and Jessica were distracted, talking among a small group by Jessica's desk opposite me, and slipped out. Upstairs to grab my wallet and coat, and straight out again by the emergency stairs so I couldn't be grabbed in the lift lobby or the lift and forced to talk about it. I didn't want to talk about it. I just wanted a drink.

Three beers later the answers were no clearer, but one thing was coming into sharp focus: Marcus. Somehow, this was all Marcus's doing. He was behind everything. The fat spider in the middle of the whole sick web. He'd tried to force us into the Big One. He'd forced Jason out of Miltons. And now Jason was dead. Marcus. It was all Marcus.

I picked up my mobile, looked up his number and dialled. I was three pints down, not too drunk, but drunk enough not to care. Marcus was going to hear some truths from Alex Konninger.

The phone rang four times and then went through to voicemail. Fine. I could tell him what I wanted to in a thirty-second message as easily as I could on a call, or face to face for that matter. Let him hear what he'd done. I didn't care any more that he held the upper hand, or that he could have me fired or arrested or whatever else he'd threatened.

"Marcus. It's Alex Konninger. I…"

That was as far as I got. I felt a sudden lightness, looked at my hand. The phone wasn't there.

"Don't do it, Alex."

It was Liz. She was stood there with my phone in one hand and the other hand open and raised like she was about to slap me. I took a step back and stumbled. The bar was there to stop me, otherwise I'd have been on the floor. For a moment I was furious, and then I was just confused. I wanted to say something but I didn't know what. Liz was staring at me, lips pursed, frowning. She looked angry enough herself. Or maybe it was just concerned. Finally I thought of something to say.

"What are you doing here?"

"I spoke to Jessica. She didn't know where you were. She was worried about you. I told her I'd find you. I'd like to say I've been looking everywhere, but the truth is this was my first guess."

I managed a rueful grin.

"You know me too well."

"What are you going to do?"

"Do? Well, I was going to call Marcus and tell him he's an evil fucker. But you seem to have put a stop to that. So I think I'll drink."

"OK. What are you having?"

"Eh?"

"I said, what are you having?"

"Aren't you going to try to talk me out of it?"

"Alex." She laid her hand on my shoulder and squeezed.

"Alex, given everything that's happened, I think the most sensible thing you could do right now is get very, very drunk as quickly as you possibly can."

"You're on. Guinness, please."

And so it began. Liz matched my Guinness with a pint of lager, and then again alongside one of those bowls full of miniature sausages so small you're not sure if you're supposed to eat them or politely applaud. But at least Liz was still sober and sensible enough to think of food. The pub started to fill up with groups wandering out of Christmas lunches, and the wait at the bar was growing. A bunch of lawyers from the floor up from mine walked in. I put my head down into my drink, the place was crowded enough for them not to notice me, but I didn't want to have to talk to anyone. Anyone except Liz. We decided to move on, decided on the West End where there would be no chance of bumping into anyone we knew.

A few more pubs, a lot more drinks. I was on bitter, Liz was on Jack Daniels and coke.

Liz pulled me out of one bar when I started getting aggressive with a party of Christmas revellers. One of them had lurched over and asked me "why the long face?"

I thought he was lucky he still had a face at all.

We got something to eat from one of those huge places in Chinatown that can fill you up for a fiver. We carried on drinking, some wine I'd not have touched with a nine-foot pole if I'd been sober and thinking about what I was throwing down my throat.

And then (and this was a bad idea), onto the whisky club. I don't remember discussing it, but since Liz had never been before, it was probably my doing. I remember getting in there, and giggling a lot, and then getting out, but not much in between.

By now it was getting late, and we were getting to the point where we couldn't carry on much longer anyway.

Outside in the street, Liz lost a shoe and hopped over to a nearby wall for support while she put it on. She started to fall, grabbed my arm to stop herself, and the next thing I knew we were kissing like the world was about to end. Good thing it was something past one on a quiet back street, because within thirty seconds I had my hand up her skirt and she didn't seem to want me to stop.

This isn't right, I thought, but it was the place rather than the act that was bothering me. I dragged us both onto the main road and into the back of a miraculous taxi. *Now she'll fall asleep,* I thought, but she didn't, and we spent the next twenty minutes getting reacquainted with each other's mouths. And then we were back at my place, and I'm not going to go into details; it's enough to say that it was good, it went on for a long time, and was interrupted only when Liz, in the middle of the action, suddenly gasped, dragged her phone out of the handbag lying next to her on the bed, and punched in a number.

"Michael," she said.

Oh fuck, I thought. Michael's her husband.

"Michael, I'm working late, OK, and then, I'm out with the girls, OK? I'll stay" – she paused, for a moment, and slapped my hand away from her left nipple – "I'll stay at Sophie's, OK?"

She hit "end call" and that was it. Appalling. I could have told her that when you've got two stories to choose from, choose one, don't use both. But all I did was giggle and carry on where we'd left off. Which, judging from her reaction, was exactly what she wanted me to do.

17: The World Explodes, 2008

It wasn't long after the christening that things started to go wrong. Wrong for everyone, to be honest, and there have been enough books and documentaries on the subject without me adding my opinion on how and why it happened. But I'm a pretty opinionated guy, so I will anyway.

The way I see it, everyone's got their share of the blame. If you're reading this, you either added some shit to the pile, or you know someone that did. Point at any one group and suggest they're the ones that did it, just them and no one else, and you're lying to yourself. If you want to say everyone ought to get shot but the bankers should be first up against the wall, I'm not going to argue. Because, after all, we were the ones who ought to have seen what was coming and hit the brakes, but instead we just closed our eyes and let the good times roll, and, well, look where that got us.

The thing is, building, buying and selling securitised products wasn't just an act of collective madness. Do it the right way and it makes perfect sense, and it did in 2008 just as much as it did in 2002. No one was supposed to get hurt; no one should have got hurt at all. There were so many reasons to create these things, to sell them, to invest in them.

There were the good reasons: the risk was low, the return was predictable.

Then there were the bad reasons: you could buy it without even looking at it, bundle it up with a load of other crap you hadn't properly analysed into a CDO and charge someone else a fee for finding it in the first place. You could fund it short-term (rolling every thirty days or so with commercial paper and hoping to god the market's still alive in thirty days' time), at a lower interest rate than it paid you in the long term, and pocket the difference.

There was, as Greenings and the hedgies have shown us, a downright evil reason: you could buy the nastiest bits of the dodgiest deals, sell them into a CDO so toxic you needed gloves to handle it, and then use a credit default swap to bet the house *against* it. Because you knew it was going to fail.

Most of all, there was the worryingly common reason: everyone else was doing it.

There was a crash. That's how it all started. American houses that had gone up hundreds of per cent in the blink of an eye suddenly weren't worth the sub-prime money that had bought them. And if it had stayed like that, a crash in an obscure sector of the American housing market, it wouldn't have been a big deal. What made this crash different, though, was the way everything was suddenly connected in a giant financial chain, and you couldn't pull out a single link. The fact that a bubble burst – well, that kind of thing happens every few years. But the fact that a bubble bursting halfway across the world should have such an extraordinary effect on individuals and companies who had never heard of US sub-prime mortgages – on individuals who'd never even met an American – taught us a lesson that we'd never really taken on board: everything is correlated. Everybody got hurt.

Let's take an example, a parallel. It's purely hypothetical; I'm quite sure it's never happened this way; but hopefully it'll go some way towards explaining the chain reaction that dragged us all into financial hell.

It all begins with a bunch of Australians buying surf-boards. Not any old surf-board, though. Designer surf-boards, hand-made, by local artisans from organic materials at thousands of dollars a go. Sounds crazy, but all of a sudden it's the next big thing, because some genius has come up with the idea that they're a great investment, and while they're waiting to become millionaires the investors can actually have fun falling off them and getting eaten by sharks. And you can't do that with a share certificate.

An ambitious bank from New Zealand sees a chance to grow. The bank sends out thousands of fliers and makes tens of thousands of calls to Australians offering them loans to buy their boards. They'll finance at 100%, low interest: why not? Surf boards are a sure thing, everyone knows that. The price of a good board can only go one way.

But as wiser heads have predicted (or claim to have predicted, conveniently, some time after the crash), the boom is over before it's even begun. The shark community hears about all the novice surfers taking to the water and decides to party on delicious human flesh. Surfers panic, stay at home, sell their boards. Suddenly ten thousand-dollar surfboards are worth nine thousand, eight thousand, five thousand. The investors sell their boards but still can't pay their loans. The New Zealand bank starts to shake, rattle and roll.

So do its lenders. The Kiwis have loans in the hundreds of millions from big Japanese banks – the same money they've been using to fund their surf-board experiment in the first place. But they're not stupid, the Japanese. They're not ones to take crazy risks on surf-boards. So when they saw their client going surf-crazy, they took out an enormous insurance policy – a credit default swap – against the Kiwi bank going bust.

And bust it goes.

OK, say the Japanese. We've got some of our money back from the Kiwis. But for the rest, they turn to the guys who wrote them the CDS, a bunch of smart ex-traders working out of a small office in Frankfurt. Hermann

Hedge-Fund, we'll call them. Hermann Hedge-Fund pays out, as it has to, and suddenly has a massive hole in its own finances. Which is unfortunate, as it tends to borrow short-term, and just three days later is due to repay a loan of, I don't know, eight hundred million euros, to a small Dutch bank.

Payment day comes. The money does not. Hermann Hedge-Fund is nowhere to be found. The Dutch are sitting around in their beautiful glass-walled offices wondering what the hell's gone wrong.

"What do you mean the companiesh not there?" asks one.

"It'sh jusht not there," says another. "No one ish anshwering the phonesh."

"They can't jusht elope with our Eurosh!" screams the first. "Thish ishn't a Charlotte Bronte novel!"

He means Jane Austen, of course. But Charlotte Bronte had a thing about the low countries.

What do the Dutch do? They're not having a fantastic year themselves. They're not exactly bust, but now they haven't been repaid, they'll probably end up breaching their capital ratios, which means their regulator – and their shareholders – will be very angry indeed.

But there is a solution. Do what bankers always do in a crisis (at least, on TV they do). Pick up the nearest phone – doesn't matter whose phone it is or who's on the other end – and scream "Sell!" at the top of your voice. The Dutch bankers sell anything that comes to hand – say, local commercial mortgage loans and obscure CDOs which no one really knows how to value. And because they're desperate, they sell dirt cheap to a bunch of smug bastards who worked for Hermann Hedge-Fund until three days ago and who probably think they've got the deal of the century.

But the thing about these commercial mortgages and CDOs is that, although they're everywhere, they're not usually traded in quite these quantities. And because of an interesting accounting device called "mark-to-market", a lot of the other banks and funds sitting on a pile of the same things now have to value their own holdings at these new, ultra-low prices. Suddenly, there are banks everywhere making losses. The giant Bank De Gauloises in Paris has made what it thought was a shrewd strategic move into Dutch commercial real estate. Not looking so shrewd now, mes amis. The rating agencies are straight on the phone with the bad news: the Bank De Gauloises is being downgraded.

This is an A-grade disaster for the Bank De Gauloises. It's written lots of credit default swaps, interest rate swaps, currency swaps, with other banks and institutions all over the world. Now it's been downgraded, they're all on the phone at once, demanding more collateral in case it can't pay what it's supposed to. After valiantly fighting on all fronts for four, maybe five minutes, the Bank De Gauloises surrenders, throws all its assets at the problem and hopes it'll go away.

The thing is, how much collateral is enough to solve the problem? They've given away billions, maybe tens of billions, in all kinds of bonds and smart financial instruments, but it's up to everyone else to decide how much it's all worth. And the answer comes back: "Please sir, can I have some more?" Scrambling around behind the sofa, the French find some US treasury bills to solve their own problem, but the big damage has been done – all the other financial instruments it's handed over as collateral have to be revalued – by everyone else who holds them – at the new, low, "marks".

"Golly." "Gosh." "My word."

The management of the Bank of St-John Farquhar Farquharson, one of London's most venerable institutions, are in session. They've just been through their books and seen to their horror that all those clever thingies with names they don't understand that their smarter friends in hedge funds and other banks told them to buy, all those thingies are suddenly worthless. Oh dear. Tomorrow there should be some money coming in, because one of their biggest clients, a car-parts manufacturer in Westumberlandshire called "Aye Oop Exhausts", is due to repay its own three hundred million pound loan. The trouble is, there's been a handshake, an understanding, don't you know, and it's assumed that The Bank (they call themselves "The Bank": what other Bank is there?) will lend all the money straight back to them. Aye Oop haven't even bothered trying to scramble the funds together. Now, The Bank needs the money itself.

A short-term cash crisis. A delicate situation. What are they to do? Times like these call for the gentleman's touch and the old school tie, and the Board adjourns while a few discreet calls are made to a few old friends. "Hello old chap, long time no see, how's the wife, how are the horses? It's terribly embarrassing, but I don't suppose you could scrape together a little, erm, a little loan for us at The Bank, could you?"

A few hours later, the Board reconvenes. Shaken heads. Looks of disappointment. "How could they let us down? Don't they realise who we are?"

There's nothing for it. Aye Oop's finance director is informed that The Bank will need its money back tomorrow after all. The poor FD tells the rest of the board, who respond calmly and reasonably by firing him on the spot. Aye Oop calls up its parent company in the Good Ol' US of A, who rise magnificently to the challenge and put together an emergency package consisting of a statement that "in difficult economic times, difficult decisions have to be made, and it is with great reluctance that we announce the imminent closure of Aye Oop Exhausts, our British aircraft engines business."

And if you're working on the assembly line, that's you out of a job. From surf-boards to spark plugs. Everything is correlated.

We got hit at Miltons. You know the story. We got hit badly and the upshot was – is – that we're mostly owned by the taxpayer. Redundancies aplenty, bonuses squeezed, salaries kept tightly in their place. Still, I was grateful I hadn't taken up the offer from Sterlings, who went from the big bad boys in the City to dead dust in a few short months. Again, you've heard and read enough about that. Crash, shipwreck, and down they went, bankrupt and drowning, and all those guaranteed bonuses and big-time salary offers so much flotsam on the waves.

I'll never know for sure why we got hit quite so hard at Miltons. Maybe me and Jason weren't the only ones, maybe there were dozens of little saboteurs like us spread around the bank, creaming a few grand off the top here and there and lying to Finance. But dozens wouldn't have done it. Write-downs in the billions, in the tens of billions, that's what brought Miltons to its knees. Hundreds of us couldn't have managed that. Even thousands would have struggled.

The truth is, we were as surprised as anyone else. What the hell was going on? It must have been someone else, somewhere else, some other team, department or division in the bank. Maybe some other bank we bought. Not us, your honour.

It's all bollocks, of course. We might have been surprised at the time, but we shouldn't have been. We'd been making the wrong bets for a couple of years, all over the bank, and those bets had been getting bigger and bigger until there was only one way things could go.

We got into the whole game late, that was the problem. Dirty sub-prime mortgages from Hicksville, Alabama, commercial mortgage platforms like Alchemy, betting your own balance sheet – *Originate to Distribute*, they called it, which was just fancy-talk for shoving your own money on black alongside all the investors – we spent years shaking our heads at all that crap and saying "no thanks". And finally, just when everyone else was starting to realise it was all just a gigantic game of musical pyramid schemes and the ones still in when the music stopped would lose everything, we changed our minds, threw all our money at it, and spent the next few years praying and holding on for dear life.

So: the credit crunch hit. Remember that, when it was a credit crunch, back before it became a credit crisis, a financial crisis, a global recession? A few faces disappeared, but not many, and it was clear enough to everyone that we weren't going to get paid like we had been any more, but nothing much else seemed to change, at first. The deals were smaller. There weren't so many people investing. They were investing less. They wanted guarantees and AAA and a liquid market, they wanted the kind of things we'd have told them to fuck off for even thinking about twelve months earlier, but now we were nodding politely and saying *OK* and rushing off to try to find it.

And bit by bit, we couldn't. No one was giving guarantees, the guys who'd always done that sort of thing were sitting in holes so deep you couldn't even hear the poor bastards scream. AAA wasn't what it used to be, it was harder to get, the agencies weren't playing ball, and when we did get it the investors didn't treat it like gold any more. And the markets just weren't there. We couldn't make this stuff liquid, not if we pulverised it for fourteen hours and boiled it at two hundred degrees.

So the deals got harder and harder, and then, one day, they just stopped.

Everyone was screwed. In corporate we could afford to sit and wait, because even if there was nothing on the horizon, all we needed was a hint of an elephant lumbering towards the water hole and we knew we'd be OK. Over in conduit and FI they still had a little work, joke deals, make-believe deals with central banks investing in their friends so they could all pretend the market wasn't in a fucking coma. But Emma was screwed worst of all, because while everyone else in the market had spent the last year cutting and saying "no", Karl had carried on jumping into every real estate deal he could smell, with Emma trying and failing to hold him back. Now they were sitting on billions worth of loans and it was worthless, all of it, even the few that hadn't been that bad in the first place, because Miltons was starting to run out of money, desperate to sell, and no one out there was buying.

Emma had thirty people in the front office alone at the peak, making loans and restructuring them into deals like Alchemy. By the time Mortensen and Karl finished their cull, there were three left, and they spent their days fighting their way through the war-zone their business had turned into. Emma was the first to go, which was a loss to Miltons, but no great personal disaster for her. She got snapped up within a fortnight by a hedge fund that was looking to buy up all those loans on the cheap and thought no one would be able to value them like she could. True to form, Karl expressed shock at the scope of the disaster it had become, and hinted Emma had been pushing through deals without his knowledge. He knew enough about the business to shift the blame, but he was so deep in it this time even he couldn't pull himself out.

Karl outlasted Emma by three months. Mortensen couldn't protect his protégé, not with the guy's name over four billion and change in loans so bad you couldn't give them away. The only shame in Karl's departure was that it happened too late for most of his victims to celebrate it. Over in corporate we weren't shedding any tears, that was for sure. But the rejoicing didn't last long. Marcus was taking us over, now.

Meanwhile in leveraged finance, Liz didn't have the time to shake her head and commiserate, because whatever was going on in real estate was happening in her world too. All the deals going sour and all the bankers looking around wondering what they were going to do now, because sure as hell the bank wasn't giving them any more money to throw away. I couldn't figure out if Liz was the unluckiest girl in the world, or the luckiest – her men, her jobs, she ended up in the worst fucking places, but she got herself out every time. This time she escaped to credit trading, and like I said before I really couldn't figure out what it was she did there, but I reckoned I did a good enough job of nodding along when she talked about it.

In FI and conduit, well, you could hardly say that things were sweet, but they were better than the mess Karl had left behind. You had to give the bastard some credit, Marcus had positioned his businesses well before the world fell off a cliff; he'd gone the opposite way to Karl, focussed on fees, cut down Miltons' risk. So when the shit hit the fan, his investors suffered, sure, but he didn't. He'd been brutal with headcount in the previous twelve months, too, so even when the deals started tailing off, it wasn't like there were dozens of people sitting there surfing the net. And for those left behind, business was hardly booming, but this was one of the few places it was happening at all.

The thing was, there might have been less of Miltons' own money in the deals, but if our investors lost out, they'd try to sue us, because it was around this time that suing your bank suddenly went viral. Everyone was doing it. Some of them were even winning.

The lawyers already knew it, but for the bankers it was something new: if someone's trying to sue you, sue them back or find someone else to sue, fast. Donkeys and tails again, just on a bigger scale. There wasn't much point suing the investors who were coming after us; they didn't have anything left to take. We needed someone else to sue. So Marcus started looking for the right donkey.

With the deals we'd been doing, there were herds of them.

You start with the lawyers: if the documents don't work, if anything's gone wrong, you go after them. Suing a lawyer is a serious ask, because these guys know how to look after themselves. But they're also insured to the hilt, so if you win, you'll be quids in (unless the insurer happens to have a sideline in writing credit default swaps for sub-prime residential mortgage-backed securities, but that would never happen, right?)

Next up, you try the accountants. Have they made a mistake with the numbers you've shown the investors? Is there a misplaced decimal point in the pool audit? But ever since Enron these guys are as slippery as a fish. Takes a sharp eye and a swift hand to pin a tail on them.

And then there's all those other advisors. You know, the guys who write the valuations, structural and environmental surveys, market reports, whatever – the due diligence providers. If they've written something and it turns out not to be one hundred per cent on the nail, then you might be able to go after them. Some of them are tough guys, but some of them aren't; and Miltons will only use due diligence providers that are well insured.

Bingo.

First thing Marcus did was summon the guys in legal and analytics and send them out hunting. Go through the documents, go through the numbers, and find me a mistake. And then he started looking elsewhere, and really, that should have been it for me and Jason, because we'd charged for reports that didn't even exist, and if anyone went looking for us, they'd find us soon enough. But we got lucky.

The first stroke of luck was that most of the deals we'd scammed weren't underwater, or weren't underwater yet or enough to really worry anyone. And you can make as many mistakes as you like; no one's going to notice a thing or give a damn unless your mistake's hit them in the pocket.

Second stroke of luck was that Jason was sitting there doing nothing in particular when Marcus strolled up to Jessica and asked for her help. He wanted someone from her team to go through the remaining deals and start looking at all the reports, see if there was anyone we could sue, any mistakes, anyone with enough money or insurance to make it worth our while.

Jessica must have been having a bad day or something because the way Jason told it, she launched into Marcus so hard she might as well have kicked him in the balls and had done with it. Why was he picking on her? She was doing deals, making money, working; so were the rest of the team. Why the fuck didn't he wander upstairs and have a chat with Russell, get someone on *his* team to do something other than sit there waiting for the next fucking elephant to wander out of the jungle and drag them out of the shit.

And maybe Marcus was having a bad day, too, because he nodded and walked away and Jason was on the phone to me ten seconds later scared shitless and gasping like he was having a fucking baby. Once he'd calmed down and told me what I needed to know, it was simple.

But I needed that third stroke of luck, and thank fuck, there it was. Not that I was sat there in Russell's office complaining about being bored and wanting something, *anything* to do, when Marcus walked in; not even that Marcus didn't seem to mind me being there, maybe he didn't even notice, at first, while he outlined what he wanted done and when he wanted it finished. That wasn't luck, that was exactly what I intended to happen, and if the cards happen to fall just like I say they will then it's me that deserves the credit, not fate or God or anyone else.

We listened to Marcus, Russell and I, and before Russell even had a chance to say anything there I was, humble little voice in the corner, saying I didn't have a whole lot on my plate right now and I wouldn't mind helping out, saying I'd been through so many of these reports over the years I could figure out what I was looking for quicker than anyone else on the team, saying x had a pitch on and y might not be busy and might be a fucking genius when it came to negotiation but she didn't have the eye for detail the job required, nailing every other door shut before Russell or Marcus could even reach for the handle. Marcus looked at me like I was crazy and I thought maybe I'd overdone it, maybe I'd buried us, but the guy didn't know me, not well, anyway, so after a moment he shrugged and turned to Russell and said "if it's OK with you, I'm happy for Alex to run it."

And that was the third stroke of luck. Because Russell *did* know me. He knew what I could do and what I couldn't, he knew my boredom threshold wasn't any higher than the next guy's, he knew I was aching for an elephant as much as anyone else on the team and that doing this was beneath me and would have been beneath me back when I was running the back office. Russell was the weak link, he could have turned and stared at me and asked why in hell I'd just put my hand up to do something he could have some fresh new associate run, with a couple of interns to help, and they'd be glad to do it.

But he didn't. He shrugged, and smiled at me, like I'd just done him a massive favour, and said sure, and that was it. I mean, yeah, I still had to do the work, I still had to dig us out of our own very real hole, but I'd just bought myself a shovel and the way I saw it, getting the shovel was nine tenths of the job.

The other tenth was persuading Jason that now wasn't the time to be running even more scams, but this time even he seemed to realise the deals were too thin and the spotlight was too close. A break, he said. I had something more permanent in mind, but a break would do.

There were two deals I had to worry about. Two deals we'd milked that were far enough underwater to make Marcus's hit-list. One of Jason's, one of mine. Tax consultancy and a market report, that was what we'd come up with to justify our fees, just the kind of thing I was supposed to be poking away at right now till it gave way. And to make matters worse, we'd used the same company for both deals, even though the services provided were completely different, which meant that anyone taking a close look would figure out pretty fast that there was something not quite right.

There were seventy or so deals on Marcus's hit-list, hundreds of reports; I couldn't be expected to look at them all myself. I had a couple of interns on Russell's team and a couple of juniors in legal, going through the easy stuff, filtering out the obvious no-hopers like firms that were already bust or had fuck-all insurance (and it turned out more of those had slipped through the net than should have done), or outfits that hadn't done anything important enough to hang for it. All I had to do was assign these two reports to myself and give them a clean bill of health. I'd back it up (just in case) with a couple of documents summarising what the reports had said. And what they'd said would turn out to be precisely what had happened – these particular consultants were as close to the mark as I could make them without looking like they had a time machine. So the market moved like the market consultant said it would; Her Majesty's Revenue and Customs did pretty much what the tax advisers had predicted they'd do. A week later I was there at Marcus's door with a dozen angles on guys who *had* left us an opening to go after them and had enough money to make it worth our while. And nothing at all on the two deals I really cared about.

We celebrated, Jason and I, with a couple of beers in the Nightingale. He wanted to carry on with the scams right away, had a deal in mind already, some credit card thing for a Portuguese bank, but I cut him off before he'd finished the first sentence.

"We need more time," I told him, and I must have looked like a man who meant what he said, because for once he didn't argue. The couple of beers turned into four, six, eight. We were out of the woods. God alone knows why we thought that was it, why we just assumed the bullet we'd dodged was the only one out there, maybe it was the beer, maybe it was the fact that we still had jobs when half the City seemed to be losing theirs, maybe we were just idiots.

I guess it doesn't really matter why we thought like we did. The only thing that matters is that we were wrong.

WEDNESDAY

18: Aftermath

Wednesday 16th December, 2009

I woke Wednesday to an urgent appointment with the bathroom. I didn't know what time it was, because for some reason I couldn't see the clock, but it was still dark and I bounced off a couple of walls before I got there. The en suite's got more bulbs and switches than the Royal Opera House so there's got to be an option for something gentle and subdued, but I didn't have the time to find it. I hit every button I could feel, knelt down in front of the toilet and didn't get up until there was nothing left to come out and the light was starting to hurt. I was tired. I was thirsty. My head felt like it'd slammed into the side of the toilet, and I was pretty sure it hadn't. But other than that, I didn't feel so bad. I crept back through the bedroom, still dark, into the kitchen, and switched on the coffee machine. Yeah, I know, I don't even like the stuff, but there are mornings when you need it, and I had those mornings often enough to make the machine worthwhile.

It was eight o' clock. While I was waiting for the heat to build up I returned to the bedroom to see how Liz was doing.

It wasn't good. I could smell it before I was two steps in and I didn't need to turn on the light to know what I was going to see. I turned it on anyway. She was still in the bed. She looked awful, probably much like I'd looked half an hour earlier, but the difference was that she hadn't made it as far as the bathroom.

I've spent most of the last few years living by myself, and I've spent a fair bit of that time either about to drink, drinking, drunk, or hungover. And one of the people I had lived with was Jasmine, whose idea of cleaning herself up was to splash a little cold water around and walk straight back out with a smile on her face. When it comes to cleaning up the morning after a good night out, I'm a stone-cold killer.

Towels, three, to wipe down Liz. Sheet to drape over leather armchair; Liz parked on armchair while I stripped the bed. I rolled the mess into a ball and pushed it into a black plastic bag. It was beyond rescue. I took a quick look around. The walls and the floor didn't look too bad. The clock was on the floor, in three pieces, and I had a feeling that however it had got that way the warranty wouldn't cover it. I turned my attention to Liz.

I'd got the worst off her with the towels. She hadn't been able to move, hadn't really been able to say anything, just grunted in discomfort. She was sitting up now, smiling, white as the sheets had been before she'd redecorated them. She reeked of it, I could still see bits I'd missed.

I didn't care. Vomit doesn't turn me on; I'm not a fucking pervert. But even in this state, Liz looked just about good enough for another round. And this time I was sober.

I restrained myself. It wasn't easy, mind. She was still in her underwear and I had to strip all that off her too before helping her into the bathroom. The shower's big enough for two, which was useful because she was in no state to clean herself up and I wasn't exactly wholesome myself. I thought about Mintrex, Primora, I thought about Marcus, I thought about anything I could other than the beautiful naked woman in front of me.

In the end, the only thing that worked was thinking about Jason. After a few minutes she nodded at me, finally spoke – "I'm OK, thanks" – and that was my cue to leave. I hung a fresh towel on the rail for her, went back to the bedroom and dressed.

She took a while. I heard the water stop after another ten minutes and remembered the coffee. Another five minutes and I was back in the bedroom with two cups, but she still wasn't out. I remade the bed and I sat down on it and thought about the last eight, ten hours, how stupid I'd been, the kind of shit I'd got myself into.

I didn't regret a thing. She came back, wrapped in the towel, still smiling, and got back under the fresh covers. I regretted it even less.

In another life, we'd have stayed there in that room and had a good talk about what had happened. We'd have agreed it shouldn't have happened, that it wouldn't happen again, maybe we'd have decided to pretend it hadn't happened at all. She was married, she was a friend, every sensible cell in my head knew it was wrong.

In another life, that's what we'd have done. But I didn't want to. I couldn't vouch for what Liz wanted, I'm not sure she knew herself, other than coffee and some more sleep. I didn't say anything but whatever those cells said, there was something louder, and all it was saying, over and over again, was *I don't regret it*. And right now I couldn't think beyond that.

So we sat there in silence and sipped the coffee, and I watched her. She was looking round the room. She'd never been to the apartment, I'd still been in Holloway when we'd last been together. Her eyes rested on the painting and she sat up, frowning slightly, her chin resting in the palm of her hand. She was looking at the painting and everything outside the room was starting to flood back and hit me, everything I'd used in the shower and then discarded when I didn't need it. Mintrex. Primora. Marcus. *Jason*.

I got up, walked to the phone, dialled the house. Sally could shout as much as she liked, I didn't care, I just wanted to make sure she was OK.

Of course she wasn't OK. But I needed to speak to her.

No answer.

I thought about going down there myself. I could show up, she'd have to face me if I was there, I might find out what the hell was going on. I decided not to. If she wasn't there, there was no point. If she was, she didn't want to speak to me. She wouldn't have to face me at all, she could just keep me there outside shouting and hammering at the door until I got bored or one of her neighbours called the police. It wouldn't make things any better.

So there was work. The office. Mintrex, to drag over the line, squeeze some money out of, dig Primora out of its hole and dig myself out of my own little hell. And keep trying Sally until she gave up and spoke to me.

There was one other thing calling me to the office. The Christmas party. It was tonight. Team meal, team drinks. Always horrible. But if I could get everything done that needed to be done, I wouldn't miss it for the world.

I walked back into the bedroom. She was still looking at the painting, but she heard my step and turned.

"I like it," she said. "You didn't have this before, did you?"

Before. I knew what she meant by that. *Back when we were having sex.*

"No. No, I didn't. I got it just after I moved into this place. Not sure it would have fitted in the room in Holloway."

She nodded. I could only see the back of her head; she'd turned back to the painting.

"What's this bit?" she asked.

"What bit?"

"Here."

She stood up on the bed, still wrapped in the towel, and pointed at the painting.

"I don't really understand this kind of art, but should this be here?"

I squinted, got up onto the bed myself so I could see what she was pointing at. There was something there. Where a block of red hair met a block of yellow body. The outlines of the blocks were black, like you'd expect, but the black had run, and there was a smudge, a couple of centimetres long. I couldn't believe I'd never noticed it. Maybe it had only recently appeared, maybe it was something to do with humidity, the frame, the conditions in the bedroom. I didn't understand it.

"I don't know," I said, and got back down. She nodded and sat down beside me.

Time was getting on and I had a lot on my plate, so I told Liz where I was going, where she could find some clothes, left her a set of keys, explained the alarm system and the coffee machine, and hoped for the best. All she did was nod and smile. I wasn't sure whether hoping was enough.

I took the Tube again, I didn't trust myself on the bike today. As I pulled my Oyster card from the depths of my coat pocket my hand brushed against the flash drive Lorraine had given me yesterday. A wise man would have looked into its contents last night. You can call me many things, but wise isn't one of them. I'd rather spend the time getting drunk and having sex with a woman just four months married to a hedge-fund heavyweight with six years in the SAS.

Hadn't I mentioned that?

Once I'd waded through all the standard crap about bonuses and days of reckoning, the morning paper had a couple of interesting pieces.

There was a paragraph on the death of a city banker at the station the previous morning. No name, and short on detail. A single witness quoted, "it was very icy there so he must have slipped", and a reference to ongoing investigation.

The other story was in the business pages.

Mintrex. But not our deal, not the deal I'd been busting my balls on for so long. This was much bigger.

Mintrex had launched a bid for Orresco. You'll know Orresco, or at least, you'll recognise the name: another giant mining business. Operations all over the world, shovels in minerals I'd never even heard of. Mintrex were offering a fortune, twenty-three billion US, and even if the Orresco board didn't like it, even if it turned hostile, the shareholders would sit up and take notice because twenty-three billion was what Orresco had been worth back in 2005, its all-time high, and a lot more than it was worth right now.

Miltons were all over the deal. First off, we were Mintrex's principal advisors for the bid, which made it far and away the highest-profile deal we'd ever been involved with. Even "our" deal – my deal, as I thought of it – even that was mentioned, since it would give Mintrex the last few bucks they needed to fund the bid. In an opinion piece beside the main article, the business editor raved about it all. A return to the days of the great British takeover, he said. Could kick-start the market, could be the shot in the arm the City and Wall Street had been waiting for. And the secrecy, he loved all that, too. No mysterious spikes in the share price in the last few days, which was pretty unusual; these things always get out, somehow and there's always someone looking for a fast buck. Yeah, it was secret, all right, I'd had no idea what was going on. But I wasn't so sure everything had been as above-board as these guys seemed to be making out. Billy D talking tax. Credit committee not questioning a damn thing. Even the way I'd got the mandate. I might not have known what was going on but a lot of other people had.

So I was mixed up in something big, then. Yippee. Right now it was way down my list of priorities. First, Sally. Second, Primora. Third, coffee, bacon roll, Nurofen, anything to kick the hangover into touch. After that I'd get round to Mintrex, to the actual deal rather the one I was stealing from. I was running late again but as long as I got through what I needed to it didn't matter.

The office was quiet. Anthony was leaning back in his chair, conducting a no-doubt critical conversation through his remote headset and flicking through his emails with one hand on the mouse and his mouth set in a narrow line. A lord dispensing judgment, that would be the effect he was hoping for. I hated the guy but I had to admit it, he wasn't far off.

I'd left my BlackBerry at my desk when I went to the pub yesterday, so I expected a mountain of email and voicemail to deal with first thing. But before my arse had even hit the chair I heard my name called from across the floor. Russell was waving at me, gesturing into his office.

Russell was never one for small talk, which was just as well given what I had to deal with today.

"Have you heard the news?"

This was a tough one. What qualified as "news" these days? Jason's firing was news a day ago; by now even his death was probably an old story. Twenty-four hours is a long time in banking.

"Not sure. Try me."

"I'm leaving."

Good. OK. He'd listened to one of the things I'd said. I could only hope he'd listened to the other one, too.

"Congratulations, mate. What do we call you now? Your Majesty? Your Grace? Baron von Calman?"

He paused. Didn't quite seem to know how to answer.

"I'm not sure you've followed, Alex. I'm leaving."

"Yes, got that, mate. Pretty clear. You're heading upstairs. Whose arse are you going to be kicking up there?"

"No one's arse, Alex."

Now it was my turn to look blank.

"What do you mean?"

"I'm not going upstairs."

Again, a pause. This time he chose not to fill it.

"Why the hell not?"

"You know what they offered." (I didn't, actually, he'd kept that one pretty close, but now didn't seem the time to remind him). "It wasn't bad. Fuck, who am I kidding, it was fantastic. But I thought about it, you know, and I decided I didn't want it. I didn't want to be a manager."

"What do you think you've been for the last few years? You're hardly down at the coalface getting your hands dirty, are you?"

The moment the words were out I realised they weren't the right ones. But it was too late now. Thankfully, he didn't seem to mind.

"Precisely. It was what you said the other day. Can't stay here forever. You were right. I already knew I didn't want the new job but suddenly it was pretty clear I didn't much want the old one either."

"OK, OK, I get it."

I got it, alright. Change of scene, change of lifestyle, whatever. I'd heard it all before, a hundred times.

"Yeah, I get it. So where are you headed?"

He smiled. Nothing.

"Come on, Russell. You can give me all the crap you like about not wanting to be a manager, blah blah blah, but I know what this is about."

"And what's it about, Alex?"

"You've got yourself a hot offer, haven't you? Who is it? One of the Americans?"

"Nope."

"What, a European house? Hedge fund?"

He shook his head. "Nothing."

"Nothing?"

"Seriously. I've got enough money, Alex."

Again, my turn to say nothing. Just stare.

"I've had enough. It's time to get out of the game, Alex. I'm leaving."

I'd have liked to chat it over with him. Had a beer, chewed the fat, really got to grips with this. Russell had made a big decision. A real decision, not one of those turn left or turn right decisions I'd been making all my life. He'd done something different. Good for him. I didn't have time to talk it all through, not now, but I still wanted to know who'd be stepping into his shoes. He was in an expansive mood, I thought. Maybe he'd let something slip. I opened my mouth to ask and before a single word got out there was a tap on the door. We both looked round. The door opened, a hesitant cough, and a head appeared, tight black curls, a bright little smile, a Yorkshire accent so strong you could stuff it in a pie and have it for tea. Suzie, Russell's PA. I'd know that voice anywhere, even without the hair.

"Sorry to interrupt," she murmured, "but Marcus has been trying to get hold of you."

I got up, told Russell to give me a shout when he'd finished the call.

Wrong again.

"No, Alex, it's you."

I must have looked as blank as I felt.

"Marcus wants to speak to you," she said, peering at me, gently, like she was talking to a child. "I'll put him through to your desk."

This couldn't be good.

"Marcus."

"Alex."

I thought for a moment about the rant I had planned for him yesterday before Liz had stopped me, and then I thought maybe not.

"Alex, can you spare a few minutes?"

If I were Marcus I'd want to speak to me, too. Could be anything, really. Could be Jason, could be sorrow, sadness, even guilt. Could be Mintrex, he'd have seen the stories today like I had, he might want to shake me by the hand and give me a well done and a thank you. Could be the Big One, could be he just wanted to remind me why it was Jason had been canned, to let me know I'd be going the same way if I didn't play ball. If I had to bet, that would be the one I'd go for, but even then I'd be surprised. I'd have thought he'd let things simmer down a bit before he went back in for the kill. If he even knew I was involved. There was that comment, that cryptic little warning on Monday, but that was all and by itself that wasn't enough. I was clinging to that. *If he even knew.*

I suppose I'd better explain how Marcus got involved in the first place.

"Sure," I said. I was shooting for bright and eager but the hangover let me down. "I'll be down in a minute."

"Good. See you shortly."

Anthony had finished his call. As I walked past his smirk widened to a full-on grin.

"Looks like you guys bagged the big one with Mintrex. Congratulations."

"Thanks." You insincere little bastard.

"Hope it all works out for you."

And there was that grin again. I didn't like the guy at the best of times, but right now something about Anthony was making me distinctly uncomfortable.

19: Caught in the Web, 2008-9

Looking back on it now, on how we thought we'd got ourselves out of Marcus's firing line, I can't believe how naïve we were. Back when we started the scams, even though I knew the chances of getting caught were a thousand to one, occasionally I'd lie there sweating a sleepless night thinking about everything that might go wrong. As the deals went by and the money poured in the sleep came back and I forgot to worry, even while I was telling Jason I wanted out I wasn't worrying, not really, and now there was someone actually looking, and we wrote ourselves a nice little cover story and got on with life.

But if you were working in a bank, life at the back end of 2008 was full of surprises. You never knew from one day to the next who'd be bust, who'd be nationalised, who the hedge funds and the BBC would turn on next. There had been whispers about Miltons for months, and now they were getting louder. People in the bank were starting to worry, years after they should have been worrying. And we were still sitting there waiting for another elephant to get things moving again.

There was no elephant. Instead there were new teams springing up all over the bank, non-core, distressed assets, capital management, risk reprofiling, regulatory liaison (which was just the old Sup Comms team reborn), team after team with innocuous-sounding names that scared the living daylights out of you if you found out they were taking an interest in one of your deals.

It turned out they were taking an interest in more than just our deals. I got a call from Russell one afternoon, must have been late September, maybe October. I sat down and he rubbed his eyes and slumped and generally looked like he'd been up all night struggling with something. They wanted bodies, he said, and I asked him who, and he told me, one of the new teams, Portfolio Assessment, and I laughed and asked how harmless they were, and he laughed back and said it depended whether you were the one being assessed. We all knew what *assessment* meant, or *management*, or *reprofiling*. It meant reduction, meant getting rid of things, loans, assets, people. Ideally bad ones, but anything would do, because we weren't the only ones in trouble: everyone's clothes were the emperor's new clothes, and all the banks were naked.

I didn't mind. It wasn't like there was a whole lot going on in corporate these days, just a bunch of people trying to position themselves at the front of the line for a deal that didn't yet exist. This Portfolio Assessment gang might be interesting, I thought. I might get to see something useful. It wasn't a big team, just eight of them, all smart, men and women who'd been at the bank a long time, longer than I had, who knew their way around, who knew who to speak to if they hit a roadblock. Useful people to know, I thought.

They had no particular specialisation – or, rather, they had *all* the specialisations. Their brief was to shift loans, risk, whatever, and they did it however they could. They securitised, they sold and sub-participated, they did whatever they needed to do. I didn't realise it at the time, but I know it now: these guys were the black ops team. They did the dirty jobs that no one else could be trusted with, and they did it so quietly and efficiently that you wouldn't know a thing about them until you woke up one day and all your loans were gone.

So I sat there with them for a month or so and worked out how to shift two, three billion pounds worth of loans to another bank. A rarity at the time, a European bank that was keeping its head above water, and apparently they owed us a favour. They'd agreed to take what was called an unfunded sub-participation, which meant they'd bear a chunk of the losses, if there were any, in exchange for a fee.

I'd been working with these guys for a month or two and we were getting towards year end when the bombshell hit. Jason called up and suggested a coffee. I'd like to say I could tell something was wrong from his voice, but I couldn't. I had five minutes to spare and I fancied a break.

The moment I saw him, though, I knew what had happened. He looked like he'd been sick, or was about to be sick, either way you wouldn't want to be in the room with him if you didn't have to. He saw me and shook his head, slowly, and I knew it was over.

If only I'd been right.

Jason had been busted. Just him, he said, not me, not yet anyway – I didn't ask, I wanted to, the moment I realised what was going on, but I kept my mouth shut and he didn't make me wait more than thirty seconds. Marcus had called him in and shoved a load of paperwork in front of him and the moment he'd seen the names on the deals he'd known. His deals, three of them, his paperwork, his KYC.

He didn't know how Marcus had found out and Marcus wasn't saying, he didn't need to, Jason had tried to play dumb but there was too much to explain, and he was never that great on the spot anyway. He'd shrugged and caved and when Marcus had asked who else was involved, he'd said no one. Marcus had nodded, apparently, and moved onto the next question, so there was no way of knowing whether he'd believed it, but at least my name hadn't come up.

He hadn't been gentle, Marcus, but then he had a plan, as it turned out, and being gentle wouldn't have helped it along much. Jason had the words, the exact words, he hadn't forgotten a single one, and when I heard it I understood why because you wouldn't, not hearing something like that.

You're screwed, he'd said. *You're screwed. Fired. The FSA won't let you work in finance again, but I wouldn't worry, because no one's gonna hire you anyway.*

The way Jason told it, he'd just sat there slumped in a chair with his head in his hands wondering what the fuck he was going to say to Sally. And then he'd thought about Emily and he'd slumped even lower. Marcus went on.

There's the police. There's the clients you stole from. Anything you took, we'll be getting it back, so I hope for your sake you've got all the money tucked away on deposit somewhere.

There wasn't a lot Jason could say. He was fucked. And Marcus being Marcus, there wasn't much point begging for mercy.

But there might be some way to make this easier. If you're prepared to cooperate.

Jason hadn't known what to think when he heard that. He just sat there, head down, and nodded, slightly. That wasn't enough. Marcus hadn't said anything more and eventually Jason had glanced up to see the guy looking at him expectantly. It was his turn. This was a dance, even I could see it at second hand half an hour later, it was a ritual, you scratch my back, I won't flay yours. But there was a way of doing things, Marcus wasn't going to make all the running, Jason had to meet him part way. Eventually Jason had realised what he was supposed to say and said it, had swallowed and looked Marcus in the eye and asked him what he had in mind.

The answer was a big surprise.

Marcus wanted more of the same. He wanted more scams, bigger scams, he wanted us – not us, Jason, he wanted Jason to carry on doing what he already was, skimming the top off the juiciest deals, and he wanted the cream for himself. He'd let Jason hold on to a little, he wanted his man to have some skin in the game, I'd have thought saving his job and keeping out of jail would be enough of an incentive but Marcus probably knew what he was doing.

He had it all mapped out. He'd start with close to a hundred grand, which took us way beyond anything we'd done before, but then, we hadn't had someone at Marcus's level to help cover our tracks if we needed them covered. If that worked, Marcus was expecting half a dozen, maybe ten more deals, each one bigger than the last, until he'd pulled out a couple of million for himself. After that, the whole thing would be forgotten.

There wasn't much for Jason and I to discuss. He'd accepted Marcus's "offer", of course – he didn't have a whole lot of choice. And I had to play along. Neither of us trusted Marcus, there was nothing to stop him shooting for more once he got his two million, but short of asking him to swear on the bible there was nothing Jason could do. The rules might have changed, but the game was back up and running.

You don't need the details. We did it. I kept myself a little further behind the scenes than I had done in the past, but Jason still needed me, he needed me to come up with the bullshit we peddled as "services", and he needed me to sit there holding his hand on the cashflow calls. It worked out exactly as Marcus planned: seventy grand for him – he emailed account details to Jason the moment the deal closed – and a few thousand left over for Jason. After Paul's split, Jason and I barely had enough for a Big Mac.

Four more deals over the next three months, while I finished up with the portfolio black ops boys. Marcus had us tucking into anything that looked big enough. It was reckless, I thought, but I didn't have any say in the matter. As far as Marcus knew, I wasn't involved. He made about three hundred thousand, all told, with a little morsel left over for us, not that it made the tension worthwhile. He'd been called the Spider for years – not to his face, of course – the guy who just sat there in the middle of it all and knew exactly what was going on. And now Jason had stretched out one little leg and that was it, stuck in the web. He threw a different bank account at us every time, no problem covering his own tracks, but we were still using the same companies, the same directors – fresh deals were being sprung on us every time we came up for air and there wasn't time to come up with anything new. I didn't like it. I was waking up at two, three in the morning and staying like that till the alarm went off, certain we were going to get caught. Caught again. By someone who wouldn't offer us a get-out, like Marcus had. And one thing I was sure of: if we were caught again, it wouldn't be Marcus standing there with his hands in the till. I argued with Jason. Jason argued with Marcus. Marcus gave him nothing.

Meanwhile my Portfolio Assessment stint was coming to an end. The project with the European bank was almost done, would be finished within the next couple of weeks, that was the idea, anyway – and suddenly the other side started talking about cancelling.

They weren't going to cancel right now – they were happy enough to get the deal done. They just wanted to rip the whole thing up early next year. And OK, we could stop paying them if they did, but the way I saw it, it made the whole thing kind of pointless. We'd get these assets off our books for, what, a month, maybe two, and then we'd have them straight back again. I couldn't believe it when they told me, I ranted and raved for a minute, and then I looked round the room at the rest of the team – you know, I can't remember a single name, it wasn't much more than a year ago and they're all just a blur of glasses and frowns – and they were looking back at me like I was some kind of idiot. *Don't worry about it*, I was told. *They can tear the thing up if they want. Just keep it out of the documents.*

It took me a couple of hours to figure it out. We wanted the assets off our books, sure – but only when it mattered, year end, when we'd show off how well we'd done to all our shareholders and bondholders and lenders, and the regulators too. *Excellent job*, they'd say, and the CEO and his chums would smile diffidently and talk about their "people", and how important is was to rebuild all that lost trust, the same old shit they'd been peddling for the last year and still are today. But once all that was over, once we were into the next year – well, I don't know what the wizards in Portfolio Assessment were really thinking. I was thinking everything was just going to blow over and this time next year we'd be as greedy for new loans as we had been five years back. They were probably thinking we'd be bust anyway, and they were just trying to keep us alive another few weeks. Next year might as well have been next century. As long as it was all kept quiet, everything would be just fine. The other side wouldn't be happy, I thought, because I was going to have to tell them *yeah, sure, you can tear the whole thing up next year if you want – but that's just between us. Nothing on paper. You'll have to trust me.* They'd tell me to go fuck myself, that's what I'd have said to them.

I couldn't have been more wrong. They laughed and said *si, si, no hay problema*, and we went ahead and closed the deal and I went back to my old job and forgot all about it.

There was something else going on when I got back downstairs. Something I hadn't seen before. Every day, some time after 11, a laugh would ripple across the floor, little pockets in different places.

"What's going on?" I asked Jane.

"It's LIBOR," she said, and went back to whatever she'd

been doing before I interrupted her. *It's LIBOR*, as an explanation, hadn't really helped, but Rachel filled me in on our next coffee break.

It was the LIBOR sets. Each bank was reporting whatever the rate was they were borrowing at that morning, so an average could be announced and used as a reference rate for everyone else that day. The thing is, those banks included us. And half a dozen others who no one else was lending to, not on normal terms, anyway. We were all getting asked what rate we could borrow at and instead of saying "erm, sorry, we can't borrow at any rate at all right now," we were just making up a number. A low number, a number that made us look solid and reputable and not at all the kind of bank that would piss all its money away on sub-prime and inflated commercial real estate and buyouts so leveraged you couldn't for the life of you work out if anyone else out there was putting their hands in their pockets at all. And we weren't the only ones. They were all doing it, making the numbers up, trying to keep their banks alive a little longer. I was shocked, for a moment, and then I laughed too. Hadn't I done just the same thing, back in '04, back when Alchemy needed saving and someone had to lie to save it? It wasn't exactly clean, but it wasn't really dirty, either.

Five deals we'd done for Marcus, and then – as if they hadn't already – things got serious. Jason called me up, didn't even wait for me to speak, just said "*It's a fucking monster.*"

A million pounds. Marcus wanted to take a million pounds out of a near-billion pound deal set to close in four weeks' time.

The way Jason told it, Marcus still didn't know I was involved. But I couldn't see things staying that way for long. If we tried to pull a million quid out of something we'd only just heard about, it wouldn't take a genius to notice us and catch us and bring us down. Maybe with a few months, time to set up some new companies, bed in some new services, maybe it would be feasible, not that I'd have looked at it if I didn't have a gun to my head. Or Jason's head, but still, I preferred Jason with his head intact. It didn't matter. We didn't have a few months, we had weeks, and that wasn't enough time to do this and get out clean. We'd shine like a firework on a November night.

Which was what I told Jason. He nodded, and shook his head, and said maybe, but it didn't matter. We were looking at it from different angles, of course: as far as he was concerned, if we didn't do the Big One, as we'd started calling it, then Marcus would pull that trigger. Jason didn't need to say it, but I'd probably get some shrapnel, too, my luck couldn't hold out much longer. If we did the deal, at least we both had a chance.

My angle was different. I could see Jason's point of view, sure, but Marcus made no sense. Yes, it was an unusual opportunity: a big deal, a cash-rich client who'd been pushed into doing a deal he didn't really need to do by a cosy little ring of small-time advisors who'd take a percentage and couldn't believe their luck; a client who didn't understand the deal, either, and accepted everything he got told as par for the course; yes, it was true, a chance like this might not come again for years.

But surely Marcus could see it would end everything. He could have us do ten deals, do fifty, do them sensibly and cautiously, and make a lot more than a million. I didn't get it. Not that it mattered. Jason went through all my arguments, he told me, hammered them down Marcus's throat. I'd even laid out possibilities for the first half-dozen deals, worked out where we could get into them, how much we could get out. But Marcus wouldn't buy it.

Part of me didn't believe it. Literally. It wasn't like I thought Jason was lying, but maybe he hadn't explained it properly, maybe he hadn't understood what Marcus was saying. And then I saw it for myself, I took the lift down to four to grab Jason and try to shake a bit more fucking backbone into him, because the way he was talking he was about to cave and send us both to jail. I got out the lift and through the glass doors and stopped short, because Marcus was standing right next to Jason's desk and I was just close enough to hear what he was saying, which was "*This is the big one, Jason. You've pissed around on the little stuff too long. You need to do this.*"

I backed away and called Jason as soon as I got to my desk. He didn't sound good, but at least I knew why. I told him what I'd heard. It was pretty clear. I think that's when we started calling it the Big One. The way Jason told it, the Marcus I'd heard was the reasonable one, the one that showed his face in public. No anger, no threats. He saved that for the privacy of his office.

I couldn't see a way out. I hinted to Jason that maybe, this time, he could fly solo. I'd give him some ideas, sure, but he didn't need me on the calls. He waited till I'd finished and started on the usual, the pleas, the grasping at straws, the odds on getting caught. It was like he hadn't even heard me. And that was probably best, because maybe Jason could fly solo but this wasn't the deal I'd have picked for him to do it on. And if he did get caught – again – chances were I wouldn't be as lucky as I had been first time round. Marcus was unusual: he'd spotted the crime and swooped in to make something for himself. Most people wouldn't have thought of that, they'd just have kept on digging until they found some more names.

And those names would all be Alex Konninger, because I'd tried every trick I had to find out what happened to Marcus's share once it left our accounts, and all I'd got out of it was a big old fuck-all. If Jason was going to do the Big One, I might as well be doing it with him because I'd be screwed either way when it all went wrong.

The days went by and I kept on pushing back. Eventually even Marcus would see it was too late, I thought, but right up to the fortnight mark he was still pushing and pushing and nothing I told Jason to tell him seemed to get through.

And then it got delayed. Another six weeks, on top of the two we had left. Still tight, still crazy, only a little less so. I thought about it. If Marcus hadn't given up when we were only two weeks away, he wouldn't give up now. Eight weeks. Seven weeks, if I spent another week pushing and seeing if maybe, just maybe, he'd see sense.

And that was the funny thing. One more week. If Marcus had waited one more week, maybe if I'd told Jason, one more week, we'll try one more week and then fuck it, we'll do it, then none of this would have happened. Sure, we might have got caught. I still thought the chances were we would. But not till later, at least. Jason would have his job and he'd still be alive.

I hadn't told Jason because I didn't want to weaken him. I'd even started planning, looking into the services, the cashflows, figuring out which companies were fit to use and which had already put in more big-money reappearances than the Rolling Stones. I didn't tell Jason about that, either. I could see how it would go, if he knew he only had a week left to push back he'd hardly bother pushing at all. I needed him desperate.

The rest you know. Up to Monday, I'd never have believed it would happen, that Marcus would really go through with it. I thought either he'd see sense, or he'd carry on fighting till the week I'd given myself had passed by and he'd finally won. The idea that he'd just end it all and fire Jason that week, it hadn't even crossed my mind. But if the last couple of years have taught us anything, it's that bankers' predictions are worth less than the paper they don't have the guts to write them on.

Jason was history. And now, maybe, my past had caught up with me.

20: The Iago of Fixed Income

"Thanks for coming down. Take a seat."

He wasn't smiling. Marcus usually smiled. He didn't mean anything by it, it wasn't a sign that he liked you or wished you well, but I didn't like that it wasn't there. He was too formal. As I turned to the seat he'd pointed at, I saw why.

There was someone else in the room. Double, double toil and trouble. If *she* was here, there was only one way this conversation was going.

"Coffee?"

So she had another role, too. Coffee-maker. Coffee-maker and Witch. Witch, coffee-maker and career-breaker.

"Yes, please." I replied. Coffee, tea, eye of newt and toe of frog. I didn't want a coffee. But I needed something in my hand to stop it shaking.

It worked. I sat there in the moment of silence the coffee gave us, the gentle sip and sit back, and I wasn't shaking at all. I felt at ease. Stupid, I know, but I'd come in here expecting the worst anyway. Marcus's office wasn't like Russell's. He'd opted to stay on four with the troops, but if he wasn't going upstairs he'd made damned sure the mountain had come to Mohammed. The desk in front of me was solid wood, not veneer. The room was bigger. Even the carpet felt thicker, but surely I'd imagined that? Marcus's chair was behind the desk. Once I'd sat down, I couldn't even see the Witch. She was behind me, "observing".

Marcus started gently.

"There are a few things we need to discuss this morning, Alex."

"OK, fire away."

An unfortunate choice of words, but I didn't mind. I was more than at ease. I felt energised. If I was busted, I was busted, but in the meantime I might as well play my hand as well as I could and have fun while I was doing it.

"Let me cut to the chase. I've been in this business close to twenty years. And I have never, in all that time, seen anything as surprising as what I've seen this morning."

This wasn't quite what I'd been expected, but then Marcus could hardly come out with the truth. Not in front of the Witch. *I've been blackmailing your dead buddy and now I've found out you're involved too.* It wouldn't have gone down well with Human Resources.

I didn't say anything. They didn't seem to be expecting me to. Instead, the Witch stood, reached over me, and handed a thin blue file to Marcus. Uh-ho. By the pricking of my thumbs, something wicked this way comes.

Marcus opened the file and pulled out a couple of pages. He sat there, frowning, looking at them and shaking his head, like he'd never seen them before, like all this was news to him. And then he looked up at me and started talking, and given all the things I could have been in the shit for, this one came as a shock.

"Do you know how important to the firm this Mintrex deal is, Alex?"

Mintrex? What was he talking about Mintrex for? I nodded. I was taken aback, but he hadn't shaken my strange sense of ease.

"I read the papers this morning, so yeah, I guess I do now."

Marcus nodded.

"Good. You should know I've been talking to Billy D this morning. To say he's fucking furious would be an

242

understatement. Do you realise what you've done?"

I didn't, and the sense of ease was fading. I mean, I'd done a lot of things, many of them highly questionable, and I'd been intending to steal close to two hundred thousand pounds from some people who now turned out to be Billy's pet clients. But I hadn't done anything yet, your honour – or at least, not to Mintrex.

I think it was a rhetorical question, because Marcus went on without waiting.

"Do you recognise this?"

Well, yes. It was a Milton's comp slip, one of those bits of paper you shove in with a bundle of documents, your name scrawled in the corner, when you can't be arsed or don't have the time to write anything more.

"It's a comp slip."

"Look closer."

It was an *old* comp slip. There was no name on it, just a department reference, "Investment Banking", which is what our Financial Markets and Corporate Banking division had been called a while back. I couldn't even remember when – the names change every couple of years and no one ever really knows why.

There was a signature scrawled across the bottom right corner, and as I read it that sense of ease disappeared faster than yesterday's food and drink had this morning. Suddenly, I felt cold, hungover, terrified.

It was my name. "Alex Konninger", it said, clear as day. And underneath that, a handwritten message: "*items enclosed – you may find these useful.*" It didn't make sense. It looked real enough, even if I couldn't remember it. But how could something this old matter now?

Marcus was looking at me. I didn't think I was shaking, but I'm sure he could tell I wasn't feeling quite so relaxed. He smiled.

"As you're no doubt aware, this is one of three. The other agencies haven't sent theirs over but they assure me they have your name on them."

He paused for a moment, watching me. I couldn't think of anything to say. Even if I had, I'm not sure I'd have been able to get the words out. My tongue felt the size of a tennis ball.

"Yesterday afternoon we received a frantic call from your friend Ahmed. He couldn't get hold of you, of course, but I've taken a close personal interest in Mintrex, so I spoke to him myself."

Close personal interest. Christ, this guy was good. He'd have taken a close personal interest in the Crucifixion if it had gotten him a few brownie points with the Romans.

"Ahmed had just heard from Hardings." Hardings. One of the rating agencies, the one that had spotted the tax problem back on Monday. It was only a couple of days ago but it felt like another lifetime. "They told him they were pulling their rating. He couldn't understand why, and we promised to investigate. But we didn't need to. We got calls from all three of the agencies within the next hour and they all said the same thing: they'd re-examined the tail and they couldn't rate the deal."

"What?"

"Yes. They couldn't rate the deal. It wasn't that they'd have to re-examine the rating, or retranche it, delay things a little, anything like that. Just that they couldn't rate it. At all."

One word, four letters, all in capitals, hammering inside my whisky-bruised head.

SHIT.

Some genuinely professional part of me, a part I didn't even realise was there any more, was shocked. In spite of everything, I wanted this deal to work out. I know. Weird. Banker, fraudster, seducer, all-round egotist. And yet.

"But it's already priced. Why did they – why did they wait?"

I blurted out the first thing in my head and for the first time Marcus looked a little unsettled. I'd always known what was going on, whenever I came up with an alibi, but I guess genuine ignorance doesn't hurt either.

He stared at me. I suppose he'd thought I'd give up then and there.

"Yes, Alex. Very good. And indeed that's exactly what we thought. You'll believe me, I'm sure, when I tell you that I argued rather strongly with all of the agencies. I told them not to pull the rating, I told them that pulling it now would kill the deal, and I told them that wouldn't just hurt Mintrex."

Of course. Miltons had run the deal pretty much single-handed but if the shit hit the fan, you could be sure we'd be spreading it as far as we could. There were five banks and three agencies on the deal and none of them would get away clean.

"And as to why they'd waited, well, I think we can point to your little packages for that, Alex."

Again, I was at a loss. Marcus went on.

"Delivered by hand late Monday night to all three agencies, all identical, all with your signature on them. So do you mind explaining why you've chosen to fuck up the deal of the decade?"

And suddenly, he wasn't so calm. He wasn't sitting any more, he was standing, hands balled into fists ready to come smashing down on the desk. And even though the volume hadn't gone up a bit, the voice had turned into a low-pitched angry growl that had me thinking of campers and wildlife documentaries and the moment before the bear ripped some poor bastard's puny little head off.

In the circumstances, I was grateful for the Witch's presence. I was hunched up in the chair, looking at the man who looked like he was about to kill me, so I couldn't see her, but somehow I could feel she'd stood up herself. Whatever she was doing, it worked. Marcus sat back down and allowed himself a weary smile.

"So what, I wonder, could have caused the agencies to change their minds at the last minute? What could it have been, inside your little packages?"

I've never been so frustrated in my life. This one was definitely a rhetorical question, because I knew what was in the packages, and he knew I knew it. Except I didn't, and he was wrong, and there was nothing I could do about it. Innocent, and no alibi. I couldn't believe something like this could happen to me.

"Four things, Alex. As you know. One was the forecast we'd prepared with Mintrex for reserves and resources during the last few years of the deal." ("*We'd* prepared?" I liked that).

"Two was the notes on how the forecasts were prepared. Three was the minutes of the meetings of the planning committee at Mintrex. Of course all of these things had been sent to all three agencies before. But the fourth item, that was new. Again, *as you know.*"

He waited. I couldn't think what to do, so I shrugged, and regretted it straight away because it seemed a touch too couldn't-give-a-fuck for the situation I was in. Marcus shook his head and slid a single piece of paper across the desk to me. I picked it up and scanned it.

One sheet of A4. Six lines.

"The forecasts for reserves and resources are based on the stated assumption of 95% planning success (as demonstrated by the historic planning records), stressed to AAA.

The historic figure of 95% does not take into account those sites in relation to which it was decided internally that a planning application should not be made. If these are taken into account, the overall success rate for applications that are either considered internally, or actually made, falls to 38%, which cannot support the transaction."

It was pretty bald, but at least it was the truth. I'd had deals collapse on me before for worse reasons, because some idiot refused to listen to reason. I nearly smiled, and then I remembered where I was. The deal was dead, sure, but at least it had died because a bunch of idiots had suddenly had reason thrust upon them.

But who the hell had done the thrusting? Not me, that's for sure. I'd been in the pub Monday evening. I could count on one hand the number of people who knew the truth about the reserves calculations, about what we'd found when we dug through the planning committee minutes. And I couldn't see why any of those that did know would want to fuck the deal up and blame it on me.

Marcus was quiet, watching me reading the note, over and over, looking for a clue. I thought back to Monday night. Conference call. Everyone on it. And the end, just a few of us left.

And then it hit me.

Four beeps.

The end of the call. Me, Sergei, Joe and Ian. A little joke about the agencies not looking too closely at the tail.

Four people on the call, and four beeps when it ended.

But I was still on the line.

What I'd heard was the sound of four *other* people hanging up.

Sergei; Joe; Ian. And someone else. Someone who'd heard my little joke, and done a little digging, and then quietly gone about the business of destroying the deal, the takeover, my career.

He was still watching me. He probably expected me to deny everything. I could almost hear myself doing it, saying it, *it wasn't me, it must have been someone else*, but the words wouldn't come. I hadn't done it, but what difference did that make? I might as well have done. Marcus shook his head, slowly.

"I've been thinking, this morning. I've been scratching my head, Alex, and I still can't get rid of the itch, because for the life of me I can't imagine why you'd do something like this. What the hell was in it for you?"

Again, he paused. If I was going to say something, now was the time, but there wasn't anything to say.

"Was it about Jason? Did you really do it for Jason, brought the whole deal down just to get back at Miltons?"

I almost laughed. *This* was supposed to be the motive? Better just say there wasn't one, there isn't one, Alex Konninger's just the kind of guy who does stuff like this for no reason. The Iago of Fixed Income.

"Billy's furious. I've never seen him so angry, Alex. And now the press have got hold of the story."

He shook his head, and looked back down at his desk. The atmosphere had suddenly changed. He wasn't waiting for me to speak any more. He was looking at something else, some other papers, and for an instant a small part of me thought that was it, the whole thing was over, somehow I'd got away with it.

Just a small part, though. The rest of me wasn't that dumb.

Marcus looked back up.

"Incidentally, Alex, I hear you've offered to help out on the Primora default."

Oh. That's the trouble with lying: on the rare occasions you are innocent, it's difficult to remember the more common occasions you're not.

"Very kind of you. Of course the boys in legal had already made a start. They got a surprise there. Everyone did. We all thought Primora was covered. Silly us, eh? I asked someone to look back through the forms that went to Finance when the deal was done. And do you know, whoever signed those forms seemed quite certain that we'd be covered on Primora for as long as we needed to be. Who do you think that was?"

Well, if I could play dumb when I really was dumb, I might as well try it when I wasn't. In for a penny, as they say. I could see my defence taking shape, a huge, decade-long conspiracy, all centred around forging the Konninger signature. He who takes from me my good name. Not that it was that all good in the first place.

"Not playing, Alex? OK. That's fine. There are a lot of people here who remember that deal. I wouldn't think you'll get yourself out of the woods on this one just by keeping your mouth shut."

And he had a point, the fucker. I'd been expecting him to fire me because I wouldn't do the Big One. I'd been expecting him to use all those scams I'd pulled with Jason as the punchline, and I'd assumed he'd have to tread carefully, what with his own involvement, even if I couldn't prove it. But the guy seemed to have his hands full fighting off reasons to fire me. The way things were going, I wouldn't have been surprised to see JFK, Jimmy Hoffa and Shergar march into the office and point two fingers and a hoof at me.

"You'll need this," he said, and slid another set of papers across the desk. I didn't need to look down to know it was a copy of my infamous Alchemy checklist.

"Oh, and there's just one other thing."

There is? I thought, and then *Of course there is.* Marcus might have anything down there. For all I knew, the ghost of Christmas future was about to walk in and damn me for crimes I hadn't yet committed.

Two more bits of paper slid across the desk. I'd done OK so far, I thought. Sure, I was screwed, even I couldn't come up with an alibi, but at least I hadn't made it any easier for him. Until I did, because he was looking right at me when I glanced at the papers he was giving me, gaped, snapped my mouth shut, and tried to act like nothing had happened. You can lie your way through life and get away with it ninety-nine times out of a hundred, but it doesn't matter. One day you'll forget how to lie at all.

"These were picked up from your printer last night, Alex. You should have followed the clear desk policy."

He was enjoying himself.

I'd forgotten about them. Completely forgotten. I'd gone downstairs, seen Lorraine, Jessica, gone out, got drunk, made what might have been a terrible mistake with Liz – and I'd forgotten the last thing I'd done before I'd left my desk.

Those faked invoices. Sitting there on the printer until someone decided to figure out where they'd come from. I might as well have stuck a "Fire Me" sign on my back.

I didn't speak. There was nothing I could say, and it didn't look like I was expected to.

"Obviously, in the light of these developments, and some other matters that have come to light in the last week –"

I looked him hard in the face and nearly said something. *In the last week.* Lying bastard. But I kept my mouth shut. He frowned at me and went on.

" – we have good reason to suspect your involvement in at least one case of fraud against the bank's clients." He looked down, and then back up, but not at me, at something behind me. The Witch. He was into the formal part of the process. Needed to make sure he was doing everything right. Wouldn't want to screw up the firing with a procedural mistake. After the last year Marcus should have been an expert at this.

"We have concluded that we have grounds for your

summary dismissal. Given the circumstances, we would like you to collect your possessions and leave the building as soon as possible."

I could hardly complain.

"Don't forget to hand in your pass and your BlackBerry and any other bank property on your way out. You'll have a security guard with you to ensure you don't take anything you shouldn't."

Not much on my desk anyway. Never was one for souvenirs. No family photos. Just some booze.

"We're going have to report everything to the FSA. We'll also put these matters in the hands of the police."

For the second time in as many minutes my mouth fell open. Sure, Marcus had protected himself, we'd tried digging into his bank accounts ourselves and got nowhere. But I'd never expected this. When you're neck-deep, however well-hidden, calling in the police might be described as a little ballsy.

I decided to throw in a final comment. It wasn't like I had a lot to lose.

"I guess you're pleased about Jason?"

"What?"

"Oh come on. Don't pretend you haven't heard." (And then I remembered that Marcus hadn't been around when Jessica went looking for him. Maybe he really hadn't heard).

In which case I'd be delivering the news.

"Heard what?"

"Jason's dead."

I delivered the line, stood up and walked out of the office.

A few faces were looking my way as I stepped out. They'd seen the Witch on the floor, everyone would have known what was going on. Closer at hand, though, was something a lot bigger and more immediate. The Beast. He was waiting for me, I almost walked straight into him. I'd have bounced.

The guy stuck to me like a bad smell to old trainers the whole way across the floor. The people who'd been looking at me turned away. A sacking's like a car-crash. You want to see it, sure, but not close up. He squeezed in next to me in the lift and stayed by my side all the way to my desk. Someone had thoughtfully put a small cardboard box on my chair. He stood back and watched me, stone-faced, while I threw in some things. And the whole time, he didn't say a word. At least, not to me. After a couple of minutes, I looked up to see him walking away, over towards the lift lobby. Someone was standing there. The lobby at our level was shielded by a strip of frosted glass, I guess once upon a time the people who'd worked up here had needed their privacy more than we did, but it meant I couldn't see who it was the Beast was talking to. Height and hair colour said Marcus but it could have been any one of a hundred others. They exchanged a few words, no more than fifteen, twenty seconds, and then the Beast turned and rolled back to my desk.

I was done. BlackBerry, pass, the lot, all handed over. Russell was in his office, door shut. I could see Jane in there, shaking her head, not looking happy at all. Looked like decisions had been made. Anthony was leaning against a wall nearby, looking the same way I was. I couldn't make out his expression. No sign of Rachel, no one else around at all. That was it. There was nothing left for me to do.

Almost nothing. There was one thing left. And no reason not to.

"Anthony. Hope things work out for you."

He looked up. Hadn't noticed me. Didn't seem to know what to say.

"I'm off, Anthony. Good luck."

"Oh, yeah. You too."

He was grinning now, smug bastard. He'd got it. He'd got the fucking job.

"Oh, Anthony – one more thing."

His gaze had shifted again to Russell's office. As he reluctantly turned back towards me I drew back my fist and delivered a sharp crack to his left cheek-bone. Bruised rather than broken, I'd imagine. My hand hurt. His face would hurt more.

I turned to the Beast, who'd watched the whole thing from three feet away without the slightest alteration in his expression.

"OK. Let's go."

21: It Never Rains But It Pours

Wednesday 16th December, 2009
11:00am

Walking down the street in the City with a cardboard box is a strange and horrible experience. Everyone who sees you knows what's happened. You've been fired. If you'd planned this, you'd have come up with a better way to get your stuff home. They see you alone, jobless, miserable, and what do they do to make you feel better? Nothing. Nada. Fuck all. Most of them look away, look at anything rather than meet your eye. The way they see it, you're lower than the guy selling *Big Issue* down the road.

But the ones who avoided me were the good ones. There were others, and you'll love this, who pointed and laughed. It happened three times, and every time the laughter came from a group of young men in suits. I might have understood if they were builders or couriers or cabbies, real people with a real grudge against City boys like me. But these *were* City boys, bankers or lawyers themselves, laughing at one of their own as he fell off the gravy train and into the sewers.

Lovely people, as my old nan used to say.

I did get one break. The girl at the Starbucks stand. I didn't know her name, she didn't know mine. She was Starbucks girl, Polish or Russian or Lithuanian. I was espresso man. She called out as I strolled past. What the hell. It wasn't like there was anywhere I had to be.

"Hi."

"Hi yourself. Why you carrying a box?"

I was stunned. Someone didn't know. Someone who hadn't watched all the gleeful live footage of Sterlings going down, TV crews waiting outside to ambush the miserable bastards walking out with their boxes and their bags and no jobs any more.

"They fired me. This is all my stuff."

"They fired you? I am sorry. Here."

There. A coffee. A double espresso, a gift from someone who earned less in a year than I'd have made in a good week.

No one looked at me on the Tube, no one said a word, but that was probably just the Tube, and nothing to do with the box. I was glad when I finally got to my door. It was unlocked, and I was surprised until I remembered what I'd left in there this morning.

She'd made it out of bed, at least. She'd even got dressed. But yesterday's clothes weren't looking good. And on an average morning Liz might be one of those girls that doesn't need make-up, but after a night like we'd had, *anyone* would have needed make-up. I could have done with some myself.

She was in the kitchen, trying to engage with the coffee machine and not getting very far. She looked surprised to see me back already, but I guess her brain was still sleeping off the whisky, because I managed to fend off any questions with a wave of the hand and a "nothing to worry about." The Liz I knew wouldn't have been put off that easily, but that was fine by me. I wasn't in the mood to talk.

I didn't bother explaining the coffee machine again. I steered her to a chair and made her a strong americano. While she drank it I returned to the bedroom. There was a drawer, I hadn't opened it for a long time. Jasmine's "things", for when she stayed over. Bottles of stuff that meant nothing to me even when I read what you were supposed to do with it, some make-up, some bath stuff. I got the bath running, put it all in Liz's arms, and left her to it.

While she was soaking, I dug out some of Jasmine's old clothes. Underwear in the drawer and a couple of dresses and skirts and tops hanging up. The stuff didn't look cheap, but it wouldn't have been her style to come back for it. None of it was what you'd call sober-business-wear, but it had to be better than the clothes Liz had been wearing yesterday. We hadn't exactly been in the mood to fold things neatly away. I hoped Jasmine's gear would fit. She was a big girl, but she liked things tight.

I laid out all the stuff on the bed and got myself changed. I was unemployed now. I knew it hadn't hit me yet, what it meant, but that was fine, because right now I couldn't think past today and what clothes I should be wearing. Jeans and a T shirt, I decided. I knocked on the bathroom door and asked Liz if she was OK.

"Yes, thanks. Much better for the bath. Thanks."

She sounded better.

"Good to hear it. Fancy something to eat when you're out?"

A few seconds' silence while she thought about it. About what she was going to do now.

"Yeah, maybe. I should get to work. Or home. Or something. But another hour won't hurt."

"OK. There's some clothes on the bed. I don't know if they're the right size, but you might as well take a look."

"Thanks, Alex. Oh, a package came while you were out. It's on the kitchen table."

So it was. A tall cardboard box with a logo I knew only too well. I tore it open and freed the contents: a 35-year old Spey that Jason and I had tasted last time we'd been at the club. A scrap of paper – "Merry Christmas mate. All the best, Jason." It had been a good drink, I thought. Must have set him back close to two hundred quid. I'd raise a glass to him later. Which reminded me I still hadn't spoken to Sally.

I tried her again, and again got no answer. Which was better than a mouthful of abuse, I suppose.

The whisky brought back something else Jason had left me. The flash drive. I unpacked the laptop onto the kitchen island, booted it up and plugged the drive in.

I couldn't think why he'd kept this stuff at work, but after everything else that had happened over the last couple of days, I wasn't surprised to see it. Everything was there. All the invoices, all the cashflows, all the bank accounts, layer after layer, all the companies we'd created. If he'd been planning on blackmailing himself, he had everything he needed right there.

I'd been looking through it for fifteen minutes when I heard footsteps behind me. She spoke before I had a chance to turn round.

"What the fuck is this?"

Now I had turned.

"What?"

"This. In my hand. It was on your bed. What are you doing with this?"

The first thing I noticed was that the clothes fit perfectly. You'd never have known they weren't hers.

The second thing was that she looked angry. When I'd come back to find her engaged in a battle of wills with the coffee machine, the coffee machine had been winning. There'd been nothing there, nothing behind the eyes. There was now, and it looked like it wanted me dead. I found myself backing up to the kitchen island.

The third thing was that she was holding some papers. The papers Marcus had given me. I don't know how far she'd got, and the Mintrex stuff wouldn't have meant a lot to her anyway. But the document sitting right at the top was the last thing I wanted her to see. The Alchemy checklist.

I didn't have much time to think. I went for disarming.

"You look fantastic. A hell of a lot better than this morning, right? Don't worry about the files, just some stuff Compliance wanted me to have a look at."

Compliance might have been useful. No one really knew what they did, after all. But it was too late for disarming.

She'd stepped closer. The eyes still looked like I didn't want to know what was going on behind them. She spoke slowly.

"Do you think I'm fucking stupid, Alex?"

There's never a good time to get asked that question. I shook my head.

"I can see what the form is, Alex. And I'm not a fucking goldfish."

I couldn't think what a goldfish had to do with anything. I worried, for a moment, that she was cracking up, and at the same time it occurred to me there were knives in the kitchen, there was gas, there was glass. Then I realised what she meant. She had a memory. She remembered Alchemy. She remembered what I'd told her.

If disarming wasn't going to work, maybe aggression would be better.

"If you can see what it is then what the hell do you want me to say?"

"Just tell me. Why did you sign this?"

I had to remember to keep the aggression going.

"Why? Do you remember crying your fucking eyes out because you thought the deal was dead? Boo fucking hoo. And you couldn't do a thing about it. But then suddenly the problem was gone. Yes. I signed it. I lied. I got the deal done, and you got to stop crying. What the fuck did you think I'd done, rewritten the rulebook?"

Aggression worked. The fight dropped out of her instantly, like a machine shutting down. She looked beaten. She was beaten.

"No. I didn't. I didn't know. But I never thought it

could be something like this."

She was close to tears. I felt horrible. She'd been in the business all this time and she still didn't know the rules of the game. She took a step back, and I followed, closing the distance between us. Her head was down. I put out my arm, touched her shoulder, and she shook it off. She might have wanted comfort but she didn't want it from me. We were silent, both of us, for a moment. I could hear my own heart beating, her breathing, the buzz of the fridge, cars going by outside. And then she spoke again.

"You should have told me."

She was quiet, calm. I nodded, but she was still looking down, at the floor, at the tiles that would have cost the Starbucks girl half a year's salary. She carried on.

"Are you seriously saying you did this for me?"

She looked back up now. The murder was gone from her eyes, but so was the defeat. There was an answer, the answer was yes, I had done it for her, but it didn't seem the right thing to say. I kept my mouth shut.

"No way." She was still calm, but a little louder, a little faster. "If you knew a thing about me you'd have known I'd never have wanted you to – to do this." She thrust the papers at me in disgust. "You'd have told me what you had in mind, and I'd have told you I'd rather lose the deal."

I wanted to interrupt. I didn't believe her. Or maybe I just didn't want to believe her. I'd thought she was like me, I'd assumed everyone was like me, maybe not as dirty, but hardly clean. She was getting louder.

"What the hell have you done? You lied to everyone, to me, the bank, the investors. For one fucking deal. You idiot. You fucking idiot. How can you pretend you did this to help me?"

By the end she was shouting. She'd got her fight back. If it hadn't been me she was fighting, I'd have been cheering her on.

I had nothing to come back with. She was right. Sure, she could have asked a few more questions. But why should she? I'd told her everything was OK, we were friends, we trusted each other. One of us was a liar and the other one didn't know it, that was all. I stood there with my mouth open like the fucking idiot she'd called me, and I watched as she marched out of the kitchen and into the bedroom, grabbed her handbag, and stormed right out of the flat.

There was no point in saying anything. No point in following. She was right.

Now, you might think that given what I'd just been through, the next thing I decided to do was stupid. Myself, I'd rather see it as thinking of others, putting someone else's feelings first. But to be honest, it was probably not thinking at all.

I called Sally again.

And this time she answered.

She didn't shout at me. I don't know what I'd have done if she had.

I said her name. "Sally," I said, and I didn't get any further.

"Why did you do it?" she asked.

I didn't understand.

"Sally, what do you mean?"

"Why, Alex?"

And so it went – round and round in circles. I didn't understand her, she wasn't listening to me.

It ended as it had to, when she'd finally had enough of the circles. Quiet. No shouting, no drama. Just weary.

"Go to hell, Alex. Don't call me again."

Jason was dead. His widow wasn't speaking to me. I'd lost my job. The married woman I'd fucked the night before had stormed out of my flat as angry as I'd ever seen her. What do you do at a time like this?

You drink, of course. And when you've got a decent bottle of Scotch, 60% ABV, sitting there right in front of you, you don't think too long about what it is you're going to be drinking. I carried on looking through the flash drive, trying to find something that might explain Sally's question, but all I could see was more of the same. After a couple of glasses I couldn't see much at all. I switched off the laptop, put some Cowboy Junkies on the stereo, and poured myself another glass. A big one. And then I poured another one, raised it, and toasted my absent friend.

Now, there's nothing more boring than a man sitting alone, at home, drinking. Maybe in a movie, with the right lighting and the right music, it might work for a minute, but not in real life. I reckon I'm a pretty interesting guy, and my thoughts, even blurred, were probably fascinating, but I wouldn't give you the detail even if I could remember it. A bit of self-pity, a bit of self-reproach, the odd sideways drift into Liz and last night, sorrow for Liz, sorrow for Sally, sorrow for Jason, a bit of anger with the three of them, and then a lot of anger with Marcus.

At a certain point I stopped thinking about what had happened and feeling angry and sorry and started trying to work out what to do. It might have been a good idea to do that in the first place, but by this time I was drunk, and what I decided was that I was going to the Christmas drinks. Sure, I'd been fired, the police were involved, chances were no one would want to see me there, but I didn't care. I hadn't missed the drinks since I'd first arrived at Head Office and I didn't plan on missing them now.

My team (my old team, I had to remind myself) would be at the tail-end of lunch by now. I wasn't sure who'd be there, though. Russell, no doubt, presiding over his final banquet. But Jane? Rachel? If Anthony had got the job chances were he'd find himself sitting down to a half-empty table. With a bruised cheek, I reminded myself. No, the others would be there. The job wouldn't matter tonight. They'd eat and drink and act like they didn't hate each other, for one night, and tomorrow the shit would fly again. I wondered what Russell would have told them about me. Maybe they'd be raising their own toast to an absent friend. They'd be drunk, anyway, and hopefully more cheerfully drunk than I was. It was a steak place, a good one, but the meal would be over and they'd be having a last few drinks before the next stage.

After lunch, a whole fucking regiment of bankers would meet up. Six o' clock, some bar, in Shoreditch, I thought. I hadn't taken note of the name, I'd assumed I'd be lurching around with everyone else and we'd get there in the end. But before six, in that limbo between lunch and drinks, no one would be heading back to the office. They'd find a bar somewhere and settle in. Somewhere near the steak place. They'd be drunk, and they'd be loud. They wouldn't be difficult to find.

I was out of the apartment and halfway to the tube before I turned around and headed back. The bottle. I didn't have a job and the police probably had my name on a list by now. After everything else, drinking in public couldn't make things any worse.

22: Bad Language, Drink and Violence. At last.

Wednesday 16th December, 2009
3:30pm

I hadn't found them yet. All I'd found was that swigging from a bottle on the street in broad daylight (alright then, dusk) wasn't too different from walking round the City with a cardboard box. No one wanted to be my friend. I'd like to have pointed what it was I was drinking, the quality, *this isn't meths, you know*, but I don't think it would have made much difference. Apparently if you're a frightening, lurching drunk, no one really cares how much it cost to get you there.

If the street wasn't welcoming, hopefully the Nightingale would be kinder. I got myself a pint and a table and sat quietly, drinking, alone. The bottle was under the table, hidden in a Tesco's bag I'd found in the street. It was fairly busy, still a little early, but no one except me wanted to sit right outside the door to the men's toilet. I didn't recognise any of the other drinkers.

Correction. There, in the corner by the quiz machine, a small group from legal. I knew a couple of them by name, recognised one other. Unlikely they'd have heard about this morning.

"Hi guys."

They looked over, three men, two women. But they didn't move. I caught a muttered "Hi Alex," but nothing more, and that from about ten feet away. I was drunk, sure, but I didn't smell that bad. Not yet, anyway. I guessed they had heard something after all. It would have been one of those sweaty little bastards in legal who'd have spotted the problems on Primora. Yeah, they'd have known. They'd have known before I did.

Returned to my pint. It was halfway gone when my phone rang. It was an old phone and I rarely used it, but I'd been relieved of the one I did use by the Beast from security. I didn't recognise the number.

"Hello?"

"Hi, is that Alex Konninger?"

I didn't recognise the voice, either; I could hardly hear it. Too much noise in the Nightingale.

"Hang on, let me just step outside. I can't hear you."

"Hello?"

"That's better. Yes, this is Alex. Who's that?"

I did recognise the voice – I'd heard it recently – but couldn't quite fit a name to it.

"Alex, it's Grace. From Greenings."

Oh. Yes. Of course. What the hell did she want? She sounded quite perky.

"Hi Grace. What's up?"

"Alex, I just wanted to offer my commiserations."

Legal was one thing, but Greenings? How the hell did she know?

"I heard about this morning. And all that stuff with the agencies. Such a shame."

"Hang on - Grace?"

"Yes?"

Things were starting to coalesce in my brain. Dark, jelly-like masses of information were coming together, slowly, like drifting continents. But the booze wasn't helping.

"What did you hear? How – how did you hear?"

"Oh, you know. I heard about your job. That you lost it. And the agencies, and the tail, and pulling the ratings. Such a shame"

"But how did you hear?"

"Oh, you know how these things happen. Of course it's

a disaster for the bid. I don't see how they can do it at all now. It's dead, I suppose."

She was still talking, wittering on about the deal, but there was something there, just out of reach. An idea. How had she heard? What did she know?

"And of course I know your chums at Miltons really wanted this mandate, but really, I can't help thinking that Graham would have been a *much* better choice."

Graham? What the hell did Graham have to do with anything?

"But, well, now your bid's dead, Orresco's in play, isn't it? They won't be able to fend off a buyer forever. Or maybe someone'll take a look at Mintrex, now they've shown themselves to be weak, right? So I suppose Graham will get a mandate after all."

It might have been the drink, but I couldn't see where she was heading with this.

"But as to why the agencies decided to take that second look at the last minute, well, that *is* a mystery, isn't it?"

I didn't say anything. I could see it now, or almost see it. The continents were getting closer.

"Yaar?"

Asia slammed into Europe. The data fizzed, reshaped itself and came out suddenly clear.

"You bitch. You fucking bitch."

"I'm sorry, Alex? What's wrong?"

She was gloating. She'd been the one. She'd been lurking there, throughout the call on Monday night, quietly waiting for something. I doubt she even knew what she was hoping to get, she couldn't have imagined I'd hand it to her on a plate. She could kill the deal, get her own back on me, and maybe something for her bastard of a husband. She was right. If anyone was interested in Orresco or Mintrex now, they wouldn't look at Miltons. They'd go straight to

Graham.

Now those old comp slips made sense, too. I'd shoved them in with the packages I sent to her office all those years ago. What kind of person would have kept them all this time?

"You bitch."

"I'm so sorry Alex. I'm not sure I understand. But I hope everything turns out OK for you."

"Fucking bitch." I looked around. I was standing just outside the pub, but I was shouting at my phone and the people inside were looking at me and then quickly away. Before, I'd just been a drunk, and even then no one wanted to talk to me. Now I was an angry and possibly violent drunk, no one was even risking eye contact.

There was no point going on. I knew everything I needed to know, now, and anything else would just make me angrier. I ended the call and turned off the phone .

The Nightingale wasn't so welcoming any more. Another venue was called for. I hadn't even figured out where I was going, and there was another familiar face. Walter, and he'd seen me.

"Alex!" came the bellow from across the street. He bounded over. Arm on my shoulder, shake of the hand, shake of the head.

"So sorry to hear you'd got the chop, Alex. Now I don't know why, and nor would I care to, but I'm sure you'll land on your feet."

Walter wasn't in Finance any more; he'd landed yet another plum role "managing" a new, important team doing something strategic that I didn't understand and he probably didn't either. But even if he had still been in Finance, he'd never have understood why I'd been fired, wouldn't have realised it was all about him and his team and their bastard checklist with its bastard boxes. But at least he was wishing me well, which made a nice change from everyone else.

"Thanks Walter."

"Got to dash. Have a lovely Christmas."

Next stop was the King's Arms. The Kings was a dirty little pit a half mile further south, and probably out of range for the Miltons mob. I wanted to see them, sure, but not right now.

I was sitting on a stool at the bar. The bottle was still in the Tesco's bag; I'd put it on the floor when I sat down, trying not to be too obvious, and then I'd looked around and remembered where I was and put it on the bar in front of me. As long as I wasn't actually drinking it, I wouldn't be too out of place here. The phone started ringing again and I pulled it out of my pocket and stared at it.

I was sure I'd switched it off. But it turned out I'd just changed the ring-tone. Some Coldplay track that had been all the rage back when I was actually using the thing.

The staring went on so long the ringing stopped.

Good. Whoever it was, they could wait. And if it was Grace again, she'd be waiting a long, long time.

I'd just settled back down to another beer when it started ringing again. It wasn't Grace again, as it happened, it was some other number I didn't recognise. A mobile. Twice, on this old phone, in just half an hour, that was some kind of luck. Whether it was good or bad luck was another matter, but bad was edging it so far.

I didn't even have time to say my name.

"Konninger?"

"Yup."

"I'm going to break your fucking neck."

Bad. Definitely bad. There was no mistaking the hoarse, impatient bark, and it didn't take a sober genius to figure out what he was talking about.

"Hello Michael."

Michael was Liz's husband. I'd only met him a couple of times, most recently at their wedding back at the end of summer. He ran a hedge fund, which had made him a multi-millionaire before he was forty. He was six five and built like a wall. His army chums called him Mickey Mouse. He'd served six years with the SAS. And he was threatening me with violence.

"I'm going to break your fucking neck, Konninger."

"I heard you the first time, Mick. Look, don't be an idiot. What's she told you?"

I could give as good as I got. As long as I was drunk and he wasn't actually standing there.

"I know what happened. Don't you worry, she'll get hers. But I'm not going to break her neck. Just yours."

"Calm down, you moron. These things happen. I'm very sorry. I'm sure Liz is too. If you love her-"

I didn't get a chance to finish.

"You think I give a fuck whether you're sorry? You think I give a fuck whether she is? She can't keep her knickers on, she's history. End of story."

So maybe *if you love her* wasn't the right approach. But half a ton of angry soldier didn't really frighten me right now, not with everything else I had to deal with. And if this was the way he reacted to a little slip, then maybe I'd done her a favour. She really didn't have much luck with her lovers, did Liz. I've said it before: her taste in men is shit.

"Michael. You're being a cock. You do realise that, don't you?"

"Listen to me Konninger. You don't know what I'm like when I'm angry –"

Now it was my turn to interrupt.

"Like a big scary mouse, I'm sure. Look. She fucked up. I fucked up. It's all a terrible, drunken mistake. If you can't figure that out then you're even more of an idiot than you look."

He wasn't an idiot, as it happened. But he certainly looked like one, the great big lump of meat.

Call over. I wasn't getting anything out of it, so I might as well kill it. And this time, I made sure I switched the thing off.

I sat back down. I hadn't even realised I was standing. My beer was still there, the bottle was in the bag, no one was staring at me. I'd kept my cool this time.

There was a table behind me, unoccupied, with an Evening Standard open at the business pages. I reached over and grabbed it. Late afternoon edition, and a great headline to accompany my misery:

"Orresco Sell-Off Weighs On Stock Markets"

There was a smaller sub-heading below:

"How Milton Shearings turned gold into lead."

The article skirted around precisely why our deal had failed, citing vague "investor concern". But the story was pretty clear from there. The bid was dead. Orresco shares had crashed, as you'd expect, and everyone, everywhere, had started to panic. International stock markets down three per cent and the only reason anyone could give was Orresco. Should have felt a twinge of pride, really. All my own doing. With a little help from my enemies. Turned out I could do more damage than a couple of days' delay after all.

I read the article, slowly, and then tried to read it again. I got halfway through and gave up. By now I was starting to feel very drunk. People. What I needed was people, friends, my old friends from Miltons. They'd understand. They'd help me. I had to find them. They could have some of my lovely whisky.

It was dark out. I hadn't expected that and for some reason I didn't like it. I needed to catch my breath. I leaned against the glass window of the estate agent opposite. Take a breath. Feeling a bit sick now.

Not sure how long I stayed there. I felt better, a little. Well enough to get moving. Stiffen the sinews, summon up the blood. One foot in front of the other. Keep going. Onto Bishopsgate. Easier now, hundreds of people around. Most of them drunk. Lurching not really a problem. Lots of shouting, laughing, the traditional sounds of December in the City.

Some of the shouting was angry shouting, and that wasn't so unusual, either. But the voices were familiar. There was a small crowd gathered round the entrance to one of those little arcades that sprout like tumours off the end of City side streets. I edged my way through it.

"Do you think you're the only one with friends at Greenings?"

The voice seemed calm, but the edge of contempt was unmistakeable. Jane.

"I don't know what you're talking about."

Anthony. He drawled the words, slowly, lazily, like he wasn't really sure why he was bothering to reply at all. Sounded drunk, but not too drunk. Still some way off my state.

"Don't bother, Anthony. I know all about it. I know it was you."

I could see them now. There were a few others from the team in the crowd, but no one seemed to be thinking about getting between them, getting them away from each other. Anthony was quiet, but only briefly. Anthony was never quiet for long.

"They were on the deal, Jane."

"Don't give me that shit, Anthony. This was confidential stuff. Us, the agencies, the lawyers, the client. There was no reason any of the other banks had to know. And you, you little bastard, you *weren't* on the deal. But you still went and fucked it up, didn't you?"

"Sorry Jane. Don't know what you're talking about."

Anthony turned around, turned his back on her, made to walk away. He didn't get very far. Jane's hand fell on his shoulder. It was just a touch, a gentle touch, but I could see him flinch like her hand was ice.

"The swaps, Anthony."

He'd turned again, and he was trying to look blank, but he wasn't very good at it. Amateur. Most of what I could see was blurry but even I could see it, the guilty dismay that passed across his face before he remembered to look dumb.

"The swaps. The little problem we had with the swaps, Anthony. And Greenings prowling around, smelling raw meat. They wouldn't have been prowling unless someone had told them about the meat, would they?"

It hadn't made sense, this conversation, but now, suddenly, it did. I remembered Monday, that message from Grace. She'd started the whole thing, not me, I'd forgotten that detail. She'd called to see if she could slide in and take our swaps away, and I'd wondered how she'd even known they were there to be taken, but there was too much other stuff going on to really care. Someone had failed to keep their mouth shut, that was obvious. And Anthony hanging around my desk, the Bloodsucker, asking to "pick my brains". Even in the state I was in I could put the pieces together, Grace, Graham, Greenings, and now Anthony. Sold us out? The bastard had sold *me* out. I felt better about hitting him earlier.

Anthony changed tack. Didn't bother denying it.

"So what? Don't tell me you wouldn't have done exactly the same thing."

"No, Anthony. I wouldn't. I'm not like you. And by the way, there's one more thing."

Anthony was grinning at her now, the piece of shit. I edged closer. I'm not a violent man but I really wanted to hit him again, harder.

"Yeah?"

"Yes. You're fired."

I didn't understand. Sure, Anthony had fucked up. But he'd got the job – that's how I'd read things earlier, anyway. I couldn't see how it was Jane doing the firing. Nor could Anthony.

"You're firing me?"

She nodded. He shook his head.

"I don't think so, dear. You'd have to be head of the team to fire me, and, well, you're not."

"*Dear*". He'd called Jane "*dear*". I couldn't stand the guy but he had some balls. I'd seen Jane angry before and it wasn't something I'd ever wanted to be on the end of. I waited for the explosion. But all she did was step back and smile at him.

"What? What are you smiling at?"

"So who *is* head of the team, Anthony?"

"Well, now Russell's gone, it's Rachel."

WHAT?

I nearly shouted it out loud. Rachel! Rachel had taken over the team! Sneaky bitch! I hadn't even realised she was in the running. Well, good for her. I took a quick look round the group. They hadn't even noticed me, too busy watching the real action. None of them looked surprised. Everyone knew.

Jane was still talking, still calm.

"But Russell isn't taking the job upstairs. You know that, don't you?"

Anthony shrugged. Didn't really seem to care.

"Do you know what that job was, Anthony?"

He shrugged again.

"New tier. Rachel's boss. Your boss's boss."

"So?"

"So guess who's taking that job now."

Anthony didn't say a word. Didn't need to, you could

see it all in his face. Smug was gone. He looked surprised, and angry. Jane continued.

"So, like I said, you're fired, *dear*."

It was too much for Anthony. His face was all screwed up, and I'd never noticed it before, but when he was upset he looked a lot like a pig. He made a noise, I suppose it was a roar, but with that pig image in my head all I could hear was a grunt. I saw his arm go back and thought *Christ, he's going to hit her*. He was a prick, everyone knew that, but I'd never have expected this.

I was drunk and wasting time thinking. Jane wasn't. I blinked, and Anthony was gone. Not gone, just down. On the ground. Blood coming out of his nose. I had a vague memory about Jane, it wasn't all polo and regattas, she did fencing and karate too. I guessed Anthony didn't know that.

Anthony gone. Rachel running the team. And Jane moving upstairs. They'd do well, both of them. At least some things had been left in good hands. Still, nothing to do with me. The whole Christmas party idea wasn't as appealing as it had been a few hours ago. Time for me to be on my way.

Passed a news stand. Headlines on the big white box.

"*Mintrex House of Cards Tumbles Down to Earth.*"

Not quite as punchy as the earlier story, but I guess they had to ring the changes.

And another headline, on the other side of the box.

"*Banker's Death Not An Accident, Say Police.*"

I stopped dead. Someone bumped into me from behind, muttered "Look where you're fucking going" and shoved me as they barged past. I didn't care. Walked over to the stand. The papers were sitting on top. Vendor eying me nervously: what was this drunk going to do? Same paper as earlier, later edition, new front page. There was the headline, I read it again just to be sure: "*Banker's Death Not*

An Accident, Say Police." Subheading below, *"New Developments in Station Death Enquiry."* And a picture, taking up almost half the page, of the mob at the station on the morning Jason died. Must have come from someone's phone.

Pretty much the same view as I'd had fighting my way out the station. Almost exactly the same, in fact: must have been taken by someone just in front of me. There was the Beast at the top of the stairs. Looking round, half-facing the camera, looking fucking terrified, like he'd get out or die trying.

Not an accident.

The Beast. At the station. Marcus's own rottweiler. Not one of our usual security team. Never seen him before this week.

Why had Marcus let Jason go? Not fired him, but literally: "let him go". Jason could talk. Jason could bury him.

Not now he couldn't. Marcus hadn't let him go very far.

Why was Jason even there that morning? Had Marcus called him in? Maybe suggested they could work things out after all? He could have said anything, just to get Jason where he wanted him.

Not an accident.

I walked over and tried to read the words, but they were too small, too blurry, they wouldn't keep still. I didn't need to read the words. It was obvious what had happened.

And then after I'd been fired: Marcus, up on my floor, behind the frosted glass, talking to the Beast. What were they talking about?

Another accident. Another not-accident.

The Beast. He'd killed Jason. He'd pushed him under a train. Jason was a threat. And now I was a threat.

I'm watching you, Konninger.

They were coming after me.

They were all coming after me. Michael was going to break my neck. But he'd have to get there fast, because Marcus and the Beast were going to push me under a train. Or a bus. Or a car. They were going to kill me.

I ran. I turned and ran and didn't get more than four steps before I was brought up short by a wall of people walking across me, shouting at me, "*Get out of the way*", "*Look where you're going*", "*Wanker*".

Don't care. Got to get through. Push through. Got to get away. Too close to Miltons. Too many cars and buses and taxis.

I heard someone shout behind me. "Hey!"

Shouting at me? I risked a look back. No. Just drunk people, more drunk people. I wasn't running now, I was walking, but fast. And then I was on the ground. I didn't think I'd been hit. I couldn't feel anything. I lifted myself and looked around. I'd tripped. There was a drunk girl on the pavement beside me, being sick. I'd tripped over her. There were people watching. She was still being sick. I didn't have time to stop.

I kept going. Another busy road but something told me I needed to get across it. Don't wait for traffic lights. Get across the road. Cars hooting. Don't care. Across the road. Side street. Quieter here. Dark enough to hide.

I stopped. If I could hide there, someone else could, too. I backed up to the nearest wall, a tiny office next to a newsagent. The newsagent was open and its light glowed yellow on a two-foot strip of slushy pavement outside. I had to think.

Where was I going? How could I get there?

It got darker, suddenly, and I realised there was more light, or had been, leaking from the main street. But now that light was out. There was someone else on the street, blocking out the light, walking toward me. Someone big.

Not Beast big, but big enough.

Michael. It's Michael. He's found me.

I was still standing with my back to the wall, in the darkness. The figure walked past and didn't even see me. It wasn't Michael. It wasn't anyone big. It wasn't even a man, it was a woman, no one I knew, no one to be afraid of.

I pushed myself away from the wall and started walking, and straight away I was on the ground again. Cold, and wet. I'd slipped on the ice, landed on my side, and it hurt, but not too much. I got up and reminded myself to be careful. Ice makes for a handy accident.

I was moving but I didn't know where. *Marcus knows where I live.* I didn't like the quiet and darkness ahead. And I didn't like the crowds either. *Jason was killed in a crowd.*

There was a junction, a bigger road, and without thinking I turned down it. Lights here, orange and red. I knew this place. Known it forever. Crowds, but not too many. No shadows. They'd never look for me here. And I suddenly realised I was starving. Hand in pocket. Nothing there.

Where the fuck is my wallet? I thought back. The pub. The Kings. I couldn't go back there, too open, too dangerous. And I'd used my phone there. Could they track me? Was that real? Michael was ex-SAS. He could do it.

Yes! A coin. One pound. Another coin, another pound. Hamburger. No, cheeseburger.

"How much? OK, two cheeseburgers."

"Thanks."

"No it's OK I'm fine."

"Slippery floor."

"Wet. Ice outside."

"Really, I'm fine."

I looked downstairs. Too quiet. Could get cornered and no one would see. Upstairs. More light, more people, but not too many. Better.

The side of my face felt warm. I touched it. Wet. My hand had red on it.

Have they got me?

I stood up and looked around. I didn't recognise anyone and none of them were looking at me. I sat and tried to calm myself down. I'd fallen over, a couple of times. Just cut my face. That's all.

Good burgers. Very good. I felt stronger, like I could carry on further, as far as I needed to. They wouldn't get me, not if I kept going. There was a strange lump in the Tesco's bag. Yes! My wallet. Things were looking up. I took the bottle out and looked at it. Not a lot left. I felt like celebrating. I was still alive and I had my wallet. One quick swig. No one would mind.

A pressure on my arm. A hand on my shoulder. *Have they found me?*

"Excuse me sir I think you'd better leave."

A young kid. Can't be more than eighteen. I could explain.

"No, see, I've had burgers. Here. Here's the wrappers. Two cheeseburgers. And if I go outside someone will try to kill me."

"Out"

He looked serious. The pressure got stronger. *Better do what he says.*

I was only just out the door when it hit me, where to go.

Out of London.

North. Kings Cross or Euston would get me there, now I had my wallet.

They'd never guess. Might even give up. Might think I wasn't worth it any more.

One step at a time.

Outside, in the dark, streetlights, traffic lights, still too many people and still too many shadows. Smell of beer and vomit. More shouting, and I'm fucking shivering. But warm in the pit of my stomach, two burgers to the good. I knew where I was. I'd crossed this road a thousand times.

There's a crowd of men on the other side. Why are they waiting? Who are they waiting for?

One of them's bigger than the others. Much bigger. Standing there right under the traffic light, face glowing green. Waiting.

Perfectly round face, short, thinning brown hair, tiny little brown eyes, boxer's nose. He's here.

And everything is clear. I know why they're waiting. I know who they're waiting for.

I have one weapon and one chance.

Get him before he gets me.

Keep walking, straight ahead, and then turn suddenly so I'm right in front of him.

I look at him. He looks at me. He seems surprised. He will be.

Swing. Up goes the Tesco's bag.

Whoosh. Down goes the bottle. He's watching the whole thing like it's happening to someone else. At the moment of impact, maybe just before, those little brown eyes widen like he's suddenly realised it's not, it's happening to him. I know those eyes. I've seen them on someone else. Where have I seen those fucking eyes before?

Crack. Hard, on his forehead and the bridge of his nose. He falls to the ground, face-first. Doesn't even have time to put his hands out. Makes no sound. Now's my chance. Turn. Run.

Make about two paces before I find myself on the ground too. Stretched out on the pavement on my belly like a worm. Can't get up – weight on my legs. Someone kneeling. His friends. Are they going to kill me? Can't. Not now. Not here. Too public. What will they do?

My head hurts and I think I'm going to be sick. People

are shouting, at me, at each other. Flashing lights, loud noises.

A little later. I don't remember what happened but I'm in a van. It's a police van. There are two policemen. They don't seem very happy to see me. Sick down the front of my jacket. The journey only seems to last a few seconds. I'm in a police station. Someone behind a desk is trying to tell me something but my head hurts. I'm so fucking tired.

A cell. Safe. Alex alone.
So tired.
Time to sleep.

THURSDAY

23: Just When You Think Things Can't Get Any Worse

Thursday 17th December, 2009
Morning. Not sure when.

A glass of water. I let the thought take shape, I saw it there, beads of condensation rolling down its sides. My head felt terrible, my throat felt like I'd swallowed a hedgehog, I needed that glass of water like I needed to breathe. I didn't know what time it was. I sat up and thought about opening my eyes, getting up, walking out the bedroom and down the hall to the kitchen and actually getting it, and then I thought *fuck it,* and I lay down and went back to sleep.

Next time I woke the head and the throat still felt like shit, but now I was cold, too. I was shivering and I couldn't find the bedclothes and the bed seemed hard. I tried to go back to sleep.

Some time later – it might have been five minutes, it might have been an hour – I gave up and opened my eyes. And then the truth came crashing in.

Forget the headache. Forget the hangover. Forget the glass of water. This is important.

I'm in a police cell, and last night I hit someone over the head with a bottle.

Someone who was trying to kill me.

Actually, don't forget the hangover. I'm going to be sick again.

An hour or so later I was sitting in a bare interview room at a table with two policemen and a lawyer who looked nearly as bad as I felt. Late thirties, maybe, but grey, bags under the eyes, burst blood vessels all over the face, dirty-looking stubble and yesterday's shirt. They'd given me the lawyer I looked like I deserved.

The lawyer wanted to speak to me alone. All I wanted to do was get home. No point in making things any more complicated than they already were. Just the truth. So here we were, and here I was trying to explain what had happened. Rights read, formalities over, plastic cup full of hot, welcome coffee on the table in front of me. Let's begin.

"They were trying to kill me."

"I'm sorry, Mr Konninger, do you mind telling us again who you think was trying to kill you?"

This was my third attempt. Telling the truth was harder than I'd thought it would be.

"That guy. The big one. The one I hit. Him and his friends."

Pause. Lawyer whispering: "Please can we have a moment alone?" Ignore.

"Right. Have you ever met him before?"

"Of course. He works at my office."

"Indeed he does. Has he threatened you at any time?"

"He killed Jason."

Another pause. All look blank.

"Jason. Jason Kennedy."

"The fella who fell under the train the other day?"

"He was pushed. I saw that – that bloke at the station."

Another pause.

"Mr Konninger, we're going to show you something now, but we need to stop the tape while we get it. We'll give you a few minutes before we recommence."

One of the policemen, the younger one, left the room. The other one shook his head and smiled like this was the kind of thing he saw every day. His colleague was back thirty seconds later with a newspaper.

"Take a look. We'll leave you alone."

And they did, both of them, and the lawyer.

It was the Evening Standard. It looked familiar – same front page I'd seen the night before, same front page that had changed everything. *Banker's Death Not An Accident, Say Police.*

It wasn't like I'd actually *read* the article last night. The headlines and the photo were enough. This time my eyes were drawn further down the page to another subheading, halfway through the article.

"Suicide Considered Likely."

SHIT.

The article continued.

There was a letter. Jason had left a letter, addressed to Sally. Turned out Jason was in debt. Hundreds of thousands, maybe a million, to brokers and traders and spread betting firms who'd all suddenly found out they were sharing the same collateral and were two steps away from grabbing the house and the flat and the car and everything else he owned.

And (of course) he'd just been fired.

The way the police were thinking, he didn't know how to tell Sally. He didn't know *what* to do. He'd gone to the City because that was what he'd done every working day for years and he couldn't think of anything else. But once he'd got there, he couldn't do what he'd always done. *"The police believe this seemed as good a place as any for Jason Kennedy to put an end to the disaster his life had become,"* as the newspaper put it with a poetic flourish.

Witnesses recalled that he'd been running. He might have slipped, too, but he'd have ended up on the track even if he hadn't.

It all took a while to sink in and I was grateful for the few minutes the police were giving me. My mind wasn't in top gear, for obvious reasons, so the train of thought took a while to get started and wandered down a random siding or two once it did.

First thing: *Jason committed suicide*. Shock. Sadness. Then, quite quickly, to be honest, a light bulb, the first diversion: *Sally thinks it's my fault*. The fraud hadn't been mentioned in the paper, but that didn't mean it hadn't been mentioned in Jason's letter, or anything else Sally might have come across. Which might explain why she was so angry with me.

Back to the main line: *Poor Jason* (I wasn't feeling very original, OK?). *He didn't have to go that far.* And then another light bulb and a further, and more interesting, side track: *at least he wasn't murdered.*

Followed, in short order, by: *oh good, I'm not going to get murdered either*, and *oh shit, I've just assaulted a completely innocent Beast.*

At which point the two cops and the lawyer walked back in and I realised that I might not be in mortal peril, but I wasn't exactly in clover.

"Mr Konninger, have you read the article?"

"As much as I need to."

"Of course it was written by a journalist, Mr Konninger, but I wouldn't hold that against it. As far as we know, it's pretty much spot on."

I looked up. I'd been staring at the newspaper, not really seeing the words any more, just the black and the white and behind them the monstrous series of cock-ups I'd made. The one speaking was the more senior of the two policemen, the one who'd waited behind while his colleague scurried off to drag yesterday's Standard out of a bin somewhere. Dome of a head and a big fat face. He was still smiling. Fancied himself a comedian, by the looks of it, but I couldn't see the joke. He went on.

"Nothing in there about murder. Our enquiries point the same way. And what with the note, and the witnesses, well, it's pretty clear your friend killed himself."

Silence. They were expecting me to say something. Fair enough.

"You have to understand where I was coming from, though."

"Excuse me" (the lawyer, again). "Might I beg a moment or two alone with my client?"

I didn't want a moment or two alone with him, though. I didn't need it. He was pawing at my shoulder, trying to turn me toward him, stop me speaking. I brushed his arm away.

"It's OK. No more secrets. Everything I've got to say, they can hear. First thing, though, is I want to know what I'm in for."

He shrugged and shook his head. He was looking at the police, now, not me, and he might not have spoken but the gesture couldn't have been clearer. *What the hell am I supposed to do with this?*

"You're here because we're investigating an apparently unprovoked –" and seeing me about to interrupt, the older policeman held out his hand to stop me "an apparently unprovoked assault last night close to Liverpool Street station in the City of London. You were arrested there a few minutes after the incident, apparently in a state of intoxication."

Right. Nothing about fraud. Yet. He'd stopped. The other cop might as well have been mute for all he was contributing. Time for my part.

"OK, first thing: yes, I did it."

The lawyer shook his head at me. I shook mine back.

"They'll have witnesses coming out of their ears. They'll be fighting them off. Not much point denying it. But the thing is, I really thought the guy was trying to kill me."

"You were drunk, were you not, Mr Konninger?"

This was the younger one, finally, frowning and looking serious and making sure every word had precisely the right emphasis. And the lawyer was back to tugging at my arm. Very annoying. What I'd give for a Tesco's bag with a heavy glass bottle in it. Part of me could see it and smile about it, *Maxwell's Silver Hammer* does *City of London Police*, and I almost laughed out loud. The other part stopped me.

"Yes. Yes, I was drunk. Look," I turned to the lawyer and removed his hand, "they know I was drunk. I'd been to a couple of pubs. I'd even" (and this hurt nearly as much as everything else) "I'd even been thrown out of McDonalds. What kind of state do you have to be in to get thrown out of McDonalds?"

"And was your purported belief that you were about to be murdered founded mainly in your drunkenness, Mr Konninger?"

Now he'd got started he wouldn't shut up. His colleague had sat back in his chair, rolling his eyes. I couldn't blame him.

"No." I paused, thinking about it. "I mean, sure, the booze might have helped, but it was everything else."

The younger cop turned and looked at his colleague, nodding, a half-smile on his face. I don't know what he thought I'd said, but I was guessing he'd be surprised by the whole story.

"Come on. I've been drunk a thousand times but I've never picked a fight in my life. But when I've explained the background you'll understand it all."

"Certainly, Mr Konninger. Please, do continue."

The older one had taken charge again.

"Right. He works at Miltons, right?"

"Indeed."

"What you have to know is that we were being blackmailed."

I was disappointed. I'd expected a reaction, I'd thought at least they'd sit up and narrow their eyes a bit. But nothing. It was like I hadn't spoken. I guessed they were used to people sitting where I was sitting coming up with line after line of desperate bullshit. They'd heard everything before. They'd probably even heard this one.

"Look, we were. Me and Jason. Being blackmailed. I had every reason to think he'd been killed."

Still nothing.

"I thought they'd got to him to stop him talking. And I thought I was next."

Older cop leaned forward. Looked like he'd had enough.

"Blackmail's a serious allegation, Mr Konninger. Nearly as serious as grievous bodily harm. Which is nearly as serious as attempted murder. You need to do better than that, son. The man you attacked, Mr Chaston-Williams, he's really very unwell. Last we heard he was still unconscious."

I felt like I'd been punched in the stomach. I'd had so many shocks lately maybe I should have been getting used to the feeling, but this was one too far. I pushed my chair back and attempted to stand, swayed and sat back down again, heavily, folded my arms on the table (knocking over a cup of cold coffee) and gently lowered my head until it rested on them, face down, eyes closed, unable to speak.

The cops looked confused, the lawyer too. That was the one thing I took in on my way back down to the table. None of them even reached out an arm to steady me. You're probably confused, too. "*What,*" you'll be thinking, "*what the hell is this all about? You've just coped manfully with the news that your best friend topped himself. Why so shocked now?*"

A few things: first, thanks for that "*manfully*". Means a lot.

Second: it's cumulative. Each shock wasn't toughening me up for the next, it was lowering my resistance till I didn't have any left.

Third: Blackmail. My story, my explanation, the basis behind everything I'd done. It's true enough, sure, but who's going to believe it? It was bad enough before, when I just had no evidence. Now I've got no evidence, the only person who could've backed me up is dead, and after last night it'll look even more like I've just made the whole thing up. To say it's implausible would be an insult to implausible.

Fourth: Grievous bodily harm. Attempted murder. Doesn't sound very promising, does it?

Fifth and final: Chaston-Williams. Not a common name. So it's a fair bet he's related to the man at the centre of the web.

Marcus.

Marcus Chaston-Williams.

All this stuff was there, buzzing around my head, but for now I didn't care. As long as I stayed like this, wherever I was, with my eyes closed and my brain locked up, it was all just out of reach. It couldn't hurt me. None of it could hurt me here. There were scraping noises, a gentle prod at my back, a cough. Quiet murmuring, possibly addressed to me, possibly not. I was vaguely aware of it but it all washed over me like a dream. None of it was real. It was all too ridiculous. A dream, yes. Just ignore it.

I came to, woke up, whichever way you want to put it, just a few minutes later. My trousers were wet; I thought I'd pissed myself. The policemen had left the room. The lawyer was still there, standing at the other side of the table, with a look on his face like I was a pet he'd just run over. I smelled coffee on my arms and face; I hadn't pissed myself after all.

"Chaston-Williams."

"Feeling any better, Mr Konninger?"

"Just tell me, who is he? Who's the guy I hit?"

He swallowed, looked like there was something he *really* didn't want to tell me. I almost felt sorry for the guy, and then I remembered I was the one in custody and he was the one getting paid to be here.

"You really don't seem very well. Would you like me to ask if you can see a doctor?"

Rich coming from him. I shook my head.

"Look, please, just tell me."

He sat. Defeated. Whatever it was, he thought I'd be better off not knowing. After everything the last few days had thrown at me I didn't think there was anything he could say that would hurt any more.

I was wrong.

"Eliot Chaston-Williams. He's twenty-two years old. His father, as you may have guessed, is Marcus Chaston-Williams, of Milton Shearings."

OK. Father. I've just put Marcus's son in hospital.

"He's -"

He started, and looked at me, and stopped. He tried again.

"He's not quite –"

Still not the right opening. Third time lucky?

"Look, Mr Konninger, he's got some kind of a genetic disorder. He may be a big lad but he's got a mental age of twelve."

I nodded. I was still trying to absorb what he was saying, what it meant, how it made everything I'd done even worse, but I could see why he'd had trouble saying it. Something didn't seem right, though.

"Can I ask you something?"

"Go ahead."

"If he's got this problem, mental age of twelve, what the hell was he doing dressed up as security at Miltons?"

The lawyer looked down at the table. There was nothing there, no papers, not even any more coffee, but he still stayed like that, staring down at bare plastic, like he'd have looked at anything as long as he didn't have to look at me. "From what I can gather, Marcus persuaded the bank to let him hang around with the security team. It wasn't really work and he didn't really do much, but, well, he's a big lad, isn't he, so I suppose him just being there would have been quite helpful. He didn't have any serious responsibilities and the rest of the team were keeping an eye on him. Marcus was, too."

He stopped, for a moment, but didn't look up. He swallowed. It sounded like there was more. He shook his head, slowly, and said it.

"The police have been talking to them all last night, this morning. When you, er, when you hit him, he was out with them for their Christmas party. None of them had a bad word to say about him."

This couldn't get much worse, could it? I'd put Marcus's nice, harmless, mentally disabled son in hospital.

"Apparently he was known as a bit of a gentle giant."

I laughed.

I shouldn't have laughed, I know. There's nothing funny. So much has gone so badly wrong in three days there's enough material for a year's worth of tears. But it was all so *ridiculous*. It was like the whole damned universe had pointed randomly, and chosen me. Me to destroy, in less than a week, every loop-hole sealed tight as a nun's knickers, and not an alibi to be found. The only way I could deal with it was to laugh. Come on! What else have you got? Marriage break-up? Suicide? The end of free-market capitalism? Throw it at me. All my own doing. I'm your man. Pin all your tails on me. Throw all your sins at me. Cast me out into the wilderness. Shoot me and stuff me, burn me, hang me, do what the hell you want to me.

But first, let me laugh.

And after that, the story. It came out smooth enough, once the laughing stopped. We were in there a couple of hours, me and the lawyer. A policeman popped his head in a couple of times and asked if we wanted any more coffee, but other than that it was just me and the lawyer and the story. He listened patiently and asked the odd intelligent question that showed he understood what I was saying, and by the time I was done I was starting to see him in a different light, not stupid at all, maybe a useful guy to have on your side. But I'm not sure he agreed. Every thirty seconds he was shaking his head, or frowning, or asking me whether I'd *known* something, or just believed it. Either he didn't believe me, or he didn't think anyone else would. I'd run out of alibis.

Either way, I was fucked.

24: Sausages, Bacon, Egg and Truth

Thursday 17ᵗʰ December, 2009
Later.

They let me out.

I don't really know why. I guess they weren't quite sure what to charge me with. On the one hand, the lad still hadn't woken up. On the other, no one was talking about anything permanent, it was just a matter of time, they said. I was still thinking about him that way, *the lad*, because every time I thought *Eliot* I felt like I needed to be sick, and I wasn't sure my body could cope with much more of that. They could see I wasn't a flight risk – flight risk, hell, I could hardly get one foot in front of the other. And I wasn't going to interfere with the witnesses, either. The Miltons security team. I could just see myself "interfering" with them. I was warned, anyway, don't speak to anyone, don't go anywhere, and I nodded and posed for photographs and walked out into the weak December sunlight.

Walking out of a police station in the heart of the City in the middle of the working day, in yesterday's vomit-stained clothes, staggering and blinking, it was a new low even by my recent standards. I'd been given my wallet and keys; the remains of the whisky was kept back as "evidence". I was starving.

There was a greasy spoon I knew ten minutes' walk to the north. A battered little parade, two shops, a pub and a caff. Ten years earlier the pub had strippers at lunchtime and the shops bought as much as they sold and didn't ask you where you'd got it from. These days the shops still bought, but only original "designs" or "pieces", and only from the "craftsmen" themselves. The pub sold more wine than beer and the beer it did sell was all Belgian. But nothing could have changed the caff. You could have stuck it in the middle of Wall Street or Westminster and you'd still walk in to half a dozen fat men with hard hats on the table and mugs of tea as big as your head, plastic tables, dirty great sugar shakers, the bacon you can almost taste every time you wake up needing bacon more than anything else in the world. I was half a mile away and the way I was feeling that ten minutes was going to be more like twenty, but all I could think about was that bacon. I looked down, at my shoes, my trousers, my shirt. Hopefully, they'd let me in; hopefully there'd be no one there that knew me. And at least I knew I wouldn't get murdered on the way, though God knows maybe I deserved to be. I started out, slowly, drifting through the squealing buses and pneumatic drills, the eternal background noise of the City.

There was something different, though, a new tone, or almost new – I'd heard it from time to time over the last year. Shouting, a vague sense of rhythm, an unstable compound of humour and rage.

The noises were separating out into individual words. I couldn't see them yet but it sounded like a fair crowd.

"Fuck the banks, fuck the banks, fuck the banks…."

Imaginative.

They were standing outside one of the other banks. It might as well have been mine, might just as easily have been Miltons, but it wasn't, it was Carlton Banking Group, Head Office, glass and steel and thirty-two floors full of bankers looking around wondering what the hell had got them into this mess. I knew the feeling well.

I saw the police first. Cars, vans, motorbikes. Dozens of men in uniform, even a few horses. There were about fifty protestors, I guessed, and despite the words most of them were grinning and enjoying themselves and looked about as troublesome as the bloke with the big Golf Sale board half a mile down the road. But some of them were armed: as I watched, an egg flew from the crowd and hit the glass a couple of feet from a banker in glasses and a grey suit who'd just stepped out of the revolving doors, face buried in a file, totally unaware what was going on outside. I couldn't imagine how he'd not known, how he'd not heard all the noise and decided to wait it out, but he had good reactions, I'll give him that. He heard the splatter, looked up, saw the mob, and before anyone was ready with a second shot he'd spun on one heel and been swallowed back up in steel and glass.

The mob were standing directly between me and where I was headed. I stopped and thought. One egg, that was all, so far, but I'd seen this sort of knife-edge on television, I'd seen how an egg could turn into a stone and then the police wouldn't seem so friendly. I looked over to them. They didn't seem so friendly now, as it happened, there were riot shields and dogs all of a sudden, all for one little egg. *Fuck this*, I thought, and ducked down a side street. It might add five minutes to the journey but I didn't fancy getting my head smashed in and I'd spent enough time in the police station already today.

There were sirens by the time I got there, and more vans elbowing their way through the traffic, plus an ambulance or two. I'd made the right call. And they didn't throw me out, either, although if the way she took my order was anything to go by, the old girl behind the counter didn't much like the look of me. Or scrap that – now I thought about it she'd always had her own grim take on customer service, whether I was dressed in Armani or last night's cheeseburgers. I couldn't have cared less. She gave me tea and a plate of sausages, bacon, chips, egg and beans, and another day I'd have struggled. Not today. I polished off the lot in fifteen minutes and came back for more. Still surly, but a little more respect this time – at least, she put my change on a plate rather than throwing it at the counter.

There were bits of newspaper all over the place, the tables, the chairs, the floor. I didn't let my eyes rest on any of them. Whatever they had to say about me, Jason, *the lad*, Marcus, Mintrex, Primora, Miltons, whatever they might drag up I didn't want to know. Not now.

After two plates and another fifteen minutes staring at nothing in particular (which might have attracted attention somewhere else but meant nothing here), I felt up to the journey home. I looked and smelled bad enough to earn me half a tube carriage to myself, which had me wondering whether this might not be the right style for travelling in London after all.

I walked in and the phone was blinking at me, and the laptop was out waiting to be woken up and tell me everything everyone wanted to say, and I couldn't handle it. If I'd been physically capable, I'd have walked straight back out again. But I didn't know where to go and I wasn't capable, not even close, so the first thing I did was take a long, hot shower.

I followed the water running down over my chest to my stomach and wondered when it had got so big. I hadn't noticed. I still wasn't fat, not even close, but I was on the way. As I reached for the shower gel I noticed an old scar running horizontally along my wrist. Twenty-something years ago. We'd been walking up Snowdon – the easy route, families and children. I remember falling, which wasn't as dramatic as it might sound. It was nothing more than a stumble, really, on a well-trodden path with rocks and stones and grass churned into mud. But in the exact spot I reached out to steady my fall, there it was, a sliver of glass, last remains of a livelier ascent than ours. My hand twisted as I fell; I came up feeling fine, but Mum was pointing, unable to speak. I couldn't see what had happened. Blood everywhere – it must have looked a lot worse than it really was. Mum was in shock. Dad didn't know where to begin. The panic probably hadn't lasted more than a minute, but in my mind it defined the whole day, the whole holiday, an entire period of my youth. Then a band of grizzled walkers passed into view, armed with a rudimentary knowledge of first aid and some plasters. There must have been some form of antiseptic involved, too – I remember the sting, far worse than anything the glass itself had inflicted. But most of all, I remember the helplessness of my parents. They couldn't solve every crisis. One day I'd have to sort out my own problems.

One day.

I shook my head and dismissed the thought. The shower had made me feel a bit more like myself. Clean clothes helped, too. Sonic Youth on the stereo, tea and a biscuit – not exactly Teenage Riot but I felt maybe I could face the rest of the day after all.

There were a whole bunch of messages, and I knew before I even started who they were from and what they wanted. At least, I thought I did. The very first voice, though, was a surprise. Liz. I hadn't thought she'd want anything more to do with me. She sounded shaken. I played it back, and noted the time. During my binge, but well before I'd gone all Texas Chainsaw with the whisky bottle. She didn't say a lot, just could I call her back. She'd heard from Michael, that would be it, she'd spoken to him and by then he'd known everything. What was it he'd said to me? *She'll get hers*, that was it. She wouldn't have expected anything like that.

Of course, since then, things had changed. Who knew what she'd heard, what she believed? I'd call her, maybe, when things had settled down a bit. But not yet. I was in enough trouble myself. I didn't need to drag anyone else down with me.

There was a message from the lawyer. He hadn't wasted any time. No need to speak again today, he said, but he'd be grateful if I could give him a call again first thing tomorrow so he could get started on preparing our case.

Preparing our case. I don't know why that made me shiver – maybe some part of me had thought that there would be a miracle, no charges, I'd be free to – to beg for work from anyone that would take me, I guess, but not in Bankers Town, not any more.

There were four more messages, the ones I'd expected. Press. Three tabloids and a broadsheet. So this was my shot at celebrity. They all wanted "my side of the story", and the way they said it made me think they already had someone else's.

I walked into the kitchen and nearly walked straight back out. Didn't really want the reminder. Coffee cups. A brown mass of coffee, Liz must have spilled it while I was out getting fired. Two glasses, a whisky-shaped mess of cardboard and paper, a laptop with a flash drive stuck in its side like a knife. I stood still and counted to ten, breathing slowly. Might as well clear up.

I'd washed the glasses and cleared up the coffee, and was about to dump all the packaging, when I saw it. An envelope. Stuck to the outside of the box, I hadn't noticed it yesterday. But I could see it now, it had my name on it, and the name was handwritten, and the handwriting was Jason's. I tore it open. Inside was one sheet of plain A4. A letter.

"*Dear Alex,*" (it began, somewhat formally).

"*I'm not sure when you'll get this. I'm not sure where I'll be, either. There's so much to say, and that's just to you. What I've got to tell Sally – I'm not sure I can do it at all.*

I'll have to, of course. Whatever else, she has to know it's not her, it's nothing to do with her, or the children, it's just me, the King of the Fuck-ups. Me alone."

Not quite alone, I thought. I'd managed some pretty impressive fuck-ups myself lately.

"But I might as well start with you, and the money.

You wouldn't believe the money I've lost, Alex. I could give you the amounts, the details, but to be honest I've lost track of it all. Let's just say if I can't get my hands on close to a million quid in the next few weeks, I'm history. Lose the house, the apartment, the cars, bankrupt, lose everything. Not my kneecaps, at least, because spread betting firms don't work like that. I suppose I should be thankful. I'm not.

You know what did it? It was the upturn. The recovery. The V-shaped fucking recovery which everyone knew was an illusion, right? Couldn't carry on. We'd crashed and bounced and the only way to go was back down again. Except things kept going up, and everyone suddenly forgot what a mess we were in, like it had never happened, they were all out there calling the bottom, buying away, talking about the future like it was a good thing, and I thought mugs, idiots, you don't know how wrong you've got it. "

I stopped, put the paper down. I remembered. We'd talked about it, me and Jason. He had his idea, everything was heading back to the shitheap, and the longer it took everyone to spot it the shittier the heap would be. I'd nod, agree, he was probably right, I didn't really know. Or care. As long as I still got paid. Thought it was just an idea, a theory, something Jason liked to rant about. Guess I was wrong.

"I went short. I went short FTSE, S&P, Nikkei, Hang Seng, Dax, you fucking name it. I went short USD against euro (which was

about as bad a bet as I could have made), I went short banks, property companies, developers. I went short copper, nickel and oil. It was a joke, this recovery. It couldn't last. And it all kept going up, so I doubled the bets. Tripled them. Quadrupled the fuckers. It was a sure thing and the only question out there was how much money I was going to make and how long I was going to have to wait before it started to roll in."

Too long. Because when you're betting against the market, it doesn't matter if you're right in the end. You've got to be right at the right time, now, before your bets expire or your margin gets out of control. That's why I don't bet. I'm cocky enough to think I know better than everyone else. I'm just not sure when everyone else'll wake up and agree with me.

"But the markets carried on going the wrong way and suddenly I was running out of cash for margin. I remortgaged the house (Sally doesn't know). I put everything I had into the system just so the bastards wouldn't close out my bets. And on they went, up and up and up, further and further away from me. The margin calls were coming in thick and fast and I just didn't have the cash. And there was only one place I could find it.

Have you figured it out yet?

So if I seemed desperate when you wanted out, when you said you'd had enough of the scams, well, I was. I couldn't do it on my own. I needed to pull something big, and I needed you in it. I know you thought I could do it on my own, but you were wrong. I needed you. I needed the aliboy.

I'm sorry, Alex. I really am. But I made it all up."

I made it all up.
Suddenly the room felt cold.

"Marcus never knew a thing. There was no blackmail. There was

no Big One. First thing Marcus knew about it was today, and he had me out quicker than you could say "fraud". I was desperate and I made it up, and I never really thought you'd fall for it. Why would someone like Marcus stick his neck out that far for a couple of stinking million? I kept thinking you'd wise up, but somehow you never did. All that stuff about Marcus thinking I was some lone wolf, it must have sounded more convincing to you than it did to me when I heard myself saying it. And Marcus's share, all of it, it all went straight to the betting firms, and it still wasn't enough. The only thing that would have done it was the Big One."

I put the paper down again and tried to work out how I felt. I should hate the guy. He'd been pulling me along for months and I'd never known a thing.

But he'd been desperate. And now he was dead.

"Marcus isn't stupid, Alex. Yeah, sure, I told him this morning I was on my own, but Christ knows if he believed me. And let's face it, your name's all over this stuff, the accounts, the companies. So watch yourself. Use this letter, if you have to. I don't mind. Use whatever you need. And I'm sorry.

I've fucked up, Alex. I've fucked up so badly there isn't anywhere left to turn. Sally thinks I've come home early with a headache. Tomorrow she'll expect me to walk out of the house and get the train to work like it's a normal day. But it won't be. There won't be any normal days again. I've lied so much and every lie has let me down, and every time it's someone else who's got to pay. Sally, David, Emily. Maybe even you. I'm poison, Alex. You're all better off without me. You can see that, can't you?

I'm sorry."

I'd thought I'd already had all the bad news I could get, but it looked like the world was in a mood to keep on giving. For a moment the anger welled up. *He makes a dick out of me for months, and then he decides to kill himself, and I'm the guy he's writing his note to?* I saw myself tearing the thing up, burning it, just getting it out of my face, and then I saw Jason writing it, and the anger was gone. I sat down and looked at it again, and the torn-up cardboard, and I thought I could have handled that whisky now. If he'd told me, if he'd only told me, I could have helped. Not a million pounds worth of help, sure, but something. And none of this would have happened. And even then, even if he hadn't told me, even after he'd died and I'd fucked Liz and got fired and fought with Liz, even after all that, if I'd seen the letter instead of jumping straight into the bottle there wouldn't be a hospital bed somewhere in London with half a ton of harmless Chaston-Williams in it. From where I was now I could look back at every step that had got me here and see how close I was to not taking it. One dead, one in a coma, one in a cell. Jason wasn't the only one who could call himself poison.

There was no whisky but there was beer in the fridge and shit on the TV and after a few minutes self-pity I realised that was what I needed. The phone rang half a dozen times and half a dozen times I let it ring. The first five were journalists, but the last one was something different.

"Er, Alex, Alex, are you there?"

I recognised the voice.

"It's Lucas. Lucas Montague. From this morning?"

So that was his name. He must have told me, earlier, but it wasn't the kind of detail I was going to remember from today. He didn't look like a Lucas Montague, with the crumpled face and clothes and the unhealthy mix of red and grey. But what was in a name?

"Pick up the phone, Alex."

I didn't want to. He was trying to help me, it was his job. But I didn't fancy his chances.

"Alex, please can you call me back as soon as possible.

We need to talk. I've just heard from the hospital. The boy, Eliot, he's, er, he's gravely ill."

Another pause. Maybe he thought I'd pick up. He'd have to do better than that.

"They still think he'll probably pull through, but – erm – they can't be completely certain."

He stopped. There was something else, too, I could tell because I could hear him swallowing like he'd swallowed at the police station when he was getting ready to say something he didn't want to.

"The other thing I have to tell you is that his father wants to meet you. He said he wants to see you alone. I don't know why, and I wouldn't advise going, but he has asked me to tell you that he'll be at the coffee shop on New Street at eleven o'clock tomorrow."

"Are you there, Alex?"

"Look, just please, call me before you decide what to do. And we really need to start working on your case right away."

"Goodbye, Alex. Don't do anything stupid, OK?"

Beep.

I went to the fridge and pulled out another four beers. I wouldn't need to get up again this evening.

FRIDAY

25: Smudge

Friday 18th December, 2009
8am

Another day, another hangover. Fuck it. Don't think there's going to be much chance to earn a hangover in Pentonville or wherever it is I'm headed, so I might as well enjoy myself while I can. I felt a bit sick, my head was banging away like a porn convention on speed, but this time there was no memory loss.

I could have done with a bit of memory loss, to be honest. The headache and the nausea were bad enough but they were nothing next to waking up and remembering I had an appointment with the totally innocent man whose totally innocent son I'd almost killed.

It was only eight o'clock. Plenty of time to go, but things were looking blurrier than they should. A shower and a smoothie later I could walk straight and see straight enough. I made myself a coffee, picked up Jason's letter, put it back down again. Every word was burned into my brain. Didn't think I'd need to read it again. I booted up the laptop instead. What Jason had written, it was so fucking extreme I hadn't even thought to check it was true.

While I was waiting for the hard drive to wake up the phone rang and I answered without thinking.

"Mr Konninger, this is Gary Billings from the Morning Post. We'd like to know how you can justify your recent actions."

"Huh?" (I wasn't feeling very eloquent).

"Mr Konninger, our readers would like to know why you attempted to kill a man in broad daylight in the middle of the City."

"Eh?" I managed to blurt out. "It wasn't daylight. It was night-time." In retrospect, probably not the most convincing defence.

"What about your affair with a colleague? What about the death of Jason Kennedy? Can you shed any light on all of this? We understand that the man you attempted to murder is the son of the man who fired you. Was this a revenge attack?"

For a moment, I couldn't think what to say, and then my mind jumped back a couple of years and there it was.

"I'm sorry, I'm afraid I can't comment on that."

Thank you, Milton Shearings.

I hung up, and let the answerphone handle the rest.

I'd already glanced at the data on the drive, of course. But I hadn't been on the look-out for anything unusual then, just wondering why on earth he'd done it, put all the details of a crime on a little stick and shoved it in his desk drawer. *Idiot*, I'd thought, and nothing more.

Now I was looking closer and it was obvious things weren't the way they were supposed to be. The last few scams, the ones we'd been running for Marcus, or so I thought. The bank account details were there, the ones Jason told me he'd been given by Marcus. But what I hadn't noticed when I'd looked before was the next level, the next set of accounts, because the cash looked like it was sitting in the "Marcus" accounts for all of five minutes before it was off again. If I'd looked more carefully and seen this, I'd have realised Marcus wasn't running the show after all, because how could Jason know where the money was going after that? I suppose at the time I'd had other matters on my mind.

And these weren't just fourteen random numbers. These were numbers that rang some very loud bells. You give me six digits followed by another eight and if I've seen them before I'll turn your sort code and account number into a bank, branch and beneficiary. I knew these numbers. I'd set the accounts up myself – with Jason – back when we started all this. KenningCo. The first company we'd set up; we hadn't used it (correction: I'd *thought* we hadn't used it) since the very first scam. Looked like KenningCo was back in business.

I shut down the laptop and made myself another coffee. I could do some more digging, check out Companies House, find out what had happened lately with KenningCo. But there didn't seem much point. The bank accounts were enough. It had been Jason all along.

And Jason was right. I'd helped set that company up. I was a director and a shareholder. My name was all over it. It hadn't taken me more than a few minutes to get there, so I guessed even the police would manage it in a week or two. Maybe I could prove it was bullshit, maybe I couldn't. The letter would help. The scams I *had* done wouldn't. It was a quarter to ten and I was tired, like I'd been up twenty-four hours hard at work. I was hungry but I couldn't think of anything I wanted to eat. I stood up and the room moved around me, just a little, just a moment, before it settled back into place. I stumbled back to the bedroom and sat down. There was the painting. There was the smudge. It had probably been there all along. I just hadn't noticed.

26: Spilled Milk

For someone who didn't work in the City any more I'd spent a lot of time there since I'd lost my job. I'd even spent the night there, which wasn't something I'd done since my early days in the front office. And here I was again, back on the Honda, heading the same way.

I parked up by a small green with a little bowling lawn on it, and a bar, and a hill covered in sandwich wrappers and drink cartons. Centuries ago there was a monastery here, then a brothel, then a plague pit. Now it was where you had lunch if it was sunny and you only had twenty minutes. Five minutes walk away was New Street; just fifteen minutes till eleven. I'd always been early for meetings.

The coffee house was busy – I'd never seen it quiet. Queues at the counter, and it took a while to get my coffee. A big one, for once. Something to warm my hands. Something to hold onto. The place was full inside, but it was one of those classic winter mornings, cold but bright, so I took my drink and headed outside.

A couple of familiar faces at one of the tables, looking surprised to see me. What was it, I wondered, jeans on a work day, or just me being here at all?

I took a seat and a glance at the paper someone had left on the table. Clear enough. It was me being here at all. If I'd seen the front page before I'd left home, I'm not sure I'd have been able to show my face.

The whole story was there, or as much of it as the reporters had managed to glean from the odd ill-informed leak, some opaque statements from the police, semi-reliable comments from drunken witnesses, and their own ability to join the dots.

They hadn't done a bad job.

First off: a photo of me. Taken a few years ago, at the annual industry conference in Barcelona. It had been fun, Barcelona, a yearly dose of drink and sun and food and sex, when I was lucky, but once things started going bad in '07 it was never going to last. Barcelona turned into the Edgware Road, North London, and the sex disappeared as fast as the sun. I was drunk, of course – if you were in Barcelona and you were awake then twelve out of every eighteen hours you were drunk. It was a group shot, when it was taken, but all you could see now was me, winking, tongue out, leaning at an impossible angle, one hand groping towards a sliver of bare flesh just visible at the edge of the shot. It was just a night out, Paddy, Jason, Jess, Russell, a few others I couldn't remember next morning let alone now. And me. There would have been other faces, other arms, arms round shoulders, arms holding me up, but they were gone, airbrushed out of the photo like they'd never been there at all. Paddy had stripped off his shirt and posed like Mr Universe, which is funnier if you know what Paddy looks like. *Brain of a scientist, voice of a salesman, built like a software engineer*, that was how he used to describe himself. The rest of us pulled stupid faces and lunged for him, it was good-humoured and good-natured and you couldn't say a word against it, not really, and someone, I've forgotten who, said 1-2-3, and there was a flash, and there we were. Except this time it was just me, face grey-blue in the flash, ill-looking, demented, sick. The headline above was

"**Milton Shearings Rocked by Fraud, Assault and Suicide**"

and underneath the photo, the caption.

"Alex Konninger, fired on Wednesday, is suspected of involvement in multiple frauds and of assaulting a colleague later that evening in an incident which left the victim in a coma."

Like I say, they hadn't done a bad job. Sure, they didn't really understand finance, but then I didn't really understand journalism. They had unattributed quotes from someone in the bank suggesting the frauds might have gone back nearly a decade and involved tens of millions of pounds (*ouch!*), another that linked me with the failed Mintrex deal (*bang!*), and a note that I was a close friend of Jason Kennedy, who had died in a suspected suicide earlier this week. I sensed a hint that it would have been better if I'd chucked myself under that train instead, but maybe I was being paranoid. They'd got hold of a vague rumour about a drinking binge on Wednesday and linked that with the marital problems of an unnamed female colleague. The assault itself was a mixed bag: one witness had me "*charging at the victim, head down and with a demonic look in his eye*" (how anyone could have seen that look if my head was down wasn't explained); another had me attacking with a baseball bat, chanting throughout the assault. A third, though, had me striking with "*something concealed in a carrier bag*", in an assault that was over in seconds against a man twice my size. They'd also figured out that the victim, "*who has not yet been named by police,*" was a close relative of "*a senior manager at Milton Shearings, thought to be the man who was responsible for uncovering the fraud and firing Mr Konninger on Wednesday. Although the police,*" they concluded, "*have not yet responded to speculation concerning the motive behind the assault, insiders at Milton Shearings are convinced that this connection was behind what is believed to have been a revenge attack.*"

Christ. Look at me. Animal. Barbarian. Savage. And I thought I was a magician. Show's over, I guess.

There was some light relief. A side banner headed *"Further Misfortune Plagues Miltons: Seconds Out As Work Rivalry Fuels Fist Fight"* was followed by a wildly-exaggerated account of a punch-up between a Mr Anthony Butler and yet another unnamed female Miltons employee. Mr Butler had been arrested and subsequently released; the other employee was not being sought and witnesses confirmed she had acted in self-defence. Mr Butler had been fired that very evening, but had apparently already accepted an offer from Greenings, the US investment bank that stood to gain most from the Orresco fiasco (that was what they were calling it now – had a certain ring, I thought). But it didn't end there. There was a statement from Greenings, and it couldn't have made pleasant reading for Anthony. "In the light of this incident we have withdrawn our offer to Mr Butler. Greenings has a reputation to protect and does not look lightly upon violence, alcoholism or other antisocial behaviour."

I stopped for a moment. Greenings did have a reputation, that was true enough, but it wasn't what they seemed to think it was. And Greenings also had Graham, so their claim to the moral high ground looked pretty fucking shaky to me. Greenings claimed to be relieved that the incident had occurred before Mr Butler had an opportunity to start working with them. There was a similar statement from Miltons, expressing relief that Mr Butler was no longer an employee of Milton Shearings when the events in question occurred. I thought about that, and decided it was probably true. *You're fired*, she'd said, and moments later he'd swung at her. I couldn't be sure precisely what it was he'd been fired for, but there probably wasn't much of a notice period.

Poor Anthony. I don't know which circle of hell I was

headed for, but I wouldn't have to look up too far to see him burn. Unattributed sources hinted darkly that Mr Butler may have been somehow involved in the failed bid that the newspaper had covered so exhaustively (cue photos of their own front pages) over recent days. I grinned. Misery loves company.

I flicked through the lead article again. Hoping there was something that showed me in a more positive light. No such luck.

A shadow fell over the paper.

Really. I'd thought that could only happen in the movies, with hours of careful planning, lights, camera angles, windows and walls. But this was real.

A shadow fell over the paper.

I looked up. It was Marcus.

I'd decided to turn up, I'd not even considered staying away, but if you'd asked me why I couldn't have told you. And I didn't know what to say – what *do* you say to the man whose disabled son you've just put in a coma? So it was a relief when he sat down opposite me, set down his drink – a pot of tea for one, with a china cup and a neat little jug of milk, and started talking before I even had a chance to look blank.

"I don't know where to begin, Alex. I have to let you know before we start that apart from what's happening with Eliot this is all pretty much out of my hands. The stuff that went on at Miltons, well," (with a glance down at the newspaper), "if there ever was a chance of dealing with it in-house, that's gone now."

"OK." I'd managed a word, at least. Now for some more. "OK, Marcus. I can see that. How is Eliot doing?"

"He's come round. He'll live, at least. As for any damage, it's too soon to tell."

"Thanks. I need to tell you-"

I didn't get any further. Marcus is intimidating, in his own quiet way, when he wants to be. I'd seen him reduce a room buzzing with fifty separate conversations to complete silence merely by clearing his throat and raising a hand. This time he didn't have to clear his throat. The hand cut me off mid-sentence.

"Look, Alex. I shouldn't really be talking to you, and you certainly shouldn't be talking to me. I have no idea what impact this meeting could have on the legal stuff, and if anyone from the press hears about it all hell's going to break loose. And whatever we say to each other, well, it's just between us anyway, so I'm not sure what use it is. But as far as I'm concerned this is about my son. I want to know what's between you and him and I want to know why in God's name you decided to smash a bottle over his head."

I nodded. It was all clear. Marcus wanted to know, and that was convenient, because I wanted to tell him, however bad it might sound. The truth wasn't nice. But it wasn't as bad as what the papers were printing, what Marcus probably believed, that I was a vicious con-man who'd driven one friend to his death, ended another's marriage, and tried to kill someone else because his father was on to me.

"OK. I can tell you everything. Just bear with me, because it'll take a while."

"I thought it might."

"Right." I sat back, took a sip of coffee, and began.

"It all goes back to Jason. You know what me and Jason were up to. What you probably don't know is how it started and why it carried on so long."

Marcus nodded, and I spent the next five minutes explaining how we ran the scams, how we'd got started, all those years ago. Maybe I skipped over my own financial aspirations a little, maybe I hurried past the Porsche, the apartment, the artist. And maybe I dwelled more than I needed to on Jason's problems, Charmaine, the builders, the rent-free albatross in Docklands. I was just a friend, helping him out. I thought about mentioning Emily, and then I remembered what I'd promised. Jason might be dead, but that was still private.

Ridiculous. I'd been looking down at the table as I spoke, occasionally glancing up, but those glances were enough. Marcus had looked calm from the moment he arrived. Not calm, perhaps, but restrained. He was holding something in, and if I had to guess I'd have said it was a burning desire to grab me by the neck and squeeze till there was nothing left. But even as I spoke, he seemed to be losing interest. He wasn't looking at me; his eyes flickered around, from a point on the building behind me, to the trio at the next table, to the people walking by. His mouth was a thin red line. I hadn't expected a smile, but the frown was getting deeper by the minute. I was losing him.

"I'll stop. I need to go back. I haven't been completely honest, and if I'm not completely honest there's no point in doing this."

The mouth didn't move. The frown didn't soften. But he looked at me.

I started again. It was the same story, but there was more of me in it. There were model Ferraris and swaps income, bonus pools, apartments and 911 Turbos. There was greed. It was the truth. He didn't say a word and I couldn't tell any more if he was listening or just waiting for me to finish, but he didn't move, so I didn't stop.

And then I got to the meat, the stuff he couldn't know, but had to.

"I wanted to get out, Marcus. I asked Jason, I told him, we've got to stop this. I won't pretend I had a crisis of conscience. I just didn't see the benefit in taking the kind of money we were taking with the risks we were taking to get it. It wasn't enough money, and I was too scared to do anything bigger."

"But you did. All you've told me about so far is forty, fifty grand each. From what I've seen you did a hell of a lot more than that."

So he was listening. Good. He'd need to be listening, because now it got complicated.

"Exactly. I tried to get out but Jason didn't want me to. And you probably aren't going to believe what I'm about to tell you, but it's important that you do because it's the only way I can explain what happened the other night."

"Go on, then. How did Jason force you to keep stealing money from your clients?"

A smile; a sneer, almost. He was still listening, I reminded myself. Even a sneer was better than nothing.

"It was all about you."

"Me? How? How on earth was it about me? I didn't know a thing about this until the end of last week."

"That's when you got to Jason, yeah. But the way he told it, you first caught him a year ago."

"But – but" (he was spluttering now) "that's nonsense. Why? Why did he say that?"

"I can explain."

Suddenly I was back in that office, on Wednesday morning, just 48 hours ago, a bastard in front of me and a Witch behind and completely, unnaturally in control. I had the facts, the motivation, the background. It was worth nothing to me, but he wanted it, and if he believed me, maybe he could make my future a little less hellish. If he didn't believe me – well, it wasn't like I had a lot to lose.

"I can explain," I repeated. "One word. Blackmail."

Marcus looked blank.

"Jason blackmailed you?"

"Nope. Jason told me that you were blackmailing him."

He'd been leaning forward, getting progressively closer

to me with each new line. But at this one, he sat back, all the way, and let out a long, deep breath. And smiled.

"Do you really expect me to believe you?"

"Probably not. But it's the truth. And when I've finished I can show you something that might convince you."

He was still smiling, gently shaking his head. But when he spoke the words – again – were "Go on."

"Back when you had us looking through all those old deals for accountants and lawyers and anyone else we could find to sue, remember that?"

"Yes. You found nothing."

"Well, a couple of the ones you had me looking at were deals we'd taken a cut from, me and Jason." I hadn't mentioned Paul yet. I wasn't going to fall on my sword for the guy, but he'd never really known what we were doing. It was just a bit of fun as far as he was concerned. A favour for a mate. Dodgy, maybe, but no real harm. No point letting the guy down for no reason.

"Jason told me you'd caught him out. Not me, though. Just him. You said – he said you said – he was for the chop, FSA, police, the whole lot – unless he carried on milking the deals, but doing it for you."

"That's preposterous."

Marcus had started to get up. I could see where he was coming from. He was right, it was preposterous. Even Jason had thought it was preposterous. But I hadn't. Hindsight's a wonderful thing.

"You're right. It's ridiculous. I know it's not true, now. I know there's nothing in it. But at the time, you have to believe me, I fell for it completely. I had no idea Jason was lying to me until yesterday."

"What happened yesterday?"

He was still standing but he hadn't moved away from the table. There was a chance. I'd been saving Jason's letter for the end, but unless I did something now, this *was* the end. I took it out of my back pocket and gave it to him. He sat.

"This."

He read quickly. Finished. Held up a hand to stop me interrupting, and started all over again. The frown got deeper, but otherwise the expression didn't change at all. He put it down, on the table, between us. I started to reach for it and changed my mind. Marcus wasn't speaking. He was looking at me. My hand was still out there, purposeless. I picked up my cold coffee and drained it. Marcus spoke.

"You could have written this yourself."

I nodded.

"But you didn't, did you?"

"No."

"You know what? I think I believe you. You're a fucking idiot, Alex, but I believe you. But I don't see what that's got to do with Eliot."

He was right, of course. It didn't explain a thing, not by itself. I picked up the letter, put it back in my pocket, and went on with the story. The seconds crawled by. It sounded worse than bullshit, I knew that. It just happened to be the pure, unvarnished truth.

Jason's sacking, Marcus's warning, Eliot's appearance at the station and later across the road, paranoia, whisky and a glimpse of a newspaper, they were the main ingredients, but I didn't stop there, I threw in Primora and Mintrex, Grace and Graham, Anthony, even Michael and Liz. I talked and talked and every now and then Marcus would interrupt with a question, an expression of disbelief, a nod of understanding; but he didn't stand up again. I was getting somewhere.

I'd finished. There was silence. I didn't even know what I wanted, so I wasn't about to ask for anything. I picked up my cup, saw it was empty, looked around. It was still light, but the sun had disappeared for lunch behind a towerload of lawyers and insurers and I was suddenly cold. I looked back at Marcus, and he was smiling.

"It's a good story, Alex."

"It's true, though. You know it's true. You saw the letter."

"I did. And I believe you."

In different circumstances I might have punched the air.

"But," he continued, "it's really not very plausible, is it, Alex?"

I didn't get it. He believed me. What did plausible matter?

"The thing is, Alex, you and I might know there's shades of grey here, but as far as anyone else is concerned, you're the bad guy."

I couldn't argue with that. I think the lawyer had been trying to say the same thing, but it had taken him about forty sentences to get there and by that time I'd lost his train of thought.

"Look at the stories in the paper, Alex. And I don't mean the stuff about Eliot. I mean Mintrex, the fraud stuff, everything hitting the bank just when everyone out there thinks we're no better than Nazis. What do you think they want to hear? That it's all a matter of degree, unfortunate circumstances, a few moral slips and minor lapses of judgement? Or that it's all about some bastard son-of-a-bitch who wants money and doesn't care who gets hurt? What do you think, Alex? What do the readers of that paper want to see?"

I couldn't tell where this was heading but I knew I didn't like it.

"But the letter. Marcus, you saw the letter. I understand what you're saying. I'm telling a complicated story, and people won't like it. But the complicated story is the truth. That's the important thing."

He shook his head.

"No, it's not. What's important is the simple story. Cops and robbers. Cowboys and Indians. Angels and demons. Guess which one you are."

I shrugged. He went on.

"As for the letter, have you shown it to your lawyer yet?"

Suddenly I was sweating, in spite of the cold. I swallowed. I could feel my heart beating.

I shook my head. "No. You're the only person who's seen it."

He nodded, briefly, not even a nod, just a slight drop of the head. Silence, for a brief moment. And then, eyes firmly fixed on mine, he spoke again.

"When did we lose sight of responsibility, Alex?"

It didn't seem like he was expecting an answer. I didn't offer one.

"It's all about big, institutional guilt, isn't it, Alex? No one's willing to take the blame for anything any more. They just want to blame something else, something abstract and gigantic, hold a public enquiry and get on with their lives. When a child gets killed, it's social services. When someone blows up a shopping centre it's foreign policy. When someone lies on a mortgage application form, the liar's a victim and it's the broker who's a criminal. The broker blames the lender, the lender blames the regulator, the regulator blames the government. Everyone's saying *they should have stopped it, they should have stopped us.* When did we forget how to stop ourselves?"

Another pause. This one went on long enough that I opened my mouth to speak, even though I still didn't know what to say. I couldn't see where Marcus was heading but it didn't look like it was going to be anywhere nice. Not for me, anyway. I didn't get the chance, though. Marcus continued.

"Everyone's got an excuse. And when it comes to bankers, well, we're full of excuses, aren't we? It's always someone else's fault. We were all along for the ride, someone else was at the wheel. Weren't we? Weren't we, Alex?"

This time it looked like he did want an answer. I nodded, dumbly. It seemed to do the trick.

"But we *chose* to get in, didn't we?" On *chose* he hammered his fist down on the table. I couldn't look him in the eye. I was watching the cups, the little jug of milk, the drops spilling out as the table shook.

"As for you, Alex," he continued, his voice softening, "well, you've got your excuses, too. Not a bad set of excuses, not bad at all. But really, it's the same thing, isn't it? You weren't making the decisions. You weren't responsible for it all. Someone else was at the wheel, right?"

He waited, and I nodded again.

"Your driver's dead, Alex. You want to point your finger at him, go ahead. But maybe it's time you looked in the mirror."

He'd finished. But I wasn't looking at him. I was looking down, at the table, where I'd been staring for the last minute or so, since he'd smashed his fist down and spilled the milk. The paper napkin had floated away on the breeze and there was nothing to clean up the mess. I sat back, and raised my head to look at him, and thought, about everything he was trying to say, about everything that had happened in the last week, the last year, the last decade, about what I could do, now, if I wanted to. Thirty seconds, maybe a minute, of silence. People were walking and talking around me, cars and buses driving by, but I blocked all of that out. He was watching me, frowning again, assessing.

And then, without warning, he stood, raised his hand to stop me getting up or saying a word, and walked away.

EPILOGUE

Time

Friday 11ᵗʰ October, 2013

> *But this rough magic*
> *I here abjure, and, when I have required*
> *Some heavenly music, which even now I do,*
> *To work mine end upon their senses that*
> *This airy charm is for, I'll break my staff,*
> *Bury it certain fathoms in the earth,*
> *And deeper than did ever plummet sound*
> *I'll drown my book*

The Tempest, Act V, Scene i

You know, my friend, I can predict your sales, your profits.
I can tell you when you're going bust before you think you even
have a problem.
But Alex Konninger? Nobody saw that coming.

Sergei Kuznetsov

The limo slid out into the Friday evening traffic. In the pools of light cast by street lamps and oncoming cars I could see the rain pounding down, but all was silent. I settled back into the leather and found a button that suggested warm air. I pressed it. I was right. I closed my eyes, then opened them. I didn't want to fall asleep. I wanted to watch the world go by.

There would be a few miles of it to see, of course, because home wasn't West London any more. It wasn't HM Prison Belmarsh, Category C, either, so things could be worse. An hour or so, I reckoned. I shook my head. I still couldn't get used to it. Alex Konninger, back out in the fucking shires.

Things change, though. Time does that. Four years, another life, hardly a surprise. The apartment was history. So was the car. But I'd kept the bike. If 2009 didn't kill me, or Belmarsh, I figure I'll outlive the Honda.

First question, I guess, is what the hell I'm doing in a limo heading out of West London. Well, if you tune in to BBC1 later tonight for your regular instalment of Britain's most popular weekly chat show, you'll find out. If you can't wait till then, I guess I can spill the beans.

I've just been on the couch opposite Gillian Welch (and if you don't know who *she* is, you're probably Category A), and alongside a host of fairly major celebrities, answering questions in front of a live studio audience and an estimated TV audience later tonight of twelve million plus. I won't pretend the viewers are tuning in for yours truly. I'll probably bring in half-a-dozen family and friends. The rest are there for a multi-platinum-selling New York pop-star with the longevity of Dracula, an ex-MP turned erotic novelist, and a young, gifted and extraordinarily good looking British actor who plays the lead in a major movie set to open next week in London and LA.

I emphasise the "good-looking" element because I'm rather pleased about it, although it won't reflect too well on me, what with his craggy yet somehow innocent face right next to my humdrum mug.

The actor, you see, is Charlie Hemmings. *The* Charlie Hemmings. The film tells the story of my final, fateful days at Miltons, and what came after. The role? Come on. It doesn't take a brain surgeon.

I did OK, at least, I think I did. I wasn't fazed by the lighting, the cameras, all the beautiful people milling around with clipboards and headsets and important things to do. I held my own with Gillian, managed a little banter with the politician-novelist. I couldn't think of anything to say to the singer ("I used to fantasize about you when I was a teenager" seemed somehow inappropriate), but I think there was enough going on around us for that to slip by. Hell, she could have said something to me. She probably had no idea who I was. Why should she?

Of course, what Gillian really wanted to hear about was the sordid story of 2009, as if any of that was still news. You've got to wonder why. There's nothing secret about it (well, actually, there is one thing, but that's another matter); everything that ever will come out came out at the time, in the papers, in court, in the interviews afterwards. So I tried to talk about the film (which, as the producer had pointed out repeatedly on the phone earlier this afternoon, was the only reason I'd been invited on in the first place); I managed a word or two on the other stuff I've been doing (because that could use the publicity more than the film could); I talked about prison; I made a couple of jokes. Charlie, who's well used to all this, told me I'd done well when we parted outside (where I noticed his limo was *significantly* longer than mine, but who's checking?) That'll do for me.

I was in familiar territory now, not far from my old apartment. There was the tube station on the left; the pub a little further on the right; the Chinese restaurant a hundred yards down a side-street. Did I miss it? A little, yes, no doubt about it. Who wouldn't? If you'd told me four years ago I'd be living in a cottage on the edge of a Hertfordshire village four miles from the nearest train station I'd have told you to fuck off. Even now it seems strange. I don't know if I'll ever really fit in. But the pub's decent and so are the locals, and there's no trouble. Things are quiet. I'm better off where I am.

That's another reason I need the bike, because I'm not cycling four miles and it seems to me if you want to park your car at the station you've got to get there the night before. I'm in London a couple of times a week, most weeks. Astonishingly, I'm in demand: people want to know what I'm thinking, on white-collar crime, the prison system, the financial system. I do radio interviews and a little TV, I write magazine articles, I try to keep myself sane on those phone-ins where people get so angry with each other they sound like they're about to explode. Weirdly, though, it's not me they're angry with. Not usually. I had six months, maybe a year, as the man everyone loved to hate, and then suddenly I was out and it was like I was a different person, I was just the man with the inside track. Prison does that, sometimes, if you're not a rapist or a murderer, at least. The book helped, of course. I wrote most of it inside, and I wrote it about the one thing I know. Me. In part, at least, and that's the bit the film's based on. But also about the madness of the world we'd filled with flashing screens in fifty-storey buildings which might as well have been empty shells. I argued like hell with the publishers, I wanted to call it *"Our Revels Now Are Ended"*, Prospero's line, near the end of *"The Tempest"*. Dad would have liked it, I thought, but the readers wouldn't, apparently, and they were the ones with the chequebooks. "*Bankers Town*", that's what we agreed on, no apostrophe, and that's what the film's called, too. Turned out the publishers were right. People liked the title.

The thing is, all that stuff about the revels and the broken staff and the hollow pagodas and the baseless fabric, all the stuff I wrote about the City, I'm not sure how much they cared. People took in the bits they liked and ignored the rest. A few might have got the message, but most just saw it as another dirty City memoir, lying and fraud with a little sex and violence thrown in for good measure (more sex and violence than I'd have wanted, ideally, but the publisher won that fight, too). I suppose I should be grateful – if I'd written what I wanted to write, I doubt anyone would have read it at all.

So when someone calls up and asks if I'd like to do some radio, write a feature, all that, my first reaction is always to back away, a little, and ask what they *really* want. If it's Alex Konninger, the crook with the smile and the way with words, they can take their expenses cheques, I tell them, and stick them where the sun don't shine. And they always say no, no, it's not that, we'd like to hear what you think about the Eurozone, or LIBOR, or rehabilitation, and although they always try to sneak in something about 2009, nine times out of ten, to my surprise, they're telling the truth.

I can oblige, because it turns out I know this stuff after all, and I've got opinions that make me stand out from the rest. I try not to give the interviewers *exactly* what they want – I do have some loyalty, and most of the people I worked with back then were decent enough. But I won't shy away from the truth, either. The giant pay-cheques. The short-term scams like the ones I used to pull on our Finance team, with nasty little stings in their tails. The media love all that, but what they really want is the bubbles, and I can talk bubbles till someone sews up my mouth. Whole continents are screwed, economies are stagnant, so what the hell is going on with house prices, consumer credit, stock indices, even commercial real estate and leveraged finance? Jason was right all along, but too far ahead of the game. Everything had fallen right back down again, and he'd have made a killing, but knowing him he'd have hung on for even more money and lost the lot twice over. There's another crash coming, folks, and I'm not foolish enough to tell you when and how, but when it comes, it'll be worse than the last one. That's what I tell them, on the radio, and they wait for me to go on, because anyone who says what I've just said always follows it up with the end of capitalism as we know it, or the dollar as a reserve currency, or the banking system, or the hegemony of the stock markets. But I don't give them that. Because it won't happen. It'll just be another crash, and by the time we're halfway out of it we'll have forgotten it already, and within a couple of years we'll all be out there rushing to buy tulips or South Sea Company shares or synthetic CDOs of non-performing German real estate loans.

I get asked about prison. I get asked about court, too, because even though the media were all over it like a hedge fund on a busted currency, no one's ever really understood what happened there. Ten months, I got, and out in six. Fraud. That was it. Ten months for fraud and nothing else, and a guilty plea, too, which no one was expecting. I stood there in that court, waiting for it all to kick-off, and I looked around and I saw it was right. Marcus was right. The plea was inevitable, from the moment I looked down at the milk on the table and realised I did have something to clean up the mess with after all. All the mess.

Me.

"Guilty," I said, and I looked around again and I saw how surprised they were. Except Marcus. He didn't smile.

He just looked at me, and nodded, and that was enough. The aliboy had grown up.

As for the other little matter – you know, attempted murder, grievous bodily harm – that was all set for later in the year. Except it never happened, and that's the one thing they're still trying to wring out of me, how I got away with it. The truth is pretty straightforward, as it happens. It was Eliot.

He recovered, as fully as he could. His brain would always be years behind the rest of him. But that didn't stop him doing what only he was in a position to do: dropping the charges. And behind him, Marcus, because once Eliot had made up his mind the police and the CPS were onto him five times a day to change it, but he didn't, because Marcus was always there to remind him it was his choice and no one else's.

That guilty plea stopped a lot of unfortunate things coming to light. Paul, for starters. And Graham and Grace, the whole Greenings connection. I don't really know what crime they'd committed, or whether they'd committed one at all, but it wouldn't have looked good for either of them if the truth had come out in the trial, or afterwards in the book. We'd all done things we shouldn't, though. Just because I'd been caught with my hands where they shouldn't have been, no reason to drag them down with me.

Actually, that makes me sound more generous than I was. The truth is, I'd have taken Graham down all the way, if I could, but not Grace. I know, I know, and after everything she'd put me through, but there's still something I like about her, the bitch. I didn't want to damn her along with Graham, and I couldn't damn Graham without her, so it looked like the bastard had got away with it.

But it turned out I needn't have worried about

Graham after all (and I'd been right about him all along). While I was inside, another scandal hit: bribery, backhanders to clients and bidders, inside information doled out like gruel in the workhouse, and (this being Graham), the inevitable garnish of prostitutes and drugs. Greenings dropped him like a stone, and Grace followed their lead, coming out of the whole thing smelling fresh as a dew-dappled daisy. She just kept on going, onward and upward; head of the team, and starting to make a big name for herself.

The other thing that didn't come out was Jason.

Because that was what I'd decided, sitting there outside the coffee shop with the milk starting to drip onto my shoes and Marcus's words ringing in my ears. I could turn him into my alibi, sure. I'd save myself a couple of months. Was it worth it?

The way things turned out, the press didn't have anything on Jason after all. Marcus had kept it all quiet, even managed to get Sally a pension and an insurance payout so she could keep the house. All the clients we'd scammed were too embarrassed to clear their collective throat and say *hang on, wasn't there someone else?* Me. It was just me, and that suited everyone, except me. And in the end, it even suited me. Sally was there at the sentencing, crying. She caught my eye, and smiled. It was a start.

They let me go home, after I'd been sentenced. A few days to sort things out, which was unusual, I was told, but by this time my lawyer had given up on things being usual with me. I called Sally, and she didn't shout at me, but told me to come over. It was late March but it was still winter out there. Snow on the common, home-made sledges, snowballs, a few tears, milk and mulled wine in the pub. I won't pretend there wasn't some initial awkwardness, but Emily knew who I was, at least, and seemed better than I'd seen her for ages. By the end of the afternoon it was like it might have been all along, just with a big Jason-shaped hole in it. Sally promised to visit when I was inside, and I wasn't too proud to be grateful.

A package came, just before I left for Belmarsh, by courier. A big carton of cigarettes, a Greenings comp slip, a handwritten note:

"items enclosed: you may find these useful."

Now, you can look at this any way you like, but it was true. The cigarettes were useful. I've not heard from Grace since, but I don't think we're enemies any more.

As for prison itself, I'm not going to pretend I enjoyed it. There were some decent enough people there. But (and bear in mind this was low-security) there were some vicious bastards, too. On the whole, I'd say it was shit. And at the beginning, it was scary, too, because it came out pretty fast that I was a banker. Not a cop, but not a whole lot better. They didn't like me. They had this idea what a banker was like, and once you've decided something's a certain way, then the rest of the world has to fit. I kept myself to myself, mostly, kept out of trouble. Didn't try to tell them they were wrong, I was different. And that gave me time to think about all the things I'd got wrong myself, and all the worlds I'd twisted to make them fit.

The idea that there was ever anyone in control, that any of us ever had the faintest idea what we were really doing, with all those CDOs and credit default swaps and numbers that went on so long the whole universe ended up looking like just another buy-to-let in Barnsley. If I'd looked closer I'd have seen it. The driver's seat was empty. Always had been.

The idea that it was OK, the tricks we pulled with that Spanish bank on the black ops team, that this was normal, that there was nothing wrong with it.

The idea that the scams I *knew* I was pulling weren't so bad, either. That there was any difference between what I did with Alchemy right back at the beginning, to save the deal and keep Liz on the team, and what I did years later to get myself a bigger car. The motive doesn't matter. The guys who gamed LIBOR thought the same way, they weren't dirty, they said, not at the beginning, they just weren't clean. Bollocks. When some poor sod's lost all his money because you lied to him, what does he care how dirty the lie was?

Eliot, of course. The idea that he was a Beast, a monster, a killer.

And Marcus. Everything about Marcus. I had him down as a spider at the centre of a web and I was right, it turned out, but I had the wrong web. He *does* know what's going on, everywhere, and he *is* the kind of man who can make things happen. Just not the things I thought were happening. That time I overheard him, talking to Jason, telling him he had to step up. *"This is the big one, Jason. You've pissed around on the little stuff too long. You need to do this."* That wasn't blackmail. That was Marcus offering Jason a step up, because Jessica was moving on and from what Marcus could see, Jason had everything he needed to run the team except the confidence he could do it.

I'd been right about Karl, though. You can't be wrong all the time.

So I did my time. I learned a lot, in those first few weeks alone with my thoughts and the hard stares of men who didn't like me. But they got bored, after a while, and I stopped being scared, and I wrote a book. Sally came to visit, every couple of weeks, and now and then she brought the kids with her. It probably wasn't the gentlest setting for David to get to know his godfather or for Emily to be in at all, but it wasn't all dogs and guns, either.

We talked about so many things, but never the fraud, never what had driven Jason to the final desperate act. I'll never know why she was so angry with me, after Jason died, why she assumed it was all my doing. I guess Jason just told her what he thought she needed to hear, and if that put me front and centre, I could understand why he'd done it, and I wasn't going to tell her anything different. Fact was, none of it mattered any more, and we both knew that without having to say it.

The closest we've come to discussing it at all was the day after I was released. I'd stayed away from Jason's funeral, given the press attention I was getting at the time (not to mention the alcoholic stupor I tended to find myself in by the middle of the morning); this was the first time I'd visited his grave. A blazing September morning in the flat middle of nowhere, no trees or shelter to speak of. As we approached the grave, Emily, David and Sally formed a small group ahead of me – just half a step ahead, but enough to make me feel like an outsider. It was an unremarkable stone, an unremarkable place. I stood looking at it and hoping that somehow I'd get a sense of Jason from a lump of rock. I got nothing. I looked at the stone and the backs of their heads, and close as I thought we'd become, I didn't know what to say.

And then without a word they all stepped back, surrounding me, drawing me in. The children were either side of me, Sally the other side of Emily, holding her hand. And then David looked up at me and put his hand in mine and I felt his little fingers close as tightly as they could. I know it seems trite, but it happened and I won't apologise: I've told the truth about enough shameful history to entitle me to tell this one too, however unreal it might seem.

I made a vow then, the vow I should have made when he was christened instead of that nonsense about protecting him from the devil. I swore (to myself, of course) that I'd never let anything happen to him. And that really *is* unreal. I had to revise it within fifteen minutes, when he tripped, grazed his knee, and collapsed into a heaving ball of tears. I can't protect him from everything; it'll be impressive enough if I protect him from anything at all.

But at least I can try.

There's not a whole lot left to say.

Grace might have got Graham wrong, but she was spot on with Mintrex, who'd pulled down their pants and shown everyone what they'd got, and then failed to deliver. A lot of people liked what they saw, which put Mintrex "in play", but the bid that got furthest was a hostile one from a Chinese sovereign wealth fund with the kind of money that only a Chinese sovereign wealth fund could get its hands on. It all got a bit political and nasty and the Chinese pulled out, in the end, and you couldn't blame them. As I write, history repeats itself: Mintrex has just announced a new bid for Orresco. Orresco's CFO is the man everyone wants to talk to right now, but he's playing coy. Can't blame him, either – it's once bitten twice shy for Ahmed, and he's got no more reason to love the press than he has to trust the bankers. I hope it all turns out better than last time.

I spent a short time trying to track down Charmaine, and I made it pretty loud and pretty obvious, so the fact that I've not had any luck makes me think she doesn't want to be found. After all that practice in the gym, I can't see her not landing on her feet.

Jasmine's still in New York. For reasons that shouldn't require much explanation, I never managed the trip I'd planned, but I did get over to see her a year later, in a purely platonic capacity, by which time she'd married a billionaire art collector who claimed to have spotted an extraordinary talent. I remember noticing at the time he didn't say what for. She managed a couple of exhibitions before things started to unravel, and by the time the divorce is finalised she'll probably be able to buy her own gallery if she wants. The art's as terrible as ever.

I'm still in touch with Paul, usually by email, because he's in India now. I don't think he ever really understood what had happened, but the tragic final act was enough to make him see how far out of control everything had got. He went to India to escape from it all, to find himself, he said: he went to live in an ashram for a year. I'm not sure he did find himself there, but on a couple of trips to Mumbai he found something far more valuable: a new business model for running call centres. He's got half a dozen now. Says he'll come home one day. But I doubt it'll be to Dagenham.

Mum's not gone back there, either. I never made the millions I'd hoped would keep her in luxury cruises till the day she dropped, but it turns out the Essex coast and Dad's pension from the Plant are all she really needed.

Jane's doing a great job upstairs, I hear, kicking crap out of half the people she used to work for and keeping at least part of the bank on the level. She knows all the tricks, plus a few more she's since learnt from me, because she was the first person in touch once I was out, asking for advice on how to spot "*little shits like you*", as she put it. So I ended up working for Miltons again after all, even if it was unofficial, and even if I do get paid in karate lessons.

Doug's rise continues unabated. He's got his own hedge fund now, and a white Ferrari to match the wardrobe. He's done well out of the last few years, seems to have an eye for the next domino to fall, and unlike most of the hedgies, he's not afraid of the limelight, so from time to time I find myself up against him on a radio debate or a phone-in. I think I've won more times than I've lost, but we've found ourselves agreeing more times than the rest put together, which might not make great radio but is probably more instructive in the long run. And he's always good for a drink or two afterwards.

Walter was found out in the end. He never was much good at anything except surviving, and finally even that wasn't enough. Milton's made him redundant at the end of last year. He won't be sobbing into his cornflakes, though. Thirty years with Miltons adds up to a hell of a severance package, and he's just set up some kind of advisory business. I can't imagine what he's advising on or who's prepared to pay him for it, but Walter's got the knack of landing butter-side-up. I doubt the City's seen the last of him.

Russell's "travelling". He's been travelling for three years now. He disappears into the middle of nowhere – the Siberian steppe, or an African jungle no one's heard of except a few elephant hunters and the odd rebel army – and a month or two later writes it all up on his blog. He can't write, his photos are terrible, and Christ knows who he thinks is reading the stuff. But I guess he's enjoying himself.

Marcus is still sitting there in the middle of his web. The web's got bigger, though, and my guess is when the next crisis hits, it'll be Marcus sweating in front of the Select Committee, trying to explain what's happened to a bunch of politicians who don't actually care what's happened as long as they get their faces on TV. And no doubt he'll get blamed for something that's nothing to do with him, and hammered for it, and people who haven't a clue who he is or what he's accused of doing will curse his name. And knowing Marcus, he's prepared for this and he'll deal with it when it comes, because amongst the many things he's taught me is that you can pretend you're drifting, but you're not, so why bother?

As for Rachel, she doesn't answer my calls or emails; I haven't heard a word from her since I walked out of Miltons carrying my box. You never can tell.

And then there's me. The newspaper and TV stuff isn't exactly a full-time job, but I have other things to keep me busy. Things even less likely than a cottage in the middle of the Hertfordshire countryside.

One afternoon, about halfway into my stretch, I heard I had a visitor. I wasn't due a visit so I thought it was probably a mistake, they made a lot of mistakes like that in Belmarsh, but I went along anyway, just in case. I wasn't expecting anything. And I was expecting Stephen even less than nothing at all.

I'd never bothered finding out where Stephen went when he left us. Turned out he hadn't gone back into banking at all. I hadn't realised, but he already had a foundation, a great big box of money he dragged in from his millionaire friends and doled out again to the charities he thought could use it best. He wanted to get out and spend more time doing that, he'd been wanting to for years, but he couldn't bring himself to step away from everything he'd built at Miltons.

It had taken Marcus to convince him he could do that, if he wanted, he could step away and the rest of us would somehow get by. It wasn't a stab in the back Marcus had given him after all. It was a ladder and an open window.

Even if I'd known about the foundation, I wouldn't have bothered finding out what it actually did, and if I had I'd have forgotten by the next day. What the hell could it have to do with me?

Quite a lot, as it turned out. Stephen's foundation specialises in integration, in getting people into work, people with the odds stacked against them, people who might not manage it without some help. There are as many difficulties as there people with them. Time constraints, care obligations, physical disability, mental illness. Sometimes it's not about the present, it's about the past. Difficulty adjusting from military service. Too many years doing something you just can't do any more. Or maybe something as simple as a criminal record.

Thanks to Stephen, I have (I flatter myself) been "successfully re-integrated". I've got a job, at least, and I've found to my surprise that all those negotiating and juggling and whip-cracking and bullshitting skills that were so indispensable when I was a banker are pretty handy when it comes to running a charitable foundation, too. All the cheques from the press and the radio end up with the foundation. I get paid a half-decent salary in turn.

Incidentally, the only other full-time employee is another ex-charity-case, a good friend, now, although our only acquaintance until four years ago was from the wrong end of a half-full whisky bottle on a cold dark night in the middle of Bankers Town. Once you look past the disability, he's a good man to have around. And not just for security.

Like I said, way back at the start: I never wanted to be a banker. Who does? I never wanted to do anything that wasn't right in front of me, and the bank just happened to be there at the right moment like a cherry on a fruit machine. But it's not something I regret, either. Being a banker isn't the end of the world. It's the kind of banker you are, the kind of person you are at the end of the working day, or the end of the career, that makes the difference. I was a bad banker – one of the worst. I thought I knew everything. But now I've realised I knew nothing at all, I'm lucky enough to have the chance to be something better.

What I'm doing right now, though, feels a bit like having your brains slowly squeezed out of your ears. I'm sitting in the back of a limo – a limo stocked with wine and whisky and a fridge full of beer and fine food – and I'm sucking on a complimentary BBC mint whilst trying to concentrate on all the crappy details of a ten-page expenses form. The charity needs every penny it can get, so I've got to claim for travel costs for a couple of interviews last week and any other incidentals I can think of. The publishers will pay; no problem. But there's a fine line between claiming for everything you can, and claiming for things you can't – and given my history with this kind of thing, it can be a little difficult to remember which side of the line I'm supposed to be on. But I manage it. Less creative, more time-consuming, and the amounts concerned seem so small the old Alex Konninger wouldn't have bothered with them at all unless there was somewhere he could squeeze in a couple of zeroes. But it's got to be done.

I put down the paperwork. I'm tired, and I can finish it off in the morning. It's been an hour since we left the studios and we're driving through the village, pub on the left, the old post office on the right, and out again. Two minutes later I'm home.

I tell the driver goodnight and wait for him to drive away. I can see the lights are on inside. It's so quiet here. I stand in the road for a moment and marvel at the silence, the occasional owl, and on the edge of earshot, aircraft circling thousands of feet above, lights turning in the darkness.

The door is open; she's waiting, just inside. We'll watch my TV performance together later; if it's good, she'll be happy for me, and if it's not, she'll know what to say. People can be very direct: some of my friends, the old ones and the new, have asked me why the hell someone like her would marry someone like me. Some of them have even asked her. I know what they're thinking: she was on the rebound, falling into my arms the moment the divorce was done, the usual story. But it wasn't that, not really. There are a thousand nameless things that bind us together, and somehow we understand each other like no one else can.

When people ask, she'll just smile at them, and shake her head. I can't do that. I have to say something, it's who I am. But all I can come up with, when pressed, is a character flaw that should be pretty damned clear by now.

Her taste in men is, quite frankly, shit.

GLOSSARY

ABS   See Securitisation

ABCP   See Conduit

Agency   A business model based on standing in the
Business middle, arranging deals for borrowers,
bringing investors to the table and taking a
success fee at the end. Slow, steady, and as
close to risk-free as you can get - in contrast
to "Principal Business".

Analytics A team at the bank who are the real-life
"rocket scientists" of banking legend. They're
all geniuses with computers and numbers and
speak a strange language of "cohorts" and
"financial models", yet they're surprisingly
human when you actually talk to them.

Back Office The guys at the bank who make sure that all
(or "Ops") the money and all the bonds and all the other
critical bits of paper end up where they're
supposed to.

Blue Screen When your monitor goes blue and your
of Death computer just dies. It's not just an everyday
crash. It's much worse than that.

Bond   A loan broken up into little bits each of
which can be sold or traded on exchanges or
in banks or in rooms full of guys with a
dozen monitors in front of them and a
Ferrari each in the car park (also known as
Hedge Funds).

CDO (or Collateralised Debt Obligation)	A bunch of loans or bonds bundled together and turned into another kind of bond, usually with the aim of spreading the risk and creating a nice safe investment. Like that's ever gonna work, right?
Commercial Real Estate	The team at the bank that lends to or arranges deals where the underlying assets or cashflows are based on commercial real estate – shopping centres, office blocks, pub chains, even crematoria.
the Conduit (or "ABCP")	Securitisation, but with a short-term bond that typically gets repaid and then reissued every thirty days. It's cheaper to raise money that way, because the people whose money you're taking know they're getting it back in a month's time, but it's riskier too, because in a month's time who knows if anyone's going to want to lend to you again?
Corporate	The team at the bank that arranges deals for corporates that don't fit into the FI or Commercial Real Estate world.
Credit Committee	Where senior bank executives decide whether a given deal can go ahead or not. Kind of like a job interview, but you don't get to ask about holiday entitlement.
Credit Default Swap (or CDS)	In simple terms, a way to insure yourself against a company going bust or defaulting on a particular bond or loan. Famously described by Warren Buffett as "financial weapons of mass destruction", which just goes to show that everyone's a poet these days.

Credit Team	The guys at the bank who assess the level of risk the bank will be taking on a specific deal, help the structuring team minimise that risk if they need to, and (if they're helpful) steer the deal through the rocky shoals of Credit Committee.
Credit Trading	Trading CDOs and credit default swaps. Insanely complicated.
Default	When someone's supposed to pay something, or do something that they've agreed to under a legal contract, and they don't.
Derivatives	See Hedging
Finance Department	a team inside a bank who specialise in accounting and arcane stuff like that, but also the all-important decisions on Regulatory Capital.
Financial Model	See Model
Financial Institutions (or "FI")	The team at the bank that lends to or arranges deals for financial institutions – other banks, pension funds, insurance companies and so on.
Fixed Income	The area of banking and finance that deals with bonds and loans as opposed to shares and takeovers.
Flow	The bread-and-butter deals of the finance world, usually mortgage and credit card deals done through FI or the Conduit.

Hedging (or "rates" or "swaps" or even "derivatives") — A way of eliminating the risks involved with movements in interest rates or exchange rates (usually), or share price movements or pretty much anything else with an element of uncertainty. The bank takes your dollars and throws you pounds in return, takes your fixed rate income and pays you floating, whatever it is you need, your friendly banker will provide. And you wouldn't believe the money he's making from it.

KYC — "Know your customer", a set of requirements to make sure a bank isn't being used to launder money by Al Qaeda, the Mexican drugs cartels or Arthur Daley's used-car yard.

Legal Team — The team at the bank who make sure the legal boxes are all ticked. At their best they can get you out of a world of trouble you didn't even know was waiting for you. At their worst they spend all their time making sure the name of the bank is always correctly followed by "plc".

Leveraged Finance — Lending to companies who use the money to buy other companies. The client's usually a private equity fund, which means they might be nice to your face but you don't want to know what they're saying about you behind your back.

Liquid — Something's described as "liquid" if you can sell it, quickly, for a clear and easily agreed price. Gold is liquid. Shares traded on major stock exchanges are liquid. Securitisation bonds used to be liquid and then the shit hit the fan and they weren't any more.

Liquidity Facility (or "liquidity line")	A loan into a structured finance deal to make sure everyone gets paid on time when there are cashflow problems that might otherwise bring everything crashing down.
Margin	In business generally, the bit of money you make on each deal you do. In trading or spread betting, the amount of cash you have to set aside to make sure you can cover your debts when your trade comes to an end.
Model (or "Financial Model")	A computer simulation demonstrating what will happen to a bond or any other financial instrument or business, in a given set of circumstances.
Offering Circular	A long and boring document that dissects the deal in the kind of detail only a lawyer or a lunatic would care about.
Pricing	The moment when you find out whether anyone's actually going to invest in the bond you've been working on for a year, and how much interest they're going to want. So quite important, really.
Principal Business	A business model based on actually putting your money where your mouth is, risking your own money, trading, putting your balance sheet on the table, typically getting greedy and fucking everything up.
Rates	See Hedging

Rating Agencies	A bunch of organisations that look at a bond, or a company, or even a country, and then tell everyone how good it is and how likely it is that it'll actually do what it's promising to. It's fair to say these guys have screwed up quite badly in recent years, but then who hasn't?
Regulatory Capital	A bit of cash that a bank has to set aside for each and every bet it makes. The riskier the bet, the more the cash. Banks like risky bets, but they hate regulatory capital, so the game is to make every bet look less risky than it really is.
Sales Team	The guys at the bank who know the investors, personally, and try to convince them to buy the bonds we're putting together.
Securitisation (also "ABS")	The art of taking an income stream, like mortgage or credit card payments, music royalties or property lease payments, turning that income stream into a bond, and selling the bond to anyone who wants to join the party. Single-handedly responsible for the end of civilisation as we know it.
SPV	A company set up to sit in a specific place and perform a specific role in a transaction. In a securitisation, the SPV usually issues the bonds.
Stress Test	Trying to work out what'll happen if the shit *really* hits the fan.

Structuring and Origination Team	The guys at the bank who bring in the client, put together the bond, basically do all the work, and do we get thanked for it, eh? Do we? Yes, I suppose we do, actually.
Sub-Prime	A polite way of saying you're lending to someone who's get less chance of paying you back than you have of pulling Naomi Campbell.
Swaps	See Hedging
Syndicate Team	The guys at the bank who "understand" investors and what they *really* want and try to make sure the bonds we're putting together taste just right to the potential buyers.
Tax Department	A bunch of people at a bank who specialise in tax. Sometimes there's no great mystery, right?
Tombstone	A lump of plastic sitting on your desk that reminds you of a deal you did ten years ago and on balance you'd rather you'd forgotten.
Tranche	When a lot of bonds are issued by a borrower or an SPV, they might not all be the same. Some might be riskier than others, some might pay more or less interest, or pay at different times or in different currencies or using different exchange rates, some might last a year, some might last thirty. Each group of bonds is called a "tranche".

AFTERWORD

For several years now I have resisted the entreaties of the great and the good to put my experiences at Milton Shearings on the public record, but when, in the space of a single week, two ex-Prime Ministers and a serving Chancellor of the Exchequer contacted me privately and expressed their fervent desire to see my words in print, well, such resistance can only go so far.

Senior figures within the Bank of England, the ECB, even the Federal Reserve, had already urged me to commit my recollections to print; comments had been made in the House of Commons; editors and proprietors of major newspapers had endeavoured to tempt me with offers of fame and fortune to which, I am happy to say, I remained entirely immune. An Irish rock star of global renown and the manager of at least one Premier League football club had joined the throng. Other bankers, understandably, had been more ambivalent; whilst seeing one's name in lights is always gratifying, nobody wants to be the bad guy.

With this in mind, when I finally succumbed, it was with one significant stipulation: that whilst the names of well-known institutions could remain unchanged (Milton Shearings, of course, but also Sterling Walton, Greenings, and the law firms Sommerson & Co and Morder & Chay), the names of individuals would have to be altered for their own protection.

Society has already judged these men and women, and judged them harshly. My own views may be seen by some as the extreme reactions of the sinner reformed. And as is always the case in such situations, we remain too close to the events in question to be truly confident in our own verdict. In years to come, new causes and effects may be uncovered, patterns of behaviour may be better understood, all may come to be seen in a different and, perhaps, more positive light. Until history has laid these matters finally to rest, who am I to stoke the fires still further by giving more names to fuel public indignation?

I have also invented an entirely fictional character, the narrator Alex Konninger. There are those who insist that Alex is a cipher, or a poorly-disguised version of myself. To this accusation I will respond only by saying that those who know me and who are aware of my work with CERN, Microsoft, the United Nations Security Council and the World Professional Billiards and Snooker Association consider such an association entirely unfounded, and will then retreat in what I hope is a dignified silence.

THANKS

This book has been a long time coming, and there are, accordingly, far more people to thank for its eventual arrival than befits such a humble work.

Sarah, for encouraging, reading, re-reading, pulling apart and putting back together again (both me and the book), and letting me do this instead of going out and getting a proper job. Without you, this book wouldn't exist.

Mum and Dad, for their advice, encouragement and critical insight. Without you, this book would be a lot worse than it is.

Zoe and Gary, for their wise counsel and marketing genius. Without you, no one would be buying this book at all.

Gary Brookman for his outstanding design work for the cover and advertisements.

Amanda for her encouragement and expert advice on my earlier writing.

My beta readers and reviewers (particularly those who've reviewed the thing positively), "Followers" of the book on Facebook and Twitter, and readers of my blog.

The surprising number of friends, acquaintances and strangers who have showered me with good advice and encouragement.

To all – I hope you think it was worth it.

Made in the USA
Charleston, SC
21 May 2014